ETERNAL FALL

R. DEAN TAYLOR

"The Watchers fell from Heaven. Thirteen spirits not of this world, dwelling among men in eternal fall. Seeing the daughters of men, that they were fair, they departed their first estate. Violence ruled the day. Blood ruled the night."
- From the Scrolls of Enoch

CHAPTER 1

I watched.

The setting sun painted the San Francisco Bay in shades of crimson, the fires of Hell dancing upon a sea of blood. How many sunsets have I seen? More than I wish to remember. So many I want to forget. That is my curse. I will remember, forever and always. When she set, new and vibrant, upon the Garden of God, I was there. When she adorned the skies above the first cities of men, the first kingdoms, from Babel to Babylon, I bore her witness. When she rose on Egypt's greatness and set on its tragic demise; shed her light on glorious Rome and set on empty, broken ruins, I was there. My eyes have seen the walls and gates of Heaven and have known the mysteries of the universe. I beheld the splendor of the cherubim and the magnificence of the Almighty, the beauty of planets without number, worlds without end.

No glory, no beauty, no magnificence, will ever compare to Marah, the woman I loved; she who became my Heaven. No sorrow, no pain ever upon the Earth, from the Fall to the Flood, to Golgotha's wicked tree, will ever compare to the sorrow I knew the moment I lost her.

But I digress. I am being rude. Please, allow me to introduce myself. My name is Saruel. I am a Son of Heaven. Physically beautiful, perfect in visage, formed by the hand of the Creator, I appear to be a young man. But I am not a man. My skin is alabaster. My eyes, sapphire—the blue of Heaven's throne. My hair is earthy brown, shoulder length. Once, a heavenly robe of soft, golden light robed my body, but it never shall again. I am Fallen, cast down, banished from the light of Heaven.

1

Churches and synagogues are everywhere in the city, and believers in God are, by default, believers in angels. There is a subtle difference, though, in believing in something and knowing, truly knowing, that it exists. Most professed believers in angels would be shocked to discover that I am here, in truth, telling this story in my very own words.

I enter places of worship from time to time. There is no earthquake when I cross the precipice, no sudden heavenly punishment. Being among believers does cause me pain. Not the pain of hellfire or judgment, but pain caused by my all too vivid memories. I see the joy of the Creator upon mortal, Fallen human beings. It is torture. Are they not Fallen, as I am? Love is my only sin, my only fall.

Love condemns me. Love sets me free.

It is right to cast sinful creatures from their heavenly estate. I will not argue the point. Yet, I ask you, is love a sin? To love with all one's heart, more than life and Heaven. Can a devil know such love?

No devil, I.

The sun slipped, finally, into the far away ocean. Darkness fell. San Francisco moved beneath me, human beings living their lives, unaware of my presence. The lights of buildings, ships and boats shone on the water, replacing the sun with artificial light, beautiful in its own way. Cars snaked along streets and highways. An occasional plane flew in the newly darkened sky. Looking down upon the inky bay, I remembered the abyss, the black waters of the deep. I remembered Heaven. My heart ached.

The top floor of the building below me was a softly lit restaurant, decadent and exclusive. Fine tapestries covered dark wooden walls. Bathed in the yellow glow of candlelight, well-dressed patrons dined on the finest cuisine. I hovered in the skies above, watching a couple at a corner table through large glass windows. A young girl sat with them. She wore a dress of rich yellow silk. Her skin was white as cream, her hair the color of autumn leaves. She displayed excellent etiquette; her posture perfect, delicate hands folded in her lap. She was a lady in the making, and I adored her. Her smile, her face, the light in her eyes, was lovelier to me than every sunset and sunrise since the creation of the world, of every world. At the sight of her, my memory of Heaven paled, my longing for the presence of God all but forgotten. My heart filled with love. For her, I would do it all again, turn my back on the glory of Heaven and the fellowship of angels. I would fall, not for carnal desire, not for pride or power. I would fall in love.

I spotted movement in an alleyway a block or two away from the restaurant, a man and woman running faster than any normal human beings could. Their skin held the sickly pallor of death: living corpses. Hidden by the night, they stole through the shadows with silent ease. The man was tall and wiry. His gaunt face held a look of constant hunger. The woman was small and thin. I knew them for what they were: children of the night, the servants of Sangruel. Continuing, they ran together from shadow to shadow, a part of the night, darting between cars and bushes, from alleyways to building fronts, never slowing, passing unwary mortals on the street.

My hearing is as keen as my vision.

"We must feed," the man said.

"The master will feed first," the woman answered.

They kept moving.

The girl and her parents left the restaurant, holding hands, strolling leisurely in the night along the Embarcadero. Flying high above them, I followed. The usual bevy of tourists streamed along the Embarcadero, Pier Thirty-Nine and the surrounding areas, gathering along the strip, around the shops and restaurants. A street performer juggled lighted torches, while a crowd formed around him. The servants of Sangruel watched from the shadows.

The lovely girl and her parents joined with the onlookers, watching the juggler, the flames of his torches lighting up their amused faces. For a better view of the juggler, the girl maneuvered along the edge of the crowd, leaving her parent's sight.

The servants of Sangruel left the shadows, joining the onlookers. They moved quickly toward the girl, the woman taking her by the arm, speaking softly, reassuring her. Her parents saw nothing, as the woman led her away. Murderous rage consumed me, and I moved to rescue the girl, but restrained myself. I could not risk harming her. The servants of Sangruel meant her as an offering to their master, and would deliver her unharmed to him. I followed.

The man lifted the girl and ran, the woman beside him, moving through shadows, until they reached an old warehouse. Light shone through broken windows and rusted holes in the tin walls. I heard the sounds of music playing, the tinkling of glasses, laughter and conversation. Expensive cars filled the decayed parking lot outside the warehouse. Two men in black suits guarded the front entrance, where well-dressed people stood waiting in line. The man and woman carried the girl inside, the guards quickly clearing a path for them.

Hurrying, I walked to the entrance, jostling my way through the line of humans. Some complained at my rudeness, while others stared at my beauty. My clothing, a simple white cotton shirt and dark slacks, stood out in the midst of their formal attire. I reached the front of the line. One of the guards, a burly man, stepped in front of me.

"You can wait in line like everyone else," he growled.

His partner—a tall, thin man—looked me up and down, leering.

"Oh, but he's such a lovely thing. Let him in."

"Everyone waits," the burly one said, "even the pretty ones."

I took a step toward them.

"Tell your masters that I am here."

The burly man put his hand on my shoulder, his steely eyes boring holes. His hand held the Grigorian mark: a tattoo of black folded angel wings.

"What do you know of my masters?"

"Remove your hand from me," I said.

He pushed me, surprised to find unyielding flesh. His eyes were angry at first, then horrified.

"You're one of them?" he said, his voice shaking. He lowered his eyes in deference to me and his growl became a guttural whisper. "Have mercy. You don't look like the others."

"If I were one of your masters there would be no mercy," I said. "Take me to their dwelling."

He turned toward the entrance.

"Please, follow me," he said, keeping his eyes turned to the ground.

The warehouse was dim inside, lit by muted red lights and low burning candles. Carpets covered the concrete floor. Black leather couches and chairs lined the walls. Humans drank red wine from antique glasses; affluent men and women, desiring immortality, willing to pay whatever cost, not understanding the true nature of their request. Some would achieve their ultimate goal, becoming Sangruel's servants, cursed to eternal darkness and the thirst for blood. Most would be used to quench that thirst. Their eyes watched me intently as the man led me to a heavy wooden door, before unlocking it with a large key. I followed him down a long lighted corridor. The concrete floor gave way to ancient stone. Smooth rocks in mortar centuries old replaced metal walls. The man stopped, motioning to stone steps spiraling downward into darkness. He bowed his head.

"Forgive me. I can't go down there. It's not allowed."

"You will go further," I said.

His voice shook as he stared into the darkness below.

"Please, I can't. Only the masters go down there."

I moved behind him and, placing a hand on his back, propelled him to the steps. He trembled under my touch.

"Rejoice," I said. "Tonight you will meet the one you worship."

I led him down the long winding steps into the heart of darkness.

I found myself within an immense chamber of catacombs. The walls were made of stone, stained over the years by a dark fluid I knew to be blood. I heard the sounds of dripping water. The smell of death filled the sour air. Bodies in varying stages of decay were scattered without ceremony along the stone floor. Skeletal remains littered the area, skulls and bones forming a wall to my right. On the far side of the chamber, I saw the faint glow of torchlight. I turned the man toward the light, guiding him forward.

He was weeping.

We walked for several minutes before reaching the torch. A statue the shape and size of a man stood in the torchlight, the graven image of Sangruel, formed from a single black stone. His shadowy robe flowed around him like pointed wings. His clawed hands held wide out in front of him, accepting worship, or sacrifice. His monstrous face looked down at an altar of stones. Congealed blood glistened on the stones in the flickering light. At the sight of the statue and the bloody altar, the man fell to his knees, sobbing.

"Please," he said, his voice faltering, "let me go. Take me back."

I pulled him to his feet.

"You should be honored. You are in the temple of your god, in your master's chamber."

Taking him by the back of his neck, I lifted him into the air. He cried out, struggling to break free of my grip. The sound of his voice echoed through the underground chamber. Hearing movement behind me, I turned to find half a dozen servants of Sangruel running toward me, shouting, hissing in rage. I called out:

"Sangruel! Sangruel, come to me!"

A powerful hand grabbed me from behind. I turned to see a servant of Sangruel, his eyes blazing furiously in the darkness, his mouth open in a snarl of jagged, pointed teeth. Moving faster than even he could see, I took him by the throat with my free hand. Holding him, I squeezed hard, feeling bones and cartilage breaking beneath my grip. He dropped to the stone floor. The others of his kind, jagged teeth bared, faces filled with rage and confusion, drew warily away from me, realizing for the first time that I was something other than human.

"Hear me," I said. "My business is not with you, but with your master."

The servants of Sangruel fell suddenly to their knees as a shadow fell from the darkness above and landed before me. The human in my hand wept in terror. Sangruel stood, watching me. A cloak of darkness surrounded him. A bone-white face, twisted into an eternal grimace, had replaced his former angelic beauty. Pointed teeth showed between thin, ashen lips. Dark circles surrounded his jaundiced eyes. I recoiled at the sight of him, as I had long ago on the night of his judgment. He stared at me, studying my face, my clothing, the human in my hand. He spoke, his voice a raspy whisper, sand on glass. "You are so beautiful. Your burden is light compared to the weight of my judgment."

"My judgment is more than I can bear," I said.

"Judgment!" he hissed. "What do you know of judgment?"

"I know judgment," I said, "for I, also, am cast from Heaven."

He shrank back at my words. His eyes narrowed into slits. For a creature of such darkness, the memory of Heaven must have been an unspeakable torture. I had the beauty of this world, sunrises and sunsets. Sangruel knew only darkness and eternal thirst. He looked upward, as if to see Heaven through the ancient stones above us. His eyes brimmed with tears of blood.

"Heaven," he said. "I wanted only to live as a man, to know their fellowship, to dwell in the light of the sun."

Behind me, I felt his servants tremble at his words. I lowered my voice.

"Do your servants know? Do they know what you were? Do they know about us?"

"They know nothing of Heaven or Hell. They know only thirst and the eternal curse, for I have robbed them of their natural death."

I looked upon Sangruel's face, his twisted hands, the darkness surrounding him, recalling the beauty he once possessed before his terrible fall. How had we come to this? We, who had once been holy, innocent, and pure?

Forgive me. I am rambling. There is much you need to know in order to understand my predicament.

It is time to tell my story. I want to tell it. I need to. Heaven turns a deaf ear to me. Perhaps you will listen. It is a long story, and I must start at the beginning. Not at my beginning, of course, for there is not enough paper in the entire world to hold the full tale of my existence. Let us start at the beginning of Earth.

Take my hand, if you will. Walk with me. Come. Our story begins. The Earth is far below us now. It is not Earth as you know it today: blue skies, flowers and trees, clear oceans teaming with life. It is without form, and void. Darkness is upon the face of the deep.

CHAPTER 2

In the emptiness of space, we watched; two figures robed in soft light, staring down at a planet covered in darkness. Shadows moved, darkness swirled. Faces appeared, breaking through the gloomy veil of mist, crying out, twisting in rage, shaking fists, gnashing teeth, before the shadows swallowed them again.

We had watched the scene below us for eons, time untold, aware of other activity in the universe, having felt many times the subtle vibration of creation, as, somewhere, far away, life began, brought forth by the spoken word of the Creator. Even from our great distance away, we had felt the joy of Heaven, the angels rejoicing and worshipping God.

Suddenly, there came a pulsing beacon of radiant light, brighter than any sun. We heard a call, low and gentle, vibrating through the vacuity of space. It was a crucial moment in history, for your kind and for mine.

Return.

Ariel, my companion, turned toward the light. I looked at him and nodded. We glanced back at the swirling mass of darkness then flew together toward the light, the glow of our bodies trailing behind us like the tails of two small comets. The light grew brighter as we flew. A great city appeared below us.

Heaven! How can words describe her? Compared to Heaven, the sun is night, its rise and set ashen gray. It is unspeakable joy and eternal pleasure. It is love unfathomable, without measure, without end.

Throngs of angelic beings were gathered below us in front of a translucent podium lifted high above the crowd. On the podium, eleven angels sat on majestic thrones. A twelfth throne sat alone and empty. Each throne glowed with internal light, every color and shade of the rainbow, and colors unknown to the human eye. Six thrones sat on one side of the podium and six on the other with a large space between them. We headed toward the multitude of angels, landing gently on a ground made of pure golden light.

Two Watchers approached us. Azazel was Captain of the Watchers, powerfully built and tall. Erozel was sleek and beautiful, his features soft and smooth, lovely to the point of feminine. His face held a dainty, graceful smile.

"Ariel, Saruel, join us," Azazel said.

We embraced.

"It has been a very long time," I said.

"Longer than usual," Azazel said. "It seems that your time of watching over the abyss has come to an end."

"We live to do the bidding of our Lord," Ariel said.

Azazel nodded.

"Tell me, what is the plight of the Fallen?"

I shuddered at the thought.

"They are without light," I said, "imprisoned in a world of shadow. Darkness is upon the face of the deep. They cry out and Heaven does not hear."

Erozel frowned.

"Such frightful punishment," he said. "What of their lord, the traitor, have you seen him?"

Ariel answered: "The Son of the Morning has become the prince of darkness. He shakes his fist toward Heaven."

"It is a fitting end for such rebellion," Azazel said.

Ariel motioned to the multitude of angels.

"Why have we been summoned? Why does all of Heaven gather together?"

"I do not know," Azazel said.

We followed him to where more Watchers, two-hundred in all, were gathered behind the multitude of Seraphs and Messengers. We turned our attention toward the podium as the eleven archangels stood, their heads bowed. A brilliant blue light appeared, moving toward us from the direction of the Temple of Heaven, God's dwelling place. We erupted into song.

"Hallelujah, hallelujah to the I Am who sits upon the throne! There is none like Him, perfect in beauty, the Creator of All That Is!"

The song continued, sweet, worshipful, as the object grew closer, revealing itself to be a throne of sapphire blue. Four winged cherubim, their faces glorious, carried the throne. Flying in unison and singing the praises of the Great I Am, their powerful voices mixed in with the multitude of singing angels. The Great I Am sat upon the throne. A rainbow circled his head. His face was smooth, magnificent, exuding love and peaceful calm. He was robed in light, brighter than the light of Heaven, because He is the source of all light.

The throne descended to a place above the podium, held in place by the cherubim. We fell to our knees, silent and still before the throne. The cherubim continued to sing, for they never cease to worship, both night and day. The I Am spoke, His gentle voice sending a ripple of pleasure among us.

"Stand to your feet and hear my word. I am about to do a great thing." At the words, "I am," all of Heaven quaked. We stood in reverence. The cherubim sang,

"Bless the Lord, all of Heaven, for He has done great and marvelous things. The works of His creation are wondrous to behold!"

The Great I Am said, "Behold the Earth. It is without form. Darkness is on its face. The inhabitants of Hell are there. Watchers, hear me. Go to Earth and behold my works, for I will do what has never been done."

We bowed before him, lowering our heads, shaking in awe and reverence.

"We hear and obey," Azazel said.

Chosen and led by Azazel, thirteen Watchers (Asriel, Marachael, Moroniel, Lascivuel, Sodomel, Arachiel, Paruel, Gomhorel and Sangruel) including Ariel, Erozel and myself, flew to the planet over which Ariel and I had watched.

Inside Earth's atmosphere, the darkness swirled, excited by our sudden arrival. The Fallen stirred in the darkness below, watching us, calling out.

"Have you come to bring greater judgment on us?"

We remained silent. There was a great trembling as the voice of the I Am sounded. The Fallen cried out in terror, hiding, seeking refuge in the shadows.

"Let there be light."

Light flooded the Earth, vanquishing darkness, revealing the Fallen below. Despite the light of God, the shadowy darkness remained around them where white robes had once been. The Lord of the Fallen, an angel both powerful and beautiful, shook his fist toward Heaven and cursed the light of God. The voice of the I Am sounded again, scattering them. The Lord of the Fallen screamed in rage and gnashed his teeth.

We watched as a new star formed, bathing the Earth with its warm glow, the first sunrise. The moon appeared after this, reflecting the light of the sun. We shouted with joy and worshipped.

The Earth shook violently. The waters parted and reddish brown land appeared. Waves crashed, lightning flashed and thunder roared. The sun rose and set six times as new life took form. Great whales and fish filled the waters, sea animals of every kind. Birds flew under the canopy below us. Plants and trees grew, clothing the planet in various shades of green and flowers of every color. Animals formed from the ground, prancing and running, playing, both male and female. We wondered at this, for we did not know what sex was.

I heard shouting from the Watchers and Fallen alike and looked around to see the source of the commotion. The throne of God sped toward us from the direction of Heaven, carried by the four cherubim. The Fallen hid their faces from His glory, crying out as the throne settled on Earth.

The Great I Am stepped from His throne. We descended en masse and hovered above where he stood. Flowers bloomed in His presence; trees swayed together in worship. Animals gathered around Him.

We watched, transfixed, as He knelt down and touched the reddish brown clay with his hands. We had never seen him bow, much less kneel. He pulled the clay from the ground and formed it with his own hands. His face shone as he worked. Little by little, the clay became a body, perfectly formed. After a time, he stood, revealing his handiwork.

For the first time in the chronicles of the Watchers, the cherubim fell silent. We cried out in surprise. The Fallen shouted, forgetting their terror. On the ground, formed from lifeless clay in meticulous detail, was the image of God.

The I Am looked up at us.

"Behold my son!"

He knelt at the side of the clay form, his face close to its mouth. He breathed. Light flowed from him into the mouth of the clay form. The clay became a living man. A rainbow appeared around his head. A robe of light covered his body. His eyes looked upon the face of God.

The Great I Am took him by the right hand and, pulling him up, embraced him.

"You are Adam, made in my own image. I am your father, and you are my son."

A cry of fury came from the direction of the Fallen. The Lord of the Fallen shot forward, then stopped and hovered in the air several feet from where the I Am stood with Adam. His beauty was second only to their identical images. His hair was black, flowing behind him.

"You have made yourself a son? Are you so lonely, now that I have left your presence?" He floated toward Adam, studying him. "He looks like you, but he is not the Son of God any more now than when he was clay."

Adam looked troubled.

"Is this true, Father?"

The I Am answered him:

"All creation comes from me, and is, therefore, part of me. The Son of the Morning came from me. He is a spirit, and I am the father of all spirits. He is not made in my image. He is the Son of the Morning. You are the Son of God."

The Lord of the Fallen clenched his fists. His face contorted in anger, his eyes flashed madness. Though the scene was far below me and the other Watchers, I hid my face from his terrible wrath. The Son of the Morning screamed. The Earth trembled. He shook a fist at the I Am.

"I should be your son! I sat on your right hand, greatest of the twelve, your crowning glory!"

Adam stepped away from him. The I Am said,

"You were the Son of the Morning, but you never were the Son of God. You are Fallen."

At the words of the I Am, the Lord of the Fallen fell backwards to the ground. Scrambling to his feet, he rose again into the air, fixing Adam with a hateful stare.

"Perhaps one day you will fall as I have. What will you think of him then, when he casts you out for all eternity?"

Adam watched as the Son of the Morning returned to the Fallen.

"Is what he said true, Father? Will I fall beyond redemption?"

The I Am said nothing. He held his hands out wide and hanged his head. He stayed with Adam until evening, and the cherubim carried him away.

Every evening the I Am walked with Adam in the Garden of God. The Lord of the Fallen watched them from a far distance. Adam named the animals, both male and female coming to him at his call. We marveled as the animals had sexual relations with each other, producing offspring each after their own kind. One day, Adam asked the I Am about this. Why, he wanted to know, did he not have a female counterpart?

"You have me, my son. You need nothing more."

"When you are not here, I am by myself," Adam said. "I do not wish to be alone."

For a long time, Adam did not broach the subject again. Then, one evening, when the I Am was preparing to leave, Adam said,

"Are you delighted in me?"

"You are my son."

"And I am in your image and likeness?"

"You alone are in my image."

"Then I desire a son of my own, as you once desired me."

The I Am answered, "It is true. Your desires are like my desires. I create, and you are right to want to create as I do. It is not good that you should be alone."

He caused Adam to fall into a deep sleep. Reaching into the light covering Adam, he removed flesh and bone from Adam's side. Far away on the horizon, the Son of the Morning looked on.

We watched all this from high above Earth.

"Will he create a son for Adam?" Ariel said.

The I Am formed the flesh and bone with his hands. It grew sinew, tissue, organs, muscle, a female body, smaller than Adam was, and slighter in build, with supple breasts, softer skin, and wider, rounder hips. Her face was narrow, fine and feminine. Her hair was long, reddish brown like the earth in the Garden of God. Her skin was the purest of white.

Erozel drew closer to the scene.

"Lovely," he said. "Beautiful is our God's creation."

She opened her eyes and looked around. Adam awoke, seeing her for the first time. He stood to his feet, his eyes never leaving her. For a long time, he did not speak. He felt his side with his hand, examining it.

"You are woman," he said, "flesh of my flesh and bone of my bone."
He stepped forward and, lifting her to her feet, held her close to him. The
light around Adam wrapped around her, clothing her nakedness. "You are
Eve," he said.

"She is lovely," Erozel said. He hovered below us, descending, drawing
ever closer to the Garden of God, his eyes fixed on the woman. "So
lovely."

"Erozel!" Azazel called. "Return to us."

Erozel turned, as if awakening from a trance, and flew back to where we
were. His face was flushed. A thickness protruded from between his legs,
jutting obscenely through his robe of light.

"What is this?" Azazel asked.

Erozel stared down at the hardness between his legs.

"I do not know." He touched the place with his hand. The thickness
swelled, increasing in size. He trembled, closing his eyes, with a look of
pure ecstasy. "It feels wondrous."

Azazel drew close to him.

"Ours is to watch, Erozel, not to feel."

There came a shout from the far horizon, as the Lord of the Fallen flew
with great speed toward the Garden of God, stopping in midair between
the garden and the Watchers. Pointing toward us, he called out to the I Am.

"Do you see your holy angel, how he worships your creation? It will not
be long before he joins me!"

The Lord of the Fallen called to Erozel.

"Tell me, Watcher, why has the Creator given you the member that is
between your legs? You have never known its purpose. Since your creation,
has it acted as it does now? Is the reason not plain? On the day of your
making, he foresaw your fall. Feel the desire and burning of your loins. Join
me now and experience so much more. The I Am treats you unfairly,
expecting you to watch life, eternally in front of you, but to never live."

Ariel shot forward toward the Lord of the Fallen, his countenance one
of fiery indignation.

"Will you accuse our God in His very presence, you who were greatest
of us all?"

The Lord of the Fallen looked coldly at Ariel.

"I do accuse your God, I who am still greater than all of you. Still,
before you judge me in your anger, answer my question. Would rebellion be
found in me if the I Am had not placed it there on the morning of my
creation?"

"He is perfect and right in all that he does. He is the Great God, who
created all things, and shall not be questioned this way," Ariel said.

The Lord of the Fallen answered Ariel.

"Then feel with your own hand, down between your legs. You, also, have a member, as Erozel does. Answer me, Watcher. Why is it there?"

Ariel answered,

"Mine is not to question, nor to experience, only to watch."

"Then you are a fool."

The voice of the I Am sounded from the Garden of God.

"Return to your place, Watcher, and hear my words, record what is taking place upon the Earth."

Ariel returned to us.

"Watch," Azazel said, pointing below to the Garden of God.

The I Am spoke to Adam and Eve.

"My children," he said. "I have placed you in my garden to rule over it as I rule over Heaven. Adam asked for a son. I have given him, instead, a companion, a soul mate. Flesh of his flesh, bone of his bone, taken from his side, she shall ever live beside him." Eve moved close to Adam who placed his arm around her.

"My son, I have given you life eternal. The woman is not as you are. You alone are eternal upon the Earth. Animals have a span of life. Afterwards, their spirits return to me. The woman will also return to me with time, but behold my plan." He lifted his right hand and, out of the ground, a sapling sprang forth, its leaves and branches forming together, reaching to a height of about twelve feet. Fruit, round and golden, appeared among the leaves. Light shone from within the fruit. "This is the Tree of Life. Its fruit will renew and refresh the woman. As long as she eats of this fruit, she will live. If she chooses to not eat it she will die, and her spirit will return to me."

The I Am raised His left hand, and, on a rocky hill in the center of the garden, another tree grew up from the ground, the same size and shape as the Tree of Life. Fruit the color of flesh appeared among its leaves.

"In the center of the garden, I have placed another tree, the fruit of which is flesh. It is the Tree of Carnal Knowledge."

The I Am looked up at the Watchers, then toward the Fallen, a mass of shadows on the horizon. He turned again to Adam and Eve.

"Love given freely is what I desire. For that, there must be a choice between what is right and what is wrong. You must not eat the fruit of the tree in the center of the garden. If you do, you will surely die."

Eve took Adam's hand in hers. Facing him, she kissed his lips.

"I will remain forever with Adam. I will love and cherish him."

Next to me, Erozel said, "So lovely, so beautiful."

Time went by. The sun rose and set day after passing day. Animals were born and animals died. Adam and Eve lived and loved below us in the Garden of God. The I Am visited every evening and Eve joined him and Adam on their walks.

Erozel was first to notice subtle changes in Eve's appearance. Slight

13

wrinkles appeared on her forehead and at the corners of her eyes and mouth. Her hair had lost some of its luster.

"What is happening to Eve?" He said.

Evening had passed, the I Am had departed and the sun had gone down. Adam and Eve held each other, sitting on the ground under the moonlight. Ariel watched them thoughtfully. Our vision is far greater than the vision of mortals, and we saw them clearly in the light of the moon.

"I believe she may be aging," he said, "as the animals do. Did not the I Am say that she would?"

"Then why does she not eat of the Tree of Life?" I asked.

CHAPTER 3

I placed the human on the ground in front of me. He hid his face, shaking with fear. His pants were wet with urine.

"My judgment is more than I can bear," Sangruel said. "I tire of night. I tire of blood. I want to taste the bread of Heaven and dwell in the light of the Great I Am."

"It is terrible, my brother," I said.

Sangruel studied me for a long moment. His eyes fell on his servant whose neck I had broken.

"What brings you to me, Saruel, after so long a time?"

I motioned to his servants.

"Those who serve you took something of mine, and I have come to retrieve it."

"Something of yours." He motioned with his hand toward his kneeling servants. "What would they want with something of yours?"

"She is a human girl," I said. "I watch over her."

A mocking smile crossed his lips.

"You continue in the duties of a Watcher, then? You watch over humans? For what reason? "

"I watch because that is what I have always done. You are as I am. Surely you understand my loneliness. What am I to do?" I nodded to his servants. "You have your children, but I am alone."

Sangruel bared his teeth. I felt his servants tense behind me. He turned away from me.

"I have not left this pit for more than two-hundred years. You live in the light of the sun and eat the good of the Earth."

"You speak the truth," I said. "Your judgment is beyond my understanding. I could not begin to imagine. You were once so full of light, now to dwell in darkness."

He turned toward me. His face softened.

"I do not blame you for my curse, for you did try to prevent me from devouring the fruit of blood." He stepped toward me. "Who is this girl, Saruel, and why are you so interested in her?"

I lied, knowing that I must keep my love for the girl a secret.

"There is nothing special about her, for sure, but she means something to me. Your servants chose her for you. I ask that you let them choose another, for my sake."

Sangruel turned to his kneeling servants.

"Who is responsible for my nightly offering? Bring them to me."

Several servants of Sangruel turned and ran to the far stairway with tremendous speed. Sangruel watched them as they went.

"My blood flows within them," he said, "and the blood of the fruit. They do not see me as the demon that I am, but as their father, their god, worshiped and adored." He walked to the servant whose neck I had broken, and knelt down. "You have injured one of mine. Why should I not injure one of yours?"

I looked down at the lifeless body.

"He will heal," I said.

"Yes, but my servants saw you inflict injury on one of their own. It must not go without payment of some kind."

I looked into his face, trying to see beyond the monster he now was, my brother from before time began, once beautiful, as I am. How had this happened? If only we had never come to Earth. All would be as it once was, we holy angels, Sons of Heaven, dwelling among the stars, in the glory of God. But then I would never have known Marah's tender love, never known the beauty of her face, the joy of the songs she sang to me, her soft and warm embrace.

I cannot bear the thought of it.

There was movement on the far side of the chamber, as the servants of Sangruel returned. I recognized the man and woman from the Embarcadero. The woman held the girl, unconscious in her arms.

"Bring her to me," Sangruel said.

The woman moved quickly, stopping in front of Sangruel.

"Is she alive?" I said, struggling to retain my outward composure. Sangruel looked at the girl. Hunger filled the awful contours of his face.

"Living blood flows within her," he said. He turned from the girl. "Saruel," he said, "I sense that you have kept something from me. I believe this girl is more precious to you than you say."

"I watch her," I said.

Sangruel motioned to the woman. She placed the girl in his arms. He held her close to him, running his fingers through her autumn hair.

"You do more than watch her. You are in love with her, are you not?" I did not answer. His lips drew close to the girl's throat. He looked up at me, baring sharp teeth. "What would you give to me in order to spare her life?"

I held my hands out to him.

"What do I have to give you?"

"You injured my servant. You must pay for that and for this girl as well."

"What do you want?" I said.

"I want you to bring me a fruit from the tree of blood."

"You know that is impossible," I said.

His eyes flared with hunger, boring hard into me.

"Then bring me two children, taken by your own hand. Share in my curse. Deliver to me life for life, one for injuring my servant and one for this precious girl."

I gazed in horror at Sangruel.

"I am a Watcher," I said, shaking my head.

Sangruel pointed a clawed finger at me.

"You are a devil," he said, "as I am. You will bring to me the blood sacrifice tonight, taken by your own hand. I will feed very soon, either on the blood of this child, or on the ones you bring to me."

I moved toward him, my anger getting the best of me. He placed his hand around the girl's throat.

"You cannot rescue her. I am as powerful as you are and have my servants besides. Go, if you want her to live. Do what you must."

"Do not do this, my brother," I said.

He grabbed the weeping man from off the floor with one hand. His teeth ripped and tore at the man's throat. He drank deeply, blood flowing down his chin, all the time watching me. I remembered the garden, the fruit of carnal knowledge. I remembered being holy. Sangruel threw the man's lifeless body to his servants, who fell on it with a fury, shredding flesh with sharp teeth, wrenching limbs from the corpse in a frenzy of need and bloodlust.

"Go," he said.

Blood poured from his mouth, staining the yellow dress of the girl that I loved.

CHAPTER 4

Adam and Eve walked with God in the Garden of Eden. The sun set low on the horizon, an exhibit of marvelous colors and shades: pink, lavender and azure. Streaks of gray ran through Eve's thinning hair. Small webs of wrinkles lined the corners of her eyes and mouth. The rainbow around Adam's head joined with the rainbow around the head of the Great I Am. We delighted in this visual display of communion. Eve walked behind them in silence.

God turned to her. "My daughter, walk with me." To Adam he said, "Please leave me alone with Eve."

Adam left them, returning to where he dwelt in the garden.

Taking Eve gently by the hand, the I Am led her to where the Tree of Life grew. Around the tree, flowers bloomed and flourished like in no other place in the Garden of God. The grass appeared more vibrant, the colors sharper, flowing with life.

"My daughter, I delight in you. You are as much my child as Adam is. Do you know this?"

"Yes, Father, I know that you love me. I love you, also, with my whole heart."

"Why is it, then, that you have not partaken of the fruit I prepared for you?"

Eve lowered her eyes.

"You know all things, Father. The thoughts and intents of my heart are open before you."

"You are not content to live in the garden."

Eve frowned. "I see the animals in the fields and the birds of the air, male and female. They come together." She paused, and looked up at the I Am. "They have offspring."

"And you wonder why the lower creatures have something that you do not."

Eve stared at the ground. "I do, my Lord."

"And why do you think I withheld this from you?"

"Adam is eternal, as are the angels of Heaven. You alone must have the power to make such a creature, one that will live throughout eternity."

"Yes, my child," he said. "Consider the Fallen dwelling in shadows outside of the garden. They are my creations, made in purity and light. They chose to rebel, leaving their first estate. They are eternal, and their rebellion will grieve me without end."

Eve embraced him. He held her close. The light surrounding her body brightened.

"I do not wish to grieve you. You are my father and I love you with my whole heart."

"Then you will eat of the Tree of Life?"

"I will eat of it."

They returned to Adam. The I Am sat upon his throne and the cherubim spirited him away. On the horizon, the Lord of the Fallen hovered in the falling darkness, watching the throne of God leave Earth.

The next morning, Eve went alone to the place in the Garden of God where the Tree of Life grew. Its golden fruit sparkled brightly in the light of the sun. She reached for a piece of the fruit, and plucked it from the tree. A vapor of light trailed from the branch where the fruit had been. She heard a sound and looked up to see a serpent coiled in the branches.

"Did you say something?"

"I did," said the serpent. "May I approach you, Daughter of God? Might I speak with you?"

Eve looked at the fruit, hesitated, then said, "You may speak with me."

The serpent uncoiled its body from the branches. At that time, serpents had legs at the rear and front of their bodies and walked upright. "As you know, the I Am filled my kind with wisdom and cunning. I wish to share my wisdom with you."

Eve nodded her head toward the serpent. "Speak your heart to me, creature of God."

I was with Azazel and Erozel. Ariel flew to us, red-faced. His eyes flashed angrily.

"What is it, my brother?" I said.

He pointed toward the western horizon. The Lord of the Fallen hovered there, his hands pointed toward Eve and the serpent, his lips moving, speaking the same words the serpent said to Eve.

"We must stop this!" Ariel said.

Azazel looked at the Lord of the Fallen.

"We will not interfere. We are Watchers."

Ariel pointed at the Lord of the Fallen. "He must be stopped!"

"The I Am has Warriors, Ariel," Azazel said. "He will send them if He sees the need. We will watch. We are not made for war."

"Ariel," I said, "what possesses you? Since our creation, I have not seen you behave in this manner. Adam is the protector of the Earth. Eve has freewill. If we fight against this, it may be that we fight against the plan of God."

"Saruel speaks wisely," Azazel said. "We will not interfere."

Ariel looked angrily toward the Lord of the Fallen, his fists clenched, his body shaking with rage.

The serpent, under control of the Lord of the Fallen, said, "I have noticed that in the midst of the Garden there grows a tree unlike any other. Its fruit is untouched."

"We may eat of any tree in the garden, but we may not eat of the fruit of that tree. If we do, we will surely die."

"Did the I Am tell you that you will die? You will not die. Your eyes will be opened and a new understanding will come to you."

The woman shook her head.

"We must not so much as touch the fruit of the Tree of Carnal Knowledge," she said.

"The fruit that you hold in your hand, what is it?"

"This is the fruit of the Tree of Life. If I eat of this, I shall live."

"Forgive me, Mother of Earth, but are you truly living? The Creator keeps you in the Garden of God, where you do the same things day in and day out. You do not experience the joys of life that the beasts of the field enjoy. They couple together, and offspring are born to them."

Eve looked doubtfully at the golden fruit in her hand.

"Forgive me for saying so," said the serpent. He softened his voice and bowed his diamond head. "You are called Mother of the Earth, but you are not a mother at all, and, if you partake of this fruit, never shall be."

"Wisest of creatures," Eve said, "I am not dismayed. I want nothing more than to dwell in the Garden of God, to enjoy sweet communion with Adam, my love, and the I Am. That is my only desire."

"It is your only desire," said the serpent, "because it is all you know."

He approached the Tree of Life, his long body reaching up into its branches, coiling around the trunk of the tree.

"I submit to you, Mother of Earth, that you have never known your husband. Consider my kind, the creatures of the Earth, the beasts of the field, the inhabitants of the sky and the deep. Our spirits will return to God. Dust we are, and to dust will we return. Forgive my boldness, but if we were allowed to eat of the fruit of this tree, if it meant giving up the joys of our flesh, the ability to couple with our mates, to have offspring, we would not eat of it, though it gave us life eternal."

Eve stared down at the fruit in her hand.

"I must be eternal, for the one that I love shall never die," she said.

"What is life without knowledge? The fruit of the tree in the midst of the garden will give you true life. To live, you must be willing to lay down the life you have. If you seek to save your life, you will lose it. If you lay down your life, you will find it."

Eve started to protest, but stopped. She frowned, looking again at the Fruit of Life. She placed it on the ground beside the Tree of Life and walked away.

That evening the I Am returned to Earth, his throne carried by the cherubim. He and Adam walked in the Garden, enjoying the cool of the day. Eve followed behind them. A sheep stepped out of a clearing, bowing her head in reverence at the sight of the I Am. Her newborn lamb, just learning to walk, stood beside her. The I Am beckoned Eve to join him, motioning to the sheep and her lamb.

"It is a beautiful thing, the sight of a mother with her offspring," he said.

Eve watched the sheep and the lamb.

"It is lovely, Father."

The animals went their way. Adam and Eve continued walking with the I Am. Night drew near and the I Am approached his throne. The wings of the cherubim vibrated, ready for flight. The I Am turned to Adam; His eyes showed a hint of sadness.

"What is it, Father? What troubles you?"

The I Am pulled Adam close and embraced him.

"My son," he said.

He watched Eve over Adam's shoulder. She turned away from His gaze. He held Adam for a long moment before kissing his cheek and releasing him. He then sat upon His throne and the cherubim carried him away.

The next morning, Eve arose early, leaving Adam still asleep. She walked quickly, her face set as flint. She did not take time to smell the flowers, as was her custom. She did not eat. She walked on until she reached the center of the Garden where grew the Tree of Carnal Knowledge. Yellowed clumps of grass grew around the tree and along the path leading up to it. The side of the hill facing her was a cliff of rough-edged rock. She stopped in front of it and gasped. A face, a natural formation of the cliff, stared back at her with dark, empty eye sockets and a skeletal grin, the image of a human skull. She took a step back, then, slowly, made her way up the path to the Tree of Carnal Knowledge.

The tree was twelve feet high at the top, its branches reaching downward to about six feet. Its broad leaves were green with purplish veins flowing through them. Its trunk was smooth as skin. The fruit of the tree was bulbous, the color of flesh, held to the branches by a network of dark red veins. She reached out with her left hand and touched one of the bulbous fruits. It pulsed at her touch like the beating of a human heart. The light of God surrounding Eve dimmed. A look of ecstasy and rapture filled her face. Her body trembled. She drew her hand back. The fruit stopped pulsating and the light of God surrounding Eve brightened again.

Biting her lip, she looked around her, then back at the tree. Reaching out, she touched the fruit a second time. The look of ecstasy filled her features once again. The tree shuddered as she plucked the fruit from its branches. Dark blood poured from the severed veins that had held the fruit to the branch. The fruit throbbed and pulsed, a beating heart in her hand.

She brought the fruit to her mouth and bit into it, her white teeth piercing flesh. Her eyes widened, her body trembled and shook. The light of God around her body died out, revealing her nakedness. Moaning, she held the fruit with both hands, gripping it tightly. Blood flowed in unseemly amounts from the fruit as she kept it to her lips. She devoured it hungrily, eating its flesh and drinking its blood, her throat moving up and down with every swallow.

Blood flowed downward along the contours of her naked body, reaching her breasts. She shuddered and gasped, touching her breasts with her empty hand, greedily licking and sucking the bloody juices of the fruit as she rubbed her hardening nipples. The blood stained her alabaster skin crimson, discovered her smooth chalice, streamed to it, around it, entered her. She cried out, violent spasms rocking her body.

The Earth trembled.

"Do you see this beautiful thing?" Erozel said. His face blushed crimson. His engorged member protruded out through his robe of light. The thought crossed my innocent mind for the first time that something was happening to him. Something was terribly wrong.

Adam looked for Eve, having awakened alone for the first time since Eve's creation. Troubled by her absence, he followed the path to the Tree of Life. Finding the meadow empty, he turned to walk away, when a flash of gold on the ground drew his attention. He knelt down and picked up the Fruit of Life, turning it over in his hands. At that moment, the Earth shook beneath him. He stood up, facing toward the middle of the garden. Dropping the fruit of the Tree of Life, he ran.

Reaching the middle of the Garden, he saw her, standing naked above him on the rocky hill, holding the fruit of the Tree of Carnal Knowledge to her lips, the front of her body thick with blood. She moaned, frantically rubbing her chalice with her free hand, her hips thrusting in a lustful rhythm. She dropped what was left of the fruit; the grass withered where it fell. While one hand rubbed her chalice, the other found her breasts, following the path of blood. She fell to her knees, rocking her hips back and forth against her probing fingers.

Adam climbed the hill, standing before her. Tears ran down his face.

"Woman," he cried, "what have you done? You have eaten the forbidden fruit, and shall surely die."

Eve gazed intently at Adam, her face hot and flushed.

"Mount me, my lover!" she cried, "Quench my desire!" She knelt on all fours, arching her hips. "Mount me like the beasts of the field!"

"I am not a beast. I am the Son of God."

Her probing fingers found her chalice again.

"You are male," Eve groaned, "I am female. Mount me!"

Adam stared at Eve with terrible sorrow. Tears soaked his face.

"You will surely die, and I shall be alone in the Garden of God."

Eve pulled her hand from her chalice, placing her fingers in her mouth, sucking and licking madly at the bloody juices.

"I am not dead," she said, "but alive as never before!"

Adam wept loudly, his face hidden in his hands. From where I watched, hovering high above with the Watchers, I felt as though my own heart would break. I had never experienced such emotion.

"He loves her so much," I said.

Beside me, Erozel watched, his hand exploring his engorged member.

Eve stood up, controlling herself with what appeared to be a great effort. She walked with caution, carefully, to Adam, her voice soft and pleading.

"You do not have to be alone, my love. We can be together for as long as we both live. The I Am is merciful. He will forgive us. To truly live, you must be willing to lay down the life you have."

Adam wiped tears from his face.

"You have broken my heart," he said. Eve reached toward him and he pulled away. "Do not touch me. You are full of sin."

"I am filled with love," she said. "I desire you as never before."

"I am the Son of God," Adam said.

"You are also my mate. I need you with me." She drew closer to him. He stepped away from her. "Do not deny me, my love. Partake of the knowledge I have. Do you no longer love me?"

His eyes softened. "I love you more than I love myself," he said, his face contorted with grief.

Eve touched him lightly and he allowed her touch.

"Would you lay down your life for me?" she said. He did not answer. She moved closer to him, her breasts inches from his face. "Will you join with me?"

Adam fell to his knees in front of her. She pressed a breast to his lips. The light of God around Adam dimmed. A look of rapture replaced his grief.

"Kiss me," she said. "Touch me. Taste me."

Adam kissed her breast. She groaned, pulling his face against it. His lips found the pink of her nipple. The rainbow around his head went out, though the light of God remained dimly around him. Eve held his face in her hands, directing his kisses slowly downward, from her breasts to the roundness of her bloodstained belly.

"This is where your children will grow within my womb," she said.

Softly, he kissed her belly. She pulled him further down. Blood covered his mouth and face. She guided his lips to her chalice, spreading her legs wide apart, her hips thrusting forward.

Beside me, excitedly, Erozel said, "What is this new thing?"

Eve spread her legs wide and Adam kissed where the blood of the fruit flowed together with her juices. He sucked hungrily, his mouth covering her chalice, drinking her in. His body shuddered violently as the light of God around him went out, revealing his nakedness. Eve moaned as she rocked her hips and pressed hard against Adam's mouth.

There was an earthquake.

We heard laughter and shouts of triumph coming from the west. I looked to see the Fallen gathered on the horizon. The Lord of the Fallen left the mass of shadows and flew to the Garden of God. He smiled, cruel and iniquitous, looking up at us.

Pointing to Adam and Eve, he said, "Do you see, Watchers? Behold the handiwork of the Creator. The Son of God has Fallen. Record this in your memories, in the chronicles of Heaven! Adam chose flesh over God, the woman being his flesh. Dust he is, and to dust will he return. I should have been the Son of God, I who lived longer in purity than any other creature. Remember my words!"

He turned from us, returning to the jubilant Fallen. They disappeared over the horizon.

CHAPTER 5

I left the girl with Sangruel and his servants as I passed through the humans in the warehouse above, before departing through the rear door. Such foolishness! If they knew what existed in the dark caverns under their feet, they would run from that place as fast as mortal legs could carry them. I lifted into the air, my heart hammering in my chest. What was I to do? Curse you, Sangruel! May you never know peace! May God cast you into the Abyss, there to thirst forever without respite!

I flew high into the night sky, tears blurring the lights of the city below me. Is that the mark of a devil, to weep over the welfare of a human being? Does a devil know concern for another? Does a devil know love? I am no demon. Sangruel—he is the demon.

I decided then that whatever I had to do, whatever it took to return the girl to safety, the guilt would fall on Sangruel. Is it a sin to do a thing against one's own will, when forced to it by another? I think not, but I am not the judge of Heaven and Earth. Soldiers fight wars to protect others, invariably killing innocent bystanders. Are soldiers guilty of the murder of innocents? A hundred times no. The blame is on whatever tyrant, whatever enemy forced them to fight. Of course, some soldiers do go rogue, killing for pleasure and bloodlust. Such soldiers are guilty of murder. I am not a rogue. I am not a soldier, either. In many ways, what I am is the innocent bystander.

I know San Francisco well. It is a city of both high society and naked poverty. Drug addicts piss against marbled walls. The poor and destitute are so plentiful they are invisible to the well-heeled passersby.

Would Sangruel accept such a sacrifice, an addict, a homeless person? No. He required children, the monster. I watched the city below me, feeling precious minutes slipping away. How long would Sangruel wait?

Focusing on the lights of cars below, I allowed the wind to carry me, looking with my angelic eyes at the drivers and their passengers, at people walking along the sidewalks below me. Thirty minutes passed, then an hour. I began to despair for the girl.

That's when I saw them.

Two beautiful twin girls, five or six years old, slept in the back seat of a white sedan as it crossed the Golden Gate Bridge. They were identical, dressed in matching red dresses with white lace. Pink bows held their blonde hair behind China doll faces. Sangruel would approve. But two girls for the price of one; How can such a thing be justified?

I flew toward the car, faster than any mortal eye could see, pushing it with enough force to flip it over the side of the bridge. The driver—the mother of the girls—screamed. The car fell in a downward spiral toward the dark waters. I flew quickly after the car, and tore a door off its hinges before removing the twin girls. I then flew with them, one under each arm, away from the falling car.

I could have been a Guardian angel.

The car continued its spiraling descent, crashing with terrible force into merciless waters, swallowed by blackness. The girls stared after it, wide-eyed, terrified.

"Do not be afraid," I said, my voice soft, reassuring, angelic. I am not a fiend, after all. I held them close to my body, warming them, comforting them, an ability that all angels possess. One of the twins looked up at me, her innocent face frozen with shock.

"Are you an angel?"

My heart nearly broke. I fought back tears.

"Yes, darling girl," I said, "I am an angel from Heaven."

"Where's my mom?" The other twin asked, staring down at the waters below.

"Your mother is with other angels," I said. "You will be with her soon."

Damn you, Sangruel.

Holding the twin girls, I returned to Sangruel's lair, landing in the back, behind the warehouse. I opened the rear door and ran. I fought against panic. Would he be true to his word, evil as he was? Would I return only to find the remains of my girl, her body torn, eyes lifeless? I could not bear such a thing.

I reached the bottom of the stone stairway and found the servants of Sangruel gathered where I had left them. I ran to the altar of stones and the graven image of Sangruel. The twins wept in my arms.

"Do not be afraid," I said. I felt them grow calm. I called out: "Sangruel, I have returned. I have fulfilled your words."

I heard spiteful laughter from Sangruel's servants behind me.

"Perhaps the master has already devoured your precious girl," one of them said.

I turned toward them.

"If she is harmed, I will cast each of you into the light of tomorrow's sun."

They trembled in fear.

"What are you?" one of them, a woman, asked. "You are neither human, nor one of us."

"He is an angel from Heaven," one of the twins said.

There was movement above me, and Sangruel appeared. I whispered for the twins to shut their eyes tight. Sangruel landed before me, my girl in his arms. She was awake, eyes wide with terror. Sangruel's servants fell to their knees. He studied the twin girls in my arms, his cruel lips curled, showing teeth.

"Saruel, an angel from Heaven," he said. "Is that what you told these poor girls?" He reached out to stroke the hair of one of the twins. Hunger filled his face. "They will do nicely." He looked up at me. "I am surprised at you."

I placed the twins on the stone floor. They tried desperately to cling to me, but I pushed them away.

"Keep your eyes closed," I said, calming them with all the power I could muster. "You will be with your mother soon."

Sangruel's servants laughed behind me.

To Sangruel, I said, "Their blood, as well as their mother's blood, is on your hands."

"Will you place the blame at my feet? Will you hide behind Pilate's excuse? You made the choice; not I. The reaper grim will collect three souls instead of one. It is your sin that ends the life of these girls. Whether it is for love, or for hunger, the result is the same."

I reached out for my girl.

Reluctantly placing the girl in my arms, Sangruel said,

"Tell me, why do you love her?"

I held my beautiful girl close, comforting her. I looked at Sangruel.

"That is not part of our bargain."

I turned from him. His servants stood, blocking my path.

"Let him leave," Sangruel said. They parted in front of me, eyes filled with hatred.

One of the twins called to me, her small voice shaking with fear. "Please, Angel, don't leave us!"

I left them there in that dark place. At the foot of the stairway, I heard the tortured screams of the twin girls, the terrible sounds of pitiless laughter, the tearing of flesh followed by the sickly smell of blood.

I wept.

CHAPTER 6

Adam and Eve played and laughed together, walking hand-in-hand, stopping frequently to explore each other's bodies. If they had considered that the I Am would return for his evening walk only to find them Fallen, they did not show concern. Evening drew near. I turned and looked toward Heaven. Soon the light of the throne of God would appear. Azazel placed a hand on my shoulder.

"It is a terrible day, Saruel," he said.

"It is," I said. "What will the I Am do?"

Azazel looked down at Adam and Eve.

"He will bring swift and terrible judgment on them as he did with the angels that sinned. It is the only way."

I shuddered. Imagining Adam and Eve cast into darkness without hope of redemption saddened me. I said, "The I Am judged the Son of the Morning and his angels for seeking to usurp the throne of Heaven. That judgment was swift and just. Eve fell, deceived by the lord of the Fallen, tempted by her desire for offspring, and the carnal knowledge of her husband. Adam fell because he loved Eve and felt he could not live without her. Will the I Am judge them as he judged the Son of the Morning? Is love not a better reason to fall than is rebellion?"

Azazel shook his head.

"Who are we to know the judgments of our God?" he said. "He alone made Heaven and Earth. He made the Son of the Morning. He spoke the stars into existence and called each one by name. Who can tell the Creator what to do with his creation? If the I Am chose to destroy us all without reason, would it be unjust? Life is His to give and His to take away."

Just then, the other Watchers shouted. The light of the throne of Heaven appeared in the sky, heading toward Earth with tremendous speed. I saw the cherubim with their lightning faces. I saw the rainbow around the I Am. He was so beautiful, good and true. Who could ever sin against him? Below us in the Garden of God, Adam and Eve also saw the light of the throne. Their faces filled with dread.

Eve turned to Adam. "What shall we do? He will see our nakedness!"

Adam watched the throne of God descending to the Earth.

"Quickly," he said, "We must hide ourselves."

They ran, holding hands, into the thickest woods of the Garden and hid under a great tree, peering out through the branches as the throne settled on Earth.

The I Am stepped from his throne and looked around him.

"Adam! Adam, where are you?"

Eve pulled broad leaves from the tree, using vines to tie them to Adam, covering his nakedness. She did the same for herself.

"We must go to him, my love," she said, "Surely he already knows what we have done."

Adam lowered his head in shame. "I am sore afraid."

Eve took him by the hand.

"Come, my love." She led Adam away from the shadow of the tree, toward the throne.

When the I Am saw Adam and Eve, He ran to them.

"Why did you not come when I called to you?"

Adam's face reddened. "When we saw that we were naked, we were afraid," he said.

"And how did you come to be naked?" The I Am looked westward to where the Lord of the Fallen watched in silence from the horizon's edge. "Did you eat the fruit of the Tree of Carnal Knowledge?"

"My father, the woman you gave me, to be with me in the Garden, ate of the fruit and offered it to me. I knew that I would lose her and it was more than I could bear."

The I Am turned to Eve.

"What have you done?" He said.

"The serpent spoke to me and told me I could know my husband if I ate of the fruit. He said I could bring forth offspring. And behold, I know my husband like never before, and I still live."

Gray clouds filled the sky, blocking out the sun and hiding the scene from us. For several minutes, we could neither see nor hear the I Am speaking to Adam and Eve. The clouds cleared as quickly as they had formed. The I Am wept. He turned His back to Adam and Eve and walked to His throne. Sitting down, He said, "Hear the judgment of the one who made all things."

The Lord of the Fallen drew closer to the garden. "Adam and Eve will no longer dwell in the Garden of God."

Two bright lights flew from Heaven. Two Warrior angels, powerful and mighty, carrying swords of fire, landed before the throne of God.

"I will put my angel before the Tree of Life to guard it from mankind both day and night, lest they should eat of it and live."

One Warrior flew to the Tree of Life. The Lord said to the other angel, "Bring to me the serpent that deceived Eve."

The Warrior bowed and departed.

"Adam and Eve will surely die. They will dwell upon the Earth for a limited time. Then will their spirits return to me. Dust they are and to dust shall they return."

The Lord of the Fallen drew closer, no more than a hundred yards from the throne of God, his eyes blazing with fury.

The Warrior angel returned, carrying the serpent by the neck. He placed it in front of the throne. The I Am looked at the serpent.

"You are cursed. You will be far below all the animals of the Earth and the beasts of the field. You will dwell in the dust all the days of your life."

Immediately, the legs of the serpent curled up like dead things and he lay on his belly before the throne. The I Am looked to where the Lord of the Fallen hovered.

"I will put enmity between you and the woman, and between your offspring and hers. You will bruise his heel, but he shall crush your head."

Eve brightened a little at the mention of her offspring.

The I Am turned again to the Warrior angel.

"Fly to the northern edge of the Garden. There you will find a sheep in the grass, sleeping with her lamb. Bring them both to me."

The angel flew with great speed, returning with the sheep and her lamb and placing them before the throne. The sheep bowed low on all fours. Her lamb nuzzled close to her.

"Adam, step forward," the I Am said. Adam obeyed, stepping closer to the throne. "Take the sword from my Warrior and slay the sheep with her lamb."

Adam frowned, looking at the sheep.

"Father, I cannot do such a thing."

The sheep bowed low again, trembling.

"I require life for life. If you and Eve will live, innocent blood must be shed."

"My father," Adam said, "I have never taken a life."

The I Am commanded the Warrior, "Bring the woman to me."

The angel took Eve by the arm and led her to the foot of the throne. The I Am looked at Adam. "Life for life," he said. He turned to the angel. "When I give the word, slay the woman before me."

Adam started forward.

"No, Father! Please!" He drew close to Eve, taking her by the hand. He looked down at the sheep and the lamb. "I will do it." The sheep shook with fear as Adam took the sword from the Warrior. "I am sorry," he said.

He raised the sword, then brought it down on the neck of the sheep. She fell, her blood spilling onto the ground. The lamb nuzzled her, stepping in the blood of its mother. Adam wept. Raising the sword again, he slew the lamb.

"It is finished," the I Am said. To the Warrior, he said, "Retrieve your sword, remove the skins of the sheep and lamb and bring them to me."

The Warrior did as he was told, cutting the skins away with neat precision. The I Am took the skins in his hands and formed them into robes. Adam grimaced.

"This will be your covering," the I Am said. "You were clothed in spirit; you will now walk in flesh. Adam will toil in the fields for his sustenance and work by the sweat of his brow."

He stood, pointing toward the gates of Eden.

"Depart from me. I cast you out."

"My father!" Adam cried.

The Warrior held his flaming sword toward Adam and Eve, forcing them from the Garden of God. The I Am sat again upon his throne, weeping, holding his head in his hands.

I watched all of this with terrible sadness. I wished for someone to comfort my Lord in his time of grief. The Lord of the Fallen flew to the throne, lighting on the ground before the Great I Am. The Warrior bristled, holding his sword at the ready. The Lord of the Fallen curled his lips in scorn.

"Are you so grieved over the loss of this creature?" Reaching down, he scooped up a handful of earth and held it out. "Here is dust. Why not make you another son?"

The I Am looked at the Lord of the Fallen. His face showed great sorrow.

"You were once my friend," he said. "Why was I not enough for you?"

For a small moment, a look of loss replaced the disdain on the face of the Lord of the Fallen.

I heard a shout behind me.

"Behold the Fallen! One of them flies to the Tree of Life!"

I looked to see a shadowy figure approach the Tree of Life. I remembered him from the time before the rebellion: Hemael, a former Messenger of God. He stood, staring hungrily at the Tree of Life. Plucking one of the golden fruits, he closed his eyes and bit into it. Light sprang forth from the fruit, flowing around him.

The I Am spoke to the Warrior.

"Go to where the Tree of Life is. Bring me the Fallen angel who has partaken of its fruit. He will receive my judgment."

The Warrior bowed and flew to the Tree of Life, taking the Fallen angel roughly by the arm. Hemael did not resist. His eyes glazed over. His hand held the fruit. The Warrior carried him in his arms and placed him before the I Am. Hemael fell in a heap before the throne.

"You are Hemael," the I Am said, "my Messenger before the fall."

Hemael looked up at the I Am, shaking himself from his stupor. Dropping the fruit on the ground, he scrambled to his feet, trembling before the I Am with a furtive glance at the Lord of the Fallen.

"You have partaken of the fruit of the Tree of Life which I made for the woman. Why have you done such a thing?"

"I desired it, Holy One, for I am Fallen and dwell in death. I thought perhaps it would make me live again."

"And did the fruit give you life?"

Hemael looked at his hands. He studied the shadow that surrounded him.

"I remain in darkness," he said. "The life of the fruit has not entered me."

"You are mistaken. The life of the fruit has entered you, but I created it for humankind, not for angels. That which would have given the woman life eternal will bring to you death in greater abundance."

"I am already dead in my sins."

Hemael then cried out. His body jerked in great convulsions and he fell to the ground clutching at his abdomen. The Lord of the Fallen stepped away from him. His convulsions stopped. His eyes stared upward, open and unblinking, empty holes, black as onyx. His hands turned white as bone, his fingers elongating into skeletal claws. The dark shadow already around his body grew in size, cloaking him in blackness, hiding his face in a hood of shadow. He came to his senses, crying out at the sight of his transformed hands.

"Kneel before me and know my judgment," the I Am said. Hemael knelt before the I Am, his body jerking, shuddering. "I say unto you, thief of life, that you are death's Messenger. You will walk alone upon the Earth, drawn to the dying, delivering my judgment upon all humanity. You will reap the spirits of the dead, returning them to my storehouse. Where the dying are, you will be, to steal their life from them as you have stolen from the Tree of Life. You will dwell not with the Fallen, nor with humankind. Graveyards and sepulchers will be your respite."

Hemael did not answer. His body shuddered a final time and he shot up into the sky, flying from the presence of the I Am toward the setting sun, his shadow around him like the wings of a great black vulture.

The Lord of the Fallen flew from the presence of the I Am without another word, returning to the Fallen.

The sun set on the Garden of God. The moon shone yellow light on the scene below. Sangruel, a Watcher with us, came to where Erozel, Ariel, Azazel and I were. He watched the spot on the horizon where Hemael had disappeared.

"What will happen to him?" Sangruel asked.

Azazel shook his head.

"He will be a Messenger of death to mankind," he said.

"There has never been such a punishment," Ariel said.

Sangruel looked down at the garden. The I Am remained upon his throne, his light and rainbow piercing the darkness. His Warrior stood at attention.

"Why does he wait?" I asked.

Sangruel looked at me. "He waits because he knows what it is I am about to do."

"My brother," I said, "What is it that you are about to do?"

Sangruel looked back down at the garden. "Do you not see? Hemael chose the wrong tree. Life, true life, is in the blood. Is that not where the life of the sheep and her lamb dwelt? Blood is life." He pointed to where the Tree of Carnal Knowledge grew in the garden. His face showed hunger. "The fruit of that tree is filled with blood."

Azazel moved in front of Sangruel, blocking his view of the tree and the garden below.

"Return to the other Watchers," he said.

Sangruel shook his head. "I will do this thing, Captain of Watchers, for I hunger for the fruit of Carnal Knowledge. I thirst for its blood. I tire in watching. Tonight, for the first time since my creation, I will truly live."

With that, Sangruel flew, his light flowing behind him as he headed toward the midst of the Garden of God. Azazel followed him, shouting for him to return. I followed also, Ariel and Erozel beside me. Sangruel landed on the rocky cliff before the Tree of Carnal Knowledge.

"Sangruel, return with us!" Azazel shouted.

We landed together with Azazel. It was the first time we had ever entered the Garden of God. It troubled me. It was dark, with no light besides the moon and stars. Our own light shone brightly in the gloom. Sangruel reached out and plucked one of the fleshy fruits. Blood poured from the veins that had held the fruit to the branches. The fruit throbbed in his hand like a beating heart. Sangruel watched the blood flow down the branch of the tree.

"Do not do this wicked thing," Erozel said.

Sangruel did not look at us.

"Do you not see?" he said. "Life is in the blood."

"Stop this madness," I said. "What you propose to do is a sin against God. You are a Watcher and have been since your creation. Will you join the ranks of the Fallen?"

Sangruel turned to me. Blood from the fruit covered his hand.

"I do not wish to join the ranks of the Fallen," he said. He looked at the bloody fruit. "I will join mankind. I will drink of the blood of life and take my place with humankind. The blood of life will flow through me. I tire of watching life lived before me. Today I will be created anew."

Ariel moved toward Sangruel. "We will not allow you to do this thing," he said.

Sangruel's eyes fixed on the fruit in his hand. "Will you stop me, Ariel, you who only watch? Would that not be interfering? Do I not have freewill? It is the height of hypocrisy, is it not? You are a Watcher, but you long for war. Why must you only watch when you have the heart of a Warrior?

Erozel longs for Eve's body. His member tells the tale." He looked at Erozel. "Will you watch for eternity, never knowing more, never fulfilling the burning desire of your loins?" Erozel blushed and said nothing. "Your silence speaks volumes," Sangruel said. He lifted the fruit to his mouth.

"Please do not eat of it, my brother," I said. "Your light will go out. You will never enjoy the light of Heaven again."

Sangruel said, "I choose the light of the sun over the light of Heaven and the fellowship of man over the friendship of angels."

He bit into the fruit. Blood exploded from it, covering him. He drank deeply. His light went out and he became a shadow in the moonlight. His white robe of light turned to a black cloak of shadow. He devoured the fruit with appalling lust, drinking the blood, which flowed in amounts much more than could ever be in a fruit of that size. He did not eat the flesh of the fruit. His eyes were wide open. His body shook. He dropped the fruit of Carnal Knowledge.

"Come," Azazel said, flying upward, away from Sangruel. "He made his choice. Let us return to our places."

We flew silently to our position above the Earth. The I Am spoke to his Warrior.

"Go to the Tree of Carnal Knowledge, in the midst of the Garden. There you will find an angel covered with blood. Bring him to me."

The Warrior flew to the tree, his fiery sword cutting through the darkness. Sangruel lay prostrate on the ground. He did not move. The Warrior lifted him up and carried him. Sangruel showed no sign of life. The Warrior placed him on the ground before the I Am.

"You have eaten of the fruit of Carnal Knowledge, having lusted after its blood. You set in your heart to choose the light of the sun over the light of Heaven and the fellowship of humankind over the friendship of angels. I am the Lord, and I know all these things. Stand before me and be judged."

Strength entered Sangruel. He stood and faced the I Am. His bone-white face, now blood-covered, twisted into an eternal grimace, replacing his angelic beauty. Sharp teeth showed between thin, ashen lips. Dark circles and saggy frowns of skin surrounded jaundice eyes. When he spoke, his voice was a dry rasp.

"You know all things," Sangruel said. "Therefore you knew that I would partake of this fruit from the very day you made me."

"Silence," the I Am said.

Sangruel fell silent. He continued to sneer, showing his sharp teeth.

"From this night, the light of the sun will be your adversary. For you to know the sun is to know the fires of Hell. You will dwell in darkness. You have stolen the fruit of death, lusting for blood. You will ever lust for blood. Hear me now, thief of death. You will dwell among men, stealing life from some, and death from others. Those who drink from you will be your children, between life and death, having the blood of the tree in them. They, too, will lust for blood. They will also hide from the sun, to live in darkness while the blood of the tree flows within their hearts."

CHAPTER 7

I flew, the girl held safely in my arms, softly weeping, her face buried in my chest. I wept as well, trying hard not to think about the awful thing Sangruel had forced me to do. A mother and her twins were dead, sacrificed for this one child. I thought about the father of the twins, whoever he was, the terrible anguish he was sure to experience at the loss of his family. Would it be better for him to have joined them in death? Perhaps, but I am no murderer. I left him in God's hand.

I flew eastward toward the outskirts of the city, where stood palatial homes in manicured neighborhoods, until I saw the home I was looking for—a sprawling mansion on a hill overlooking the rest of the neighborhood, two police cars parked in the long driveway. I lowered to a spot where I could see through the large living room window. Two uniformed police officers stood by while a plain-clothes detective talked with the girl's parents on the couch. The mother, a petite blonde woman, wept. Her husband, a handsome man who appeared to be in his early thirties, looked stunned and concerned. I listened in.

The detective was an older man, graying and tired-looking. He spoke calmly, asking questions and jotting the answers down in a small notebook.

"You are her adoptive parents, then?"

The man nodded. The concern on his face made him look much older.

"And how long ago did you adopt her?"

"We raised her from when she was a baby," the man answered. His wife held a handkerchief to her face. Her shoulders shook. Her husband placed his arms around her.

"Do you know the birth parents? Is there any way they could be involved in this?"

The man shook his head. "No. We never knew them."

The detective looked around the living room, his eyes falling on the luxurious furniture, the trappings of wealth. "Do you own this house?"

"Yes," the man said.

"Then I assume you have money. We have to look at the possibility of kidnapping for ransom."

The woman's eyes widened. "Oh, do you think that's what happened?"

"At this point, anything is possible. Do not lose hope. I have been doing this for a long time, and more often than not, we find the missing child. For all we know, she is safe with a private citizen. It happens. Whatever you do, do not lose hope."

I waited for the police to leave, and then landed. I entered the house, uninvited, through the front door. The woman bowed her head when she saw me. She looked with relief at the girl in my arms.

"I must speak to Jonathon."

"He is in his study, my lord," she said.

The study was on the third floor of the house. I climbed the stairs and, without knocking, entered. Jonathon sat at a fine wooden desk. He looked up at me, worry on his face. I pointed my finger at him.

"The servants of Sangruel took her last night, while you were distracted. I paid a steep price for her safe return."

Jonathon's face paled. He stood up from his chair.

"Servants of Sangruel? How? She was with me the entire time. She just disappeared."

"If I had not been watching over her..." I said.

Jonathon bowed his head. "Forgive me," he said. "I am at fault."

I felt my anger slip from me. It was not Jonathon's doing, after all.

"I forgive you," I said. "You have been true to your charge, and she is unharmed. Still, I am disappointed in you, for you of all men should understand her value to me."

"It will not happen again," he said.

I placed my hand on his shoulder.

"It is not your fault," I said. "All that matters now is that she is safe."

I left the girl with Jonathon and headed home.

The place where I reside is a spacious penthouse on the very top of a high-rise building. The top three floors of the building are mine, lavishly decorated, though I care little for decadence. The ceilings are vaulted, the middle floor mostly removed to make space. A staircase connects all three floors together in the heart of my dwelling. I descended to my marble balcony. The glass doors leading to my living room were open and the curtains fluttered in the wind.

I am a lover of great works of art. Paintings and murals adorn my walls. Sculptures and statues decorate my hallway. Masters of art, most long dead, painted and sculpted each work. I enjoy paintings that depict Heaven, sunsets, nature, but it is easy to know where my heart truly is. The majority of the paintings and statues are of women, and every woman depicted has alabaster skin and autumn hair. The painted and sculptured women vary in age, from small girls, to fair maidens, to stately matriarchs. Above the mantle of my fireplace is such a painting. The subject is a young girl holding a bunch of violets in her dainty hand. Her hair is autumn, her skin the color of cream, her eyes alive, as though the artist captured a part of her soul with his artistry. She is the very image of the girl I rescued from Sangruel.

I do not tire, and though I take a respite, I need no rest. I never sleep. Therefore, I have very little furniture. A sofa (rarely used) and two comfortable, padded leather chairs, sat before a large window. I looked out over the city, in the direction of the girl's home.

There came the soft sound of footsteps on the staircase leading up from the lower floors, pausing before reaching the top.

"Come," I said.

I find the terms valet and manservant to be obsolete, and perhaps even a bit degrading. Andrew was in his late fifties, and was much more than a servant to me. His hair was black, salted with a generous amount of gray. He wore a dark suit with a white shirt and black tie. It is what he always wore. I did not require such a uniform, but Andrew would have it no other way. He was the curator of my art, the protector of my dwelling. He picked out my clothing and polished my shoes, and he was my friend. He was also my girl's driver. He entered, carrying two wine glasses and a bottle of my finest red.

"Wine, my lord?"

I nodded. "Yes, thank you."

He placed the glasses on the small table between the two leather chairs, opened the bottle of wine and filled my glass, holding it out to me, his head bowed. I took the glass of wine from him and glanced at his right hand. A tattoo of small folded wings in black ink marked it. The mark of the Grigorian, an Order of humans who know the truth about us; a remnant of those who worshiped and served Fallen angels in ages past. Members of the Order choose which Watcher to serve, and are usually very much like their Watcher—Andrew was like me, a man in love, though widowed now for many years.

"Andrew," I said, motioning to the empty glass on the table, "you were presumptuous enough to bring a second wine glass. Fill it and have a seat."

Andrew smiled and nodded. He filled his own glass and sat in one of the chairs. I took the other seat. We watched the city together while sipping wine. It was very good, aged and delicious—though, after my ordeal with Sangruel's servants, I might have preferred white wine over the red.

Andrew was good company. He talked little. He would have been a good Watcher. I thought about the events of the night, of the demon hidden in the catacombs below the city, satiated by the blood of the beautiful twin girls. I took a sip of the wine.

"I committed murder tonight, Andrew," I said.

Andrew did not look at me. His eyes remained on the view of the city.

"I am sure, then, that you had a good reason for it, my lord."

"Please," I said, "do not call me that. We are both children of God."

I sat in silence again, slowly emptying my wine glass, savoring each sip. My girl was safe. Nothing else mattered. Sangruel be damned.

"The servants of Sangruel took her tonight," I said.

Andrew stood up in shock, spilling wine from his glass.

"How can that be?" he said. "What about Jonathon?"

"He failed to protect her," I said.

I told him the entire story. He shook with fear and anger for the girl, cringing with revulsion when I spoke of Sangruel and the twins. I did not mention the Grigorian who I had forced into Sangruel's pit.

After a time, Andrew left me alone, returning to his own chambers on the first of my three floors. I poured the last of the wine into my glass and watched the city until dawn.

CHAPTER 8

As the population of Earth grew, I saw my fellow Watchers less and less. Ariel remained with me, my eternal partner for time without measure. We watched, chronicling the events below us. I was content to return to the trance-like state of watching, welcoming its familiarity. Perhaps the madness was over and we would simply watch until the end of the world. One-hundred, two-hundred years passed before us, then more, five-hundred. Humankind formed families, built cities, tilled the ground for their food. Adam and Eve had dozens of children together, Cain being the first, Abel the second. How Eve exulted at every birth, taking pleasure in even the pain of childbearing.

Adam built an altar of stones at the garden's entrance, and there, weekly, every man joined together as Adam sacrificed a lamb on the altar, spilling its blood upon the stones. This they did in the evening time. Unseen by humankind, the Fallen watched the sacrifices week after week, year after year, hovering together on the horizon. Hemael watched as well, his dark cloak of shadow billowing around him, his skeletal hands pointing toward the sacrificial lamb. A tiny trail of golden light would leave its body, flowing to Hemael. At that time, no human had yet to die, and I did not know the extent of Hemael's curse, his eternal banishment as the role of death angel. I would soon learn.

Sangruel came one night, after sunset, when Adam and his sons had departed. He stood blended in the shadows, weeping bloody tears before the altar of stones, crying out for mercy, begging to be freed from his thirst, to be returned to his former state. His pleading unanswered, he drank the blood of the sacrificial lamb. I sensed a strange restlessness in Ariel that night. He had taken delight in the sacrifice, his eyes wide and face intent, as Adam drove the knife blade into the lamb. Ariel watched closely as Sangruel tore the body of the lamb apart, drinking its blood.

"Beautiful," he said. His words and apparent delight troubled me. How could he consider such a thing beautiful?

One night, he left me without warning. I had been in the trance of watching and had not noticed his departure. I sensed something was wrong and found that I was alone for the first time since my creation. A feeling of dread and apprehension fell over me. I flew as quickly as I could, circling

Earth, searching for Ariel.

I found him after a time, just outside of the Garden of God, and I was even more alarmed. Ariel had descended to a spot mere feet above the Earth, hidden only by a clump of bushes. He sensed my presence and, looking up at me, pointed to an open, moonlit field. Two men stood in the field, voices raised each against the other in intense argument. I recognized them as Cain and Abel. Ariel watched them with mounting excitement, beckoning to me. Finally, I joined him, descending to a spot beside him.

"You left me alone," I said.

He ignored my accusation. "Listen to their anger, Saruel. Feel the violence in Cain's voice."

"It is terrible," I said.

Ariel turned toward me, scowling. I felt fear again. "Just watch."

I looked again at Cain and Abel. Their voices were angry, heated. Cain yelled loudly, standing face to face with his brother, his body tight with aggression. Spittle flew from his mouth as he shouted. Abel pushed him away. Cain stumbled over a stone, falling backward to the ground. He shook with rage, his eyes crazed.

"I will kill you for that!" He leapt from the ground and ran at Abel, before grabbing him, throwing him off balance. He then fell on him, pinning him to the ground. Beside me, Ariel tensed. I felt his excitement. His hands clenched into fists.

"Cain!" Abel cried, clearly in shock at his brother's terrible wrath. Straddling Abel, Cain's hand found the stone over which he had tripped.

"You are no longer my brother!" Cain yelled, lifting the stone, then bringing it down hard on Abel's head. Abel screamed, trying desperately to free himself from Cain's hold.

"My brother! My brother!"

Cain hit Abel again. This time the stone found its mark, sinking deep into his skull with the sickening sound of breaking bone. Ariel floated closer to the scene. I followed him, pleading with him to remain hidden. I placed my hand on his shoulder in an effort to stop him. He turned to me, his face contorting into a mask of rage.

"Do not touch me," he said. I let him go. He turned again to Cain and Abel. Blood flowed from Abel's head wound. His body convulsed. His eyes were open, glossed over, unseeing. Cain stood up. The stone fell from his hand. The angry look on his face turned to disbelieving terror. He fell to his knees beside Abel's seizing body.

"Abel?"

A final violent spasm racked Abel, and he became still. He did not move again. There was movement in the shadows to my left. I turned to see Hemael, hovering low, staring down at Abel, his bony hand outstretched.

Cain shook Abel, trying desperately to revive him. "Abel, my brother!

What have I done?"

He wept, crying loudly, burying his face in Abel's chest. Then he stood, looking fearfully around him. With one final glance at Abel's lifeless body, he turned and ran away.

Hemael moved from the shadows, drawing close to Abel's body, engulfing it in the darkness of his shadowy cloak. Abel's life left him, the light of his spirit illuminating the darkness. Hemael grasped the spirit of Abel, holding it fast in his hand, and flew, a great black vulture silhouetted against the night sky.

"Let us leave this terrible place," I said. "It is a place of death."

Ariel moved nearer to Abel's body, the light of his own body revealing Abel's face. Blood formed a halo on the ground around his head. More blood trickled from the corners of his open, dead, staring eyes.

"It is very beautiful," Ariel said.

With increasing horror, I saw Ariel's member protruding through his robe of light. Suddenly, Sangruel, a ghastly apparition in black, landed next to us. Kneeling before Abel's body, Sangruel snarled, showing sharp teeth.

"The body is mine! Leave me, holy angels, to my appalling curse."

He ran a clawed finger through the blood seeping from Abel's head wound, then placed it in his mouth.

"At last," he said, falling upon Abel's body, tearing into it with his awful teeth, drinking greedily of Abel's blood, seeming for a moment to forget our presence. He turned his head to look at us. Blood covered his mouth. "Leave me to my curse."

"We will stay," Ariel said.

Sangruel bared his teeth. "Will you look upon me in this dreadful state? I drink the blood of a righteous man. Will you behold this evil? I am a demon. Depart from me, hide your holy eyes from this cursed place."

"We are Watchers," Ariel said. "We will watch."

Sangruel fell again on Abel's body, tearing flesh, drinking human blood.

"Beautiful," Ariel said.

I flew, leaving Ariel behind. I wanted to hide my eyes from the sight of Earth. I wished Heaven had never ordered us to this planet, that it had never known creation, but remained the formless abyss it had once been. Ariel's delight in Abel's murder troubled me deeply, the pleasure he had shown in the mutilation of Abel's corpse, a body formed in the image of the I Am. What Ariel delighted in repulsed and sickened me. Such violence, such wickedness, was the murder of Abel.

Ariel did not return to me.

Children playing in the field discovered Abel's corpse the following day. The entire city gathered around the scene of Abel's murder. Adam and Eve arrived just before evening. Adam looked only slightly older than he had while in the Garden of God. Eve was just as lovely, though her hair had turned completely white. They walked hand in hand through the crowd to the spot where Abel's body lay. Eve fell to her knees, her face in her hands. Adam stood beside her, staring in silence at the body of his son. He looked up at the sky, as if the return of God's throne was imminent. Heaven remained silent. His eyes turned toward the Garden of God. He wept. Eve cried out, sobbing. The city joined in their grief, women wailing and men weeping.

Adam told the men of the city to dig a deep hole in the ground. When the hole was deep enough, he wrapped Abel's body in fine white cloth and, with the help of the men, lowered it into the grave, burying it in the earth. After these things, Adam stood before the crowd.

"Hear me now, sons and daughters. This place shall be called the Field of Blood, a place of death."

Adam and his children then returned to the city.

Far below me, Hemael lighted on the Field of Blood. His sepulcher white, skeletal hands folded in front of him, his face hooded in shadow, he looked down at where Abel's body rested in silence beneath the earth. There he stayed, the Field of Blood his dwelling place.

It was a terrible experience, being alone after so much time with Ariel as my companion. In vain, I searched the Earth for him.

He never returned to me.

Several hundred more years went by. During that time, Adam and Eve had another son who they named Seth. Eve held him in her arms and said:

"May the Lord use you to crush the head of the serpent. May the birthright of Cain fall to Seth and may his descendants return humankind to the presence of the Lord."

Death, unheard of before Abel's murder, increased in the passing years. Cain's single act of violence spread virally among mankind. Quarrels normally solved by peaceful means now often led to fighting, and fighting to murder. Natural deaths occurred as well. Hemael collected the spirits of all the dead.

A man, a son of Adam and Eve, died from an illness. His children cleaned and dressed his body and were in mourning for him. Others in his city prepared his grave as Adam had taught them. I flew to a spot above the Field of Blood, finding Hemael there, his hooded face turned downward to Abel's grave. I waited.

Finally, Hemael lifted his head, looking eastward toward the dead man's city. He rose up from the Earth, flying very quickly, faster than any other angel could fly. I flew after him with all the speed I possessed, barely able to keep up. It helped to know where he was heading. I arrived behind Hemael, just in time to see the man's spirit leave his body. Hemael pointed one long finger and the spirit flowed to him. He turned, flying toward the abyss.

I followed as quickly as I could. The land below me gave way to ocean.

The skies grew dark, the clouds sinister shadows. Lightning flashed around me. Hemael slowed his flight, descending to the dark waters. A great whirlpool of pitch black churned below him. He held the glowing spirit of the man tight in his hands. It struggled, taking the form of the body it had inhabited, thrashing and turning as Hemael drew nearer the abyss. Screams of terror came from the spirit as the mouth of the abyss yawned open to receive him, flames of hellfire leaping upward. Hemael cast the spirit down into the abyss. Black tendrils shot out from Hell's open mouth, wrapping around the man's spirit like so many serpents, pulling him down into the belly of Hell. The fire engulfed him. The mouth of the whirlpool closed, silencing his screams.

I flew to Hemael and hovered in front of him. He looked up at me, his gaunt face peering with empty eyes from the midst of his shadowy hood.

"What will become of the man's spirit?" I asked.

Hemael pointed toward the swirling darkness. His voice was death's rattle.

"All mankind will enter there," he said.

"Do they suffer, Hemael? Is it a place of eternal torment?"

"You know the answer, Watcher," he said. "You watched the abyss while I was still in its clutches. Mankind is the new Fallen." He looked down at the abyss. "They are tormented day and night, for all eternity."

CHAPTER 9

Alone.

I never quite understood the word. I knew that the I Am was alone; God alone, both in status and in reality. The I Am did not have a partner, did not have an equal. I had never been alone, for Ariel had been with me since our creation. I watched the Earth below me, my heart aching for the companionship of my brother Watcher. I worried for him. Had he joined the ranks of the Fallen? The other Watchers did not mention him when they visited the place where I watched the Earth. I had asked Azazel about him, but he knew nothing. Erozel, ever by Azazel's side, seemed preoccupied, wanting to return to where he watched the Earth. They came to me less and less.

I watched humankind, studied their ways, followed the births and deaths in the cities below me with renewed interest, living vicariously through others.

That is how I first saw her.

I was there when suns were born, witnessed their first glorious rise and their explosive demise. My eyes have seen the walls and gates of Heaven and have known the mysteries of the universe. I beheld the splendor of the cherubim and the magnificence of the Almighty. I was present during Earth's first sunset. I have witnessed the beauty of planets without number, worlds without end. None of these sights compared to her beauty.

I heard her before I saw her. She sang a song, sweet and soulful, in the language of Heaven, for the tongues of the Earth were not yet confused. I have heard the incomparable choirs of Heaven, but her song, unaccompanied by instruments, made the music of Heaven seem flat to me. She sang soft, yet strong; soulful, yet delicate. She sang of beauty, she sang of longing. She sang of love. I felt as though my heart would break. I had to stop myself from falling, forgetting that I hovered above the Earth.

Every sunrise I ever witnessed, the rainbow of God, the glory of Heaven, faded in my memory when first I saw her. Her alabaster skin was perfection, her autumn hair shone like the sun itself. She was a flower, her voice a running stream—pure, refreshing. Wearing a robe of light green cloth, she walked barefoot in the grass of a solitary meadow, toward a pool of slow flowing water. Stopping near the pool, she undressed. Her beauty overwhelmed me. Her soft breasts, the graceful curves of her body, the roundness of her hips, the fullness of her thighs; her belly a fine work of art, her chalice a goblet of sweet nectar. Stepping into the pool, she waded into the deep. I envied the water as it enveloped her, caressed her.

I watched her, drawing closer to the Earth, realizing that I had descended entirely only when my feet were already on the ground, yards away from the pool of water, standing in plain view. She stopped singing and listened, sensing my presence. I remained where I stood. She turned and looked at me. She gasped, covering her breasts with her arms, attempting to hide herself from me.

"Please," she said indignantly, "you must turn away from my nakedness."

I turned my face from her.

"I apologize," I said, "I mean you no harm."

I heard her move hastily from the water.

"You meant no harm? Are you in the habit of watching maidens while they bathe?"

"I regret that I have offended you."

She dressed quickly, and I looked at her.

"Please, sir, leave me alone with my shame."

Blushing, I turned to leave, my heart aching.

"I am deeply sorry," I said.

"Wait."

I turned back to her. She stared at me in wonder, seeing me clearly for the first time, having settled from her initial shock. "Who are you, son of Adam?" She stood, unmoving before me. "You are not a son of Adam," she said. "Who are you?" She stepped back. "What are you?"

I came to my senses then, realizing that I had broken the rule of all Watchers, revealing myself to this woman, taking part in her life. I panicked, flying away from her as quickly as I could, appearing to vanish.

"Wait. Come back!" She called out to the empty meadow, "I wish to know your name!"

I did not answer her, but, high in the sky, I remained, watching her, my heart filled with emotions I had never known before.

CHAPTER 10

I watched the rising sun before getting up from my chair. Andrew had left the penthouse earlier to pick my girl up, and drive her to her school. As was my custom, I would follow, watching over her. I changed into the clothes Andrew had lain out for me, a blue suit with a white shirt, no tie. I enjoyed the cut of the suit in my full mirror.

The day was cool, but the sky was clear. I stepped out onto my balcony and rose into the air, flying with great speed. I found Andrew's black car heading north on the highway. The girl attended a traditional Catholic school, nuns and priests providing her education. My Fallen brothers shied away from such places, which is why I chose to send her there. I followed until Andrew pulled the car up to the church, a building of ancient stones occupying several acres. Manicured ivy covered the walls. A statue of Mary Magdalene, the church's patron saint, watched serenely over the uniformed students below her. It looked very little like the real Mary.

Wearing a red school uniform like the other girls did, and carrying a backpack, my girl made her way into the building. I waited, hovering above the chapel where the students gathered together for their daily prayers. I listened to the prayers for forgiveness and for salvation, led by a priest. I prayed with them,

"Our Lord, deliver us from our sins and transgressions, save us from our iniquity."

I felt the presence of ministering spirits, as two angels descended to a spot above the chapel. They wore the white robes of Heaven. The light of God surrounded them. They hovered just below me, offering me not so much as a glance, listening to the prayers of the humans in the chapel. I repeated the prayer, personalizing it,

"Hear me, oh God, attend unto my prayers, deliver me from my sins, save me from my iniquity. Let me enter into your holy presence again."

One of the angels looked up at me.

"Will you deliver my prayer to Heaven?" I said.

The angel remained silent, looking down at the chapel again. I called out to him, pleading.

"Let my cry be heard in Heaven, for my judgment is more than I can bear."

The angel looked at me again. "Salvation is not granted unto you, Fallen spirit," he said. "Your prayer will not reach the Temple of God. You are in eternal fall."

I held my hands out wide. "The I Am is merciful and sovereign. He can do as He pleases. He can return me to my first estate."

The second angel looked up at me. "Be gone, unclean spirit," he said. "I cast you from this place."

At his words, an unseen power propelled me backward, away from the chapel, away from the school. A barrier formed around the entire school, keeping me away. I cried out in anguish and frustration. "Is it a sin to love one of God's own children?"

I flew from the angels, circling the Earth, tears staining my cheeks, until I saw Jerusalem below me. I found the place of the skull and descended, my feet landing hard in the dust below the hill called Golgotha. Though the area was worn by time and the elements, I could make out the natural formation of a skull in the rocky crevasse of the cliff. I remembered the cries of men two millennia ago, the agony of the one crucified there, the terrible darkness that followed. I felt a tremor in the air, and looked up to see a dark figure flying toward me. It was Ariel. He was the only Watcher I kept in contact with, and we met here once every month. He landed in front of me. He wore the uniform of a bronze era soldier. His armor was black leather with the emblem of a silver dragon, a sword fastened to his waist. Dried blood covered his hands.

"Where do you come from, my brother," I said, motioning to his blood-stained hands. His eyes flashed with madness.

"I am the spirit of war and destruction. It is from battle that I come. What of you, Saruel? Rumors of you have reached my ears."

"I do what I have always done," I said. "I watch the Earth."

Ariel laughed.

"That is my Saruel," he said, "never changing, desiring to return to his former glory."

I said nothing in reply. Ariel frowned.

"Forgive me, Saruel, for you are my brother. I love you with my whole being."

"Love," I said. "What does the spirit of war know of love?"

"I love violence; I love destruction, with a love as pure as yours. The I Am placed a love for these things in my heart. I do his bidding, for war, pestilence, unrest, death; all are part of his will and plan."

"He made you a holy angel. You chose violence over him."

Ariel shook his head.

"Do you fill a creature with desire and tell it not to act upon it? You loved your maiden from the moment you saw her, didn't you? And who gave you the ability to love her, if not the I Am at your creation?" He pointed toward the worn face of the skull. "Do you see how it all fits? We stand now at the place where it all happened. Here lies the former Garden of God, where Adam and Eve fell, where Hemael ate the Fruit of Life, and Sangruel the fruit of blood. Here, Adam built the altar of sacrifice, Abraham offered up Isaac, and Solomon built the temple." He looked up to the top of the hill. "Here, the Son of God was slain."

"What are you saying?" I asked. "Do you believe that God wanted you to fall—planned it, even? I cannot believe such a thing."

He looked at me intently. He pointed westward to the open plains. "Don't you see? Behold before us the Field of Blood, where the war to end all wars will take place, where Abel was slain and Hemael finds respite. It is where I first knew the thrill of violence. Hemael will be here at the great battle, and so will I. We all do God's will."

"And what about me," I said, "where do I fit into this supposed plan?"

Ariel studied me for a moment. "I heard about your actions in Sangruel's pit," he said. "I found Sangruel and he told me everything. I was intrigued by his tale, and Sangruel's description of the girl whose life you saved, her hair autumn, her skin ivory white; a familiar description." His eyes met mine. "Who is the girl, Saruel?"

"I have watched her family line," I said.

"And what family line is that, Saruel?"

"One that has no interest for you," I said.

Ariel studied my face. "After leaving Sangruel, I found Hemael. I asked him about your maiden, and he did not remember her."

"The girl is only six years old. Her time for meeting Hemael is many years away."

"Not that maiden," Ariel said. I stiffened. "The one you fell in love with, the one that caused you to sin. Hemael did not know her. How can that be?"

"Many have died."

"Yes, Saruel, many have died. Only two men escaped death: Enoch and Elias. Hemael remembers each and every spirit he collected, yet not your maiden."

I waved my hand dismissively. "This is absurd," I said.

"Then tell me, Saruel, how did she die?"

"She died like all the others of her time."

Ariel was silent for a moment. He rose slowly into the air. "I'm not so sure of that," he said.

"If only I had such power," I said, "Marah would still be alive."

"Marah would be alive," he said, "but what about Asherah, the woman Erozel loved? Would you have saved her from death as well?"

"Erozel does not know love," I said.

"He loves perversion," Ariel said, "with a love as pure as your love was for Marah. As for Asherah, if you could have saved her, and chose not to, who knows what Erozel might do if he discovered it?" He turned from me.

"I hope for your sake you have spoken true."

With that, he flew away from me. I stood, my eyes following him until he disappeared over the horizon. I was trembling.

I turned to the place of the skull, recalling the horror of that place two millennia ago, smelling the blood again, the pungent gall, hearing the groans of pain; seeing the cruel soldiers of Rome, the jeering mob and weeping women and the face, the blood-marred face of the image of God. I remembered Sangruel's appalling sin at the foot of the cross, and his subsequent curse. I looked upward toward Heaven.

"You gave your life for love," I said. "Did I not do the same as you?" Dark clouds appeared in the sky, shading Golgotha from the rays of the sun. "Hear me," I said, "will you hide your face from me forever?"

I lifted from the Earth, flying through dark clouds, seeking the light of the sun, on a path toward Heaven, the Earth behind me diminishing in size. I saw the abyss below me, swirling in the deep, hidden from the eyes of mortal man. I flew on, miles above the planet. I flew faster, hoping to escape the bonds of Earth.

"City of Heaven," I called, "Open your gates to me. Let me dwell with the angels of God!"

I hit an invisible wall at the edge of Earth's atmosphere. Pain racked my body and I cried out, losing control of my flight. I fell toward the earth, paralyzed. "My God," I cried, "why have you forsaken me?"

I fell for several minutes, helpless, my eyes fixed on Heaven. The water of the Pacific Ocean hit me with meteoric force. I sank down, deep into the water, my eyes open, watching the light above me disappear, leaving me in utter darkness.

CHAPTER 11

Adam and Eve passed away together, Eve's head on Adam's shoulder, leaving this world as she had come into it, at Adam's side. Hemael came for them as he did for every human being. Their spirits did not struggle. They went calmly, together, into the abyss. I marveled at the bond of love they shared.

After the death of Adam and Eve, tensions arose between the sons of Abel and the sons of Cain. Abel's descendants were herdsmen, while Cain's descendants tilled the ground. It began with a small argument that blossomed into something much more. That is the way of such things. Wars are fought, lives wasted over petty differences, even to this very day.

A herd of goats belonging to a son of Abel trampled and devoured the vegetables of a field belonging to a son of Cain. The son of Cain demanded that payment for the field should be the goats that had destroyed it. Abel's son disagreed. I watched them together in the field.

"Have your father, Cain, pay you for the field," Abel's son spat, "does he not owe us an unpaid debt?"

At this, the son of Cain struck the son of Abel with his fist.

Abel's son said, "Will you murder me, as your father murdered my father? Surely, all sons of Cain have slaughter in their hearts!"

The son of Cain looked at his fist, his anger subsiding. He turned and ran, distraught at his own violence. It would have ended there.

I saw a flash of light in the sky, an angel flying at great speed. My heart rejoiced when I saw that it was Ariel, my brother. He had not Fallen, for the light of God shone around him. My delight turned to dismay, as Ariel landed in the field, standing before the son of Abel.

"Hear me, son of Adam, son of Abel," Ariel said. His voice was strong and powerful, his body shone with angelic glory. The son of Abel fell to his knees, worshiping. "Stand to your feet, son of Abel, for you must only worship the Great I Am."

Did Ariel have a message from the I Am? Is that where he had been? Had Heaven called him away?

"Speak, my lord," Abel's son said.

"Hear the word of the Lord. Behold, my son Adam is dead. It is time to avenge the death of Abel, his son."

"What will you have me do?" The son of Abel said.

"You must destroy every descendant of Cain," Ariel said, his face hard, his eyes fire, "every man, woman and child."

Abel's son looked at Ariel in astonishment. "Surely, my lord, this cannot be. It cannot be right, returning violence for violence."

"Will you question the will of your God?" Ariel said. "Even now, the sons of Cain are conspiring against you. They are violent men, murder lies within them. They desire the blood of every son of Abel and the chalice of every daughter. You must do unto them what they will surely do unto you."

I watched, horrified, as hate filled the features of the son of Abel.

"I will obey the word of the Lord," he said.

Ariel rose into the air above the son of Abel. "Make the children of Cain a blood sacrifice on the altar of the Lord."

He flew then, to a point high above the Earth. I heard him laughing, wicked and evil. The angelic light surrounding him went out, revealing his nakedness.

I wept.

The sons of Abel attacked the children of Cain without mercy, with terrible violence, using stones and knives. The sons of Cain fought back, their plowshares and farming utensils as weapons. Bodies of men, women and children littered the cities of Cain. Blood and the anguished cries of bereaved mothers filled the Earth. I hoped for Heaven's intervention, but Heaven was silent. Ariel stood at the outskirts of the city, watching the violence with exhilaration, drawing near whenever a battle was particularly brutal. Hemael was also close by, fulfilling his curse. A dark cloud appeared on the horizon as the Lord of the Fallen and his angels arrived to watch the bloodshed on the Earth below.

Not only was Heaven silent about the violence on the Earth, but Ariel's sin was not punished. He no longer shone with the light of God, but the I Am had not judged him beyond that. His robes were not black like those of the Fallen. He looked like a man. I wondered at this.

The Lord of the Fallen flew to Ariel, landing before him.

"We welcome you, Ariel, to the ranks of the Fallen," he said.

"I do not wish to join your ranks, Son of the Morning, I choose to remain alone."

The Lord of the Fallen frowned. "Of course," he said. "I wish only to applaud your decision, your choice to fulfill your own desire. Your heart has always been that of a Warrior. The I Am made you this way. It should not be a sin to be what you are."

Ariel looked at the Lord of the Fallen. "And what is it that you desire? What is in your heart?"

The Lord of the Fallen looked toward Heaven. "I wish to rule Heaven and Earth. I will sit upon the throne of God. I will be worshiped and adored."

"Your passion has robbed you of sanity," Ariel said. "Whatever you and I do, it is the will of the I Am. My fall, your fall, only serves his purpose. I am no god, you are no god, nor shall we ever be."

"But we are gods!" The Lord of the Fallen said. His face was angry, his beauty eclipsed by madness. "You are the god of war, Hemael the god of the abyss. I am the god of gods."

"You are mad," Ariel said. He flew into the sky, leaving the Lord of the Fallen behind.

The war between the descendants of Cain and Abel continued. I saw innocent, peaceful men turn savage, lusting after violence and blood.

The beautiful maiden was my only respite.

I watched her daily, delighted by her every move, her every action. She was a descendant of Seth, the son of Adam, and her people had not yet joined in the violence. She walked to the meadow every day, bathing in the pool of water, looking around her whenever she undressed, as if expecting my sudden appearance. I was tempted several times to land near her, but mine was to watch and I reminded myself of this. I would not follow in the way of Ariel.

Azazel came to me one day. His face was marked with sorrow. Erozel was not with him.

"My captain," I said, "What has happened?"

He shook his head. "Erozel has Fallen. The other Watchers have followed him into sin."

I did not know what to say.

"What have they done?"

Azazel shuddered. "I loathe even to tell you, for their sin is very great."

"Tell me," I said.

Erozel had shown untoward interest in the animal coupling of human beings, delighting in their physical relations, his member engorged, protruding through his robe. He fondled it openly, without shame, watching humans couple together on the Earth. The other Watchers joined with him.

Erozel discovered a young maiden, voluptuous and well formed, by the name of Asherah. Humankind was relatively innocent concerning physical relationships. Asherah was an exception. She lusted brazenly after men. Her sexual appetites captivated Erozel's attention. She seduced many men, coupling with them in the seclusion of a wooded area near her home. Erozel and his followers watched her, lowering close to the Earth. Azazel rebuked them, but to no avail.

The maiden's appetites grew over time. She brought two men to the forest, coupling with them both, committing unnatural acts, never before known under Heaven. The men had sexual relations with her at the same time, one in front of her, one behind her, one member thrusting into her forbidden part while the other man had her chalice. Erozel watched this with wanton desire.

Finally, Asherah committed an unthinkable sin. She brought a young woman with her to the wooded area, seducing her as she had seduced the men, kissing her as a man would kiss a woman. Azazel had watched in anticipation, sure immediate judgment would befall her. None did. She undressed the young woman, kissed her breasts, exploring the woman's chalice with the fingers of her hand, her mouth working, kissing from the woman's breasts to her belly, and lower. I considered Adam's sin in the garden.

"Surely not," I said.

"It is so," Azazel said.

The young woman stopped her. She got up hastily from the ground, and, grabbing her garments, ran from the depraved maiden. By that time, Erozel had lowered all the way to the ground. Asherah shouted after the young woman, cursing her, her evil desire unquenched. Erozel stepped into sight, his member engorged, showing through his robe of light. Asherah looked up, staring at Erozel.

"You are beautiful," she said. "Delicate like a woman, yet you have the member of a powerful man. Tell me; are you a man or a woman?"

Erozel answered, "I am neither a man nor a woman."

"Then what are you?"

"I am one who longs for you."

Asherah spread her legs wide, her chalice swollen, open.

"Then have me," she said.

Erozel lay with her, committing that which is unlawful, thrusting deep into her chalice with his member. His light went out and he was naked. To my surprise, he was in nearly every way female: shapely hips, his breasts round and full, his skin smooth as silk. His engorged member filled the place where a chalice would have been.

The Watchers joined in his sin, taking turns with the wicked maiden, committing acts so terrible, so unnatural, that I choose not to describe them.

As time went by, Erozel sought new ways to fulfill his desires. He influenced humankind to commit terrible sins. Men and women, forgetting their Creator, offered Erozel their worship, dancing naked before him in large groups, performing sexual acts together in the open, unashamed, sinning against their own flesh. They built a temple unto him and an altar of stones fashioned after the altar that was before the Garden of God. They brought young women who had never known men, raping them mercilessly, leaving them bleeding and weeping, naked before the temple of Erozel. Erozel accepted their abomination as worship. I watched in anger as the young maidens cried out in terrible pain and fear.

The Fallen enjoyed the continued pollution of God's favored creation. The Lord of the Fallen influenced humankind to forget the one true God.

He chose men of arrogance and pride to rule over other men. These men led their people in the worship of Fallen angels, defiling the place of sacrifice before the gate of the Garden of God, offering their sons and daughters, butchering them on the altar of stones. In return for their worship, the Lord of the Fallen gave them knowledge, wealth and power.

Earth groaned. Violence ruled the day. Blood ruled the night. The thoughts of humankind were wicked continually. Sangruel preyed upon the living, feeding in the night, leaving corpses for the morning. Hemael collected the spirits of men and the abyss enlarged itself to contain them.

Azazel returned to me. His prior sadness was gone. He appeared excited.

"What is it, my captain?" I asked.

"It is Erozel!" he said.

What pleasure he could take in anything Erozel did, I could not imagine. "What of him?" I said.

"It is the most wondrous thing, Saruel!"

I frowned at him. He looked at me and shook his head. "No, listen to me. I know that Erozel has committed terrible sin, but something wondrous has happened. His woman, the one he fell into sin with, she has known no man, coupling only with the Fallen Watchers since Erozel's fall."

"May the I Am bring judgment upon them all," I said.

"So be it," Azazel said, "but behold, the maiden is with child! Do you know what this means, Saruel? It means that we, the angels of Heaven, can have children with the daughters of men!"

I was astonished. "How can this be?" I said. "Why would angels have seed as men do?"

Azazel looked down at the Earth.

"Why is it, Saruel, that we have members at all? Why would the I Am make us this way if not to have children?"

"It is not for me to know," I said. "Mine is to watch, not to experience, not to understand. Your words are like unto the words of the Son of the Morning."

"Yes," Azazel said, "Of course. I forget myself." He looked down at the Earth, then, nodding at me, he flew away, leaving me alone again.

Under the influence of the Lord of the Fallen, the leaders of men gathered with their followers before the gates of the Garden of God. They had cut down trees, and formed battering rams, desiring to break down the gates of the Garden in order to reach the Tree of Life.

I saw the two angelic Warriors who guarded the Garden of God. One stood directly behind the gate. The other stood before the Tree of Life. If the men did break through the gates, the Warriors would cut them down. Surely, the Lord of the Fallen knew this. Was he truly mad? It made no difference, however, for the Warriors, hearing the call of Heaven, departed the Garden, taking both the Tree of Life and the Tree of Carnal Knowledge with them. When the Lord of the Fallen saw this, he ordered the leaders of men to fall back.

I watched the Warriors depart, my heart sick, for they had stripped the Garden of God of its past glory. Would humankind ever walk again with the I Am in the cool of the day? Were they forever beyond redemption?

While looking down at the garden, I saw a glint of golden light. I looked closer. A single fruit of the Tree of Life, the very one that Eve had picked, lay on the ground where Adam had dropped it, barely showing through the overgrown foliage. I looked toward Heaven in the direction the Warriors had flown. How could they have forgotten this fruit? Could it be that they did not know it existed? That had to be it. Only the Watchers could have known.

I looked at the Earth, at fallen humanity, lost in their sin, polluted by violence and unnatural desires, worshiping Fallen angels as gods. I could not allow them to partake of the Fruit of Life, but I was a Watcher. Did I have a choice? I made my decision, flying as quickly as I could to the Garden of God, landing by the golden fruit. I picked it up carefully, remembering Hemael's curse, and hid it within my robe.

CHAPTER 12

A descendant of Seth decried the evil that filled the entire Earth. His name was Enoch. He stood daily upon a hill in the City of Lamech and cried with a loud voice.

"There is but one God and one master of the universe, who alone rules over the heavens and the Earth. He made the stars, the planets and all that is therein. He made angels and humankind alike. We must worship the one true God, and only him shall we serve!"

When people gathered around him, he taught them to follow the ways of the I Am. He caused the sacrifice of the lamb to continue, building and consecrating a new altar of stones in the city of Lamech. Therefore, the city of Lamech became a light in the darkness.

The beautiful maiden lived at the edge of Lamech. I watched her every day as she bathed in the pool of water. After a time, she stopped looking around for me, no longer expecting my sudden appearance. For a reason that I did not understand, this displeased me.

She was so lovely, more glorious to me than all the angels of Heaven. I knew it would not be long before men sought her hand in marriage. This troubled me. I did not want her to change. She was my only respite, and I did not want to lose her.

The news of what Enoch did in Lamech spread throughout the Earth, reaching the ears of the Watchers. Enoch's words angered Erozel. He stood before his servants and said, "Where is the God of Enoch? Do you see him in the heavens; does he walk upon the Earth? Will you serve a God that you cannot see, and who does nothing for you, or one that you can see, and who brings you pleasure beyond your imagination? Will mankind return to the Garden of God, will they forget the delight of offspring and the pleasures of the flesh?"

Erozel rose slowly into the air, above his servants, his androgynous features filled with rage. "Whosoever defiles the children of Seth is worshiping me. Whosoever brings this man, Enoch, to me will sit at my table and lie between my breasts."

My heart filled with dread, for the lovely maiden lived on the edge of Lamech, and was of the children of Seth.

Small parties of the servants of Erozel began raiding the city of Lamech, bringing the women and children with them to Erozel's temple, defiling them with sexual acts as an offering to Erozel, raping and abusing them until their spirits were broken or they, also, became Erozel's servants.

Enoch continued to decry the sins of both angels and men. The children of Seth formed an army to defend the city of Lamech. For a while, this stopped the raids.

Soon after, I saw Ariel land in a secluded section of Lamech. He had disguised himself as a mortal, dressed in the style of the sons of Seth. His face was dirty, his shoes dusty and worn, his clothes soiled and torn. He approached several men of the army who were gathered to protect Enoch. He fell on the ground, weeping at their feet.

"What is it?" they asked him. "Why do you weep? What has happened to you?"

Ariel cried out, his face filled with torment. "My brothers," he said, "hear me. I have escaped from the city of the wicked, where the sons of men worship at the temple of false gods. They committed terrible sins against me."

Ariel cried out again, his entire body shaking with what looked like terror. He covered his face with dust and tore at his garments. "They have defiled my wife and children, both male and female, offering my oldest daughter as a blood offering. They bound me with ropes and defiled my body. They raped me as they would rape a woman, forcing their evil members into my forbidden part as though the chalice of a woman."

At this, the sons of Seth were enraged and tore their clothing.

"Hear me!" Ariel said. "There is more. Before I escaped, I overheard these evil men, these worshipers of devils, plotting to bring war against this city. They have formed an army and will attack in three days. They have sworn to do unto you and your families what they have done to my family and to me. Now I plead with you, do unto them what they will most surely do unto you. Avenge me, avenge my family, and protect your own wives and daughters."

The army of the sons of Seth cried out and covered their heads with dust, enraged at the wickedness done to another son of Seth. They did not see Ariel depart, slipping into a secluded alley and flying away. They did not hear his wicked laughter. When the story Ariel told spread throughout the city, the men of Lamech demanded war against the servants of Erozel.

The next morning, Enoch stood on his hill, calling to the leaders of the army of the sons of Seth.

"Hear me now, for you have been deceived. The Great I Am desires peace, and not war. Defend this city from evildoers, but do not bring war to our brothers. Vengeance belongs to God, and to God alone."

At this, the leaders of the army answered, "Will we allow such wickedness? Will the worshipers of demons attack this city in full force? We must surprise them; do unto them what they would do unto us. Did you not hear what the son of Seth told us, did you not hear the terrible acts they committed upon him?"

Enoch answered, "And where is this son of Seth? Bring him to me, so that I might see him with my own eyes and hear him with my own ears."

"He has not been found in the city," they answered. "Surely he has departed, filled with shame for what was done unto him. We must attack the evildoers. We must stop them from overtaking this city."

Enoch said, "And what will you do to them? Will you spill their blood? Will you capture their women and children? Will you do unto them what they would do to you? Will you rape them and commit other sexual sins against them?"

"We will do unto them before they do it unto us," the leaders answered.

While Ariel watched, the army of the sons of Seth attacked the next day, killing many of the followers of Erozel and taking the women and children captive, returning with them to the city of Lamech. Because of this, many of the women who had worshipped Erozel, and who loved strange and unnatural sexual sin, became the wives of the sons of Seth. They taught the men their wickedness, so that soon the people of the city of Lamech resembled the servants of Erozel. Enoch continued to cry out from atop his hill, but the children of Seth paid him little attention. One day, he brought his son with him, a man of around three-hundred years old.

"Hear me, sons of Seth, for I have heard the voice of the I Am. He has come to me in the night while I slept upon my bed. God will judge the Earth at the end of my son, Methuselah's, life. Turn from your wicked ways and he will offer you and your descendants a way to escape his terrible judgment."

A man who heard Enoch laughed and said, "What did the I Am do to you while you were in bed with him? Are you now the concubine of the one who rules the universe?"

Enoch held out his hands to Heaven and said, "Hear me, one who sits upon the throne, show these men a sign that I am your servant."

The sky immediately darkened. Fire fell from Heaven and consumed the man before the people of the city of Lamech, leaving a mound of ash on the burned ground where he stood. Those around the man cried out in terror. After this, no man spoke openly against Enoch. Nevertheless, the people of the city did not change their ways.

I was intrigued, for I was a Watcher, an angel of Heaven, yet not one time had I heard the voice of the I Am since he had cast Adam and Eve from the garden. Yet here was a man that heard his voice! A Fallen man heard the voice of God! I could not help feeling envious.

Azazel had not visited me in quite some time, and my only relief was the lovely maiden. I lost myself to her song.

One morning, she walked to the pool of water. I waited for her to undress, as she usually did. She remained clothed, however, her eyes searching the surrounding woods. She looked up suddenly, in my direction. Hidden by the ether, I knew she could not possibly see me. Yet for a moment, I was not sure.

"My love?" she called. The woods absorbed her soft voice. She looked around her, listening, watching, and calling again. Was she calling for me? I drew closer to Earth. "My love, can you hear me? I am here for you," she said.

My heart pounded in my chest, yearning for her. I hovered at the edge of a low cloud, watching her. She was beautiful, wearing a robe of white. A garland of purple flowers adorned her autumn hair. I descended to a spot several hundred yards above her, visible to the eye, but far enough away not to attract attention. I wanted to talk with her, to be near her.

A young man stepped out from the thick woods. Tall and handsome, he wore the clothes of a descendant of Abel. "I am here, my love," he called.

The maiden ran to him and they embraced, holding each other, kissing. I felt a terrible stab of jealousy.

"I feared you might not come for me," she said to him. Turning, she looked in the direction of her father's house. "We must leave before my father and brothers discover my absence."

The young man stepped back, looking at the maiden.

"You are sure of this?" he said. "You will come with me?"

Her face reddened. "I will marry the man that I love, not a man chosen by my father."

The young man smiled and took her by the hand. "Then let us go, my love. My family has prepared a great celebration and tomorrow we will be married."

They traveled the rest of the day together, walking many miles. She laughed with him, talked with and kissed him along the way, hand in hand with him for much of the journey. When she sang to him, my heart ached. I told myself that I was being foolish. She was a daughter of Eve, while I was a son of Heaven. She belonged with one of her own kind. The sun set low on the horizon. They came to a pleasant meadow and stopped beside a running stream.

"Let us rest here for the night," the young man said. "We will reach my village by midday tomorrow."

They settled down for the night, holding each other as they slept. They remained fully clothed, and for that, at least, I was thankful.

The next morning, the maiden awoke, leaving the young man asleep. She walked along the stream for a few minutes, singing such a wondrous song of love that it still haunts me to this day. She undressed and stepped into the clear water. I hid my eyes from her as she bathed, for I could not bear to see her beauty while she gave her love to another.

I fastened my attention on the sleeping young man. He was very handsome and comely. For just a moment, I thought of snatching him from where he lay and carrying him to a faraway place. I did not, of course. I would not interfere. Just then, I heard movement in the surrounding woods. I looked to see four people, two men and two women dressed in the revealing garb of Erozel's worshipers. The women's breasts were bare, lifted up high by cloth halters. The hems of their robes were cut at a point just below their chalices. The men wore robes of similar length, carved wooden phalluses sheathing their members as ornamentation. They walked together, not having seen the sleeping young man. If they did happen to see him, I knew they would rape and defile him right there in the meadow. If they found him especially lovely, they would save him as an offering to Erozel. As it was, they passed him by, unaware of his presence. I held my breath as they walked, mere yards from him, talking together in raised voices. The young man stirred from his slumber, and looked around him.

Be still, I thought.

He stood up, seeing the servants of Erozel walking away, their backs turned to him. I held my breath. Surely, he would know what they were, and remain hidden. I was admittedly jealous of him, but I did not wish to see him defiled. To my dismay, the young man called out.

"I am here," he said. What a fool! Did he not know what they were?

Erozel's servants turned toward him. One of the women ran to the young man and fell to her knees in front of him, pressing her mouth to his robes at the place of his member.

"Priest of Erozel," she said. "Shall I honor you?"

"Not now, servant of Erozel," the young man said. "The maiden is nearby. Take her, bind her, but do not defile her. She will be presented as a virgin to the master."

The jealousy I had felt earlier gave way to wrath and indignation.

The two men left him, heading toward the spring. She was dressing when they found her. She screamed when she saw them. One man grabbed her from behind, holding her roughly, while the other bound her hands with chords. Together, they carried her to the young man. She cried out, "My love, are you well?"

The servants of Erozel laughed. The priest of Erozel smiled cruelly.

"My lovely young virgin," he said. "Do not fear for me. Fear for yourself. Tomorrow, you will lose your innocence, your body used, your chalice and forbidden part stretched until the blood flows. It is a great honor, but not without pain."

She stared with horror at him, confused and distraught. "But I loved you," she said. "We were to be married."

One of the women laughed. She approached the maiden and kissed her lustfully on the mouth. "When the master is through," she said. "I shall have my turn. I will do things to you that you never knew were possible."

"Leave her be," the priest of Erozel said. "She will be offered undefiled to the master."

"My waters run with desire for her," the woman said. "When she has fulfilled her purpose, give her to me, I pray you."

"That remains to be seen," he said.

Anger and hatred like I had never known before consumed me. I wanted to destroy these servants of Erozel. When I came to my senses, I found that I had lowered to a spot visible in the sky, no more than a hundred yards above the ground.

Leaving the men, the two women walked together to the flowing spring. Removing their garments, they stepped hand in hand into the water.

"She does not know her good fortune," one woman said. "How I wish the master would choose me to bring a child of the gods into the world."

"You are hardly an innocent virgin," the other woman said. "I made well and sure of that." She reached for her, pulling her into a tight embrace, kissing her neck, then lower, to her breasts. "Still, to be sure, let me defile you once more."

I turned away from them, deciding then what I must do. Erozel would not have the maiden. He would not defile her in such a way, bringing unholy children into the world. Watcher or not, I would not allow it. I flew to a spot just above where the men held her captive, then landed next to her, in plain sight. The men jumped to their feet at my sudden appearance. The maiden stared at me in surprised shock.

"Who are you?" Erozel's priest demanded. Ignoring him, I quickly untied the maiden.

"Stand up," I told her. She obeyed at once.

"This woman belongs to my master," the priest said. The men moved toward me. My anger getting the best of me, I grabbed one of the men hard by his arm and heard the snapping of bone. He screamed in pain. I released him, pushing him to the ground. The priest of Erozel stared at me in disbelief.

"You are not a man. Are you one of the gods?"

I lifted into the air with the maiden. The priest called after me.

"Do not take her! My master will hear of this. He will find her and bring punishment to her! She will not escape his wrath"

I stopped, considering his words. Erozel would hear of this, and would know me by my description. I had only one choice. I flew with the maiden, depositing her on a hill a safe distance away.

"Wait for me," I said. She nodded, looking up at me, a mixture of terror and heartbreak on her lovely face. I returned to the men. The one with the broken arm sat on the ground, rocking back and forth, cradling his arm. I picked him up and carried him high into the air. He screamed with pain and fear.

"Release me! I am a servant of the true god, Erozel!"

I released him. He fell screaming to the Earth, his body hitting the ground with a satisfactory thud, cutting him off in mid-scream. I flew to the other two men, and, seizing them both, returned with them to the sky.

"I am a priest of Erozel," the young man shouted to me over the wind. "You must not do this!"

"You deceived her, taking advantage of her love," I said. "You deserve far worse than what I will do to you."

"My master will search for me. When he finds my body, he will know how I died."

"Then he will never find your body," I said. I flew quickly, holding the terrified humans in a tight grip, until the dark ocean appeared below us. I hurled the screaming men toward the turbulent waters below, watching until they disappeared beneath the waves.

I looked down at my body, surprised somewhat that the light of Heaven still surrounded me. Could it be that what I had done was not a sin? I had saved the maiden from terrible misery, a life of lust, rape and abuse, but I had violated the rules of Watchers in doing it. I had taken the lives of human beings.

Turning toward land again, I returned to the maiden.

She sat in the green grass, weeping, her body trembling, her knees pulled up to her chest, arms wrapped around her legs. I landed quietly on the ground in front of her.

"You are safe now," I said.

She remained seated. "I thought that he loved me," she said.

"He will never hurt you again."

She looked up at me, her eyes red from weeping. I wiped her tears with my hand, touching her face for the first time. So many feelings, new and powerful, welled up from deep within me; new, yet somehow familiar. I felt alive. I felt complete.

"What is your name?" she said.

"I am Saruel."

She stood to her feet, looking closely at me, examining my face, my white robe.

"Saruel," she said, "you have saved me this day." She leaned forward and kissed me on the cheek. "My name is Marah."

"Marah," I said. Her name was poetry on my lips. I said it again, "Marah."

She smiled at me. "Do you continue to spy on maidens while they bathe?"

"I am a Watcher," I said, "an angel from Heaven. I do not have the desires of men."

She frowned. "Do you not know what it means to love another?"

"I love the one who sits upon the throne of Heaven," I said.

"Then it is all true? The garden, the fall of man, Heaven, it is all true?"

"It is," I said.

"Then why does the one you serve allow such evil on the Earth?"

I did not know.

"His will is always being performed," I said. I held my hand out to her. "Come, I will return you to the house of your father."

She took my hand and I pulled her close to me, feeling the warmth of her soft flesh, the ample curves of her body next to mine. Her hair smelled of flowers. Her breasts pressed against me. Carrying her, I rose into the air, flying at a slow speed. I felt her tremble in my arms.

"Fear not," I said.

At the speed I flew, it took several minutes to reach her home. I landed gently next to the pool of water. She stood, facing her father's house.

"They will wonder where I have been," she said. "My father promised my hand in marriage to a man I do not love. They are surely searching for me."

"You must not speak of me, Marah, for your own safety. Do not tell anyone about me. Do you understand?"

She nodded, biting her lower lip. "Then what shall I tell them?"

"Tell them the truth," I said. "You were taken by worshippers of Erozel, and you escaped."

She turned to me. Her eyes found mine. "Will I see you again, Saruel? Will you watch over me?"

"I am a Watcher," I said, "I watch over the Earth and its inhabitants."

She took my hand in hers. "Yes, but will you watch over me?"

My heart swells as I recall the way she looked at that moment, her autumn hair, and her pleading eyes. Her fair skin glowed like the very light of Heaven!

"I will do the will of the Great I Am," I said.

She smiled, releasing my hand. "I know you will watch over me," she said. "I have felt your eyes upon me many times before this day. I know that now."

Turning from me, she walked toward the house of her father.

CHAPTER 13

Several hours passed before I regained control of my body. I rose upward, cutting slowly through the dark, cold ocean water, my eyes searching toward Heaven. Thousands of years have passed since my fall, but the knowledge of the barrier between me and my celestial home is as painful to me as if I had Fallen yesterday.

I headed home, reaching the patio of my penthouse in moments. I removed my wet clothing with a heavy heart, staring at my naked body in the full mirror. I appeared in every way to be a man, absent the navel, which I do not have. I looked at the reflection of my member. Why had the Great I Am created me with one? Why, for that matter, did I have a heart, a seat of emotions, if not to love and to be in love? I dressed, choosing casual clothes, a white shirt and dark pants.

I walked to my viewing window and sat down in my chair, watching the city below me, focusing on the horizon in the direction of Mary Magdalene's, toward my precious girl. The school was several miles away, beyond the horizon, blocked from my sight by Earth's curvature.

I picked up the telephone on the table beside my chair, and dialed Andrew's number. His phone rang several times before going into voice mail. That was unusual. I stood up, looking toward the school, where Andrew waited five days a week, keeping watch over the girl. I dialed Andrew's number again and waited. Once again, it went into voice mail. I was concerned, but not unduly troubled, because Andrew was faithful and the girl was in school, after all. A heavenly messenger had cast me away from the school, and it would be several more hours before I could enter the area again. All I could do was to wait for Andrew to return my call.

An hour later, when Andrew still had not returned my call, I decided to investigate. I flew toward the school. I knew that I would not be able to enter the sky above the school, and I did not want to risk hitting a barrier, and fall, paralyzed, to the Earth.

I flew to a spot high above the city with a good view of Mary Magdalene's. I searched for Andrew's black car, and felt a sudden shock of panic when I did not find it. For, though I constantly reminded Andrew of the truth, being a Grigorian, he nonetheless revered me as a god, doing what I asked of him, religiously. He would not have left the girl.

I flew in a large circle several miles around the school, hoping to see the car, but not finding it. I focused my hearing toward the school, isolating individual voices, hoping to hear the girl. I heard priests offering confession, and nuns giving instruction. I heard the voices of children, but not the voice of my girl.

With growing alarm, I flew quickly, shattering the sound barrier, turning, looking in every direction, focusing on every black car I found in and around the city. Where was Andrew? I searched in vain for nearly half an hour, before turning toward the school again. Had enough time passed? Could I make it through the barrier surrounding the school? I had to try. I took a deep breath, gathered my strength and prayed to Heaven for mercy. I flew at my top speed toward the school, hitting the barrier in an instant, my body burning with sudden pain. The barrier remained in place, but weakened by time, slowed my flight instead of stopping me altogether. I felt what a human must feel like when running in deep water—in this case, boiling water. In agony, I pushed hard against the barrier, struggling to penetrate it. Finally, I made it through. I fell, exhausted, to the ground, lying face-down on the school lawn.

I stood up, brushing grass from my clothes, looking around to see if anyone had witnessed my fall from the sky. I ran to the main building, where my girl's classroom was. I entered the building through large hardwood doors, slowing to a brisk walk, and made my way down the hall to my girl's classroom.

I peered through a long rectangular window in the classroom door. Children were sitting cross-legged in a circle on the carpeted floor. Their teacher, a young brunette woman, was reading to them from a book. My girl was not among them.

Opening the door, I stepped inside. The teacher stopped her reading and turned, looking up at me. The children stared curiously in my direction.

"May I help you?" The teacher asked.

"Yes," I said. "Please, forgive my interruption. I am looking for Mary. Is she here?"

"Are you a relative?" The teacher asked.

"Yes," I said.

She looked at me carefully, deciding, I suppose, that someone as lovely as I am could not be a monster, or something dangerous, like a demon.

"Mary left for the day," she said. "Her driver said there was some sort of an emergency."

I fought to control a surge of panic.

"I see," I said. "About how long ago did she leave?"

The woman thought a moment. "Well, let's see. She was here for the morning snack, after devotional. So that was maybe thirty minutes into the day. Three or four hours ago, I suppose."

"Thank you," I said.

One of the girls looked up at me. "Are you an angel?" she said.

I stepped into the hallway without answering. I heard a boy say, "He's not an angel, stupid. Angels have wings."

66

I left the building, finding a secluded spot from which to fly. I returned to the girl's house, entering through an open upstairs window. I called for Jonathon, but there was no answer. I went downstairs, finding no one home. Using Jonathon's house phone, I called Andrew's mobile again, with the same results, his phone going into voice mail.

I flew home, descending the long stairway into Andrew's quarters, finding the door of his office locked. I put my hand forcefully through the wooden door and unlocked it from the inside. I had never been in Andrew's office before, and was surprised to see several lifelike paintings of my image, decorating his walls. The office was quite large. A white marble statue of my likeness, scaled to half my size, stood in the center of the room. A desk sat in the corner, cluttered with yellowed books and ancient scrolls. I rummaged through the drawers, finding nothing helpful. A book case against one wall held a treasure of occult and witchcraft books. I pulled several of them out, leafing through the pages, before putting them back again.

I stepped back, looking at the room in its entirety, searching for anything out of place. At last I saw it. The orange-peel texture of the wall behind the desk was slightly larger than the texture of the other walls. I approached the wall, searching for a lever or a button. Not finding one, I scanned the room again. My eyes fell on the statue. The hardwood floor behind the statue looked more worn than the rest of the floor. Approaching the statue, I pushed it backward in the direction of the wear. I heard a clicking sound in the floor beneath it. The wall behind the desk opened into a doorway, revealing a dimly lit room.

The room was a shrine, a smaller sculpture of my image in its center, adorned with flowers and unlit candles. A table beside it held a large leather-bound book, occult symbols etched skillfully into the leather. I picked it up. There was no title on the front cover. I opened it. The book was written with ornate handwriting in ancient Sumerian. It told the history of the Watchers. A sheet of yellow legal paper in the middle of the book acted as a bookmark. At last, something helpful. The paper contained several names: members of the Grigorian order and their phone numbers. I committed every name and number to memory and, shutting the door of the secret shrine, ascended to my own dwelling on the top floor.

I dialed the first number on the list. A woman with a clipped British accent answered.

"State your name and reason for calling, please."

"A member of your order, Andrew Lawrence, is missing," I said without introduction. "His car is gone. I believe he is in some sort of trouble."

"Who are you," she demanded. "How did you get this number?"

"You are not listening," I said. "Who I am is unimportant. You must help me find Andrew. He does not answer his phone. I know about your order. I know that you will have a trace on my phone in a matter of moments. Do not waste time sending your men to my home. You must find Andrew."

The woman sighed. "Hold for a moment," she said. I heard her typing on a computer keyboard. "We have a lock on his mobile, and are sending our people to find him."

"Where is he?" I said. "I can get there without delay."

"How..." She stopped. The pitch of her voice went up a notch. "Are you a..."

"Yes," I said. "Give me the location."

"My lord, I didn't..."

"The location," I said.

"The Golden Gate Bridge."

I hung up the phone and flew from my penthouse through the open patio doors. I had passed over the Golden Gate Bridge in my earlier search for the car, and had not seen it. I reached the bridge in seconds, searching the entire area again, finding no sign of Andrew's car. Perplexed, I flew high into the sky over San Francisco, looking down at the bridge. Where are you, Andrew? Where is my girl? There was the usual street traffic on the bridge below. I felt a tinge of guilt, remembering the twin girls and their mother the night before.

Through the sounds of wind and cars below, I heard a faint ringing coming from the south side of the Golden Gate Bridge. I flew quickly, landing on the south tower, above the passing cars, listening. Several minutes passed before I heard the ringing again. It came from the west edge of the bridge. I flew, landing near the railing at the bridge's edge, not caring whether or not anyone saw me.

I followed the ringing and realized it was coming from underneath the bridge. I climbed over the railing. The ringing came again, feet away, to my left. Andrew's phone lay on the metal edge, on the bottom of the outside rail. Holding the rail, I stepped toward the phone and picked it up. I looked down at the San Francisco Bay. If Andrew had fallen from this height, he could not have survived. Yet, why would he have fallen? Andrew was not suicidal. Besides, his car was nowhere to be seen. How did his phone end up on the outside of the bridge railing?

I felt a hand grab my shirt from behind, pulling me back toward the bridge. I turned to see a policeman. I pushed his hand away.

"Get back on the bridge," he shouted. I ignored him, turning my attention back to the bay. The officer reached for me again. "Don't jump," he said, "we can help you!"

He thought I was suicidal, apparently, and who could blame him? Placing the phone safely back on the edge, I allowed myself to fall forward, off the bridge and into the bay. I heard the officer shouting, as I hit the water.

I dove down into the murky depths, finding Andrew almost immediately. He was dead, floating, tethered by a chord of rope to a large stone on the bay floor, his right leg broken at the hip. His eyes were wide, open and unseeing. I searched the surrounding area again in a panic, praying desperately that I would not find the body of my girl.

Finding nothing else, I returned to Andrew's body. The stone was round and smooth, not so large that Andrew could not carry it, but getting over the rail with it would have been extremely difficult. I studied the stone, touching it, examining it closely, realizing with incredulity that I knew what it was and where it had come from. I rolled it over, knowing that I would see letters etched deep into its surface. And, of course, there were letters, faded smooth by time, written in a language not spoken since the tower of Babel. Etched into the stone by a devoted hand, thousands of years ago, was a name, an angelic name. There had been thirteen such stones, each with a different name, placed together, forming an altar of worship at the Temple of all Gods. I trailed a finger along the letters. They spelled my name. Saruel.

I turned toward Andrew's body, releasing his foot from the rope, holding him with one hand to keep him from floating to the top of the bay. I carried the stone under my other arm, and flew, propelling myself underwater until I was several hundred yards away from the Golden Gate Bridge. Then I flew upward, carrying Andrew's body and the altar stone, shooting into the sky with a speed that would have crushed Andrew to death had he still been alive.

I returned to my dwelling, entering through the open patio doors. I placed the stone on the floor in front of my viewing window, and carried Andrew's body downstairs to his own quarters. Opening the door to his bedroom, I placed him on his bed.

I climbed the stairs again, and sat down in my chair, contemplating the altar stone. I had last seen it thousands of years ago, and I had detested it then. I hated it all the more, now that it was tied, quite literally, to the death of a man I had called my friend. How did it get there? Where had it come from? Where was my girl? I rubbed a finger along the letters of my name. That was what troubled me the most. It was not just an altar stone, but my altar stone. I was sure of two things. One was that Andrew had not killed himself. The other was that whoever had killed Andrew knew an awful lot about me. No living person could read the ancient inscription. How could they have known this was my stone? The only answer terrified me. Andrew had been killed by an angel.

I stood up and looked out through the window toward my girl's home. Where was she? If she had been abducted, it was her second abduction in two days. Her first abductors were servants of Sangruel, but whoever murdered Andrew had done it in broad daylight. It could not have been Sangruel. Of course he had human followers, who were not harmed by the rays of the sun, but could they have done this? Throwing Andrew, tied to a large stone, over the side of the Golden Gate Bridge in broad daylight, is not the way to commit a secret murder. And yet, the murderer had gone unnoticed.

I left my dwelling, and returned to the Golden Gate Bridge. Andrew's cell phone was by the edge where I had placed it. I flew down, retrieved it, and returned to the sky. The phone rang in my hand. I answered it.

"Yes?"

"Andrew?" The voice belonged to a man. He sounded angry.

I mimicked Andrew's voice.

"Yes," I said.

"Where in the hell are you?"

"I am a bit delayed," I said.

"A bit delayed? You were supposed to be here hours ago. Do you have the girl?"

"Of course," I said. What girl? My girl? I considered my next move. "I'm having second thoughts about bringing her."

The man lowered his voice.

"Listen to me. If the girl is not here within the hour, you will pay a terrible price."

"It seems to me that if I bring her to you, others might hurt me more," I said.

"No one can hurt you like we can. Need I remind you that we have your daughter? Imagine what we will do to her."

I did not know that Andrew had a daughter.

"No," I continued in Andrew's voice. I considered this. Whoever I was speaking with did not know Andrew was dead, and, obviously, they did not have the girl. Still, I had nowhere else to turn. What did this man want with her? "I know you have my daughter," I said, "but how can I be sure that you'll return her to me?"

The man raised his voice, "You don't know. But if you don't bring the girl, your daughter will die for sure. I guarantee you that. There are men here who would love to get their hands on her. Do you understand what I'm saying?"

"I understand," I said, "but I want to be sure. If you want the girl, meet me some place neutral."

"We don't negotiate, Andrew. We will kill your daughter. You will come to us, or she will die."

I sighed deliberately into the phone. "Meet me at Pier Thirty-Nine," I said.

I hung up.

CHAPTER 14

Not long after I had rescued Marah, Azazel found me. His face held a look of excitement.

"What is it, my captain?" I asked.

He pointed in the direction of Erozel's temple. "Come and see, Saruel. Erozel's woman gave birth to the child!"

He flew toward Erozel's temple. I hesitated before following him. His excitement over the birth of the child troubled me.

"Hurry, Saruel, come and see!"

I flew, following behind him, feeling a sense of impending doom. Halting in the sky above Erozel's temple, I heard the sounds of music and celebration. Throngs of people, all carrying flowers, gathered below me, around the temple. Erozel stood with the other Watchers upon a stage in front of the crowd; beside him stood Asherah, the woman who had shared in his fall. She wore brilliant white, a robe of silk, edged with gold. A delicate crown of gold and precious stones rested upon her head. In her arms, she held a newborn baby, also wrapped in silk, matching her robe.

Azazel descended toward the temple.

"Wait," I called to him. "You must not join the Fallen Watchers."

He stopped his descent and, turning back, looked up at me. "Do not fear for me, Saruel. Come. We are Watchers, and the birth of this child is a momentous occasion. We must behold it, chronicle the event. Join me."

I shook my head. "No, my captain," I called to him. "I will watch the event, but I will not partake in Erozel's joy and celebration over the birth of this child. Return to me, I beg of you. We are Watchers. Erozel and his followers are unholy, and the fruit of their loins is an abomination."

Azazel gazed down at the celebration. Wordlessly, he descended the rest of the way and landed near the temple.

Erozel raised a hand, calming the audience. He took the infant from the woman's breast and held it up for all to see.

"Today is a day like no other," he said. "For unto us a child is born. Unto us, a son is given. He shall be called Eros, the son of gods."

The musicians played a jubilant tune. The crowd shouted with joy, throwing their flowers onto the stage where Erozel and Asherah stood with the child. Azazel lighted on the stage before Asherah. Erozel looked at him. The other Watchers tensed.

"Be at peace," Azazel said. "I will not harm the child, or his mother."

Erozel stepped forward, and took the child from Asherah's arms. To

Azazel he said, "Come and see."

Azazel stared down at the child. "He is beautiful." He looked up, beckoning for me to join him. I remained where I was, high above the temple.

He flew to me.

"Come, Saruel. Share in this tremendous event," he said. "We can have children, sons and daughters! Does this not prove the Creator's plan? Does this not show His will? He made us this way, filling our members with longing, our hearts with the desire for children of our own."

"It is not our place to judge His intent," I said, "We are to obey his word, not our own desires. What will be the end of all this? Surely, judgment will fall upon Erozel and his followers, and the child will be destroyed."

Azazel scowled, pointing toward Heaven. "And where is the Great I Am? No man alive has seen His face. To them, He is no more than a legend, a tale told by their elders. He has abandoned mankind and the Earth. We are the objects of their worship. We are their gods."

"There is only one God," I said. "He made mankind in His own image. We are not their gods, Azazel. Adam was the Son of God. We are angels, servants of Heaven, far below Adam's station. Except for the Lord of the Fallen, there are no archangels among us, and not even an archangel comes close to Adam's former glory."

Azazel looked down at the other Watchers, who stared quietly up at us.

"Yet, consider our strength," he said, "our innate beauty. Human beings are fragile and weak. They are bound to the Earth by gravity. We are immortal and indestructible, as far above them as the sun is above the moon."

"Consider the Great I Am," I argued. "He does not fly on His own. The cherubim lift Him wherever He goes. Yet, He is the Creator of all that is. Every living thing bows to Him. He is worshiped by all. Your power and immortality came from Him. He is God alone. How can you, the Captain of Watchers, speak the way you do? Will you share in Erozel's sin? Will you join the Lord of the Fallen and his angels of darkness?"

Azazel's face softened. He looked down at the Watchers.

"Is the child below us not a creature of God? Did he choose his parents? Will you render judgment upon his head even before he makes his first decision?"

"My captain," I said quietly, "my eternal brother. Do not do what is in your heart to do."

A look of terrible sadness showed on his face. He looked longingly at the scene below us. "I am a leader of angels, filled with wisdom from the day I was made. I have so much to offer humanity. It will not be long before we all fall. I see this clearly. You speak in lofty tones, yet sin surely lies at your door. Desire lays her temptress hand upon you. Will you deny it?"

I thought about Marah. "My captain..." I said.

He drew near, and placing his hand on my shoulder, said, "You will always be my brother."

With that, he left me. I watched him return to Erozel, who received him with open arms. The celebration below me erupted with renewed vigor. I watched them for a while longer. Thirteen Watchers had come from Heaven. Twelve were Fallen. I cried out in anguish, weeping tears for my brothers.

CHAPTER 15

From the air, I searched the streets around Pier Thirty-nine. After about twenty minutes, a van more rust than blue pulled up to the curb. An unkempt man in wrinkled clothes stepped out from the passenger side. He looked around, squinted in the sunlight, pulled a cell phone from his pocket and made a call. Andrew's telephone rang in my hand. I answered.

"Do you have my daughter?" I said in Andrew's voice.

"Do you have the girl?" He said.

"I do."

"Meet me in front of the pier. I'm in a blue van. If you do anything stupid, your daughter dies."

"I understand," I said, ending the call.

I landed quickly behind a restaurant and walked to the front of the pier, directly up to the man. He was in his early thirties. A jagged scar ran down the right side of his face. I smelled his unwashed sweat. A black tattoo of angel's wings on his hand marked him as Grigorian.

"Andrew sent me," I said.

The man's face turned an ugly red.

"Who the hell are you?"

I saw the driver staring hard at me through the open passenger window. He was as sullied and unclean as his partner. They might have been brothers.

"I am an interested third party," I said.

"Do you have the girl?"

I held my empty hands out. "Does it look like I have the girl?" From inside the back of the van, I heard a girl crying. I nodded toward the sound. "I can tell you have Andrew's daughter."

The man made a quick move, drawing a small pistol. He pointed it at me. I feigned fear and raised my hands.

"Don't shoot," I said.

He waved the gun. "Get in the fucking van," he said.

I opened the side sliding door to the reek of old urine. There were no seats in the back. A girl of about eight or nine, her wrists and ankles tied tightly together with nylon ropes, a red bandana gagging her mouth, lay on a filthy mattress. Pictures of naked children in unspeakable situations surrounded her on the floor of the van. Her resemblance to Andrew was striking. She stared up at me, her eyes filled with terror. I climbed into the van. The driver turned and tossed a pair of handcuffs at me.

"Put these on," he ordered.

I shackled my wrists in front of me, then sat next to the girl on the filthy mattress. The man with the gun slammed the door shut and got into the passenger seat. The driver pulled the van out onto the street. The man with the gun turned toward me. His eyes were murder.

"Where in the fuck are Andrew and the girl?"

"What do you want her for?"

His face reddened. He actually growled. "You do not ask questions. You are fucking dead," he said. "That's what you are."

I looked at him, projecting calm and tranquility, which worked to enrage him further.

"So that's what you two are, a couple of murderers, and," I motioned toward Andrew's daughter and the bloodstained mattress, "by the look of things, perverts as well. Is that what you wanted the girl for?"

The man spat on the floor beside me. He leered at me. "Oh, we're that, and so much more. We will rape and strangle the girl, and then we will do the same to you. That's what we do."

I thought of Erozel. Were these his followers?

"Please," I said, my voice dripping with sarcasm, "don't."

The man moved toward me, but his partner caught him by the arm.

"Not yet," he said.

I smiled at the man with the gun. He fought to constrain himself. I settled down for the ride. The van rolled northward away from the city. The tops of trees took the place of skyscrapers. We drove for around thirty minutes before turning off onto an isolated road. Through the front window of the van, I saw a large wooden shed. I caught the smell of nearby death and decay in the air. The van pulled to a stop and the driver turned the engine off.

The man with the gun turned to me and said, "I'm going to carve up your pretty face."

I smiled at him. The driver got out and opened the side door of the van.

"Get out," he said.

I obeyed, stepping from the van. Trash littered the ground outside. The driver walked behind me, his partner keeping the gun pointed at my back, leaving Andrew's daughter in the van.

The driver opened the door to the shed and I stepped inside. The interior was as littered as the exterior; a yellow light bulb hanging from the ceiling cast the place in a dingy light. A filthy bed was the only furniture. Cruel-looking leg and wrist restraints were tied to the bedposts. A video camera sat on the bed.

"You bring children to this place?' I said. "What kind of monsters are you?"

"Shut the fuck up!" The man with the gun struck me with a fist in the back of my head. I pretended it hurt.

A Mercedes pulled up and parked next to the van outside. A middle-aged man in a dark suit got out, nodding to the men as he entered the shed. "Where is the girl?"

I recognized his voice from our earlier cell phone conversation. He looked at me.

"Who is this?"

"This piece of shit was at the pier instead of Andrew," the man with the gun said. "He knows about us, so we brought him here."

I smiled at the man.

"Pleased to meet you," I said.

He studied me with incredulity. "Are you stupid?"

"What do you want with the girl?" I said in answer.

"I think you should mind your own business," the man said. "You should worry about your own predicament."

"She is my only business," I said, allowing anger to enter my voice. I fixed the man with a cool stare. My sudden shift in attitude made the men uneasy.

"Who are you?" the man in the suit said.

I stepped toward the bed and picked up one of the restraints, looking at it with distaste.

"This is what you do to children?" I said. "Were you never children yourselves? How could you do this evil?"

The man with the gun pointed it at me, ready to fire.

"Wait," the suited man told him.

I dropped the restraint. "It seems to me that you wanted my girl for something more than your own perversions," I said.

"Shut the fuck up," the man with the gun said. He stepped forward, swinging the gun at me in a rage. I spread my wrists apart. The handcuffs broke and fell with a clatter to the concrete floor. I grabbed the gun in the man's hand, crushing it along with his fingers. He cried out in pain. I let him go, and he crumpled to his knees.

"My hand," he cried, "my fucking hand!"

Taking the gun in his left hand, he aimed it and fired at me. The bullets burned holes into my shirt. I looked down at the holes, then back at the man with the gun. He stared at me in disbelief.

"Who...who...are you?" he stammered.

"I am judgment," I said.

His partner moved toward me. I grabbed him by his shirt, lifting him into the air, the collar of his shirt cutting into his throat like a garrote. He struggled to breathe, his arms flailing toward my head. I dropped him, and he scrambled away from me, his hands to his throat. The man in the dark suit turned to run. I moved quickly, grabbed him, then threw him toward the man with the gun. He screamed at the top of his lungs when he fell. I heard the sound of bones breaking. His lower leg turned at an odd angle.

"Now," I said, "I know what you are, and the Order you belong to. Who do you serve? What do you want with my girl?"

"Fuck you!" The man with the gun aimed it and fired at me again, putting more holes into my shirt. A bullet glanced harmlessly off my face. He fired until the gun was empty. I stood watching him. His eyes grew wide with fear.

"It is better," I said, "for a man to tie a millstone around his neck and cast himself into a river than for him to hurt a child."

He turned and ran. I let him go, knowing he could not get far. The keys to the van were with his partner. He ran out through the door of the shed. I turned to the driver.

"Who wants the girl?"

He trembled with fear, his face dawning with recognition of what I had to be.

"I don't know anything, my lord. I was ordered by those above me to take her."

"Then you were not planning on hurting her? You weren't planning on—what did your friend say—raping and strangling my little girl?"

The man's face turned pale. He held shaking hands out toward me.

"Please..." he said, "I did only what I was told to do."

"Do you plead with me? How many innocents cried out to you for mercy, how many begged you to let them go? You took them from their fathers and mothers."

He clambered to his feet.

"No. I didn't. I wouldn't..."

"You did. Their decay is thick upon the air. How many children are buried out here?"

He turned to run, but I blocked his path. He fell to his knees, trembling before me, his face in his hands, weeping.

"I was molested, too," he said. "I can't help myself..."

I thought about my girl. Was she with someone like this man? I reached out and placed my hand on his shoulder. I leaned in, drawing my mouth close to his ear.

"Believe me," I said softly, "I understand. Tell me. Who do you serve?"

He looked up at me with teary eyes. I saw for an instant a glimpse of the little boy he had once been. Perhaps someone had molested him. Perhaps he was once the victim of his own terrible childhood.

"We serve the great lord, Erozel, but we worship all of the Elohim. Forgive me," he said. "Have mercy on me. I would have delivered her safely to my master."

"I release you from your sins," I said. My voice was soothing, calm. He shook with relief.

"Thank you, my lord."

With blurring speed, I tore his head from his shoulders. His body toppled, spewing blood across the dirty floor and the bed. I held his head by the hair, blood spattering my clothes and shoes. His eyes registered a moment of shock before the light in them went out. I turned to the man in the suit, holding the bloody head out to him.

"Will you tell me what I want to know?" I said.

He looked up at me, horrified. "Yes, my lord. Anything, only let me live." I moved closer to him. He held out his hand. "She wasn't to be touched, I swear. We were supposed to get her from Andrew, nothing else. We were on orders." He looked with terror at the man's head in my hand. "I am not like them, my lord. I never hurt children."

"You serve Erozel," I said. "Rape and deviant lust is what he loves. Can you be any different? Still, tell me what you know, and you will live. Where were you to deliver her?"

"To the place of worship," he said, "to the priests of Erozel. That is all I know, my lord." He looked up at me, grimacing with pain. "You said you would let me live."

"And I will," I said, kneeling down at his side. He cringed away from me. "I always keep my promises." He looked hopefully up at me. I grabbed his spinal column in the middle of his back, crushing it in my hand. He screamed. I stood up. "You will live," I said, "but you will never rape again."

I left him there, the sounds of his cries and curses behind me.

I rose into the air and found the man with the gun in short order, stumbling in the woods behind the shed. I landed in front of him.

He stared at me, his eyes filled with fear and hate. His voice shook. "What the fuck are you?"

"Haven't you figured it out yet?" I said. "I am your personal demon, here to send you to the belly of Hell."

"There is no Hell," he said.

"Then you won't mind going there," I said. I picked him up, detesting the stench of his unwashed body. I carried him into the air, following the smell of death and decay. I found what I was looking for below me in a secluded area, the ground scarred, marking new and old graves. There was an open hole, only a few feet long, a child-size grave. I landed next to it, releasing the man. He stared at the graves around him.

His voice cracked. "Why did you bring me here?"

"Are you not proud of your handiwork?"

His face trembled. He fell to his knees, eyes welling up with tears.

"Will you weep before me?" I said. "How many here wept to you for mercy?"

"Not all were mine," he said, his voice pleading.

I stepped toward a grave, which by the look of it and smell of decay was several weeks old.

"Was this one yours?" He did not answer, and I took his silence as an affirmation. "Dig it up," I said. "Let's see your work."

He trembled before me, staring down at the grave. "I can't," he said.

I grabbed his broken hand and squeezed it hard. He cried out in pain. "Do what I tell you to do."

He fell to his knees in front of the grave, and began to claw slowly at the loose dirt with his good hand. The rotted stench of decay permeated the air as he uncovered the discolored hand of a child. He stopped digging. His body shook. He sobbed. I pushed him aside and pulled the body from the earth with one quick movement. It was a girl, about six or seven years old, the same size as my girl. Her hair was brown, her gray skin mottled and caked with soil, blackened in places. A dark ligature mark branded her throat. I placed the body of the girl gently on the ground next to her killer. He turned his face from the sight of her.

"Look at her!" I said. Reluctantly, he turned toward the body. Tears poured down his face. "What did you do to her? How could you do this?"

He shook his head. "You don't understand."

"You aren't the first monster I have come across," I said.

"What are you going to do to me?"

I placed the girl's body into the open grave. I picked the man up by the throat and threw him forcefully into the grave on top of the girl's body. He screamed, scrambling to get away. I pushed him back into the hole, feeling his ribs break under the force of my hand. He shook violently, crying out. His eyes rolled back into his head. I slapped him in the face.

"Stay with me," I said. "I want you awake for this."

He returned to his senses, screaming in fresh agony. Pulling up great mounds of earth, I buried him in the grave, saving his face for last.

"This is nothing compared to Hell," I said, covering his face with dirt, silencing his cries.

I returned to the van and opened the side door. Andrew's daughter looked up at me, her eyes fearful, the gag still in her mouth. I made to remove it and she pulled away from me.

"Fear not," I said. I removed the gag and untied her. The ropes had cut into her flesh at the wrists and ankles. "They will never hurt you again, child." I considered my next move. I could not leave the girl in that place, but time was of the essence. "Can you keep a secret?"

She nodded, and looked at me with wide, frightened eyes.

"It is a very big secret. One your father shared. Will you tell no one?"

"I won't tell," she said.

I reached out to her, but she drew away.

"Do not fear me, little one," I said. I picked her up in my arms, calming her. Stepping from the van, I rose with her into the air. She looked around, shaking in my arms, her eyes looking down at the ground far below us.

I returned to the mansion where my girl lived with Jonathon. This time, I rang the doorbell instead of barging in uninvited. The young woman opened the door. She studied the girl in my arms.

"Jonathon," I said.

She nodded, stepping aside and calling for Jonathon. He came down the stairs, smiling broadly when he saw me. The look on my face wiped the smile from his.

"What is it?" he asked.

I turned to the woman. "Please, take the girl and leave us."

She bowed her head, and, taking the girl by the hand, led her into the kitchen. Jonathon took a seat on the couch. I remained standing. I told him everything, about Ariel and his questions, my girl's disappearance, Andrew's death, and the altar stone. Jonathon was one of the few I trusted, besides Andrew. He listened without a word. Finally, he said:

"They know. Somehow your brothers know who she is." He stood up. "We must find her. Someone took her before these men could. If they were servants of Erozel, then another of your brothers must have taken her. Who besides Erozel has enmity toward you?"

"I have no enemies," I said.

Jonathon shook his head. "Perhaps you don't see them as they see you. The servants of Erozel sought to take her, but another, presumably an angelic being, took her before they could. Your brothers surely know the truth of her, and it has ignited their anger." He frowned. "I fear for her life."

I left Andrew's daughter in Jonathon's care. I needed answers. Foremost in my mind was my girl's welfare. She had to be alive. I could not live without her.

I flew, San Francisco behind me, the ocean below me. Day became night, and gray waters turned to black as I rounded Earth's curvature, flying on until the night became dark as pitch, lit only by occasional flashes of lightning in opaque clouds. The air grew thick around me. A whirlpool churned below, a black hole leading deep into the bowels of Hell. I waited, hovering high above, watching, recalling a time when the entire planet was the abyss, a prison to the Fallen. The whirlpool was larger than it had once been, enlarged over the years by the increase of lost souls. The death angel worked night and day, gathering the souls of humankind, dividing the righteous from the wicked, casting the damned into the darkness below. I waited.

Within an hour, he appeared, flying with tremendous speed; a blur even to my eyes. A silvery chord in his hands bound several screaming, writhing spirits together, struggling in vain against his sure grip. The mouth of Hell opened under his dark gaze, belching hellfire and sulfurous smoke high into the air. The cries of tormented humanity escaped from the belly of the pit. I saw movement inside, effervescent shapes, human in form, reaching upward toward Hell's open mouth. He drew near the opening and released the spirits from the silvery chord. They fell into the depths of Hell, their cries of terror and pleas for mercy silenced as the mouth of Hell closed around them. He looked up at me, his face gaunt, bone-white, his eyes two empty holes, black as the abyss below.

"Hemael," I said. "A moment, I pray you."

"The souls of mankind wait for me," he said.

"Please hear me."

He waited.

"A girl," I said. "Did you collect the spirit of a girl?"

"More than one," he said. "The Earth is vast and humanity frail."

"Earlier today," I said. "Did you collect the spirit of a girl in San Francisco?"

His eyes met mine. His voice held accusation. "I collected the spirits of twin girls and their mother in that city. Did you care for them as you care for the girl you speak of?"

He knew. Had the story spread so quickly?

"Please," I said, "will you tell me?"

Hemael looked down at the abyss.

"Innocent blood is on your hands, Saruel; three lives lost to save only one."

"You know my nature, my respect for life," I said.

He looked down at his skeletal hands. "Every life lost, every spirit departed, has felt my cold grasp. Yet I have never caused the death of another. I, who embraced life before the Great Rebellion, am forced now to embrace death." He pointed a long finger at me. "You took the life of innocents."

"Not by my choice," I said. Yet I had chosen. They had died because of me. "I had my reasons."

"On your account, I dragged from this world the wailing spirit of a mother bereaved of her daughters, only to collect their spirits soon after." He held out his hands. "With these hands, once beautiful, caressing all life. You remember my delight in these things. How I marveled at it all! From nothing, life sprang forth, spirit and being. Life is precious, yet you cast innocent children to Sangruel."

"I made the choice that led to their deaths," I said, "but to choose another route, I could not. Their blood is on the head of Sangruel. My hands are clean."

"Clean hands," he said, looking down at his own skeletal hands. His voice held regret and sorrow. "Three died because of you, yet you enquire about one girl. I sense your fear for her. Why do you worry over her? She lives still, but, in time, I shall collect her spirit."

"She is special to me." I turned to leave.

"All succumb to me in time, Watcher. How many have I collected already, torn from your heart without mercy? How many women have you loved?"

I flew from him without answering. Relief flooded through me. My girl was alive. Wherever she was, she still lived. Hemael's words echoed in my mind.

How many women have you loved?

I have loved only one.

CHAPTER 16

The sons of Seth, the leaders of the city of Lamech, grew weary of Enoch.

"Let us turn him over to the servants of Erozel," they said.

They gathered a large group of men and surrounded him, intent on taking him by force. He cried out to them as usual, warning of the wrath of God, calling for them to turn from their wickedness. The men took hold of him and bound him with chords.

"Tell your stories to Erozel's servants," one of the men said. "You will find it hard to speak with their members in your mouth."

The other men laughed.

"And not only in his mouth," another said.

I waited. Would fire fall from Heaven as it had before? Would the men turn to ashes at Enoch's feet?

Nothing happened.

The temple of Erozel was a full day's journey from Lamech. They chose a dozen men to take Enoch to Erozel. Enoch did not resist. His face looked frequently toward Heaven. I wondered at this. How was it that this mortal man knew Heaven's location?

They traveled, leading Enoch to certain defilement, until morning turned to nightfall and the temple of Erozel was only a few miles away. They spoke of the reward they thought they would receive. I followed Enoch's gaze toward Heaven, expecting the I Am to intervene for this righteous man. Heaven was silent.

They reached the temple in the dark of night. Servants of Erozel met the men, who turned Enoch over to them. Over the next hour, the surrounding city came to life. Torches lit the stage in front of the temple. Men, women and children gathered around the stage. Enoch stood before them, stripped of his garments and tied to a pole, his shame exposed for all to see.

He cried out to the servants of Erozel. "Hear me, sons of Adam, and daughters of Eve! You must turn from your ways, denounce your false gods and serve the I Am who lives beyond the stars! It is not too late for you. For, though God spared not the angels that sinned, he offers us redemption."

The crowd laughed and jeered, shouting loudly at him.

"See how holy you are when we are finished with you! Will you be so proud when blood and seed run from your forbidden part?"

Enoch fastened his eyes toward Heaven.

The crowd began to dance and worship as the Fallen Watchers appeared before them on the stage. I was saddened to see Azazel among them. He wore a robe of cloth, his robe of light having gone out. He smiled broadly at the crowd.

Erozel appeared suddenly, floating twenty feet above the stage. The worship of the crowd grew to a full frenzy. Orgies broke out in several places. The children watched their elders, delighted by the frivolity and celebration.

Erozel held out his hand and the noise died down.

"This is a night of celebration!" Erozel said. "For on this night, you will see the foolishness of men like Enoch, and the glory of your gods."

I watched as the Lord of the Fallen and his angels appeared high above the temple, a dark cloud in the night sky. The Lord of the Fallen lighted upon the Earth, hidden only by shadows.

"The man Enoch will soon know the wrath of your gods," Erozel said. "He has cried out against us, speaking lies to all who would hear him. No more! I have a special plan for him. He will soon join the ranks of my followers. He will experience the pleasure and pain of forced copulation!" The crowd roared their approval. Erozel raised his hand again. "Asherah, come," he said.

The woman who had given birth to the angelic child, the one who had caused Erozel's fall, stepped onto the stage, standing in the midst of the Watchers. She wore robes of crimson, her crown upon her head. She looked at Enoch then turned to the crowd. She dropped her robes with a flourish. The crowd applauded, shouting with pleasure. Ornate strips of blue cloth wrapped around her waist and her upper thighs, securing a large phallus of carved wood directly in front of her chalice. She stood for a long moment, the nipples of her full, naked breasts engorged to hard points, the hand-carved member jutting obscenely out in front of her.

"Behold," Erozel said, "a new thing will be done tonight. For my maiden shall lie with Enoch as a man lies with a woman."

The crowd shouted their approval once again. Erozel motioned to two of his servants, who untied Enoch, holding him, forcing him to bend over, his nakedness exposed to Erozel's maiden. Asherah stepped behind him and grabbed his buttocks in both of her hands.

"Do not worry, my virgin man," she said, "I will be gentle, at first."

The crowd broke out in laughter.

"Do not do this thing!" Enoch cried. "Do not bring this sin upon you!"

Asherah's face grew cold. Her eyes flared with lust and cruelty.

"It is I who will bring this sin upon you," she said. She spread the cheeks of his buttocks, rubbing his forbidden part with the fingers of one hand. Enoch cried out. "That was only my finger," she said. "My phallus is the size of a horse's member." She turned to the crowd. "Are you watching?" she shouted. "Behold how I worship the one I love!"

She turned again to the bent-over Enoch, spreading the cheeks of his buttocks, positioning the phallus onto his forbidden part. The crowd shouted and danced.

"Do it! Do it!"

Asherah thrust forward, her naked hips pushing hard toward Enoch's buttocks.

Enoch cried out, "My God, my God, why have you forsaken me? Why are you so far from the words of my crying?"

The crowd laughed at him, continuing to shout and dance. Asherah pushed into him, slowly at first. Enoch screamed, trying with all his might to twist away from the men's grasp.

The dark cloud of the Fallen in the sky above vibrated with anticipation.

"My darling," Asherah said, "you hurt my feelings. Do you not want me like I want you?"

She thrust her hips hard forward, driving her wooden phallus deep into his forbidden part. The front of her thighs pushed against the flesh of his buttocks. Her round hips moved back and forth, gyrating with every thrust. Enoch fell down, face forward, onto the stage, crying out. The men held him down as Asherah lay on top of him, her breasts pushing into his back, her hips driving the phallus in and out of him with quick, violent thrusts.

I looked away from the terrible sight. I wept for Enoch the righteous. I turned my face toward Heaven, hoping to see any sign of intervention from the I Am. Instead, I saw Ariel, flying toward Erozel's temple. I watched as he lighted on the stage. He looked with interest at Asherah as she impaled Enoch with her wooden phallus. Enoch's cries grew less forceful. He stopped struggling, exhausted from his ordeal.

Asherah laughed. "I believe you are getting used to this. Perhaps we should do something else?" She pushed into him, forceful and rapid. He moaned. She slowed the rhythm of her thrusts, and pulled her hips backward, removing the phallus from Enoch's forbidden part. He did not move. Asherah stood up. Even in the torchlight, I saw that the phallus was slick with blood. She turned to the audience, showing them the phallus. "Behold," she said, "the blood of the righteous!" The crowd cheered and danced before the stage.

Asherah turned back to Enoch. "Roll him onto his back," she said. The men holding Enoch obeyed her. Enoch looked up at the woman, and at Erozel, who hovered above the stage. He did not attempt to hide his shame. He turned his face toward Heaven. Asherah knelt before him, smiling. "Dear man," she said softly, "you have taken my abuse quite admirably. Now I will reward you for your pains." She trailed her fingernails lightly along his naked chest, downward to his belly, caressing him, allowing her fingertips to brush the area just above his member. She did this for a short while, finally rubbing Enoch's member with her other hand. His member grew hard. She laughed again. "Perhaps your thoughts are not quite as pure as you let on." She kissed his member and he groaned. "Would you like me to pleasure you?" she said, "just ask me to, and I will. Then your punishment will end and you will join the ranks of Erozel's servants. I assure you that the time will come when you will hunger for my phallus." Enoch remained silent. Asherah stroked his engorged member. "What do you say, my darling? Do you want pleasure, or more pain? I would love to pleasure you as much as I love punishing you."

Enoch looked at Asherah. "Depart from me, worker of iniquity and lover of demons. For your punishment will be far greater than anything I have endured."

She pulled her hands away from his member. Her face turned crimson. "You have not yet felt the sting of my whip!"

"Do your best," Enoch said. "I will worship the one true God, and serve him only."

Asherah stood up quickly, her face a portrait of rage. "Erozel is the true god!"

Enoch cried out in a loud voice. "There is only one God! He who made the heavens and Earth, who sits upon the throne of the universe, shining with light, His rainbow about His head. He is the Great I Am!"

Ariel flew forward from where he had been watching, and kicked Enoch. His eyes were fire. Violence consumed his features. Enoch cried out in pain.

"What do you know, mortal man?" Ariel said, seething. "You have never seen Heaven. You do not know the I Am. Were you there at the birth of the universe; did you see Him put the stars in place? You speak of things you cannot understand!"

Enoch held his side where Ariel had kicked him. "And yet you have held back on the strength of your kick," he said. "I am a mortal man. You are a demon. You could have killed me. Why did you spare me? Do you fear further judgment? Do you fear the only true God?"

Ariel screamed with violent anger. The crowd drew back in fear, away from the stage. Enoch stared calmly up at him.

"Bring me a spear," Ariel said to the men who held Enoch. "Release your hold on him. He cannot escape." One of the men brought a spear to Ariel. Ariel cut through the air with lightning fast strokes, causing the air to sing around the iron of the spear. "I can kill you quickly or I can kill you slowly," Ariel said. "Turn from your rebellious ways, human, denounce your service to the I Am, and I may let you live. Your life is in my hands."

"Life is the Lord's, both to give and take. My life is in your hands only because the I Am has allowed it to be."

Ariel lashed out with the spear, cutting Enoch across the face. Blood poured from the wound.

"You were raped in your forbidden part by a woman. Where was your God?" Ariel said. "I have disfigured your face. Where is your God? If you served me, no such thing would have happened to you."

"You are able to destroy my body. Only the I Am can destroy my soul. Behold, I will see Him coming in the clouds on the throne of glory."

Ariel lashed out again, cutting the other side of Enoch's face.

"Then tell me, mortal man," Ariel said. "What is the color of the throne? No man alive has seen the I Am."

Enoch looked upward toward Heaven. Tears streamed suddenly down his face. "It is blue," he said, "like lighted sapphire. His rainbow is a perfect halo about him. Four winged angels of light carry his throne."

Ariel looked astonished. He stared at Enoch with incredulity. "How do you know such a thing?"

Cries of terror erupted from the dark cloud of the Fallen. They scattered in every direction. I looked toward Heaven. I saw the light of the throne of God, carried by the cherubim. I rejoiced and worshiped. My heart was glad. I wept tears of joy. The servants of Erozel saw the throne as well. They fell to their knees, hiding their faces from the glory of the I Am. Ariel looked up and saw the throne. He dropped the spear and stepped backward, away from Enoch. The throne slowed, hovering above the temple of Erozel. The Watchers, including Erozel, fell to their knees. The Lord of the Fallen watched from the shadows. He did not kneel.

The voice of the I Am sounded, shaking the Earth.

"Enoch, Son of the Most High God, stand to your feet."

Enoch stood up, favoring the side where Ariel had kicked him. He looked around him at the kneeling Watchers and their servants.

"You are righteous upon the Earth, having turned neither to the left or the right. This night, you are reborn, recreated in my image. This night I call you my son. Come up to me, Son of God, for all is yours to command. I have placed the angels of Heaven at your beck and call."

There came a shriek from the darkness, terrible and insane. The Lord of the Fallen flew to the stage, landing in front of Enoch and retrieving the spear that Ariel had abandoned. With a cry of fury, he thrust it into Enoch's side. Enoch stopped. His eyes widened and he looked down at the shaft of the spear.

"My father!" he cried, looking up at the I Am. Light surrounded Enoch's body, a robe of the purest white. The spear fell harmlessly, clattering to the floor of the stage. The cuts on his face healed. A rainbow appeared around his head.

The Lord of the Fallen cried out, hiding his eyes from Enoch's light. He rose into the sky between the temple of Erozel and the throne of God, pointing an accusatory finger at the I Am.

"This cannot be," he said, "even you must obey your laws. Enoch is Fallen. He is dead, stillborn in original sin. The price is not paid. No innocent man has paid Adam's wages. You cannot do this!"

The I Am spoke again, his voice causing the Earth to tremble.

"I am sovereign God," he said. "You are my creation. I have no beginning and no end. Will you teach me my law? Will you instruct the source of all knowledge and wisdom? I have prepared a lamb for Enoch from the foundation of Earth. My law is not broken."

The cherubim turned from the Earth, spiriting the throne of God toward Heaven with great speed. The Lord of the Fallen shrieked again. The humans below him trembled in fear. He looked down at Enoch.

"Now then, Son of God," he said, vomiting the words, "what will you do to those who have caused you harm? Will you destroy the woman who had her way with you? Will you call fire from Heaven to consume Erozel's temple? Will you bring destruction upon the heads of his servants? If you are the Son of God, command these things to be."

Enoch rose into the air, floating in brilliant light and color above Erozel's temple. The Watchers trembled below him. He looked at Asherah, who kneeled, cringing on the stage, the phallus still tied to her. He spoke to the Lord of the Fallen.

"Get behind me, accuser of humankind, for the heart of the I Am is mercy." Enoch looked to Heaven. He held his hands out toward the crowd before the stage. "Forgive them, Father," he said, "for they know not what they do."

He rose higher into the air, the light of God around him illuminating the dark sky. When he was no more than a glow in the clouds, I flew to him. He fastened his eyes on the Earth below.

"Enoch!" I called, "Son of the Most High God."

He turned his attention to me.

"Angel of Heaven," he said. He smiled, his features dancing with excitement. "I can fly; I am covered in a robe of white like unto you!" He stared in wonder at the rainbow halo adorning his head.

"I am Saruel," I said, "servant of God, Watcher of Heaven. I bore witness to the life you have lived before the I Am, and the torture you have endured at the hands of Fallen angels and wicked humans."

Enoch frowned, looking back toward Earth.

"The wickedness of man is terrible. Their thoughts are of violence and evil continually. The Lord will not abide them forever," he said.

"When will He judge the wicked? How will He punish the Fallen Watchers? If it seems right to you, Enoch, Son of God, please tell me what the I Am has told you of these things."

Enoch kept his eyes focused on the Earth below us.

"When my son, Methuselah, is dead, judgment will come upon the entire planet. God will open the waters of the deep and tilt the Earth on its axis. Water will fall from the sky until it covers all land."

"The abyss," I said. "He will return Earth to its former state."

"Every living thing upon the Earth will die," Enoch said, "Men, women and children."

I thought about Marah.

"What of the righteous? Will the Lord not spare the faithful? Will He destroy the wicked with the holy?"

Enoch met my eyes with his. "When that time comes, will there be any faithful on the Earth?"

"How many years?"

"Only the I Am knows," Enoch said.

I changed the subject. "How, if I may ask, were you translated from mortal to immortal? You were born in sin, shaped by iniquity; Fallen."

Enoch shook his head. "The I Am is sovereign," he said. "He can do whatever He chooses."

Violence filled the Earth and the thoughts of humankind were evil continually. They worshiped devils at a temple made by hands.

Eros, the son of the Watchers, grew faster than human children did. In a matter of months, he was a young boy, walking and talking. He was brilliant in intelligence, and physically powerful. After several more months, he appeared to be in his early teens. Erozel loved him and called him the son of the gods.

Enoch's translation had enraged the Lord of the Fallen and humiliated my brother Watchers. In rebellion, Erozel invented new acts of abomination to visit upon the bodies of men and women. The Fallen Watchers dwelt in Erozel's temple, which they renamed the Temple of All Gods.

Ariel caused more and greater violence, wars and murders. He had taken to joining in battle, dressing as a man in soldiers garb, killing men, hundreds at a time, with his own sword. He invented warfare, weaponry, and gave victories to those who worshiped him and the Watchers, his bloodlust rivaled only by Sangruel's own.

I saw Enoch no more, and wondered about him. Had he gone to Heaven to be with the I Am? No man had ever entered the city of light. How all of Heaven would have rejoiced. I longed to see my home again.

I watched Marah every morning. She had changed her routine slightly, looking up into the sky where she supposed, correctly, that I was, before disrobing by the pool of water. I never tired of her beauty. I did not lust after her in the way Erozel lusted. I loved her with a pure heart. Yet, having seen the fall of my brothers, I did not dare show myself to her again.

One evening, at sunset, I flew to her father's house where she lived. The sun had lowered on the horizon, a golden glow in purplish skies. I found Marah sitting upon the ground, her robes white, green grass beneath her. Flowers bloomed around her. She watched the lowering sun, hands folded daintily in her lap. Her mother, a beautiful older version of Marah, stood behind her, an expression of sadness on her worried face.

"You must marry, Daughter. You are of age. Father agreed to the union. To deny your hand now would seem a terrible insult and bring shame upon your father's name."

"My hand, Mother, it is yet my own. I do not seek to insult the man, or to shame Father, but I will not wed a man who I do not love. Shall I give my hand and not my heart?"

"There is more to a marriage than love, Daughter. Love is fleeting, while duty remains. Time replaces beauty, emotions wax old. With life comes trouble enough to erase all early passions. Will a man who loves you for your beauty still love you when age has marred your face and stooped your shoulders to the ground? I speak to you of duty, the true life of a woman, not of frivolity or of romance. Do your duty and perhaps, with providence, you may find love with the one you wed."

Marah stood, facing her mother. "I shall not wed him, Mother. My heart does not belong to him and neither shall my body. I desire true love, not duty, not feigned devotion. I want to know the fullness of love, to give my heart to the one who gives his heart to me in return. Such love can never diminish. Eternal love never dies." Marah's gaze returned to the setting sun. "Love is real and true. I will not settle for anything less, and certainly not for duty."

"You speak, Daughter, as though your heart already knows such a love. Has a man known you? Is your field untouched or is it already plowed and seeded?"

"I remain a maiden, Mother. I will remain one until the hour my true love makes me otherwise. He will know me then, and no other before him. My lover shall desire me with a whole heart, not for duty's sake, but for love's sake."

Her mother sighed. "There is no man on Earth as you describe. Desire, lust, love, it is all the same emotion. What love has to do with the bond of marriage, I do not know. Perhaps you will find one who feels like you do, but duty will replace such nonsense. I admonish you not to bring shame upon the head of your father, but to perform the duty of a good and faithful daughter."

Marah turned her eyes to the setting sun. "It is not good and faithful, Mother, but decidedly evil and faithless to deny the heart its true love, for not only would I deny my heart, but also the heart of the one meant for me.

Somewhere, my love waits, longing for me as my soul longs for him. You speak to me of duty. Is there any greater duty than to guard true love? When my love comes along will he find me wed to another?"

Marah's mother stepped toward her, taking her by the hand. "Do your duty. Obey the will of your father. He has chosen a good man, wealthy and handsome. You will never want for shelter or sustenance, but will have the good of the land and be clothed with the best garments."

"Yet I would be poor and miserable where it matters most. What good are a handsome face and much gold without love? No, Mother. Though I am cold and destitute, if I have the love of my heart, I shall be content."

With a final look of worry, ringing her hands, Marah's mother turned to leave.

"I will tell your father and it will displease him. I only pray that you find the love you seek, or come quickly to your senses."

"My love will come along, Mother. When the time comes, I will be ready for him, having maintained a faithful heart."

Left alone, Marah watched the final sinking of the day's sun. Before returning to the house of her father, she gazed upward into the part of sky where I hovered out of sight above her.

"My love will come," she said.

I watched her until the sun went down.

CHAPTER 17

Enoch's son, Methuselah, prophesied in his father's stead, crying out to the men of Lamech from the same hill where his father had. Few paid him attention. He brought his family with him, his sons, daughters and grandchildren. He warned of a great destruction of the entire Earth. Men derided and mocked him, but none dared to touch him, for the story of Enoch had spread to every part of the world.

Methuselah called a young man to him from among the members of his family. He was handsome, tall and comely. Methuselah placed his arms around him and, looking up to Heaven, cried out, "Behold Noah, God's chosen vessel! Behold God's plan of salvation from judgment to come!"

I was lonely, longing for a companion. I watched Marah more and more, following her with my eyes whenever she left her father's house, envious of any that spoke with or touched her. Nevertheless, I had decided not to interfere again with the affairs of men.

Then one day, unexpectedly, Heaven summoned my return by the beacon of pulsing light. I was shocked, having been away for so long. I turned to follow the call and return to Heaven, but hesitated. I looked down upon the house of Marah's father. Would I return to this place? Would I see her again? My heart ached to see her one last time, but she remained in the house. I shook myself from my hesitation and flew obediently to Heaven.

I forgot the evil of Earth and humankind as soon as I entered the gates of Heaven. Such beauty, such light! The aching in my heart turned to pure joy. I worshiped, praising God with a loud voice, gazing with rapture upon the streets of golden light.

I took my time, flying along its streets and rivers of light, seeing the varied types of angels around me, admiring their glory, like a man returning to the home of his fond childhood. After a time, the beacon of light drew me from my rapture, toward the twelve thrones.

The meeting place was unoccupied, save for a solitary figure sitting on one of the twelve thrones. A rainbow circled his head. I landed before him, marveling at his likeness to the Great I Am. Enoch stood when he saw me.

"Saruel, angel of Heaven," he said. He motioned to a throne beside him. "Sit with me."

I hesitated.

"Do not worry," he said. "That is now your throne, for the I Am has promoted you. Of the thirteen Watchers on Earth, you alone remained faithful."

I felt guilty, remembering that I had taken human lives, that I had loved a woman. Yet had I loved her? In the light of Heaven, my memory of such things faded.

"I live to do the will of the Great I Am," I said.

"Bless His holy name," Enoch said.

I was startled.

"The I Am has a name?"

Enoch smiled. "He has a name, higher than any other."

Enoch was not even four-hundred years old, and had been in Heaven for a very short time. I had lived for time beyond numbering, yet I did not know the Great I Am had a name.

"I did not know," I said.

"I am not surprised," Enoch said, "for I see that the angels of Heaven do not aspire for knowledge in the way that my kind does. The Creator made us in His own image. Angels are made as His servants."

"Please," I said, "tell me His name."

Enoch shook his head. "It is not for me to reveal his name, for it is secret."

"So be it," I said, but I could not help feeling envious of Enoch. "Tell me, though, why have I been summoned?"

Enoch frowned. "Your time of watching over the Earth has come to an end, for the I Am will soon visit judgment on its inhabitants. Behold, the angels of God are prepared to smite the Earth. The abyss is expanding to hold the spirits of all mankind."

"Forgive me," I said. "Did you not tell me His judgment would come when your son, Methuselah, died? Behold, he is a young man."

Enoch looked at me. "Do you not know the nature of time? Heaven is eternal. A day here is as a thousand years, a thousand years as a day. You returned to Heaven less than an hour ago, but on Earth many hundreds of years have passed."

I stood to my feet, staring dumbstruck at Enoch. Marah! When I had left Earth, she was a young maiden.

Enoch looked at me, a quizzical expression on his face.

"Are there no righteous on the Earth?" I said. "Will all of mankind be destroyed?"

"On all the Earth, there is but one righteous man, Noah, son of Methuselah. He will be saved, and anyone who joins him." Enoch studied me thoughtfully. "Earth is no longer your concern, Saruel. Your time of watching humankind is over." He pointed toward the temple, which held the throne room of the I Am. "The Creator invites you into the Holy of Holies. Enter into the joy of the Lord."

I turned and looked at the Temple of the Most High God. It was a great honor to serve in the temple. Most angels who served there had never actually entered the temple, but served in the courtyard and in the porch outside. The temple was divided into two chambers: the Holy Place, where only the twelve archangels entered (there had been eleven since the fall of the Son of the Morning); and the Holy of Holies, where only the chief of the twelve entered. The throne of God rested within the Holy of Holies. No angel had entered the Holy of Holies since the Great Rebellion.

I turned to Enoch. "This cannot be."

Enoch smiled. "Saruel, son of Heaven, the Great I Am blesses you this day, for the throne you sit upon once belonged to the Son of the Morning. You will serve before the throne of God, in his place. For the I Am finds you worthy to be chief among the twelve archangels."

I stood before Enoch, hearing his words, barely comprehending. How could this be?

"Surely not," I said, "for I am only a Watcher, one of many. There are angels far more worthy, far more powerful than I."

"And why are they powerful? Only because the I Am made them so. Can an angel glory in power granted to him through no work or merit of his own? The Son of the Morning, the most powerful of God's creation, fell to temptation. His power did not save him, his beauty made no difference. You watched others of your kind fall to sin, yet you sinned not."

I lowered my head. "I have taken the lives of men," I said.

"Heaven knows," Enoch said. "You saved an innocent woman from evil men, a noble act, above and beyond your station."

Enoch stood, motioning toward the Temple of Heaven. "Do not keep the Master of the Universe waiting."

I obediently flew toward the Temple of the Most High God, my anticipation growing. Ministering angels stood in the courtyard. Messengers flew to and from the temple. I landed before the porch, closer to the temple than I had ever been before. The ministering angels stared at me in wonder. I gathered my courage and stepped toward the shining doors leading into the Holy Place. They opened before me. I stood in awe at the sight of the Holy Place and trembled at the immense power of the Spirit of God within. I walked slowly upon a floor made of shimmering light. Ten dazzling lights, brighter than the brightest star, shone before me, leading to the Holy of Holies, five on the right side of the room and five on the left.

I heard movement behind me and turned, surprised to see Enoch standing with me in the Holy Place.

"Can humankind stand in the Temple of the Most High God?" I said.

"Mankind was made to dwell with God." He pointed to one of the five lights closest to me. "Look, Saruel. Behold the Earth, as it is now."

I peered into the light, and saw the image of Earth. The atmosphere around it was exceedingly dark and turbulent. Sporadic lightning flashed in the midst of black, ominous clouds. The ocean churned as great waves crashed angrily, battering the shoreline. Hurricanes and tornadoes moved across the land, fingers of God, destroying everything in their path.

"Come," Enoch said, "the Holy One waits for you."

Pulling away from the light, I continued walking.

A crimson veil divided the Holy Place from the Holy of Holies. A small, golden altar stood between the veil and myself, where the archangels pour out the prayers of all creation. Enoch motioned to the altar.

"Place a worthy offering upon the altar of prayers, and the veil will open, allowing you entrance into the Holy of Holies."

"What do I have to give to the Great I Am? I have no possessions."

Enoch pointed to another one of the ten brilliant lights. "Observe and understand."

I looked into the light, and saw the Garden of God as it was on the day the Warrior angels had removed the Tree of Carnal Knowledge and the Tree of Life. I saw myself, landing before the single abandoned fruit of the Tree of Life, picking it up then placing it in my robe.

I drew away from the light and reached into my robe, feeling the fruit. I pulled it free of my robes and faced the altar of prayers. Enoch stopped me with a hand on my arm.

"It is not yet time for your offering." He pointed to the light again.

I looked into the light once more. I heard a woman singing, and saw Marah as I had first discovered her, bathing in the clear pool of water. Such emotion, such tremendous love and longing filled me that I nearly cried out, forgetting that I was in the Temple of God. I saw myself lowering from the sky, landing near her. The look on my face was rapture and bewilderment. I saw again the moment of her embarrassment, and shock when she saw me. I saw again her wonder, when she realized I was not a son of Adam.

I felt Enoch's hand on my shoulder, pulling me away from the light. "Unless you love the Great I Am more than you love all others, then you are unworthy of him." He pointed to another light. "Look and see, angel of God."

Staring into the light, I saw her again, walking with the deceitful young man on the day she was abducted by Erozel's servants. Rage consumed me, equal in measure to the love I had experienced earlier. I saw myself rescuing her, killing her abductors, wiping away her tears, returning her to safety, holding her in my arms. And, suddenly, I was no longer watching. I was there again, carrying her as I flew, feeling the graceful curves of her body pressed against mine, her soft, full breasts against my chest. I smelled the aroma of flowers in her hair. I said her name for the first time, and it was poetry, music, a symphony.

Something pulled me away from my reverie. I looked around me, momentarily confused as to my whereabouts. Enoch's hand rested on my shoulder. My hand still held the fruit of the Tree of Life.

He pointed to another of the lights.

I stepped hurriedly to the light, wanting desperately to see Marah again. And I did see her. She stood outside of her father's house, conversing with her mother, on the day she had refused to marry a man she did not love. Her eyes searched the skies for me. I trembled at her words.

"My love will come."

But hundreds of years had passed in her time, and I had not come. Had she abandoned her love for me? Had she succumbed to her mother's wishes and married another? I pulled away from the light and turned to Enoch.

"Tell me," I said, my voice shaking, "where is she? Is she safe? I must know."

Enoch motioned toward the altar of prayers. "You stand just outside the Holy of Holies, where only one angel has ever entered. Forget this woman, angel of God. What is she, compared to the great honor bestowed upon you? You are First of Angels. Enter into His holy presence."

I stood, staring at the veil and the altar of prayers. I looked at the fruit in my hand. All I had to do was to place it on the altar, and I would be the archangel of God, standing with him in the Holy of Holies.

"Please," I said. "I must know."

Enoch pointed wordlessly to another light.

I saw a small house. In the distance, behind the house, stood the outline of the Temple of All Gods, silhouetted against the night sky. Lightning flashed, thunder roared. An old woman stood in front of the house, staring frightfully at the dark, roiling clouds above her. Time had marked her face and bent her body, but she was as lovely to me as the first time ever I saw her. High winds whipped against her, rain began to fall. The Earth shook, catching her off guard. She fell to the ground, the earth shaking and rolling violently beneath her. Crevasses and cracks appeared in the ground around her. Water bubbled up through fissures from underground springs. She tried to stand, but lost her balance once more, falling hard on her right leg. She cried out in pain, sitting in the mud, staring helplessly at the turbulent sky, the rain increasing to a torrent of water. Her leg was twisted at an odd angle.

I pulled away from the light. Enoch watched me in silence.

I looked at the veil separating me from the Holy of Holies and at the Fruit of Life I held in my hand.

"Tell me," I said, fighting to control my voice. "How will God deliver Noah from the flood?"

Enoch watched me with sad eyes. "He has built an ark of wood. He and his wife, his three sons, the two wives of his sons, are entering the ark as we speak. Will you place your sacrifice on the altar of prayers?"

I looked with longing at the veil separating me from the throne of God. Beyond that veil was glory that only the Son of the Morning had known. I was to minister before God as the chief of angels, seeing him as he truly is, but, if I did, Marah would die in the flood, alone.

"What will you do, Saruel?" Enoch asked.

"I am honored beyond words at the position the Great I Am has bestowed upon me, and accept it wholeheartedly. But there is something I must do first. I must return to Earth for a time, and then I will come back to enter into the Holy of Holies."

Enoch frowned, placing his hand on my shoulder. "Leave the dead to the dead," he said.

I shook my head. "I must go to her."

Leaving Enoch, I flew faster than I ever had before, reaching the Earth in moments.

Lightning flashed in the atmosphere below me. The position of the Earth had changed, tilted on its axis. I searched below me for the Temple of All Gods, but dark clouds blocked my view. I dropped below the clouds, searching the ground for any familiar landmark. I found the city of Lamech, its people in a panic, women screaming, holding their children out of the water, as it rose steadily around them.

I flew to the west, away from Lamech, arriving in the sky above the temple. Servants of Erozel surrounded the altar, calling his name. Erozel and his Watchers were nowhere to be seen. I flew backwards, facing the temple, until it appeared as it had in the vision of Marah, silhouetted against the black sky. I hovered above the flooded street, where I had seen her fall. The water was waist deep, and she was no longer where she had fallen. The roof of the small house had caved in on itself. I heard her voice, weeping, weak and faint, coming from inside the house. Quickly, I landed in the water, pulling hard on the front door, tearing it from its fastenings.

"Marah!" I called.

The sound of her weeping came to me from the back of the house. Marah sat, balanced precariously on a wooden table, the water rising around her. She was blue with cold, and wet. Her leg was broken and useless. Moving quickly, I went to her, picked her up and held her close, warming her. She looked up at me, eyes wide, lips moving soundlessly.

"I have returned," I said.

Weeping, she buried her face in my chest. "Do you come to me only now, on this, the day of my death?"

Carrying her from the house, I lifted into the air, flying with her above the clouds, out of the torrent of rain. I hovered, looking down on the terrible destruction caused by the judgment of God, not knowing what else to do. The Earth filled with water. Marah looked up at me.

"You are still so beautiful," she said, "while I am marred by my many years."

I met her eyes. "You are as lovely as the first day I saw you," I said.

"I was in water on that day, as well."

"I remember," I said.

Her face became a mask of sorrow. "I waited so long for you. Why did you never return to me? I kept my heart faithful. My love for you remained. Was my love in vain?"

My heart burned within me. "I am here now," I said. "Tell me, where does Noah, the son of Methuselah dwell?"

She looked up at me, questioning.

"In the city of Enoch, East of Lamech," she said.

I flew to where she told me, dropping through the clouds, into the rain below. There I saw the ark of Noah. It was an enormous vessel made of wood, covered with pitch to proof it against the battering rain. It rested upon the ground, the water not yet high enough to set it afloat. Hundreds of men and women waded in the rising water around the ark, pounding against its closed door with fists, crying in desperation, their voices lost to the pummeling rain and howling winds.

"I will place you upon the ark," I said.

She shook her head. "No, my love, it is of no use. I will die here in your arms. There is no other place for me. My heart has longed only for you since I was a maiden."

"Did you marry, did you have children?"

She smiled weakly. "I have never been with a man. I have never loved another."

I held her to me, my heart aching, knowing then what I would do. I flew as quickly as I could without hurting Marah, to a high mountain, finding shelter in a cave, the light of my body casting long shadows across the rough stone walls. I placed her on the floor of the cave and stood, looking down at her. I touched the fruit of the Tree of Life through my robe. My thoughts were on Hemael and his curse. He had eaten of the Fruit of Life, and God cursed him. But he was an angel, Marah a woman. Would God curse her, as he had cursed Hemael?

"What troubles you, my love?" she said.

Reaching down, I touched her face. "I may be able to give you life again," I said, "or, in trying, I may bring a curse upon you. For life is not mine to take or to give. Life belongs to God alone."

"You have taken life before," she said. "Is it better to take life, or to give it?"

I pulled the fruit from my robe and held it up. It glowed brilliantly with golden light.

"It is beautiful," Marah said. "What is it?"

"This is a fruit from the Tree of Life in the Garden of God. It had the power to give life to Eve, the Mother of the Earth, yet it brought terrible judgment to an angel of God."

"Which will it bring to me, life or judgment?"

I shook my head. "I do not know."

"If it gives me life," she said, "will I spend that life with you? For to live without you again is, to me, no life at all. I choose to die and face the judgment of my kind, rather than to live without you again. If you will remain at my side, then give me this fruit. I accept it, and the consequences. Otherwise, remain with me until I live no more."

I thought of Heaven, of the Temple of God and the Holy of Holies. I was an angel of the Most High God, offered a place that only one other had ever known. I loved and worshiped the Great I Am. To enter into His dwelling place, to see Him as He truly is, would be a delight and privilege beyond my understanding.

Marah looked down at the floor of the cave. "I see, then, that you have made your decision," she said. "Please stay with me until my spirit leaves this vessel of clay."

I looked down at Marah. She was so beautiful to me. I felt as though my heart was being pulled in two directions, torn between the Great I Am and Marah.

"Take it," I said, holding the fruit out to her. "Eat of it and live."

"Then you will remain with me?"

I knelt down and placed the fruit in her hand.

"I will remain with you," I said.

Looking into my eyes, Marah brought the Fruit of Life to her lips, and ate a small piece of it. I held my breath. She cried out, suddenly, clutching at her throat. Her wide eyes looked up at me in terror, then lost their focus and glazed over, unseeing. Her body went limp. I moved quickly, scooping her up, holding her in my arms.

"Marah!" I called.

She did not respond. She stopped breathing, her heart stopped beating. I cried out in anguish as ethereal light lifted from her lifeless body to the roof of the cave. I wept. Her spirit floated listlessly above me. I expected it to leave through the mouth of the cave. Instead, it glided downward, gently covering her body, growing brighter, revealing every recess and crevice of the cave. I placed her body on the floor of the cave, staring down into the light. Slowly, the light returned, flowing into her. What remained was a young maiden. It was Marah, but she appeared no older than sixteen or seventeen years old.

"Marah?" I said, softly.

She opened her eyes, looking around her. "Where am I?"

"You are with me," I said, my weeping turned to joy. "You are alive!"

She looked around the cave and sat up. "Where is my home? Where are

99

my parents?"

"My love, even now your home is covered by the flood waters, and your parents have been gone for many years."

She stood up quickly. I stood also, facing her.

"Gone?" she said, bewildered. "Who are you?"

"You do not remember?"

She searched my face. Her eyes narrowed. She stepped away from me, pondering, looking confused.

"You are a son of Heaven," she said finally.

"Yes," I said.

She watched me. I watched her. Understanding dawned on her lovely face.

"Saruel, you are Saruel." She looked down at her hands, her body. "I ate of the Fruit of Life and am young again." She stepped to the mouth of the cave and looked out into the darkness. Water poured from the turbulent sky. Rivers and lakes formed in the valleys and lowlands. Lightning flashed. Thunder rumbled. "And the Earth is flooding with water, as Noah said it would."

"All Earth will be covered in water. Every land creature will die, except for those who have found salvation on the ark of Noah." I said.

She faced me. "And what will my fate be? Will the water reach this cave?"

I stepped to her and held her close to me, kissing her lightly on the cheek. How wondrous it felt, my lips upon her skin. "I will not let you die," I said.

Marah in my arms, I flew from the cave. Wind and rain whipped around us, soaking through her clothes. She trembled with cold and I held her closer, her hands clinging tightly to me. I flew to the city of Lamech, then eastward to the city of Enoch, where earlier we had seen the ark of Noah. Water covered the entire city. I heard the cries of the damned in the dark waters below me, calling out for rescuers who would never come.

Carried away by the flood, the ark was not where it had been. I flew in a large circle, miles around, searching the waters below me. Finally, I saw a Warrior angel, shining in the darkness. The ark floated in the waters below him. I flew toward the ark. The Warrior stopped me, his sword lifted out in front of him.

"Son of Heaven, what brings you to the ark of Noah?"

"I have brought this maiden to share in the salvation of Noah and his family." I said.

"I am here to stop anyone, man or angel, from entering the ark," he said. "Who are you to add to the seven souls already inside?"

"I am Saruel, a Watcher of God."

The Warrior looked at me. "You are Saruel, chosen to minister before the throne?"

"I am," I said.

He lowered his sword. "Who am I to question the chosen of God? Enter with good will, Saruel, First of Angels."

The top of the ark was a covered deck with hundreds of stalls, joined together like cells. I landed on the deck, hearing the sounds of frightened animals in the stalls around me. The ark tipped and rocked, carried by the swift ocean currents. I listened for the sounds of human beings. I heard weeping and praying from somewhere within the ark.

Near the center of the covered stalls was a flight of stairs, leading downward into the heart of the ark. I carried Marah down the stairs. I found a passageway leading deeper into the ark, and followed the sounds of voices. Soon, lamplight appeared. Noah and his family knelt on the wooden floor, praying. I stood in silence, not wanting to interrupt their prayers. Noah's wife was the first to see me. My body glowed brightly in the darkness and I am sure I was a remarkable sight. She gasped.

"Fear not," I said. Noah tried to stand, but the ark rocked him violently. He returned to his knees. "I am Saruel, an angel of the Most High God. I brought this young woman to share in your salvation."

"Forgive me," Noah said, "but the door in the side of this ark was shut by the hand of God. Why did she not enter before then?" I placed Marah gently on the floor. Noah looked directly at me, his lined face unmoved by my shining beauty. "How can we trust you when it was your kind that led the world to this present judgment?"

His wife looked at Marah. "Come now, my husband, we cannot return her to the water," she said. "Shem, our son, is without a wife. Is she not his answered prayer? He will never have children unless his brothers share their wives, or he waits for their daughters."

Noah was old at the time, more than six-hundred. His sons were not much younger. Shem, the only one kneeling by himself, looked like he could have been Marah's grandfather. I could not bear the idea of him being with her.

Noah looked at me. "Is it true, angel of God? Is this young woman to be the wife of my son, Shem?"

I wanted to say no, but was afraid that Noah might actually reject Marah. Would he throw her from the ark? I could not be sure. His distrust of my kind seemed quite powerful. I looked down at Marah. "It is not for me to declare the will of God in this matter. This woman has freewill. If she chooses to dwell with your son, she may do so."

Noah's wife said, "There will be no other choice for her. Shem is the only available man."

Marah looked up at me, her eyes pleading.

"Will she share in your salvation?" I asked.

Noah studied me with a scowl. Finally, he nodded. "She may stay with us."

I placed my hand on Marah's shoulder. "Maiden," I said, "salvation belongs to you."

I knew she longed to speak, but eyes were watching us. I turned, leaving the eight humans safe inside. Passing the Warrior, I lifted to a place in the sky, high above the ark, following it as the waters flooded the whole Earth, reaching even to the highest mountains. I thought of Heaven and the Holy of Holies. I looked down at my body. I still glowed with the light of God. Was giving the Fruit of Life to Marah not a sin worthy of casting me from Heaven? Was it possible to return to Heaven and enter into the Holy of Holies? Perhaps, but my promise to stay with Marah bound me to Earth.

I heard a cry of anguish, not from the waters below, but from the skies above me. A figure hovered in the darkness, above the clouds. I drew closer, finding Erozel holding an unconscious old woman in his arms with the same care I had shown to Marah. The woman was Asherah, who Erozel fell into sin with, and who had defiled Enoch. She wore the same sort of finery as in the days of her youth. Her long, silvery hair was wet and in disarray, her skin deathly pale.

Water ran down Erozel's feminine face. His eyes showed terrible pain.

"The only woman I love," he said, holding her out to me. "Will you save her, Saruel, my brother? Will you do this thing for me?"

I lowered my gaze. "And where is Eros, her son?" I said.

Erozel's shoulders quaked. "Eros is no more. Warriors took hold of him, and his brothers, all the children of the gods, holding them until they drowned in the water below us." He wept, moaning in anguish, then, looking up at me again, said, "Will you save the woman I love?"

"Am I God, that I should grant life?"

"You are First of Angels, second only to the I Am. Your word is like unto the word of God. If you command it, it will be."

I shook my head. "I cannot, Erozel, for I have not yet entered into the Holy of Holies."

His face crumpled with sorrow. Terrible pain filled his eyes. "Hemael hovers nearby, following me, waiting for her spirit to leave her body."

I looked with pity upon Erozel. His fall, as wicked as it was, had not diminished my love for him. I felt the Fruit of Life hidden in my robe. I thought of Marah. How soon would I need to give her more?

"I understand your sorrow. All the same, life is not mine, either to give or to take. She is dust, and to dust will she return. That is the way of all flesh."

"Look upon me, Saruel, at my breasts and the roundness of my hips; I am lust embodied, but did the Lord not create me this way?" He ran a finger along Asherah's face, and kissed her. "Will He now take from me the object of my desire, a desire that He placed within me on the day I was made?"

"My brother," I said, "I cannot help her. I am sorry for your loss."

"Leave me to my misery," he said, "Pray that you never know heartache such as mine."

Leaving Erozel, I returned to the skies above Noah's ark. It was a dark speck floating in an opaque ocean, lit only by the glow of the lone Warrior above it.

It carried the future of the world, and the future of my heart.

CHAPTER 18

The ark floated at the mercy of ocean currents, jostled by frequent storms. Water poured from the sky in sheets, flurries of hail the size of stones battered the ark on every side. Thankfully, Noah had built it to withstand even the most punishing rain and turbulent waves. Finally, after what seemed like an eternity, rays of sunlight broke through the dark clouds. Torrents of rain slowed to a drizzle, then stopped altogether. A rainbow appeared in the sky.

Slowly, over the span of several more months, the water abated from off the face of the Earth. The peaks of mountains appeared, followed by the hills beneath them. The tops of trees protruded from the water, searching for sunlight. The ark floated on peaceful waters, at last coming to rest upon a high mountain. The eight humans ventured out onto the deck into the light of the sun. How wonderful it was to see Marah again. Her eyes searched the skies for me, but I remained hidden.

The Lord of the Fallen hovered with his followers just above the horizon, watching the ark. The Fallen Watchers, absent Erozel, hovered together as well, high in the sky, their demeanors sullen and filled with despair. I flew to them.

"My brothers," I said in greeting.

Azazel answered me. "Do we remain brothers, now that you are First of Angels? We are Fallen creatures."

"You will always be my brothers," I said, "and I do not yet dwell in the Holy of Holies."

"But you shall, Saruel," Azazel said. He looked at me with pleading eyes. "You will dwell in the presence of the I Am. When you do, remember us kindly. Perhaps we will find mercy in His sight, even now."

"I will remember you," I said. "Where is Erozel?"

"Erozel is alone in his grieving," Azazel said. "Asherah's death weighs heavily upon him. He is not himself. Even now, he dwells in the Garden of God, holding her corpse, refusing to be comforted."

I left my brothers and flew to the Garden of God, searching for Erozel, surveying the terrible aftermath below me as I went. The catastrophic flood had divided the single mass of land the Earth had once been into something resembling the present day continents. To my surprise, I arrived to find the Garden of God untouched by the flood. The trees stood, as large and green as ever. Flowers bloomed in vibrant colors.

I found Erozel sitting languidly against one of the great trees, his eyes haunted, staring at nothing. In his arms, he cradled the rotting corpse of Asherah, her face in an advanced stage of decay, her abdomen bloated, her skin mottled and blackened, sloughing off in places. Her eyes had receded into her skull, her head resting limply against Erozel's breasts. My eyes wandered over the former Garden of God, to where the Tree of Life had been. Was that why Erozel had come here? Had he also remembered the Fruit of Life? Looking in the opposite direction, I saw the place of the skull, the rocky hill where the Tree of Carnal Knowledge once grew. I lowered to a spot nearby. He did not look up at me, and I remained quiet. His lovely face held such terrible sorrow. Several minutes passed before he acknowledged me.

"She is dead," he said. "Her soul is in the abyss, carried away by Hemael, punished, in torment for sins which were, to her, as natural as the very air she breathed."

"God is just," I answered. "We do not know His full plan. I assure you, though, that Asherah is part of it. All things work together for His glory."

Erozel stood quickly, holding Asherah's body angrily out to me. I drew back at the sight of her, and at the fetid smell of decay.

"You assure me? Where is the glory in this? The one I loved molders in my embrace. How does this fit into His plan? Tell me truthfully, Saruel, First of Angels, before God who sees all, could you have saved her from this?"

"I am a Watcher," I said. "You know the limits of my power."

His eyes blazed furiously at me.

"I do know your limits," he said. "Even now, as second only to the Great I Am, you could restore her to life. Your hatred for Asherah and for the nature of my fall is apparent. You could have saved her, but you chose not to."

"Erozel," I said.

He turned sharply away from me, cradling Asherah's corpse lovingly to his bosom. "Depart from me, holy angel of God."

"My brother…"

"Leave me. Find me no more!"

I lifted into the skies, leaving him alone with Asherah's fetid corpse, in the Garden of Eden.

Several days later, the door in the side of the ark opened and the eight humans stepped out onto dry ground. The women began foraging for food, gathering fruits and nuts, while the men built an altar of stones to worship God. Marah left them to their work, walking until she reached a clearing in the woods. I lowered to the ground near to her, concealing myself from other angels under a dense jacaranda tree. Its bell-shaped flowers covered the green grass around me in a blanket of purple.

"Marah," I called.

She ran to me. Tears streamed down her beautiful face. I wiped them with my hand.

"Why do you weep?" I said.

"I weep for joy. My heart is glad, my eyes happy to see you. Take me away from here. Be my husband. I will be your wife."

"Marah," I said, "You must understand. I am an angel of Heaven, not a man. I do not partake in marriage. Such a thing would be outside of the natural order, an abomination in the sight of God."

She looked sadly up at me, her face wet with tears; I wanted nothing more than to take her in my arms, to hold her, to comfort her.

"Is it natural for me to marry a man I do not love, when my heart belongs to you?"

"Come," I said. "Do not be sorrowful, for I am overjoyed to see you again."

"Do you love me, Saruel, the way that I am in love with you?"

"I am a servant of Heaven," I said. "My affections are for the Great I Am. I am not a man that I…"

She placed a finger on my lips to quiet me. "I love you with my whole heart."

With that, she turned away from me, returning to Noah and his family.

CHAPTER 19

I have told my story, describing what took place on Earth, from Creation to the Great Flood. You understand my heart's intention, to the extent any person can understand the heart of another. Am I a devil, worthy of this damnation, my eternal fall?

Wait. Before you decide, before you pronounce judgment, I must first tell you how I fell.

Taking the lives of wicked men had not excluded me from heavenly service. On the contrary, I was to be rewarded for my behavior, exalted to the loftiest angelic position under God. Saving Marah from the deluge, giving her of the fruit of the Tree of Life, did not extinguish the light of Heaven around me.

I fell for love and for love alone.

One moonlit night I heard the voice of my beloved, crying out to me in distress.

"Saruel, my angel, my only love, come to me!"

She stood alone in the middle of a grove of trees. I landed beside her. She was shaking. Tears wet her face.

"What is wrong, dear Marah?"

"It is Noah," she said, sobbing. "He commanded me to lie down with Shem."

"He commanded you?"

"He said we must have children, to replenish the Earth. I would rather die. I love you, and I will not marry another. Though you are a son of Heaven, and I a daughter of Eve, we belong together."

I looked down at her, and I suddenly knew that I would not enter the Holy of Holies. I would never see Heaven again. And, at that moment, I no longer cared. My heart filled with love, pure and true, overwhelming and undeniable. I held her close to me, lifting with her into the cool night air. It seemed the most natural thing, to hold her to my heart, to feel the warmth of her soft breasts, the curves of her body against mine.

I kissed her lips.

Holding her, I headed toward the Garden of Eden, marveling that my body still shone with heavenly light. I saw the outline of the garden, lit only by a golden moon. I headed to the spot Adam and Eve had once called home. Suddenly, a rainbow of light appeared in the midst of the garden.

"Saruel, come to me." It was Enoch.

I lowered to the ground and stood before him. Marah held herself tight against me. Enoch looked at her and frowned.

"What are you doing with this woman, when Heaven is waiting for you?"

I looked down at Marah's lovely face, and ran my finger along her cheek. "I will remain here with her," I said.

"You are not a man that you should marry a woman."

Marah hid behind me, clinging to my waist.

"Then why did God fashion a heart in my chest? Why do I love, Enoch, Son of God. I love this woman, and I question why I should not have her."

"Yours is not to question," Enoch said. "Will you choose a mortal woman over eternal glory? Earthworms will devour the body you find so lovely, but Heaven remains, eternal. You are to minister before the throne. Is that now meaningless to you?"

"It is not meaningless to me," I said. "Heaven was my dwelling from before time began, but Marah is my home."

"Saruel, look around you. Do you see where you are standing?"

I looked around me and understood. Marah was standing in the exact spot where the Tree of Carnal Knowledge had once grown. Where Eve had chosen to eat of its fruit, so that she might know her husband in ways she had never known him, so that she might bear children.

"You made your choice," Enoch said sadly. "You are cast down from Heaven."

He turned his back toward me and, without another word, flew away, leaving me alone with Marah. The light of Heaven surrounding me went out and I stood before her, naked. I had never been naked. I trembled with the newness and delight of it all. It was pleasure as I had never known.

Marah undressed before me in the moonlight. I smelled her aroma, flowers and desire. She drew near to me, her naked breasts pressing against me. She kissed my mouth, my neck, going ever lower, kiss by kiss, to my chest, my belly, her lips wet silk upon my skin. My member protruded hard out in front of me. Marah touched it, encircling it with her fingers. I groaned with anticipation. We made love in the Garden of God.

It was Heaven.

CHAPTER 20

I built a house in the Garden of Eden from the wood of fallen ancient trees. Marah turned it into a home, decorating it with the flowers she gathered on our daily walk, for as the I Am walked with Adam in the cool of day, so I walked with Marah. She talked with me, laughed and sang songs of love to me as day after day, year after year, we made our own trails through dense woods to private meadows and cool running streams. We began each day with tenderness and each night with passion, just the two of us, learning what it meant to love. I was Marah's and she was mine. I adored her. Life was simple, and love was all we needed.

Several hundred years went by and she remained as beautiful as ever. One small bite of the Fruit of Life had returned my darling to me. She never fell ill and had boundless energy. What would the entire fruit have done to her? I did not know, and thought it unwise to find out.

One night, as Marah lay sleeping, the smell of smoke came to me on the wind. I left Marah, lifting into the air to investigate the source of the smoke and was surprised to find a large city only a hundred miles or so from the Garden of Eden. Several hundred years had passed since the flood, and already there were thousands of dwellings in the city below me.

The source of the smoke was a great white tower, larger than I could scarcely believe, reaching high into the night sky. It was under construction, less than halfway to completion, but was taller already than any of today's highest buildings. Fires from hundreds of smelter's pots sent smoke into the air, and the winds carried the smoke toward Eden.

Marah and I, being alone, had felt no need for garments. I searched the area below for appropriate clothing and found a handsome selection of robes drying on a tree branch by a nearby brook. Landing by the tree, I chose a blue robe of cotton about my size and dressed quickly. I walked the rest of the way to the tower, passing the city dwellers. The sounds of musical instruments and the smells of cooking food were wonderful to me after so many years. The laughter of children at play made my heart glad.

I reached the base of the tower, and stood in awe at the ingenuity of man. What a structure! Made primarily with stone and mortar, it spanned more than a square mile at its base, growing narrower the higher it went. I wondered over its purpose, seeing no practical reason to build such a monumental tower. Wide stone steps ran from the base of the tower all the way to the top, each step etched with words artistically written in golden letters: the Stairway to Heaven.

I climbed the steps as a man would. Nearing the top, I heard the voices of women and children coming from somewhere above me. I moved quietly to the top of the tower. The voices came from inside a dwelling of finely carved wood. Light shone from within through the cracks of covered windows. Two men armed with swords stood watch outside.

Far to the right of the dwelling stood an altar of large stones, similar to the altar Adam had built outside the gates of Eden. Was this a place of worship? Twelve stones of equal size and shape formed the altar. A thirteenth stone sat alone, several spans away. I walked to the stone, finding that someone had fastened a chain and ankle shackle to it. Congealed blood covered the area around the stone. My heart beating rapidly in my chest, I returned to the twelve stones. Each one had a name etched into it. There was Azazel, Captain of Watchers; Ariel my brother; Erozel and the others; and, finally, my own name, Saruel.

"Stop where you are!" The two guards ran to me with swords drawn. One of them, a powerfully built man, pointed the tip of his sword at me. "You dare to defile the Temple of All Gods, desecrating their altar with your presence?"

"Your gods," I said, "not mine."

"I should deliver your soul to the gods for such blasphemy," he said.

"Where are your gods? Are they unable to fight their own battles? Do they need you to defend them?"

He struck me across the face with the wide side of his blade. I did not resist.

"Will you speak of the gods in this way?"

"I ask you again, where are your gods?"

He brought the sword back, this time ready to cut me down with it, as if it were possible. The sword arched through the air toward me. Suddenly, the guard stopped. The sword fell from his hand, clattering to the ground. His eyes grew wide. He fell in a clump beside his sword, puzzlement on his dying face, a great, bloody hole in the middle of his back. Ariel stood behind him, the man's bloody, pulsating heart in his hand. He wore a black robe laced with silver. A sword sheathed in black leather graced his side. The second guard fell to his knees and bowed his head, shaking in fear. Ariel dropped the heart next to the trembling guard.

"Saruel, my brother, you have returned to us."

"By chance," I said. "I did not know you were here." I motioned to the altar of stones. "The others are here as well, I see."

"They will be here soon, for our blessed worshipers await our return."

He looked toward the wooden dwelling, then down at the trembling guard. "Do you not know a god when you see one?"

The man bowed lower to the ground. "Mercy, my gods," he said, his voice shaking.

"I am not the god of mercy," Ariel said. He turned to me. "Will you show this man mercy, Saruel?"

"Yes," I said.

Ariel laughed. He looked hard at the man. "Return to your post."

The man scrambled to his feet and ran, returning to the wooden dwelling.

"I heard that you fell from Heaven's graces," Ariel said. "I see it is true. Where have you been?"

"I have roamed here and there upon the Earth," I said.

"Why did you not find me?"

Before I could answer, I felt a sudden change in the atmosphere, and looked up to see Erozel and the other Watchers descending to the tower. They were so beautiful, and, though I despised much of what they did, I delighted to see them again. Erozel wore a robe of white. He was lovely, graceful and feminine. Azazel flew beside him. Erozel looked in my direction, and frowned. Azazel landed in front of me.

"Saruel," he said. "How I have missed you!"

"And I have missed you," I said.

Erozel landed with the other Watchers, at a distance, watching me with cold eyes. I held my hands out to him.

"Erozel," I said. He turned away from me. "My brother," I said.

He kept his back to me. "Were you my brother when I held dying Asherah in my arms?"

"I am and always will be your brother."

"Yet you let her die," he said. "You could have saved her."

"You judge Saruel too harshly," Azazel said. "Life is not his to give and to take."

Erozel turned sharply toward me. "Was it not yours to give?"

"If I could return her to you, I would."

"But that is not in your power," he said.

I shook my head.

"Not now," Erozel said, "for you are obviously Fallen, as we are. But it was once in your power, and you denied me, letting her die, despite my terrible grief. Is that what a brother would have done?"

Azazel said, "You have another love, Erozel. Semiramis is beautiful, the very image of Asherah herself. You have a son of your own. Is it not time to make peace with Saruel?"

Erozel turned and looked at me. "Leave me," he said. "Return to wherever you dwell."

"I will do what you ask of me," I said. I turned to the others. "Peace be with you."

"Blessed be," they said.

I nodded at Ariel and lifted into the air.

I hovered for a time, high above the Earth, watching them together. They turned toward the wooden dwelling. Women, some with children, beautiful and fair, ran out to meet them. I saw the woman who must have been Semiramis. She wore a robe of fine white cloth like unto Erozel's, embroidered with gold, cut in the fashion Asherah's had been, to the edge of her chalice. She looked like Asherah had looked in her younger years. Beside her was a young boy, also in a robe of white.

"Semiramis, Queen of Heaven," Erozel said, as they approached him, "Nimrod, my son."

I returned to Eden with a troubled heart, finding Marah waiting for me. She stood up from where she had been sitting in the lush green grass outside our home.

"Where were you, my love? I awoke to find myself alone." She touched the stolen robe I wore. "Where did you get this garment?"

"I smelled smoke, and went to investigate."

"And what did you find?"

I hesitated.

"What is it?"

"There is a city not too many miles from here," I said.

Her face filled with excitement. "A city? Oh, Saruel, you must take me there!"

I shook my head. "My brothers are there," I said. "They are worshiped as gods. I cannot bear the sight of it. It is like the former Temple of All Gods, but far worse. They are building a tower of worship, reaching to the very heavens."

Marah frowned. "You will not take me, then?"

"My darling, it is an abomination."

She looked at me in earnest. "It would be wonderful to see people again. I lived before the flood just outside of the Temple of All Gods, never once taking part in their worship. What would be the difference?"

I put my arms around her. "Are you not happy here?" I said.

"I am the happiest woman the world has ever known. I dwell in a house of love with the one who completes me. Yet it would be nice to be with other people, to spend time with other women, to see children. We have been isolated for a very long time."

"I admit that I was pleased to see my brothers again," I said.

"Then let us go together to this city, my love. I am overjoyed at the thought of it."

I kissed her. "If it will bring you joy, then we will go on the morrow."

The next morning, I carried Marah in my arms, flying at a leisurely pace. She nearly burst with excitement when the city appeared below us in the light of the morning sun. The tower loomed over the city, its shadow stretching out over the shops and homes.

"It is magnificent," she said.

"I must find proper clothing for you," I said.

I placed her on the ground and flew through the open window of a home. I found a green robe and golden sandals. I brought them to her. She dressed on a hill overlooking the city, and we walked the rest of the way, holding hands, taking in the sights all around us. The roads were paved with stones and mortar. The homes were wood and stone, well-made, even by today's standards, for the people were builders, and skilled at their craft. Men and women sold their wares at a market in the center of the city. The aroma of freshly baked bread and sweet cakes pervaded the atmosphere. Musicians played instruments and children danced. Marah looked longingly at the children.

"Do you see them, Saruel?" she said. Tears filled her eyes. "It has been so long since I watched children at play."

We joined in with a small crowd of people and listened to a man playing a lively tune on his flute. Men and women tossed coins at his feet to show their appreciation. A small clothing shop caught Marah's attention. She happily sorted through robes of a variety of colors, marveling at the new styles and material. The shop woman tended to her, and I left her there, returning to where the musician played. I was mesmerized. I had watched cities from afar, but had never shopped at a market or stood in a crowd. I loved every moment of it and found myself glad I had come, delighted by how easy it was to blend in with human beings. People stared at me, entranced as usual by my beauty, but never suspecting I was anything other than a man.

Shouting interrupted my pleasure.

"Thief, thief!" I turned to see a pudgy, balding shopkeeper holding Marah's arm in a tight grip. She winced in pain. I ran to her and pushed the man away. He fell backward, landing hard in the dirt.

"Keep your hands off of her!" I said.

He scrambled to his feet. A crowd of curious onlookers gathered around us. The man shouted to them, pointing an accusatory finger at Marah.

"She is a thief! I sold the robe she is wearing to another woman only yesterday. I made it for her with my own hands, and I would know it anywhere. See for yourselves; she came to the market without coin."

Murmurs spread through the crowd. Several people shook their fists at Marah, yelling words of anger and accusation. The shopkeeper pointed at me.

"He is with her! Strangers to our city, come in to steal our goods!"

The crowd surrounded us, quickly deteriorating into an angry mob. Marah pressed herself against me. I had enjoyed my anonymity, and did not want to reveal myself, for doing so meant never being at the market again.

"She is no thief," I said.

"Then show us your coin," the shopkeeper demanded.

"I have no coin," I said.

The crowd pressed angrily toward us.

"Kill the thieves!" someone cried, and it steadily became a chant. Several people grabbed at us. Fearing for her safety, I picked Marah up and rose into the air above them. The crowd of people drew away in fear. Expressions of anger turned to cries of terror. They fell to their knees, looking up at me.

"He is a god!" They turned on the shopkeeper. "You fool! What have you done? You have killed us this day, laying hands upon one of the gods!"

The crowd cried out in new terror, prostrating low, as my brother Watchers, led by Erozel, flew to us from the top of the tower. They hovered in front of Marah and me. Erozel studied Marah wordlessly. Azazel spoke.

"Saruel, it is good you are here, for we wanted to find you, but do not know where you dwell. Erozel is ready to embrace you as a brother again."

I looked at Erozel. "Is this true?"

Erozel nodded. His eyes remained on Marah. "It is true," he said.

"Then let us celebrate," Azazel said. "Meet us tonight at the Temple of All Gods. We will rejoice together for your return to us."

I began immediately to decline, but stopped myself when I saw the way Erozel was watching me.

"Yes," I said. "I will meet you there."

"Your woman as well," Erozel said. "Bring her with you. You are in love with her, are you not?"

I hesitated.

"Do not be troubled," Marah whispered to me. "I want to meet your brothers." Reluctantly, I agreed to bring her.

We returned to the city that night to find the tower glowing with the lights of thousands of torches, as the people of the city, all wearing white, climbed the steps to the top of the tower, finding seats around hundreds of low tables. Elegant carpets and silk pillows of purple and magenta covered the floor. There were cooking fires, the aroma of good food, and music.

Azazel met us in the air, and, carrying Marah, I followed him, landing near the wooden dwelling where I had seen the women and children two days before. Servants, male and female, clothed in robes of gray, were expecting us. They dropped to their knees in front of me, lowering their heads.

"My lord," one of them said, "May we attend to you? We have robes for the occasion, and the finest wine."

I went with the men, while Marah went with the women. They robed me in scarlet with a blue sash and gave me a golden goblet of wine, then led me to a long, rectangular table and bid me to sit down in a chair near the center. The female servants brought Marah to me. She was lovely, smiling prettily, wearing a robe of blue with a scarlet sash. The servants sat her to my right. I held her hand in mine, and kissed her.

Erozel landed with the other Watchers on a stage, itself high and lifted up on a podium of white marble. He raised his hands and the music stopped. The crowd grew quiet, men and women kneeling in reverence.

"Tonight is a momentous occasion," Erozel said, "for my brother has returned to us: Saruel, god among men. Let us celebrate!"

The people began to shout, clapping their hands, crying my name. "Saruel, god among men!"

Erozel's maiden, Semiramis, joined him on the stage. She wore a robe of costly white material, interwoven with gold, cut to a point just under her chalice. Her likeness to Asherah was stunning. A small, ornate crown of gold sat on her head. She raised her hands and the crowd grew quiet again. She motioned to several nearby servants, who carried a large object wrapped in purple silk, and placed it in front of the stage.

"We offer Lord Saruel a gift," Semiramis said, "for a talented sculptor saw you in the market with your lovely woman."

She waved a hand toward the object; the servants pulled the cloth away, revealing a life-size marble sculpture of my image, perfectly depicted, though the sculptor had added feathered wings to my back to illustrate my ability to fly. My marble likeness held an equally sculpted Marah in its arms. The audience clapped and shouted.

"Saruel, god among men!"

"There is more, "Semiramis said, "for when they came to this city, Saruel and his lovely woman were mistreated and blasphemed against. Let it be known that whoever speaks against one of the gods will be punished."

Two guards appeared, leading a naked man shackled with chains. I saw it was the shopkeeper who had accused Marah of being a thief. The guards led him to the altar of stones. The crowd watched with growing excitement.

"Chain him to the altar of blood," Semiramis said.

The man cried out, begging for mercy, struggling in terror against the guards.

"Not this! Not this!" he cried. "Please, I did not know who he was!"

The guards held the shopkeeper down on the ground, while servants fastened the shackle of Sangruel's altar stone to his ankle. He stood, pulling against the chain, crying and trembling.

"Please! Not this! Please!"

Marah turned to me, worried for the man. "What will they do to him, Saruel? He does not deserve this."

I had a terrible idea. Was Sangruel here at the Temple of All Gods?

Congealed blood covered the altar stone, but I could not imagine such a thing as turning humans over to him while others watched. But I knew by the man's terror that it must be true. A dark figure moved in the shadows just outside the edge of the torchlight. I stood to my feet.

"Hear me," I said. "I am not angry with this man, and I do not desire sacrifice. What this man did, he did in ignorance. Release him, I pray you. I have forgiven him."

Semiramis stared at me, a look of bewilderment on her face.

"Do you wish to show him mercy, my lord?"

"Yes," I said. The man looked desperately up at me. I nodded to him. "Let this night be a time of celebration, not of death."

Semiramis turned to Erozel, who nodded.

"Release him," Semiramis said.

The guards obeyed, removing the man's ankle from the shackle. He fell to his knees, sobbing.

"Thank you, merciful one, Saruel, god among men!"

Sangruel leapt from the darkness with tremendous speed, falling on the man, his black robes enveloping him. He looked frightful in the light of the torches, his teeth buried deep in the man's throat, his sharp nails ripping into the man's flesh. People shouted, horrified, drawing away from him, falling to the ground in their terror.

I placed my arms around Marah, shielding her from the sight of it, as Sangruel drank greedily of the man's blood, nearly tearing his head from his body. Sangruel turned to the crowd, his awful face glistening with blood, and let the man's corpse fall hard to the stone floor.

"Will you deny me the blood sacrifice? Would you rather I visited you and your children in the dead of night?"

"What is he?" Marah said, staring in horror at Sangruel from the safety of my embrace.

"He is a demon," I said, "and he is my brother."

Sangruel turned and looked at me, having heard what I said. Then, rising into the air, he flew, his black form swallowed by the dark night. Semiramis gazed down at the man's broken body.

"Remove his heart and bring it to me," she said.

One of the guards unsheathed a dagger and, bending over the body, removed the man's heart. He brought it to Semiramis, who took it from him, wrapping it in a cloth of white silk. She handed it to her servants who carried it away.

Erozel stood suddenly, raising his hands toward the audience.

"It is time for celebration. Receive the blessing of Erozel; burn with my delightful fever!"

I felt energy leave him in ripples, the atmosphere vibrating around me, as a power flowed through the crowd, who cried out in licentious pleasure;

men and women fell upon each other in sexual desire.

"Let the music play," Semiramis said. "Let us celebrate."

The musicians played and the dancers danced, ignoring the bloody corpse lying on the floor by Sangruel's altar stone. The crowd joined in with the dancers. Wine flowed and the music soared, higher and livelier, gaining in speed. The dancers moved to the music, drawing closer to our table, stripping their clothing off as they came. Marah watched them, and I was horrified to see the same shameless desire on her face.

She turned to me.

"Saruel," she said, "couple with me."

"We must not," I said, "for this is Erozel's unnatural influence."

Lifting her robes, she placed her feet wide out onto the table in front of us, spreading her legs. Her hand found her chalice.

"Now, Saruel. I will be satisfied. Mount me here. Mount me now!"

Semiramis walked toward us, her hips swaying seductively to the rhythm of the music, stripping her robes off as she came. She stood in front of our table, her eyes on Marah's nakedness.

"Let me have you," she said to Marah. Marah blushed, staring with hunger at Semiramis's naked flesh. Semiramis smiled at her. "Will you partake of my nectar? Do not be afraid. My waters are sweet."

"We admire your beauty," I said, "but Marah and I are bound to only each other."

Semiramis's face reddened. "You would refuse me?"

"Please," Marah said, turning toward me, "allow me this, my husband, for my chalice is a raging fire. I will love you just the same."

"No, Marah. Erozel is influencing you, causing these aberrant desires." I stood up. "We must leave this place."

Semiramis turned and looked at Erozel. Erozel frowned at me from the podium and I knew he had heard our conversation. Semiramis spread her legs, lifting one foot onto the table, revealing the full view of her chalice.

To Marah she said, "Taste and see. My nectar is sweet, my chalice is full and running over. Drink of my waters, lie in my arms, take pleasure in the comfort of my breasts."

Marah touched my hand lightly. Her eyes were glossed over, her body burned hot with fever. Was she physically ill?

"Please, my love," she said, "I thirst after her. I must have her."

"We must go now," I said. I lifted Marah into my arms, and rose with her into the night sky. She moaned as I carried her from the Temple of All Gods, away from Erozel's influence and the temptation of Semiramis. As I flew, her hands found my member.

"Mount me, Saruel. Couple with me, here in the air."

"Control yourself, my darling," I said, "for you are not in your normal state of mind."

She squeezed her legs tight around me, pressing her chalice hard against my thigh.

"Give me your body, or return me to that delicious woman," she said, "for I must be satisfied."

"I will not," I said.

"Return me," she said, struggling to break free from my hold. "I must have her!"

I held her fast in my arms.

The treetops of Eden appeared below us in the night. I landed. Carrying Marah into the house, I then placed her carefully upon our bed. She opened her legs wide, rubbing vigorously at her chalice through her robes.

"Come into me!"

"No, my love," I said. "You must control your desires. Erozel did this to you."

She cried out, lifting her robes, spreading her legs, driving the fingers of her hand deep into her chalice with such violence that it frightened me.

"Couple with me!"

I placed my hand on her forehead. She burned with fever. What had Erozel done to her? Rolling over on the bed, she knelt on all fours, her round buttocks raised, open to me, her chalice swollen, dripping with wetness, her face twisted with mad desire.

"Mount me, mount me!"

CHAPTER 21

Leaving Hemael and the abyss, I flew on until Rome appeared below me. The green waters of the Tiber River flowed through the five arches of The Bridge of Angels. Ten statues lined the bridge, five on each side, likenesses of Erozel and his followers, leading from the city of Rome to the Castel Sant'angelo. To my right lay the Holy Sea, the Vatican. A multitude of angels hovered above the city, Messengers and Warriors. A small stream of angels flew back and forth between the city and Heaven. They ignored me, and I flew on.

The dome of the Pantheon appeared. Though built for the worship of angels, the Pantheon was a beautiful work of architectural artistry, unrivaled in its time. Its design is copied even to this day; its white dome and pillars are the inspiration of palaces and capitol buildings. I found a deserted alley and landed, before walking the rest of the way to the Pantheon.

Lighted candles decorated the middle of the stairs, forming a pathway leading to the large entrance. White flowers lined the immense frame of the open doors and the outline of a lover's arch in lavish preparation for a wedding. Walking past the pillars, I then stepped inside, finding very few people—a scatter of tourists and priests. I passed by a desk where two security guards sat with bored expressions, not so much as glancing up at me. I made my way to the rotunda, standing under the enormous, vaulted dome, its large oculus open to the sky outside. In that spot, for many centuries, men had worshiped at the altar of Fallen angels. I searched the marble floor of the rotunda, finding nothing out of the ordinary. Someone stepped quietly behind me. I turned to see a gray-haired priest in a white tunic.

"Have you lost something, my son?" he said in Italian.

I answered, also in Italian: "No, Father. I am admiring the beauty of this place."

"It is one of the finest examples of architecture," he said. He looked at me. "You are not Italian, I think, though you speak without the slightest accent. Are you American?"

"I live in America."

"I see," said the priest, "and what brings you to Rome?"

"I am something of a historian," I said. "Rome is full of history, a subject I find very important. Take the Pantheon, where we stand. It has not always been a church."

"That is true. For it was, as its very name means, a temple unto all gods.

The biblical God was not the first to be worshiped in this place."

"May He be the last," I said.

"Are you a believer, then?"

I looked up at the oculus high above us, a large hole in the middle of the dome, open to the outside, where, at times, my brothers would enter this place when worshiped by their followers.

"I believe," I said, "and tremble."

"Come with me," he said, "allow me to show you the altar."

I nodded, following him to the high altar and the apse, where an icon of the Madonna was enshrined. The priest did not stop at the altar.

"Were you not going to show me the altar?" I asked.

"Please, follow me," the priest said. "It is not this altar I wish to show you."

I accompanied him along the wall of the rotunda passing the chapels and niches, all holding priceless works of art, until we reached the tomb of the great artist Raphael. The statue of Madonna of the Rock filled the niche above Raphael's sarcophagus.

"Can you read the inscription?" the priest said, running a finger along the lid. The inscription was in Latin, carved into the stone of the sarcophagus.

"Bones and ashes," I said.

"Yes," the priest said. "Here lie the remains of Raphael, the sculptor of angels." He looked up at me with a curious expression and pointed to the statue in the niche behind the sarcophagus: a woman standing, presumably the Madonna, one foot upon a rock, holding an infant in her arms. "Do you know that statue?"

I nodded. "It is Madonna of the Rock," I said.

"Do you not see it?"

I turned to the priest, puzzled. "I have seen it many times before," I said. "It is Madonna of the Rock, the Mother of the Christ, with the Holy Child."

The priest shook his head. "Is it? Look at the woman's face. Is it the Madonna, is it Mary?"

I turned again to the statue, and found myself looking up into the perfectly sculpted face of Semiramis, the lover of Erozel. Was it Semiramis? It could just as easily have been Asherah, and the child Eros.

The priest turned to the few people with us in the rotunda.

"Please," he said, raising his voice. "The rotunda must close now in preparation of a wedding."

He left me momentarily, ushering everyone through the doors, closing them out, leaving us alone. Returning to me, he pointed to the Madonna of the Rock.

"She is the Queen of Heaven," the priest said, "the goddess of fertility, holding the child, Nimrod. I see that you recognize her face." He looked around us, ensuring that we were alone, and then fell to his knees in front of me, his head bowed in reverence. "My suspicions are true. You are one of the Thirteen."

I was stunned. "What are you doing?" I said. "Are you not a priest of the Most High God?"

"I serve the Thirteen," he said. "You seek the altar of all gods. Look and see, the Queen of Heaven is the way."

"Stand to your feet," I said. "Do not worship me."

He obeyed, looking perplexed.

I examined the statue. "Do not speak to me in riddles. You know what I seek."

The priest nodded with a bow, then pulled a small lever cleverly hidden in the artwork. Three steps appeared, dropping down in front of Raphael's sarcophagus. He climbed the steps to the statue. Taking hold of the statue with both hands, he pushed. The wall of the niche moved easily in a circular motion, stone grating against stone; opening, revealing a stairway of marble leading downward into darkness.

"What you seek is down there, my lord."

"Show me," I said.

He pulled a small flashlight from his vestments and lit the way. I climbed the steps up to the niche and followed him down the stairs into a large stone room. He pulled a lever and the statue above us returned to its former place. The priest led me down a corridor lined with sculpted statues of winged angels.

"We are now directly under the middle of the rotunda, my lord. Look and see."

He pointed to an altar of stones arranged in the same manner as they first were at the tower of Babel, thousands of years ago. Sangruel's stone was several feet away from the others, in a place by itself.

"One stone is missing," I said.

The priest shone his light on the altar. He shook, visibly frightened. "My lord," he said. "I did not know. I do not know how."

"Has anyone else been down here?"

"I allowed no one in here. I am not the only one who knows about this place, but the others would never do such a thing. I am sure of it."

"What of the others like me?" I said.

"My lord," he said, "you are the first of the Thirteen I have seen with my own eyes."

"How, then, did you know what I am?"

He pointed at the wall several yards behind the altar. There, sculpted by a master hand—Raphael himself, judging by the style—were the perfect likenesses of the thirteen Watchers, though feathered wings were added to the sculptures to show our ability to fly. Raphael depicted Erozel carrying a woman in his arms, his feminine face etched into a mask of perpetual sorrow. This time I was sure who the woman was; Asherah, in her youth, instead of the old woman she had been at the time of her death. Erozel held what appeared to be a human heart in his hand. Ariel's image, wearing the uniform of a Roman soldier, his sword drawn, stood next to Erozel, the threat of violence upon his marble face. My own image stood beside Ariel's, holding a woman in the same manner that Erozel carried Asherah. Marah's face, perfectly depicted, looked lovingly into mine. My left arm held her to me, while my right hand pointed heavenward. My marble face looked down at her in eternal rapture. It was the image sculpted at the Tower of Babel on that terrible night thousands of years ago.

"It is you," the priest said, "in every detail. I am honored to be in your presence."

I looked upon the perfect images of each of my brothers. Those who had taken part in Erozel's fall knelt in front of his image. Azazel's image knelt with them, his stone face fashioned in a look of perpetual wonder, a small child in his arms. Separate from the others stood the hideous likeness of Sangruel, sculpted from black marble, the twin to the one standing in his lair in the catacombs under San Francisco.

"Is there another entrance to this place?"

"No, my lord, only the one by which we came."

No man could have taken the stone from that place, at least not without detection. An angel then, flying quickly, leaving by air, perhaps even through the oculus. My eyes fell upon Erozel's statue.

"Let us leave this place," I said.

We returned to the top, entering the rotunda. I instructed the priest to tell no one about my visit. He bowed low in worship. I turned away from him and departed, flying upward through the oculus.

CHAPTER 22

All night long, Marah tossed and turned, crying out, tormented with lust unabated. Her chalice bled, worn raw by the violence of her own fingers. I feared for her. Nothing I said or did gave her relief. I could not release her from Erozel's spell.

The sun rose upon the garden. Still she moaned with desire, calling out to me. Finally, I gave in, mounting her. She pressed herself hard against my member, devouring rather than loving me. Yet nothing I did satisfied her. Her lust only grew. The more I gave her of myself, the more she wanted. In desperation, I left her, and returned to the Temple of All Gods, landing near the altar of stones. I called out in a loud voice.

"Erozel!"

Semiramis, wrapped in a scarlet robe, walked toward me from the dwelling of the women. "My lord is not here," she said.

"Marah," I said, "Marah is not in her right mind."

Semiramis smiled wickedly. "It is the fever she burns with. If she cannot satisfy her desires, she will surely die. The fire must be quenched, or it will consume her."

"What must I do?"

"She must have whoever or whatever she lusts for. Nothing can take the place of it. She will not be satisfied until she has tasted the fruit of her desire."

"Please help her," I said.

"She desires me. I saw it in her face last night. Bring me to her. I will give myself over to her lust. Only then will she be satisfied."

"What you ask of me is an abomination," I said.

She turned as if to walk away.

"Wait," I said. She stopped. "If you can help her, please return with me."

She smiled impishly. "I will go with you," she said, "but I must have something in return."

"What do you want?"

She touched my lips with her finger, then, leaning forward, kissed me. "I want both of you," she said. "You must do whatever I ask."

Thinking only of Marah's agony, I nodded.

I carried Semiramis in my arms, hating the very feel of her. She wrapped herself against my body, laughing as I flew to the Garden of Eden.

I led her to Marah.

Marah sat straight up when she saw her. Semiramis disrobed and climbed into bed with her. She placed her hand against Marah's chalice, caressing it softly. Marah groaned.

"My darling," she said, "you are bleeding."

Semiramis kissed her deeply on the mouth. Marah returned the kiss. I turned my face from the sight of them.

"Look at us, Saruel," Semiramis said, "or I shall leave her to the fever's mercy."

I obeyed, reluctantly. Semiramis placed Marah's swollen nipples in her mouth, sucking them gently. Marah cried out. Semiramis laughed, her eyes watching me, her kisses moving downward to Marah's round belly, her tongue caressing Marah's navel. Marah arched her hips toward Semiramis.

"Watch us, son of Heaven. Behold our wondrous abomination." Moving downward, she kissed Marah's bleeding chalice, filling her mouth with it. I turned away. Tears filled my eyes. Semiramis pulled away from Marah. "Look upon us!" she demanded.

I turned toward them again. Semiramis went down on all fours, holding Marah's legs up and wide apart, devouring her chalice. She looked at me. Blood covered her lips.

"Mount me from behind, son of Heaven," she said.

I shook my head.

"Please," I said. "I have been with no one but Marah."

"Do as I say."

I knelt behind Semiramis.

"Partake of her, my love," Marah said. "I want to watch."

I mounted Semiramis, my member pushing into her chalice. I wept. Thrusting my hips in anger, I drove my member into her, deep and hard, wanting to hurt her.

She cried out.

"Yes, son of Heaven, punish me, inflict pain upon me!"

She bent forward again, her lips returning to Marah's chalice. I closed my eyes, hiding from the sight of it. Marah cried out, her body convulsing with pleasure.

"Enough!" she said. "I must taste the sweetness of your nectar! I thirst for you!"

Semiramis laughed, lying on her back, spreading her legs. "I am yours, sweet woman."

Marah lay on top of her, thrusting her hips against her, chalice to chalice, as a man to a woman. She kissed Semiramis's breasts, her lips moving lower, finding her belly, her navel, finally burying her face between Semiramis's legs, devouring the forbidden fruit with her hungry mouth. Semiramis looked up at me, leering, mocking me.

"Take her from behind, Saruel," she said. Reluctantly, I stepped behind

Marah, lifting her hips, pulling her up to her knees. "No, Saruel," Semiramis said, "Not in her chalice. Your lack of fervor displeases me. Enter her forbidden part."

"I will not," I said, "it is an abomination."

"You will," Semiramis said, pulling away from Marah. Marah cried out, reaching for her. "If I leave her now, the weight of her desire will crush her. Do as I say, defile her for my pleasure."

I stepped toward Marah, pressing my member gently against her forbidden part. She cried out. I stopped.

"Do it," Semiramis said.

Carefully, I pressed forward. Marah arched her hips toward me.

"Yes! I want you inside of me!" she cried.

I entered her. She moved back and forth against my member, moaning, her face buried between the legs of the so-called Queen of Heaven. My tears fell like rain on her white skin. Finally, Marah shuddered and cried out. Her body shook with a wave of pleasure and satisfaction. I stepped back, away from her, covering my nakedness with my robe. She fell forward, her body slack against Semiramis, kissing her softly. Semiramis caressed her tenderly, all the while smiling mockingly up at me. Marah closed her eyes and fell fast asleep, her head resting between Semiramis's breasts.

Leaving them alone together in the house, I flew upward, high into the sky, crying out with a loud voice. Tears streamed down my face. I shook my fist toward the Temple of All Gods. Damn you, Erozel. Damn you to Hell.

I went home only to carry Semiramis to the Temple. Afterwards, I did not return to Eden, but hovered listlessly, moved by the currents of wind wherever they would take me. I hated Erozel with every bit of my being, and despised Semiramis. I wept bitterly. I am, and always will be, haunted by the degradation Semiramis forced upon me. I do not blame Marah. She was a victim of Erozel. I drifted for several weeks, night and day, stricken with sorrow and grief. After a time, my grief turned to anger.

I found the Temple of All Gods. I loathed it; a colossal man-made phallus. Why had I taken Marah to such a place? It is my greatest regret. Workers stood on high scaffolding, working with stone and mortar. I landed hard without slowing, my feet hitting stone with meteoric force, shaking the tower to its foundation. Laborers fell to their deaths as a large part of scaffolding crumpled.

"Erozel, come to me!" I cried.

I waited, searching the skies for him. They remained empty. I walked to where several laborers bowed low to the ground, trembling with terror.

"Who will tell me where the gods dwell?" They did not answer. I grabbed one of them, an older man, and lifted him to his feet. "Where do the gods dwell?"

He bowed his head, turning his eyes away from me. His voice shook.

"You seek the god of gods?"

"I seek Erozel the defiler of innocence and all things pure. Where does he dwell?"

"My lord, he dwells in the holy mountain of the gods, a place I have never seen, for no man may approach it."

"Have you seen them fly from here?"

"I have, my lord." He pointed to the west.

Placing him on the ground, I then flew westward, scanning the Earth below me. Soon, a high mountain range appeared, its peaks covered by white clouds. Towers of white crystal, formed with precision and artistry, lined the sides of the mountain. Upon each tower sat a throne, fashioned like the thrones of Heaven, one throne formed from bluish crystal, sitting on a tower lifted above the others. Statues of marble, the likenesses of the Watchers, lined stairs of gold, leading upward to a city of crystal from a lush valley below. The Watchers had tried to create their own Heaven on Earth. I came to a stop, floating in the air above it.

"Erozel!" I called.

Several figures, all in white, appeared over the crest of the mountain, Erozel and his followers. I flew to them. Erozel turned away when he saw me. I landed on the ground before them.

"You have wronged me, Erozel," I said, "defiling the one I love."

He turned slowly, facing me. "Defiled?" he said. "You do not know defilement. The one I love decayed in my arms. I held her while worms consumed her. That is true defilement."

"You caused Marah to commit abominations."

"Is that what I did? Was she not already defiled, as the consort of a heavenly angel? That is an abomination in itself. It was not I who defiled her, then, but you."

"She was pure and innocent until you influenced her, causing her to burn with unnatural desire. I hate you for this."

"I did not place desire within her. I only brought to the surface what was already there. You speak of her as if she were a holy angel. Need I remind you that she is Fallen, born and shaped in iniquity? Sin is in her blood, her very nature is an abomination."

"She was pure," I said. "The harlot you call the Queen of Heaven defiled her in my very chambers."

Erozel opened his hands in a gesture of peace.

"Feel free," he said, "take Semiramis and defile her, and then you will have your vengeance. They are both just women, after all. Their lives are vapor. You will replace Marah with another. That is the way of things. There will be a new Queen of Heaven, but we are eternal. We remain."

I stepped toward Erozel. My hands clinched into fists.

"Will you strike me, brother?"

I controlled myself and stepped away from him. I bowed my head, my grief returning to me.

"You have placed a stain upon my love," I said, "but I will not strike you. For you are my brother, from the beginning." I met his eyes. "Why would you do such a thing?"

"My brother would not have allowed Asherah to die."

"How could I have helped her? She was flesh, and went the way of all flesh."

"Is not defilement also the way of all flesh? Even the innocent discover desire, hungering for more, until they perform the acts you loathe and which I delight in. Your woman tasted the forbidden fruit. What once pleased her no longer satisfies. Her lust will only grow with time. That is the nature of flesh."

"Love conquers the flesh," I said. "Love conquers all."

Erozel's face contorted with anger.

"It does not conquer death. It cannot stay the hand of Hemael. You were second only to the I Am. If you had commanded it, Asherah would have lived forever."

"If I could have helped her," I said, "I would have."

Erozel turned from me. "Leave this place. Never return."

I returned to the Garden of Eden, seeing it for the first time as a place of great sorrow. There, innocence was lost to carnal knowledge, first with Eve, then Adam, Sangruel, and now Marah. I understood the grief the Great I Am felt at Adam and Eve's fall. My love, my companion, had tasted of the forbidden fruit.

I lowered to the ground. I had not seen Marah since she had been with Semiramis, weeks before. I opened the door of our house, finding it empty. I called, "Marah, where are you?"

There came a rustling of leaves from the wooded area to my right. Marah stepped from dense trees onto the bare path. Flowers garnished her autumn hair. When she saw me, she lowered her head in shame.

Walking to her, I took her hands in mine. She broke down, sobbing.

"My love," she said.

I wrapped her in my arms and held her close to me, bathing her in my love. She wept freely, her face against my chest. I carried her into our house.

CHAPTER 23

The sun set, a cascade of red and orange on the San Francisco horizon. Somewhere out there, my girl needed me. It would not be long before the first of Sangruel's servants headed into the night to prey on unsuspecting humans. That is the order of things, whether natural or unnatural, and not my concern. What concerned me was my girl. They had touched her, frightened her, and, had I not intervened, they would have killed her. I paid a terrible price for her. Now they would pay their part.

When darkness fell, I flew to the warehouse above the catacombs, where Sangruel dwelt with his servants. The parking lot was empty, and there was no sign of life. I waited. Finally, the back door opened and the servants of Sangruel made their appearance. One by one, they emerged, hunger fresh on too pale faces, lusting for blood. Tonight they were the hunted, and I the hunter.

More than a dozen passed beneath me before I saw the ones I wanted. The woman appeared first. The large man joined her, as I had hoped he would. They left the warehouse, running toward the downtown area, blending in with shadows. I followed from high above.

They darted into an alleyway. I looked to see a man in a bathrobe walking barefoot in the alleyway behind an apartment building, carrying trash bags to a dumpster, grumbling to himself. Leaving the shadows, Sangruel's servants moved toward the man. The woman grabbed him by his throat. He dropped the trash bags, opening his mouth to scream. No sound came out. She leaned in, her mouth close to his throat, her teeth bared.

I dropped from the sky to a spot behind them, catching the male servant of Sangruel by the back of his neck. He hissed and growled, struggling hard against me. The woman turned in surprise, releasing the human. She ran toward me. I grabbed her by the arm and flew, carrying them into the night sky. I heard the human screaming in the alley below us.

The man struggled against my grip, clawing at my hand, surprising me with his strength. For a moment, he nearly succeeded in breaking free of my hold. He glared at me with murderous eyes, gnashing his teeth, trying desperately to bite me. The woman looked up at me, shouting over the wind.

"Release us, for already our master feels our distress. He will come."

"I have little doubt that he will," I said, "but what good is that to you if you have already met the sun?"

I flew on, heading toward the western horizon, catching up to the sun. The woman kicked upward suddenly. She pushed her feet hard against me, pulling her arm from my grip, falling through the dark clouds below, before I could catch her. I had underestimated her strength. I flew after her. She appeared suddenly, flying upward from the darkness, hitting me with great force. I had not considered that she might possess the gift of flight, a rare ability among Sangruel's servants. She was nowhere near as powerful as I am, but, seeing his chance, the male struggled with renewed energy. It was all I could do to keep a grip on him while remaining in the air. The woman grabbed me by my legs with both of her arms and turned, flying in a spiral, taking me down with her toward the ocean below. With all my might, I righted myself, breaking free from the spiral, before shooting upward into the sky. The woman held onto me, the man struggled, nearly slipping from my grip.

The higher I went, the brighter the western horizon grew. There was little oxygen at that height and I wondered if their kind needed air. Apparently, they did not. At last, the first light of the sun appeared. They screamed in agony, hiding their eyes. The man's face blistered. I smelled burning flesh. I stopped in mid-air, hovering between light and darkness. The woman released her grip in an effort to fall back into the darkness, but I caught her, holding her fast. She fought against me but the light of the sun had diminished her strength.

"Release us," the man said, "for the master comes."

I waited, listening, hearing only the wind and the ocean below.

"What are you?" the woman said. "You are not like us."

I looked down at her. She looked no older than her early twenties and, despite her deathly pallor, was very beautiful.

"You speak true," I said. "We are nothing alike, for you feast on the blood of children, having yourself once been a child. You prey on the living, having once been alive."

"Did you not deliver twin girls to our master just last night?" the man growled. "Was that not murder on your part?"

"That was your master's doing," I said, "and yours as well, for choosing the wrong victim."

"Our master arrives," the woman said, looking toward the eastern horizon.

I waited, holding them between night and day. I heard a whistling sound and felt a troubling of the atmosphere. I looked into the darkness below me. Sangruel hovered there beneath the canopy of night, his eyes blazing with fury, a creature of nightmares, held back only by the light of the sun.

"My brother!" I called.

He snarled up at me. "You call me brother, while threatening to destroy my children?"

"I have not harmed them," I said.

The woman called to Sangruel, "My master!"

"They truly love you, Sangruel; you who cursed them to eternal darkness."

I lifted upward, allowing sunlight to touch the man's hand. He cried out in agony, his hand blistering and charring. Black smoke filled the air around him. Sangruel shot upward to the very edge of darkness, reaching for his servants, his eyes wide with fear.

"Please," he said, "release them."

"A price must be paid," I said, "for they touched the girl that I love."

I rose slowly toward the rays of the sun. The man screamed again, the sunlight burning his face. Sangruel howled. Blood trickled from the corners of his eyes as he wept. I wondered how much of that blood came from the murdered twin girls.

"Please," he cried, "what do you require?"

"Someone took her from me, Sangruel. Was her presence in your pit last night a mere coincidence? She was abducted this morning. Her driver, my friend, murdered. I cannot help but imagine that you had something to do with her disappearance."

"Will you lay this at my feet—I, the father of nightwalkers? I dwell in darkness. The morning is my eternal enemy."

"Perhaps," I said. "Yet the other Watchers know about last night. Why did you tell them? You are as apart from them as I am."

"Azazel came to me and enquired about the girl. I told him about her. Why would I not?" He looked at his servants. "I did not tell him everything, Saruel. I kept your secret."

"What secret do you speak of?" I said.

Sangruel looked intently at me. "I know who she is, Saruel. I know the secret you keep." His gaze fell longingly on his servants. "I know another secret as well, one that Erozel kept from you. Let my children go, and I will tell you."

"Tell me now," I said, pulling the male closer to the sunlight. Sangruel cried out, reaching up to me.

"No," he said. "I will tell you. Only give me your word that you will free my children."

"You have my word," I said, "if what you tell me is worthwhile."

Sangruel's eyes darted between his servants and me. "I would not have fed upon your girl last night, even in my great thirst, for her blood is more than human blood. Its aroma gave me pause. I could not quite place its origin at the time, but I can now. She is more to you than just a girl you watch over. Of this I am sure."

I looked down at Sangruel, struggling to keep my expression neutral and my voice calm. "What are you saying?"

"She smelled to me like Hemael had on the day of his judgment. The fruit of his sin flows in her blood, the fruit of the Tree of Life."

I nearly dropped the two servants of Sangruel.

"Then it is true," Sangruel said, watching me. "It is of no great matter. Let my children go, and I will tell no one. For what is it to me?"

I stared at the demon Sangruel in the darkness below me. I had kept my secret for thousands of years, carefully hiding it from Watchers and men alike. I felt numb. Sangruel's eyes scanned back and forth between his servants and me. He held his arms out, pleading.

"I know what it is to love," he said.

"My brother," I said, but I stopped, at a loss for words. Why would Azazel inquire about my girl? The only answer was that my tightly wound deceit had unraveled. I hovered there between the night and the day, knowing firsthand the true meaning of Hell. The sun continued in its westward trek over the horizon. Darkness crept up to me. Sangruel rose with the darkness. He spoke softly, his harsh voice cutting into my thoughts.

"Please, Saruel, release my children."

"Do not come further," I said, lifting higher to the edge of sunlight.

"Saruel," he said, "perhaps there is another way."

"What other way? You spoke to Azazel about her. You put her life in danger. Why should I spare the ones you love?"

"There is more," he said. "Erozel has a secret as well, one that may change everything. Release my children and I will tell you."

CHAPTER 24

As the years went by, Erozel's passions grew, from hedonistic lust and lascivious orgies, to the killing of innocents. In the Temple of All Gods, he required a virgin's heart as a sacrifice; a yearly celebration, the Festival of Hearts. Maidens by the hundreds came, hoping to receive the high honor, to be the sacrifice presented to Erozel. The chosen maiden, dressed all in crimson, lay on an altar of stones before a throng of worshipers while priests of Erozel removed her beating heart, laying it before the graven images of Erozel and the Queen of Heaven. Though no longer a public practice, remnants of the festival survive even to this day. Every February, lovers offer a gift of hearts to the ones they love, a token of affection, but the remnants of a darker past.

Erozel's fever returned to Marah; a reoccurring disease, an uncontrollable, compelling lust that grew worse with each passing year. Unable to satisfy her in these times, keeping her identity unknown, I brought her to the temples where sexual perversion was a form of worship. There she took her fill of women, refusing the pleasure of men for my sake. The fever came upon her more frequently, increasing from once a year, to every month. Her lusts grew as well. One woman no longer satisfied her. She required several at a time, women twisting their naked bodies together, a bed of devouring serpents. How I wept at these times, hating Erozel for what he had done to her.

The day came when Marah had to partake again of the Fruit of Life. She had aged well, her face remained smooth, her beauty vibrant, though her hair had long before turned silver. Her strength was diminished. Illnesses, unknown to her in her younger years, found her all too often. I feared for her. One day, I brought the fruit from its hiding place. She was in bed when I came to her. She looked at the golden fruit in my hand.

"It is as full of life as it was long ago," she said.

"It is," I said.

"I am glad that I partook of it. I have loved my life with you." She studied my face, frowning. "What about you, my love? I know you still desire Heaven. I know you long to see the face of the Almighty. I am tormented with the thought that you gave away so much to be with me."

I looked at her, recalling her acts of depravation in the temples, the pain I had felt as she coupled with others. I touched her silver hair and kissed her lightly on her forehead.

"I would do it all over again," I said. "Heaven does not compare to you." I held the Fruit of Life out to her. "If you wish to leave this world, I will understand. I will never force this upon you."

She reached out, taking the fruit.

"You are my world," she said, raising the golden fruit to her lips. "You are my life."

She bit into the fruit. The room of our small home filled with golden shafts of light, surrounding her as it had in the cave during the flood. Her spirit left her, mingling with the light of the fruit before returning to her. I waited with apprehension. The light shone brightly around her body, hiding it from me. When the brightness of the light abated, I saw only bedclothes where her body had been.

"Marah!"

I reached quickly into the remaining light, feeling only the bedclothes. My heart pounded in my chest. Groping in the midst of the light, my hand touched soft skin, a tiny foot. A baby cried.

Babylon, Nebuchadnezzar, Artaxerxes, emperors and empires rose and fell. The Medes and Persians, Egypt, Greece, Rome. I was there, Marah beside me, a secret hidden from the other Watchers. We moved often from country to country, blending in as best as we could, living as a normal couple. From time to time, I sought out Ariel alone, if only to stop him from searching for me. I stayed away from the other Watchers.

I witnessed the influence of my brothers on every major civilization. They were the lords of Babylon, the Egyptian Rah, the Grecian and Roman gods, demons all. They coupled with human women, who bore them children, men and women of renown. Men built pyramids and towers, temples of worship, in honor of the Watchers.

Only one human worshiped me. I worshiped her in return.

Every thousand years or so, Marah required more of the Fruit of Life. Each time I offered to let her go, never once denying her the right to die. Each time, she declared her love for me. The fruit's affect on her was unpredictable. When she first reverted to an infant, I enlisted a childless couple to raise her. I did this not wanting to raise her myself. How awkward it would be for her to see me as her father, only to suddenly remember me as her lover. Twice, she reverted into the young maiden she had been, her memories of me complete and intact.

To my disappointment, the fruit did nothing to cure her of Erozel's fever. It always returned to her, her passions fermented with the passing of time. She bedded women by the thousands, while still vowing eternal devotion to me. I was in agony, but also in sweet love. For when the fever passed, my Marah returned to me.

More than two-thousand years ago, while living in Israel, I gave her of the Fruit of Life and she became a small girl. I was relieved in a way that Marah was now but a child, innocent and pure, giving me a time of rest from the pain of her fornication. I found good parents for her, a barren

Israelite couple of considerable means. They adored Marah, and called her Miriam, a name befitting the Hebrews. I watched over her, remaining out of sight.

Caesar Augustus was Emperor of Rome at the time, and by decree, ordered that all people in Israel return to their places of birth to register with the Census. Thankfully, Marah's adoptive parents were born and raised in the city where they lived and would not have to travel.

CHAPTER 25

It is with a new pen and freshly washed clothes that I write the rest of this story. I tell you now of things holy, far above the sad tale of my eternal fall, far above the judgments of God on sinful angels.

For unto us a child was born.

The Watchers dwelt in Rome, near the Pantheon, the Temple of All Gods built for them by the Roman Consular, Marcus Agrippa. Ariel especially loved Rome, a people second only to him in their thirst for war, violence and bloodshed. Under his influence, Rome attacked and conquered nearly the entire known world. Gladiators baptized Rome in the blood of criminals, war captives and martyrs, killing in Ariel's honor, under his marble likeness, Mars, god of war.

Marah, being but a small girl, did not yet know me, and I took the opportunity of our time apart to seek out Ariel. He told me of the virgin visited by Gabriel, the Chief Messenger of Heaven.

"She is with child," Ariel told me, "she who has never known a man."

"Is Gabriel, then, the child's father? Is he Fallen?"

"No," Ariel said, "of that we are certain. The Watchers and Fallen alike have watched her very closely, and with much interest. She did not couple with Gabriel, and he remains in robes of light."

"Then who is father to the child?"

Ariel frowned. "His mother is of the lineage of both the kings and priests of Israel. He may be the one foretold." He looked uneasily at me. "The Prince of Peace."

Leaving Ariel, I flew to Nazareth, the city where the maiden lived with her husband, a man who had not been with her at the child's conception. I landed in one of the dusty alleyways near the house where Ariel had told me she lived, hoping to see her. After several hours of waiting, she finally appeared with her husband, a man many years her senior. I knew her the moment I saw her. She was lovely, one of the most beautiful maidens I had ever seen. If Marah did not already command my heart, I would have fallen in love. She was no older than sixteen years, at the time an appropriate age for marriage and childbearing. Her complexion was olive, her eyes a gentle brown. She wore a modest blue robe, her head covered by a shawl. She was great with child, near the time of her delivery.

Her husband helped her carefully onto the back of a donkey, after first loading it with provisions and bedding—a common sight in Israel because of the census. I felt for her, having to travel in her condition. I approached her husband.

"Peace to you," I said.

"Peace to you," he answered.

I nodded at the maiden. "Do you leave for the census?" I said.

"We do," he said, looking a bit worried, "to my hometown of Bethlehem of Judea."

"I see. I take it you will not pass through Samaria, but will go by way of the Jordan River?" The Samaritans were not friendly to the people of Israel.

"That is so," he said. "It is a week's journey, made longer by the Sabbath, and, as you can plainly see, my wife, Miriam, is with child."

"May the Lord watch over you," I said.

"Thank you," he said, taking the donkey by its leather lead. "Peace be with you."

I returned to Marah. She lived in a wealthy part of the city known as the Towers. Sprawling mansions, all with towers of stone, lined cobbled streets. I wanted her to have the best, choosing wealthy people to raise her. She was a beautiful girl, appearing no older than two years old. I longed for the day that her memories would return to her. I longed for my lover, but delighted in her childhood as well, watching her play and laugh, wishing that I could hold her.

After a week's time, I flew to Bethlehem at night. Angels were present everywhere; holy and Fallen alike, populating the skies, hidden from mortal sight. The night was silent, save for the soft cries of a woman in the midst of childbearing. Nature seemed to hold its breath in anticipation of the event of his birth. I saw the Lord of the Fallen on the eastern horizon, his followers with him. He looked troubled. The Watchers hovered near them: Erozel and the others, including Ariel. All eyes looked down, waiting expectantly, on a crudely made stable formed from rough-hewn wood and stone. Was this humble stable the birthplace of the Prince of Peace, the prophesied King of Israel? No nobles attended his birth. There was no pomp and ceremony. He was not born surrounded by marbled halls of power.

Finally, the cries of the woman stopped, replaced moments later by the crying of a baby. Far away, I heard Heaven rejoicing. Here on Earth, angels sang.

What child is this?

I heard the heralds of God shouting, "Peace on Earth, good will to men. For unto you is born this night, in the city of David, a savior, the anointed one."

His mother named him Yeshua.

For several years, my attention shifted between watching Marah, who had grown into a blossoming teen, and watching Yeshua. Yeshua neared his twelfth year, the time of life when a Hebrew boy officially reached the age of accountability. In every way a boy, he played with the other children, developed crushes on the neighborhood girls, played harmless pranks with his friends. His mother's husband was a builder by trade and Yeshua apprenticed with him, building homes and furniture, working with wood and stone. He learned the trade of a builder, his mind wandering as any other boy's when made to work instead of play. As for him being the anointed one, I would never have guessed it, had I not been there at his birth. He was average, unassuming. People passed him on the street without so much as a second glance.

Marah was everything but ordinary. She appeared to be about thirteen years old. Where Yeshua was a diligent, obedient son, Marah was a rebellious daughter. Where Yeshua was pure, Marah was impure. She despised the heavy, modest garments of the women of Israel, and showed more of her flesh than the customs dictated. I was dismayed and greatly vexed by this, for never before had she been that way at such a young age. She skirted the strict boundaries of modesty and it was not long before she caught the eyes of men. She was too young, even for ancient standards, but one man in particular showed her untoward interest. He was a squat, portly man in his late forties. I hated him at once.

She was alone at market when he approached her, offering a gift of sweet bread from a nearby merchant.

"My little one," he said, "sweets for the sweet."

She smiled flirtatiously at him, taking the sweet bread. "You are a kind man," she said. "How shall I repay you?"

The man glanced furtively around the market. "Are you here alone?"

"I am alone," she said.

"Come to my home, then, for I have something more to give you."

Marah held her hand out to him and smiled. "I will go with you."

The man's face reddened with excitement. He licked his lips and took her by the hand, leading her away from the market to a run-down home in a squalid part of town.

"It is not the Towers—where, I can see by your finery, you must live—but it is private."

He led her inside, shutting the door behind them. I lowered to the ground near the house, listening in.

"What is it you have to give me?" Her child's voice dripped with seduction.

"I have much to give you, little one. Sit here with me, upon my bed."

"No, I will not, for your bedding is soiled and unclean."

The man's voice grew hard, demanding, its former friendliness gone. "Is my bed not good enough for you? You are a pampered thing. Sit down next to me."

"I will not," Marah said. "I wish to leave."

"You came here of your own will. Look what I have to give you. Is this not what you wanted? Will you now refuse me? Lie down on the bed, lift your robes, for I will have my way with you."

I rapped sharply upon the door. The house went silent.

"I know you are in there," I said. I waited. Finally, the man opened the door a crack, peaking out, scowling. Sweat ran down his plump, reddened face.

"What do you want?" he said.

I pushed my way inside, knocking him down. He had girded his robe up into his belt and his member showed, erect, under his rotund belly. Marah stood in the middle of the room. She looked at me and gasped.

"You are in my dreams!" she said.

The man scrambled to his feet in surprise and anger, forgetting his nakedness.

"Get out! Leave my home," he shouted.

I turned a fierce glare upon him. "What are you doing here alone with my girl?" I said. I looked down at his exposed member. His eyes grew large. His fat jowl quivered.

"I didn't…" he said. He made as if to pull his robe down over his nakedness. I moved quickly, taking him by the pearls, holding them in a firm grip. He let out a sharp squeal.

"You are a swine," I said, "for she is little more than a child."

His breathing came in short rasps. He struggled to speak through his pain.

"She…wanted…please…"

I squeezed. His body shuddered. His legs lost their strength. I let him go and he fell to his knees in front of me.

I turned to Marah. "Will you come with me?" I said.

She turned her eyes from the man kneeling on the floor and studied my face. "I know you," she said. "You are in my dreams."

"Come," I said, "I shall return you to your home."

"Who are you? I feel I know you, but I could not possibly."

"Miriam," I said, "allow me to take you home."

She stood, looking confused, a young girl in every way but her eyes. They held ancient wisdom. She shook her head.

"Not Miriam," she said, "not Miriam at all. My name is…" She bit her lip, losing whatever revelation had come to her.

I placed my hands on her shoulders. "Do you remember?" I said.

She met my gaze and her confusion gave way to astonishment. "You are not a son of Adam," she said.

"You speak true. Do you remember anything else?"

"My name is not Miriam, but," she paused, grasping at fleeting memories, "I am Marah."

"Yes," I said, "you are my Marah."

Understanding lit her eyes. She looked suddenly ashamed, glancing toward the man kneeling on the dirty floor.

"Saruel," she said. "You are Saruel!"

"Yes," I said. "Will you come with me?"

The fat man moved painfully, stumbling to his feet.

"See here," he said, "you are not the girl's father at all." He drew a dagger from somewhere in his robe and waved it toward me. "Leave my house," he said. "She stays with me."

I looked down at the dagger in his hand, at his exposed member.

"Do you wish to join the eunuchs?" I said.

"I will spill your blood," he said. "Leave my house and the girl, for I claimed her before you. I see that you desire her as I do. Perhaps you will have her, after I am satisfied."

"Then you have made your decision," I said.

He waved the knife again, pointing to the door. "Leave us. I shall take my satisfaction upon the girl."

"Very well, then," I said.

Moving quickly, I took the dagger from his hand and grabbed him by the pearls again. I lashed out with the dagger, removing his pearls with one quick cut, holding them in the palm of my hand. Blood poured from between his legs onto the dirt floor. He looked down at the pooling blood, not yet comprehending what had happened. His eyes fell on the pearls in my open hand. He screamed.

I cast the pearls at his feet.

"Pearls before swine," I said, wiping my hand on his robe. I turned to Marah. "Let us go."

I flew, carrying Marah in my arms. The screams of her would-be molester turned to deep sobs far below.

"Saruel?" Marah said, looking up at me.

"Yes, my love," I said.

She looked sorrowful and ashamed. "It was the fever that brought me to that man's house."

"You are with me now," I said.

"And where will we go?"

"I will return you to the house of your father and mother."

"They are not my father and mother," she said.

"You are still a child, even though your memories have returned."

"I am Marah, your lover, your wife."

"Yes, my darling," I said, "but in this time you are also Miriam of the Towers and your parents love you very much."

She pressed her childlike face against my chest. Her home appeared below me. The rooftop balcony was unoccupied, so I landed there. She stood, looking up at me.

"You are so beautiful," she said. She pressed herself against me. "My parents are not here, and the servants are in their quarters. Lie with me."

"My love, your body is that of a young girl's. I could not do such a thing."

"I am on fire," she said. "I am not so far from womanhood. Would you rather that I defiled myself with that beast of a man? The fever is upon me, Saruel. I may soon lose control of my urges."

I wrapped my arms around her and held her close, remembering all the times she had been with the fever, coupling with the women of the temples of Erozel.

"I cannot," I said.

She turned angrily away from me. "Perhaps I should call my servant, Gabrielle, into my chamber and seduce her," she said. "She is delightful, a virgin of only fourteen. I imagine her chalice flows with sweet wine."

"It saddens me," I said, "that the fever has come upon you at such an early age."

She frowned, the anger leaving her to be replaced by sadness.

"And, yet, I remember you," she said. "We are united once again. The fever, my sickness, does not reach my heart, only my flesh. My heart belongs to you." I held her to me. "I am sorry, my love," she said. She turned and opened the door to her chamber. "Will you come to me again?"

"I will," I said.

She walked into the house and shut the door behind her. I waited, listening, as Marah called the name of her servant girl.

"Gabrielle, come to me."

CHAPTER 26

I flew to Nazareth, landing near the synagogue, where the boys of the city received their education. The lessons were usually at an end by that time of day, and I waited, hoping to see Yeshua. Boys trickled out of the synagogue in small groups. After a while, he appeared, walking with other boys about his age. They were laughing and talking together. He was just a child, an eleven-year-old boy, yet, like Marah, his eyes told a much different story.

I leaned against the synagogue wall, watching as he passed by. He stopped suddenly and looked around. My heart leapt within as his gaze fell upon me. His friends stopped as well, questioning him. He said something to them and they went on without him. He stood there, across the street, watching me. His face held a thousand questions. Finally, he walked over.

"Peace be with you, Sir," he said.

"And with you," I said.

His blue eyes studied me. I trembled.

"Do I know you?" he said, looking me over. "For you seem familiar to me."

"We have never met," I said.

"Excuse me, then," he said, turning to leave. He stopped and turned back to me, shaking his head. "No. I am sure of it. I do not understand how, but I do know you."

"You are mistaken, young master, for we have never met." His likeness to Adam, the Son of God, amazed me. He was much younger than Adam had looked at creation, but the similarities were remarkable. Was that the plan? Was the I Am raising up a second Adam as a savior to humankind? He looked troubled. "What is it?" I said.

"It is what I see when I look upon you. I see brilliant light, a bright star forming in darkness. The light before me takes shape, a body, a hand reaching out."

He hesitated.

"Continue, young master."

"I take the hand and pull it from the darkness. The form of light steps out, and it is you." He stopped, looking up at me.

I was astonished, for Son of God or not, he could not have known such a thing.

"How can this be?" I said.

"I called you Saruel, a Watcher of Heaven," he said. "What is a Watcher?"

Adam himself had not beheld my creation, yet Yeshua had just described it to me. I remembered it clearly, before the Earth, before this physical universe. I had stepped from the darkness, newly and completely formed, holding the hand of my Creator, looking into His blessed eyes, trembling in his presence. He had named me Saruel, a Watcher.

I turned away from him.

"Please, Sir, I must know. What is happening to me? Please do not leave." I stopped and turned back to him. He looked at me for a long moment, appearing confused. "You are not a man at all," he said.

"Do not speak such a thing, young master," I said, looking around to see whether anyone had heard him.

Emotion welled up in his face. His eyes grew wet with tears. "Forgive me, Sir," he said, lowering his gaze to the dusty street. "I just want to know what is happening to me. I want to know who I am."

Compelled by an unseen force I fell backward to the ground. Startled, I jumped to my feet, nearly flying into the air. I stared at the unassuming boy in front of me. I knew him.

I Am.

I had seen those eyes before, and had no doubt. Yeshua was a boy in every way, but he was also something else. Yet what I was thinking could not be. I had to be mistaken, for neither the Watchers or Fallen had realized it. Yeshua was not the son of an angel. He was not Adam formed anew by the Creator. His body, the flesh that contained him was surely the Son of God, fashioned in the image of God, but his spirit, his soul was more than that. Looking out at me through the eyes of a boy was the intelligence, the power and authority, the presence of the Great I Am.

I found myself standing once again in the Holy Place, and there, beyond the veil of this boy's flesh, was the Holy of Holies.

CHAPTER 27

Not long after my experience with Yeshua, I flew to Rome in search of Ariel. Wearing the clothes of a Roman citizen, I mingled with an excited crowd in the common area of the Amphitheater of All Gods. My clothing stood out in a sea of tattered garments, my beauty at odds with the sun-baked, unwashed humanity around me. Covering my head with my cloak, I hid my face in shadow.

Wicked as Ariel was, he had been my companion for ages without number and my bond to him remained strong. I wanted to tell him about Yeshua. Eschewing the Pantheon where humankind worshiped Fallen angels, I refused to go there. Gladiator matches had begun anew in Rome and I knew such an event was irresistible to Ariel.

Far to my right, in a private balcony, politicians and prominent citizens dressed in the finest garments enjoyed the delicacies of Rome. Above the balcony, Ariel's image, sculpted in white marble, presided over the event. In the bloodstained sands of the arena, twelve gladiators from a sundry of nations and tribes stood ready with weapons of death: swords, spears, maces, nets and shields.

Trumpets flourished and the crowd rose together in anticipation. The announcer, a round man with a crown of gold leaf, stood in the balcony, silencing the throng with an upheld hand. His strong voice carried loud, echoing to every seat in the amphitheater.

"Citizens of Rome, visitors to the finest city on Earth and to the Amphitheater of All Gods, behold the sacrifice of lives and blood to the great gods of Rome." He gestured theatrically to Ariel's sculpted image. "We honor the great god of war. May he continue to grant victory over our enemies!"

A tremendous roar erupted from the crowd around me. I felt a tremor in the atmosphere and looked to see Ariel in the sky above the amphitheater. He wore the uniform of a Roman soldier.

The announcer looked down at the twelve gladiators standing in the sands of the arena below. "Let us begin our feast of blood!" he cried.

At the far side of the amphitheater, soldiers opened an immense iron gate. Four lions, lean with hunger, entered the arena—moving cautiously at first, eyes roaming over the shouting mob in the theater seats, settling finally on the gladiators. The gladiators formed into one solid group, facing the lions with readied weapons, man and beast locked in a momentary impasse. A lion roared and bolted toward them, the others following close behind. The thunderous shouting of the crowd drowned out the roars of the lions.

The four beasts worked together, separating a single gladiator from the end of the column. He jabbed bravely at them with an iron spear, sinking the shaft between one of the lions' ribs. The lion snarled in pain, his sharp claws flailing toward the man's head. The other lions attacked together, striking the gladiator, knocking him hard to the ground, their great mouths finding his arms and legs, the injured lion clamping its jaws around his throat, crushing the life from him as the other lions tore the limbs from his body. Blood stained the sand around him. The crowd shouted. Ariel watched without expression.

The eleven remaining gladiators formed a column and moved toward the lions who feasted on the fallen man. They moved at once, striking a lion with their swords and spears. The lion turned toward them, furious with pain, crazed by the taste of human flesh and blood. It leapt toward a gladiator, knocking him to the ground while receiving blows and slashes from swords and spears. It turned, bleeding heavily, and limped away. The men followed, striking and jabbing, hitting their mark. The lion fell to the ground, a sword buried to the hilt in its chest.

I watched the savage violence below me, man against beast. Who could take pleasure in such a thing? I looked up at Ariel and was surprised to see that he was no longer alone. Erozel hovered next to him, his white silk robes cut in the fashion of the women of Rome.

The gladiators defeated a second lion, losing another man in the fight.

Ariel and Erozel landed together on the stone roof of the balcony, next to Ariel's marble likeness. Ariel pointed his hand to the announcer. I felt the slightest tremor. The announcer stood, looking dazed. He raised his hands, beckoning silence. The shouting slowly subsided.

"Citizens of Rome, hear me. We shall add new stakes to the games today. The last man left alive shall receive much coin and, with it, his freedom. He will be a citizen of Rome!"

The gladiators looked up at him, one of them paying a terrible price for the distraction as a lion leapt on him, bringing him down. The gladiators broke off from the column, every man now the enemy of the other men. They struck out at each other, man against man, while the two remaining beasts tore their victim apart.

Erozel lighted from the roof onto the balcony below him, where the wealthy and prominent watched the event. The men and women saw him and gasped at his beauty. He closed his eyes and stretched his hands toward them. They fell on each other with a passion as the fever consumed them, tearing at each other's garments with lascivious desire. Erozel took a young man by the hand, pulling him down to his knees. Lifting the white silk of his robe, he revealed his engorged member. The young man took it in his mouth.

I turned my face from the wickedness, and, walking as a man, left the amphitheater. I took to the skies a safe distance away, wanting nothing to do with my brothers.

CHAPTER 28

"There were two trees, remember," Sangruel said, "the Tree of Life and the Tree of Blood. One gave life eternal, the other caused spiritual death, but it gave life as well. The life is in the blood, after all. Where it brought destruction to the spirit, it gave life to the flesh." He looked at his servants. "Would you be surprised to know that the woman you hold is greater than four-hundred years old?" I looked down at the woman's youthful, pallid face. "And the man you hold is not much younger than she is. It was not my blood that gave them life eternal, but the fruit of blood which flowed into them from my veins on the night I made them."

"They are not truly alive," I said. "You did not give them life, but only robbed them of death. They are undead."

He looked up at me.

"Your woman is still alive," he said. "That is plain to see. I have given the matter much thought. She partook of the Fruit of Life."

"Continue," I said.

"There were two trees in the Garden of God. One was spirit, the other flesh. Eve devoured the blood of the Fruit of Carnal Knowledge. She did not finish the fruit, but dropped the remaining part upon the ground. Adam dropped the Fruit of Life in his haste to find Eve. I assume that you retrieved it."

I did not answer. I stared down at Sangruel, recalling Eve in the garden, the Fruit of Carnal Knowledge pulsing in the palm of her hand like a human heart. I felt the two servants of Sangruel slipping from my grip.

"I have kept a secret for a very long time," Sangruel said. "Erozel is not aware that I know."

"What secret?" I said.

Sangruel motioned to his servants. I released my hold on the woman, who fell into the darkness below.

"Very well, then," Sangruel said. "At Babel, a woman we both know carried upon her the aroma of the fruit of blood. She was no child of mine. My blood did not flow within her. She was Semiramis, Erozel's Queen of Heaven."

I felt myself go numb. I released my hold on the male servant of Sangruel and he dropped below me into the night. The woman appeared, carrying him as she hovered, watching Sangruel from below.

"Semiramis partook of the Fruit of Carnal Knowledge?" I asked.

"She did."

I remembered the fruit in Eve's hand, a living thing, a beating heart. I recalled the statue under the floor of the Pantheon, Erozel carrying Asherah, a human heart in his hand. I remembered the Festival of Hearts held every year in Erozel's honor, the heart of a willing virgin, a love offering to Erozel. Semiramis had looked so much like Asherah. Erozel's lovers, numerous through the ages, had all resembled Asherah: Isis of Egypt, Venus of the Greeks, Dianna of Rome. Raphael had sculpted Asherah as a young woman, not the old woman she had been at her death.

"The fruit of blood gives life to the flesh," Sangruel said.

It was not a heart the sculpted image of Erozel held in his marble hands, but the Fruit of Carnal Knowledge. I knew. Finally, I understood. All of Erozel's many lovers throughout the ages had been the same woman.

"Asherah is alive?" I said. "This cannot be, for I saw her with my own eyes, decaying in Erozel's embrace. Hemael cast her spirit into the abyss."

"The fruit of blood beats within her chest," Sangruel said, "placed there by Erozel after her death. It gave new life to her body, though her spirit remains in the abyss. It is for this reason that Erozel hates you as he does."

CHAPTER 29

When Marah was of age, I purchased a home in the Towers, near her adoptive parent's house, and took her to live with me as my wife. How wonderful it was to have her again, to live in a house of love. I spent every day with her, and most nights, watching her as she slept. The fever came upon her from time to time, and at Marah's request I brought her servant, Gabrielle, into our home. Marah satisfied herself with the young woman. Still, I loved her with everything in my being, and she loved me.

Yeshua grew as well. I had expected greatness from him. Instead, he lived a simple life with his parents in Galilee, just a young man working with his mother's husband as a builder. Though he attended synagogue, he showed no inclination for a religious career. For one born to be king, he showed no interest in politics. After my experience with him in front of the synagogue, I kept my distance, watching him in secret.

My brothers dwelt in the palace—what is now the Castel Sant'angelo—near the Pantheon, the Temple of All Gods. I decided not to reveal to them what I had seen in Yeshua's eyes, or what had happened to me when he had uttered the words 'I Am'.

For ten years, I lived with Marah in our home in the Towers. The fever grew within her at an alarming rate. The servant woman no longer satisfied her cravings, and she frequented pagan temples, where prostitution was a form of worship. There she gave herself to wealthy women, Greeks and Romans.

One evening, Gabrielle came to me, weeping. She fell to her knees at my feet.

"My master," she cried. "Forgive me, but I must leave this house."

I placed my hand on her shoulder and beckoned her to get up. She stood, looking up at me with wet eyes.

"What is wrong, Gabrielle?" I said.

"It is my mistress." She broke down sobbing again.

"What is it? What distresses you so?"

"Oh, my master, I fear to tell you. For, surely, I will invite your wrath upon me."

"Speak," I said.

"While you are away, my mistress invites me into her bed. I am a servant, and must obey." I looked at her and said nothing. "She orders me to come into her naked." She stared down at her feet. "I am a student of the scriptures, and know such things are an abomination. I have never known a man. The things my mistress desires of me, I dare not speak of."

She clasped her hands together and trembled in front of me. I held her hands in mine.

"Does she give you pleasure?" I said. "Is it all unpleasant?" She looked up at me in confusion. "I know of her desires," I said.

"She has given me pleasure," she said, blushing, "but now, with the pleasure, she gives me pain as well."

"How does she give you pain?"

"My master, I dare not say."

"As your master, I command you."

She stepped away from me. "I cannot speak of it. I must show you."

She turned her back toward me and, leaning over, pulled her robe up, exposing her naked buttocks. Long welts, red and swollen, ran along the contours of her flesh.

"Your mistress did this to you?"

New tears filled her eyes. "She has done this, and so much more. She defiles me in unspeakable ways."

"I have seen enough," I said.

Lowering her robes, she turned to me, then fell to her knees.

"Forgive me, Master." She searched my face. "Perhaps if you joined us, she would be gentler. I am untouched by man, but defiled for marriage. Lie with us, I pray you, as Jacob with Rachel and Leah."

I turned from her. "For a long time, you have lived in my house and have known my wife in ways that only a husband should. What has changed? Why do you come to me now? You took the good. Will you now refuse the evil? Is it now an abomination? Is it any less an abomination to share the bed of marriage with us both?"

"Forgive me," she said.

"You are forgiven," I said, turning to her. "If you must go, then I will not stop you. I ask you to stay, if you will. Your mistress is good and kind, her carnal desires her only vice."

Gabrielle lowered her head. "Yes, my master. If it pleases you, I will remain."

"Leave me, then, and return with my blessing to your mistress."

She left me alone. I wept.

The next day, I watched over Yeshua. He was nearing thirty years old. His mother's husband had gone the way of all flesh, and he continued in the business of building homes and furniture. Nothing had changed. The people of Israel had not gathered around him to declare him their king. He lived the ordinary life of a skilled worker.

Still, I sensed restlessness in him that I had never sensed in him before.

Having once been a focused, meticulous artisan, he now performed his work absorbed by his own thoughts, staring often at the mountain at the edge of the city. I looked toward the mountain one evening and understood why. There in the skies, high above, was a solitary shadow, the Lord of the Fallen.

When I returned home, night had fallen. It was dark inside, save for the light coming from a small lamp. I climbed the steps to my chamber and stopped outside the door. I heard the crack of leather against flesh and a cry of pain. I waited. The sound came again, the smacking of leather on flesh and a woman crying out. I opened the door.

Marah stood, naked, leather whip in her hand. Gabrielle knelt on our bed on all fours, her exposed buttocks lifted in the air. Tears streamed down her face. Red welts appeared on her round buttocks, combined with the older ones from her prior sessions with Marah. She looked up at me, her eyes imploring. Marah turned to me, her face crimson. She looked embarrassed.

"Saruel," she said. "Please, I do not want you to see me this way, for the fever is hard upon me. My desires have consumed me."

"I will stay," I said. "For I love you, even when the fever afflicts you."

Lust filled her countenance again, replacing any embarrassment.

"Then join us, lover. Take your fill of this delightful woman. She would welcome the change, I am sure."

I moved toward Marah and held her to me. She kissed me on my mouth then returned her attention to Gabrielle.

"She is a thing of beauty," she said. She trailed her fingers lightly along the flesh of Gabrielle's buttocks. "Spread your cheeks," she ordered. Gabrielle reached back with both hands, pulling the cheeks of her buttocks apart, revealing her forbidden part. Marah placed the wooden handle of the whip to her forbidden part, thrusting against it with slow back and forth movements. Gabrielle flinched, pulling away from the wooden handle. Marah slapped Gabrielle's buttocks with her bare hand. "Do not pull away from me!"

I took Marah's other hand, which held the whip.

"Never before have I seen you so deep in the clutches of this affliction," I said.

Marah kept her eyes on Gabrielle and frowned. "It is impossible for me to resist anymore," she said.

"Do you see how you have hurt her? Do you take pleasure in her pain?"

Marah's face twisted. She bit her lip. "I repent of my ways and beg forgiveness once the fever departs, but it returns again, and I am lost to its whims and impulses. I am undone. I will understand if you choose to leave me, for I am not worthy of you."

"Perish the thought, my darling. I love you, and I always will."

"Then stay with me, my love. Share her with me."

Gabrielle looked up at me with wide, pleading eyes.

"You know that I will not," I said. I pulled away from Marah. "I will return when the fever has passed."

I left Marah alone with Gabrielle. My heart was broken. I turned my face to Heaven.

I prayed.

CHAPTER 30

"As I take blood, so Asherah takes hearts," Sangruel said. "The blood of the fruit must ever be replenished with the blood of mankind, so the flesh of the fruit is replenished with flesh."

"She devours human hearts?"

"Consider my servants. While they dwell in darkness and feed upon the blood of life, they are eternal as we are. It is the same with Asherah. She is sustained by the flesh of the Fruit of Carnal Knowledge within her."

"Yet she does not fear the light of the sun," I said.

"My blood does not flow within her. My curse is not hers."

"She is as much a fiend as you and your children are," I said.

He looked up at me from the shadows of night below and I sensed tremendous sorrow in him.

"I am hardly the monster you believe me to be. My curse compels me, not my own desires." I remembered the frightened faces of the twin girls he murdered, and frowned down at him. "It is true, my brother," he said. "I wanted only to dwell among humankind. I never asked for this. I loathe the darkness and lament the rivers of blood I have shed. My children are my only comfort." I thought of Marah's affliction. Was it Sangruel's fault that he needed and desired blood? "I wish I had listened to you on that night," he continued, "for the penalty is more than I can bear."

I slid my eyes along the gruesome contours of Sangruel's once beautiful face. His jaundice eyes held a haunted expression. For a moment, I saw the former angel of Heaven before me.

"We cannot go back," I said. "We cannot undo what is already done."

"Would you, Saruel, if you could? Would you have Fallen for your woman, knowing the full consequences?"

I answered without hesitation: "I would do it again Sangruel, a thousand times over."

I left Sangruel, returning to San Francisco and my own dwelling. The cursed altar stone sat in the middle of my living room. How much blood had fallen upon that stone over thousands of years, how many innocent lives offered as a sacrifice to the Watchers?

I looked through my window toward a silent Heaven.

"You once loved her as I do," I said. "Return her to me, I pray." I sat down in my chair, despair gripping my heart. "You loved her, also."

I gazed out at the night. Fog fell upon the city, covering it in a blanket of gloom and gray. Marah was somewhere out there.

I stood up, looking down at the cursed altar stone. I picked it up, hating the very touch of it. There was my name in heavenly script. I turned it over in my hands. What I saw made me drop it. It fell with a hard crash onto my wooden floor. There was more writing on the stone's underside. Had it been there earlier? Could I have missed such a thing? I knelt in front of the stone. Someone had etched a message to me in an ancient script. The grooves were fresh, not worn with time like the script that spelled my name. The message was short and to the point: I know. Someone had been in my dwelling. I listened closely for any sounds, searching for any other sign of their presence.

I walked down the staircase to Andrew's quarters. His bedroom door was still closed. The lights were off. Sculpted angels, depicted with wings, eerie gray in the darkness, lined the walls of Andrew's living room. I peered down over the wooden railing to the foyer below. A large, finely sculpted statue stood on the floor, facing me. It was the marble image of Erozel from the Pantheon, the very statue, brought to my home from thousands of miles away. I vaulted the railing and lighted to the foyer in front of the sculpture. I smelled blood.

The likeness of Erozel was perfect, carved by the hand of the master sculptor, Raphael. Sorrow, grief, filled Erozel's feminine features. Asherah's likeness was perfect as well. Why had I not realized this earlier? How had Raphael sculpted with such detail the face of a woman who had died during the great flood?

Dark blood ran down Erozel's marble hand, falling in droplets to the fine wooden floor. He held a small heart in his hand, not a marble heart, but an actual bleeding human heart, small in size, the heart of a child. I stood, motionless, staring down at it. Fear filled me. Panic seized me, gripping my own heart in its vice-like grip. Was this Marah's heart?

I picked it up, examining it closely, loathing the feel of it in my hand. Part of it was missing, a large chunk torn away from the left side the heart as if bitten off.

Not knowing what else to do, I called Jonathon, the only confidant I had left. He arrived within half an hour. I showed him Erozel's statue and the human heart, explaining to him what Sangruel had revealed to me about Asherah.

"If Sangruel truly knows the scent of Marah's blood, perhaps he can tell you whether or not this is her heart. At least then you will know for sure," he said. Opening the door to Andrew's bedroom, he peered inside at the motionless body lying upon the bed. "Allow me to make arrangements for Andrew's remains." He looked up at me, meeting my eyes. "I hate to see you in despair. Go to him."

I placed my hand on his shoulder. "You are forever faithful," I said.

CHAPTER 31

Yeshua spent forty days and forty nights alone in the mountain, without food of any kind. I watched him from a distance, hovering just above the horizon. The angels of Heaven surrounded the border of the mountain, but none ministered to him.

After the fortieth night, the Lord of the Fallen landed before him. Yeshua was in a weakened state from a lack of nourishment, sitting on the ground. He looked upon the revealed image of the Son of the Morning.

"Do I know you?" he said.

The Son of the Morning did not answer right away. He studied Yeshua with a look of utter distaste and loathing.

"You are Adam all over again," he said after a time. "Do you call yourself the Son of God?"

"You say that I am," Yeshua said.

The mountain trembled at his words. The Lord of the Fallen looked troubled, thoughtful. He bent down and picked up two stones.

"If you are the Son of God, turn these stones into bread."

"There is more to nourishment than bread. Every word of God is nourishment to man."

The Son of the Morning's face twisted with sudden rage, his beautiful, mad eyes burned with hatred. He grabbed Yeshua roughly by his garments, flying with him, high into the air.

"If I were to drop you from this height, would you not fall to your death?"

He carried him to Jerusalem, landing at the pinnacle of Herod's Temple. I followed at a distance.

"Cast yourself down, Son of God. For, if you truly are the Son of God, the angels of Heaven will prevent you from falling."

Yeshua stared down at the ground below him. "I will not tempt the Lord your God."

"My God?" the Son of the Morning said. "Who is my God?"

He lifted Yeshua from the temple and carried him to a place high in the sky. "Behold my domain," he said, waving a hand toward the Earth below. "Here, I am God. The kingdoms of Earth are mine to give and to take away. Make me your God, worship at my feet, and they shall be yours. You will truly be the king of kings."

Yeshua looked down at the cities of Earth. When he spoke, his face was calm, strong, his voice composed, commanding.

"Get behind me, demon," he said. "I cast you away from my presence."

The Lord of the Fallen trembled, crying out in sudden pain. His eyes grew wide with both rage and fear as an unseen force repelled him violently away from Yeshua. Free from the Son of the Morning's grip, Yeshua plummeted toward the Earth.

I waited, watching as he fell, his body gaining in speed. Would the angels of Heaven come to his aid? He continued to fall toward certain impact, but no angels appeared. Unless Heaven intervened, he was going to hit the ground. I flew as fast as I could from where I hovered over the horizon. I was afraid to touch him, for I knew who he was. Who was I to touch the very Temple of the Great I Am? Who was I to carry the Holy of Holies made flesh? But there was no one else to help him.

I caught him moments before he hit the Earth, and I lowered him gently to the ground. He sat down, trembling, looking up at me.

"The Son of the Morning is gone?" he said.

"Yes, Lord."

His eyes searched the skies above us. "I judged him in a time before time, in his pride and rebellion. I beheld him fall as lightning from Heaven. With my little finger I cast him to the abyss."

I fell to my knees in front of him. He looked at me. "Allow me to minister to you, Lord," I said.

He nodded. "Please," he said, "I must eat soon."

We were near Jerusalem, surrounded by a grove of olive trees. Promising to return, I flew to an outside market in the streets of Jerusalem, before returning to Yeshua with a loaf of bread, honeycomb and a jar of goat's milk. He lay on his side, too weak to stay in a seated position. I sat behind him and, lifting him up, rested his back against my chest and placed the jar of milk in his trembling hands.

"Drink," I said. He lifted it to his lips and drank deeply from the clay jar. I took the milk from him and broke off a piece of the honeycomb. He ate it and his strength returned a little. He finished the bread over several minutes.

"Thank you," he said, sitting up.

"I am honored to minister to you," I said.

He looked thoughtfully up at me. "It is you," he said, "Saruel, Watcher of Heaven."

"It is," I said.

"I owe you a great service."

"My Lord, I am Fallen, unworthy of your favor."

"If a man's son sins against him, is he no longer a son? Will the I Am love his children less than a man loves his?"

I fell to the ground, lying prostrate before him. "Then it is you," I said. "You truly are the Great I Am."

Yeshua touched my head gently. "I also am the son of man, a descendant of Adam. I am flesh and blood." He placed his hand on my shoulder. "Arise. Stand before me."

I stood, looking with wonder upon his face. Yeshua was the express image of the Great I Am, God robed in flesh. I had trouble reconciling such a thing with all that I had known before my fall. Yet it was undeniable. The one who had called me into existence before He created this universe, stood in front of me as a mortal man, weak, susceptible to fatigue, hunger, and human frailty. The urge to kneel before him overcame me, and my knees began to bow. He stopped me.

"You are Fallen. Still, you ministered to me in my weakness. Why?"

"Surely, Lord, you know all things," I said.

"I am a mortal man," he said. "I know only what is revealed to me, or what I have learned on the Earth."

"I helped you, my Lord, because I love you," I said. "You are the object of my worship, the focus of my desires."

He stood, looking at me in momentary silence. "Then why, Saruel, are you Fallen?"

I looked up into his eyes. How I loved him. I bowed my head. "I also loved another," I said.

"You loved a maiden." His face filled with comprehension. "I remember it now. You left your first estate, turned your back toward Heaven for a daughter of Adam." His eyes filled with tears. He reached out and touched my cheek. "You caused me much sorrow."

I touched his hand with my own, longing to kneel before him, to sing to him a song of worship and dwell for eternity in his holy presence. What would I give for redemption? What price would I pay to enter the gates of Heaven once again?

"What would you give?" he said, verbalizing my thoughts. "Tell me, Saruel, my beloved creation, if you could return to the past and alter history, would you choose Heaven and my presence over the love of this woman?"

I thought of Marah, her laughter, her singing, the way I felt when I held her. I thought also of her affliction, her lust and depravation. I hung my head.

"My Lord," I said, "I would not leave her for all the glory of Heaven, not for all the wonders of the Holy of Holies. I left my first estate and, for her love, I would surely do it again. Yet I will always love and worship you."

He dropped his hand from my cheek.

"I understand." He turned from me. "Go," he said. "You must depart from my presence, for you are a Fallen angel and I am the Holy One of Heaven. I will repay you in time for your kindness."

I rose into the air above him, my heart filled with pain, misery, and sweet love.

"Forgive me, Creator of all that is and ever will be. My love for you is genuine and true."

I turned from him, flying toward home.

Marah was in the garden behind our house when I found her. She held a fresh bouquet in her hand. A garland of flowers garnished her autumn hair. She was humming to herself, my Marah again, her affliction passed for a time. She smiled when she saw me.

"My love," she said.

I rushed to her and held her in my arms. "I would choose you all over again," I said. "I will never leave you. You are my heart. You are my love."

CHAPTER 32

I wrapped the small heart carefully in a washcloth and placed it in the pocket of my slacks. Returning to my balcony, I then lifted into the night sky. I flew to find Sangruel, entering through the back door of the warehouse, then down the spiraling stone steps into the catacombs below. Ignoring the awful smell of decay and the discarded remains of human victims, I made my way to the black sculpture of Sangruel. I felt eyes watching me and heard the subtle sounds of stealthy movement in the surrounding darkness. I called Sangruel's name. The walls of the catacombs seemed to come alive, as servants of Sangruel poured into the chamber. They stood warily before me, hunger on their faces.

"You dare to come here again?" a man growled. He was the one whose neck I had broken the night before. He stepped slowly toward me, snarling, showing a mouth filled with sharp, yellowish teeth. "You are greatly outnumbered this time."

The others moved beside him, beginning to surround me.

"Leave him be!" a woman's voice commanded. The servants of Sangruel pulled obediently away from me. I turned to see a tall woman. She appeared to be in her late forties or early fifties, and held an air of authority. Her skin was sepulcher white, her long raven hair streaked with gray. She wore a dress of red so dark that it touched on black. She addressed the servants of Sangruel again in the same commanding voice. "Leave us."

The one whose neck I had broken started to protest.

"Go," she said. He turned wordlessly away, slinking with the others back into the darkness. The woman followed them with her eyes for a moment, before returning her attention to me. "They do not understand," she said. "They know nothing of Heaven or of heavenly creatures."

"You know of my kind?"

"I do," she said. "I know my master's history. He is Sangruel, Fallen from the heavens. His blood flows within me, from his very own body, for I am the first of my kind, born to the blood when the world was young and the Temple of All Gods still stood at Babel."

I stared at her in awe. The first of Sangruel's servants still lived!

"What is your name?" I asked.

"I am called Sarai."

"I seek your master, Sarai," I said.

"My master has not returned." She looked up at me, troubled. "I am afraid, for I feel his emotions. He is in fear and terrible anguish."

"You feel what he feels?"

"His blood flows within me."

"Can you tell me, then, where he is?"

She turned, pointing toward the north. "He lies in that direction. I must go to him, for he is calling to me."

"Come," I said, "let us find him together."

Sarai did not move. She looked at me, doubtfully. "I do not know you, and am not sure I can trust you. Swear to me first that you mean my master no harm."

"You have my word that I will not harm him."

Having the gift of flight, she flew alongside me. We headed north, along the coast, the dark ocean below us, Sarai feeling the way, circling back every now and then before carrying on with our search. Finally she stopped, hovering high above a rocky cliff, her eyes searching the area. She let out a cry and fell suddenly from the sky, tumbling toward the rocks below. I flew quickly and caught her in my arms. Her body felt cold and stiff against me; a living corpse. She cried out again, her voice filled with pain. I landed near a clump of bushes at the base of the cliff.

"What is it?" I said.

She pointed to a spot midway up the rocky face of the cliff. "There," she said, tears of blood staining her pale cheeks, "my master is there."

I looked up to where she pointed. There was Sangruel, his arms and legs spread wide, wrists and ankles tied with ropes to a large wooden cross, helpless as any mortal.

"Go to him, please," Sarai said, "for I cannot approach the cross."

I left her, flying to Sangruel, landing in front of him. He looked fearfully up at me. His face showed agony, his mouth contorted in torment, his lips moving wordlessly. A cross of iron hung from a silver chain around his neck. I broke the silver chain, removing the iron cross, hiding it from his sight, within my pocket.

I untied the ropes, and carried him, lowering him to the ground beside Sarai. He sat on the ground, powerless, his body shaking, his mouth frozen in a tight grimace. Sarai sat next to him, cradling his head carefully to her chest, not as a child to a father, not as a servant, but as a lover.

"He must have living blood," she said. "He must feed."

I knelt down, facing Sangruel. "Was it Erozel? Did he do this to you?"

Sangruel lifted his head with considerable effort. He spoke, his voice a strained whisper.

"Erozel and his followers," he said. "They know about your girl, my brother. They know who she is."

I showed him the child's heart. "Is it hers?" I asked.

Sangruel looked weakly at the heart. Touching his finger to the blood, he placed it in his mouth. His eyes filled with predatory desire, feral hunger.

"It is not hers. Give it to me, Sangruel," he said, licking his lips greedily. "It is not her heart, and I must have its blood!"

"I will leave you with your faithful servant, my brother." I gave him the heart, and stood up. Turning to Sarai, I said, "Not a child. That is what I require for having helped you. When your master feeds tonight, let it not be upon the blood of a child."

"You have my word, Son of Heaven," she said.

Lifting into the air, I left her with Sangruel.

CHAPTER 33

"My lord, come! My mistress is not well." Gabrielle said. She was naked. Dark scratches marked her body, her buttocks freshly lashed by Marah's whip.

I had returned to my dwelling in the Towers, having watched Yeshua, mesmerized by his works. He healed those who were sick and afflicted of every disease and ailment. I marveled at his tenderness, for, though he was but thirty years of age, he treated every man and woman as his own child. Such uproar he caused among both the princes of men and the principalities of the air!

"What is the matter?" I said.

Gabrielle wept. "My lord, my mistress is vexed by a tormenting spirit. I cannot help her, though I tried to satisfy her desires. Please come."

I followed her to the bedroom I shared with Marah, preparing myself for a terrible sight. The chamber door was open and I heard her moans and cries. I stepped inside. Marah lay upon the bed, her naked body twisted and covered in sweat, her muscles tight as if in a palsy. She bled freely from her chalice, rubbed raw by her own fingers.

"My love?" I said.

She turned, looking insanely up at me, her eyes widening. "You are no lover of mine!" she shouted. "You cannot satisfy me!"

"Marah," I said calmly, using her true name. Gabrielle did not seem to notice. "I am, and will always be, your lover."

She spread her legs, rubbing her chalice hard with the fingers of her right hand. "Then quench the flame burning within my loins, before it consumes me! Satisfy me, satisfy me!"

I place my hand gently on her forehead. She pulled away from my touch.

"No! It is not love I crave, but pleasure!" She pointed an accusing finger at Gabrielle. "She no longer satisfies me. I desire more! I must be filled, or I will surely die!"

"Then I shall mount you," I said, lifting my robe.

"You shall not!" she said. "Bring me Semiramis! I crave the Queen of Heaven. Let me lie between her legs and taste the nectar of her chalice."

She groaned piteously, her hips thrusting violently, her fingers probing her chalice.

"She surely has a demon, my lord," Gabrielle said.

"She will recover," I said. I turned from Marah, my heart breaking.

"Remain with her."

I climbed the stairs leading to the rooftop and stood alone under the night sky, listening to her continual moans, powerless to help her. I had been through this with her before and she had always come out of it, but it seemed to worsen each time. I feared the fever would one day kill her. I returned to our chambers to find her convulsing upon the bed, in the fit of a seizure. I placed my arms around her and held her close to me.

"Let us dress her," I said to Gabrielle.

Gabrielle looked surprised, but obeyed, working with me to robe Marah's nakedness. Marah was beyond struggling and did not resist. Her eyes looked up at me with fear and madness. Once she was dressed, I picked her up from the bed.

"Leave us," I said to Gabrielle. She seemed troubled, but relieved as well. She returned to her own chambers in the lower part of the house. I waited until I heard the sound of her door closing. Then, returning to the rooftop, I lifted into the sky with Marah.

I flew to the Mount of Olives, where I had last seen Yeshua. The lights of campfires shone in the night, illuminating the hillside. Yeshua's followers clustered around the fires. I heard their scattered conversations below me and smelled the cooking of food. I searched until I found a campsite separate from the others. The men closest to Yeshua were sleeping around the fire. Yeshua sat a way off from them, leaning with his back against an olive tree, his eyes gazing down at Jerusalem below. I searched the skies around me for the presence of other angels.

"You are alone, Saruel," Yeshua said, looking up at me. "Why are you here?"

I landed in front of him, placing Marah on the ground at his feet. He looked down at her.

"Lord of Heaven," I said. "This woman is sorely vexed and there is no help for her. I have seen what you do for others. Please, I pray you, touch her, and make her whole again."

He looked up at me.

"Who is this woman, Saruel? What is she to you? There are many who need healing in Israel, yet you chose to bring only one to me."

"She is Miriam of the Towers, my Lord."

Yeshua stood to his feet, looking down at Marah. She laid there, eyes closed, body twitching, her right hand groping weakly at her chalice.

"Miriam of the Towers," he said. "Perhaps that is who she is in this age, but not in ages past."

I bowed my head. "Nothing is hidden from your sight, my Lord," I said.

He placed a hand on my shoulder. "I said I would repay your kindness to me, Fallen spirit, and I will keep my promise. I will heal this woman, but never again will I hear your prayers. You are cast from Heaven."

"My Lord," I said, "I am unworthy."

He turned his attention to Marah. "Miriam of the Towers," he said. She opened her eyes. "Look upon me and be healed."

Marah turned her face to him, seeing Yeshua for the first time. He placed his hand on her head. Her body shook violently at the touch of his hand. She clawed feverishly at her chalice with one hand, reaching for Yeshua with the other, pulling at his robe.

"Lie with me!" she cried. "I must have satisfaction!"

"Daughter of Eve," Yeshua said, "you are set free from the influence of demons. Behold, all things are new again. You are cleansed from your multitude of sins."

Marah's body shook again, her chest heaving, arching. With a retching sound, she vomited a black mist that rose above her like smoke and dissipated into the night. She relaxed, lying still upon the ground, softly weeping. I bent to pick her up. Yeshua stopped me.

"No, Saruel, for I have set her free. Would you defile her again, so soon after I have cleansed her?"

I looked down at the weeping Marah. Her body was relaxed. The fever was gone, but at what price? In my desperation to help her, I had not considered that I might lose her. Marah looked around her, blinking her eyes as though waking from a dream. Tears streamed down her face. I went to wipe them from her eyes, to hold her and fill her with peace, to tell her how much I loved her, and that I would always love her.

"No, Saruel," Yeshua said. "Salvation belongs to her this night. Would you tempt her away from Heaven? I have redeemed her from certain destruction, released her from her infirmity and cleansed her from a multitude of transgressions. I have made her pure. If you love her, you will let her go. Will you deny her the beauty of Heaven?"

I stared dumbfounded at Yeshua. Marah's gaze fell upon his face and she gasped, lifting to her knees, kneeling before him.

"You are my Lord and my God," she said. Her tears fell in great drops upon his sandaled feet, tears of love and joy. She had never looked more beautiful. Yeshua's eyes met mine. I nodded and turned away, rising silently into the night sky. Alone.

I hovered high above the Mount of Olives, watching them until morning. I hated myself, torn between my need for Marah and my love for her. On one side, she had peace. Erozel's affliction had left her, perhaps for good. She had communion with the Great I Am. On the other side, I could not bear life without her. For her to choose to remain with Yeshua meant the salvation of her very soul and admission to Heaven, a place I longed for her to see. Yet it also meant that the love we shared together was unclean and never meant to be.

I wanted her and loathed myself for wanting her. She was free from her affliction, free from sin, free from me. But what would I do without her? Losing Heaven was terrible enough. Losing Marah would be Hell. I loved her, though, and wanted what was best for her.

When morning came, I tore myself away from watching over Marah and Yeshua, returning to our home in the Towers. Gabrielle heard me when I came in and rushed to meet me.

"Where is my mistress? Is she well?"

"She is well."

"When will she return?"

I did not know how to answer. "I am unsure," I said.

"Then she remains with the healers?"

"Your mistress has left this house for a time. I do not know when she will return."

Gabrielle's eyes went wide. She looked bewildered. "She has left us? This cannot be."

I turned from her. "I will retire to my chambers now," I said.

I entered the bedroom I shared with Marah and shut the door behind me. The delicate bedding, soft fabric of Macedonian purple, held the scent of her aroma.

CHAPTER 34

I returned to my dwelling to find the glass door of my balcony open. I heard the sound of Classical music coming from inside. I landed, watching for any movement, and entered my living room. Azazel sat in Andrew's chair. He wore a finely tailored gray suit, looking every part the modern man. His face held a smile that did not reach his eyes. A glass of red wine stood beside him on the table, next to an empty bottle.

"I helped myself to your delicious wine," he said. "I trust you do not mind. We are brothers, after all."

"Where is my girl?" I said, unable to keep anger out of my voice.

Azazel frowned. "I have come to tell you where to find her, but before I do, let us reason together. I wish for peace between Erozel and you. Will you, eternal brothers, let a mortal woman come between you?"

"You call Erozel my brother? I hate all that he is, all that he stands for. He is rape where I am romance, lust where I am love. He defiles the innocent and despises purity."

"Purity?" Azazel said. "Are you not Fallen? You speak as a holy angel; is your sin not an abomination: coupling with a daughter of Eve? You also broke the law of Heaven."

"Love," I said. "I loved a daughter of Eve. Adam loved Eve, and left his first estate for her. The Creator himself left the glory of Heaven for his love of humankind, taking upon himself the sin of the world. If my love is sinful, at least I am in good company."

Azazel shook his head. "Love again, Saruel; is that all you ever speak of? Love is jealous, and as cruel as the grave, causing more strife than hatred ever could. You are right when you say that Adam fell for love, and because of Adam's love, death came into the world."

"By love was the world made," I said.

Azazel laughed derisively. "You turned two innocent girls over to Sangruel because of your love. If Erozel had sacrificed them upon his altar, would you not have condemned him for it? Yet they are just as dead, whether for love or lust."

"Enough of this," I said, raising my voice. "Tell me where to find her."

"In time, my brother, in time. But first, Erozel requires something from you. He has your girl, and I will tell you where she is when the time is right.

When you go to her, you must take the fruit of the Tree of Life with you."

I stood, speechless. He smiled, seeing my surprise.

"Of course Erozel knows of the fruit," he said, "how else could you have kept her alive this long?"

A shadow moved silently just outside the open balcony door, as Sangruel and Sarai landed together on my patio. They stood, watching us. I kept my eyes on Azazel, who did not notice their arrival.

"Why does Erozel want the Fruit of Life?" I asked.

"It does not matter why," Azazel said. "You will bring the fruit if you wish to see your beloved girl ever again."

"No," I said. "You will tell me where she is."

Azazel frowned. "You are in no position to make demands."

"Tell me, Azazel," I said. "Why did you and the others attack Sangruel?" Azazel looked surprised. "I know what you and the others did to him," I said. "I was the one who removed him from the cross."

"Then you know why, Saruel. Erozel heard that Sangruel gave you help. We punished him for it."

"What you did was cruel," I said. "Sangruel is our brother. How could you do such a thing to him?"

Azazel took a sip of wine, a look of distaste on his face. "He is not my brother," he said, "but a filthy demon, worthy of the abyss. I would that you had left him upon the cross for the morning sun."

The glass of wine flew from Azazel's hand as Sangruel, moving with a speed second only to Hemael's, hit him. Sarai followed Sangruel. Together, they grabbed hold of Azazel. I joined them and we held Azazel, binding him with our collective strength. The chair he sat on broke, and we held him to the floor. He struggled against us, his eyes registering shock, before finding Sangruel.

"Release me!" he cried.

Sangruel hissed, baring his teeth. "No, brother. Am I only a demon in your sight?"

"Let me go!" Azazel said. "This will do your girl no good, Saruel." He turned his face toward Sangruel. "What can you do to me, demon? I do not possess your weaknesses. I do not fear crosses and sunlight. You can hold me, but you cannot harm me."

Sangruel smiled cruelly. "Perhaps you underestimate my strength," he said. "Remember the night of my fall. Consider the terrible curse flowing within my veins."

Bringing his wrist to his mouth, Sangruel tore through his angelic flesh. Dark blood flowed from the open wound. He held his wrist to Azazel's lips. Azazel looked in horror at the blood. Sarai used the fingers of her free hand to ply Azazel's lips apart. She was remarkably strong for someone who had started life as a human being. The blood moved down Sangruel's wrist; a living thing. Azazel screamed, wide eyed, bucking against us. Sangruel held his wrist hard to Azazel's open mouth. The blood flowed into him. Azazel's eyes rolled back into his head. His body shook with terrible spasms, before becoming rigid and stopping altogether.

"What have you done?" I said. "What will become of him?"

Sangruel bared his teeth at Azazel. "My blood is in him and with it the blood of the Fruit of Carnal Knowledge."

"He is not a man," I said. "Surely it will not affect him as it would a mortal."

"We will soon see," Sangruel said. He nodded to Sarai. She released her hold on Azazel and, turning, stepped out onto the balcony, before flying and vanishing into the night.

I looked down at Azazel. His open eyes were turning the color of blood. The nails of his fingers were sharpening to yellow claws.

"I fear that you have made him stronger than he was before," I said.

Sangruel smiled wickedly. "Stronger, yes, but with his new strength comes new weakness."

Azazel let out a feral scream. His mad eyes focused, looking from me to Sangruel. He tried to stand, but Sangruel held him fast to the floor.

"What have you done?" Azazel shouted. He looked down at his hands. "What have you done to me?"

"How does it feel to be a demon, Captain of Watchers?" Sangruel said. "Did you believe yourself above me because you kept your former beauty? Feel the bloodlust; know the fear of the sun. Learn of my curse, walk in my path, for you are once again, and truly, my brother."

Azazel struggled to free himself, lashing out at Sangruel.

"Release me!"

Sangruel narrowed his gaze. "Did I not ask the same of you earlier, on this very night?"

"Your curse is not mine! You desired the fruit, not I. This cannot be!"

Sangruel hissed. "What recourse do you have, demon? You chose to fall, as I once did. No one forced this way upon you. Could I hold a holy angel, as I now hold you? You chose your path, but cannot choose its end. Is your judgment now more than you can bear? I wanted to live as a man. I wanted to dwell on the Earth, to feel the sun upon my skin. Instead, I walk in darkness, a creature of nightmares. Now, you will share in my curse."

Sarai returned, carrying an unconscious young man in her arms. I stepped forward.

"You will not take a life in my presence," I said. Sarai looked at Sangruel, who nodded.

"We will not kill him," he said, "but we must open his veins. Once Azazel tastes living blood, he will always thirst for it."

Azazel looked with terror at the unconscious young man. "I will not drink blood!"

"You will drink," Sangruel said.

Sarai brought the young man to Azazel. Tilting the man's neck back, she bit into his throat. Blood poured. Azazel's eyes grew wide, staring hungrily at the blood.

"Yes," Sangruel said, "you want it."

Azazel tried to pull away. The blood poured, covering his lips and mouth. His chest heaved and arched. His face contorted. His eyes filled with fear, and then madness, as the blood of the man entered his open mouth.

CHAPTER 35

Yeshua grew in fame among the people. The word of his great works and miracles spread to every corner of the known world. Marah did not return to me. My heart was broken. For a time, ever hidden in the ether, not wanting to cause her grief at my sight, I watched her. Wherever Yeshua went, she followed, becoming an accepted member of his closest companions and inner circle of friends. The multitudes knew her, calling her by the name of Miriam of the Towers, a former harlot of Pagan temples, once possessed by a demon, now set free by the hand of Yeshua. I wept when I heard this, for, if the story was true, I was that demon. Rumors ran rampant as Yeshua's followers speculated about his close friendship with Marah. Was the master in love? Would he take her as his wife? It was more than I could bear. Love, however, bears all things, and I loved Marah.

The very presence of Yeshua filled her with joy. She bubbled over with laughter and song. I was happy over her newfound joy and devastated by it at the same time. Did she not long for me? Did she think so little of our many years together? Was this why I left Heaven? Yet, I thought, to be jealous of the Great I Am, robed in flesh though he may be, was absurd. Marah was his daughter, his creation, lost to him and found again. I was pulled in two different ways, jealous of Yeshua's time and communion with Marah and envious, also, of Marah's relationship with Yeshua. In a strange, unforeseen turn of events, the two loves of my life—the Great I Am and Marah—came together without me.

In my grief, I desired solitude and spent much of my time locked away in my chambers, lying upon the bed, which still held Marah's scent, though to an ever-lessening degree. Gabrielle worried over me, preparing food and begging me to eat it, fussing about as though I was no more than a sick child, which is quite the way I felt.

One night, as I sat in my room, there came a slight rapping on my chamber door.

"Enter," I said.

Gabrielle opened the door. Her face showed shyness in the light of the lamp she carried. She was completely naked. Even in the darkness of my room, I saw her blush.

"My master," she said, "I wish to lie with you if you will have me, for I can bear your sorrow no longer."

I turned my face away from her nakedness. "I am faithful to your mistress," I said. "I want no other."

She stood before me, embarrassed by my rejection. Her eyes glistened with tears. She looked down at the floor. "I have never been with a man, for my mistress defiled me in ways no man could forgive. Will you not give me the pleasure of your body? Have I not been a faithful servant to you? As she has abandoned you, she has also abandoned me. My loins burn with desire, having grown used to her abuse. Shall I forever live with such suffering, will I never know satisfaction?"

"My heart belongs only to Marah. I will not share the love I have for her with another."

"I do not require love," she said. "My mistress can have your heart. I want only your body."

"Return to your chamber," I said.

She lowered her eyes, bowed slightly, then left me alone, closing the door behind her. I heard her weeping in the night. When morning came, she served me breakfast without a word.

I spent the days in heartache and the nights in restless thought. To watch Marah caused me the greatest pain, to not watch her was torture. I had no relief. After a time, to distract myself, I sought out Ariel.

I found him in Rome. Caesar's army had returned after a great victory, bringing captive princes and treasures with them to present to the Emperor. Ariel was with them. He wore the uniform of a high-ranking Roman officer, marching along with them as they entered the city; a thousand soldiers dressed in their finest regalia, marching to the gates of the Imperial palace, accompanied by the roar and applause of a celebrating public. I waited until the procession ended before making my presence known.

"Saruel, my brother!" Ariel said when he saw me. He embraced me. "I return from glorious battle!"

"What is glorious about battle?" I said.

He smiled. "Always the same; you will never change. I wish you could know what I know, feel what I feel, admire the courage of the valiant and the violence of the murderous."

"I prefer peace," I said, "and love."

His face fell. His eyes flashed hot. "Perhaps you should join this Adam reborn, the so-called Prince of Peace."

"Let us not quarrel," I said, "for it does my heart good to see you again."

The smile returned to his face. "As it does mine to see you. Perhaps one day you shall join with me in warfare, perhaps not, but you will always be my beloved Saruel."

"That I shall be."

I walked with him.

"Tell me what news there is of this Yeshua," he said.

I considered telling him what I knew to be true. Yeshua was so much more than Adam reborn. My heart filled with pain when I thought about it. How I missed Marah.

"His fame has spread throughout the land. His hands perform miracles. He heals the sick and commands the Fallen. They obey his word."

"Then he truly is the Son of God."

"He is the anointed one," I answered.

Ariel walked in silence for a while, lost in his thoughts.

"I would like to see him," he said. "Lead me to where he dwells."

"You would see him now?"

"Yes, for it is time that I witness his works with my own eyes. Am I not the Prince of War, he the Prince of Peace?"

I hesitated. I wanted nothing more than to see Marah, but the idea of it troubled me.

"Why do you tarry?" Ariel said. "Let us fly to him. Lead the way."

"My brother, perhaps now is not the time."

"And why is that, Saruel? Should I wait to see the anointed one?"

I shook my head.

"Very well, then," he said.

We walked to a remote place on the outskirts of the city and rose together into the air, heading to Israel.

We found him by the Sea of Galilee. Throngs of people surrounded Yeshua, to the extent that it was necessary for him to stand upon a small boat, pushed out a little into the water. From there, he spoke to the people. I had contented myself to watch from the air, but Ariel would have none of it.

"Let us go among the people, to see this Prince of Peace up close," he said.

"You would walk among them dressed as an officer of Rome? That is sure to draw attention our way."

"If that is your only argument, I shall find a change of garments."

He left me. I scanned the throngs around Yeshua for any sign of Marah. She was nowhere in sight and for that, I was both grateful and regretful.

Ariel returned several minutes later, wearing a robe of expensive blue fabric. Small drops of blood stained the cloth near his neck. I motioned to the blood.

"Imagine what violence will happen in this city," he said, "when the Romans find the body of one of their officers, absent his head."

"What have you done?"

"I traded a man my garments for his."

"You left his body dressed as a Roman officer? My brother, the Romans will certainly exact vengeance on innocent people."

"Yes, Saruel, that was my intent."

"Please, Ariel," I said.

"It is done." His eyes were cold, implacable. "Let us see the Prince of Peace."

He lowered to the ground. Reluctantly, I followed. We made our way, unnoticed, through the crowd, drawing closer to where Yeshua spoke from the boat. His voice carried across the water, heard everywhere, even to the tops of the hills.

"Not a stone will be left on top of another," he said. "Many shall say in that day: Peace, peace! Yet destruction will come to them. There shall be wars and rumors of wars. The sun shall be turned into darkness and the moon into blood before the great and notable day of the Lord shall come."

"These are the words of the Prince of Peace?" Ariel said.

Yeshua paused, looking around him, his eyes falling upon Ariel and me.

"Do not think that I have come to bring peace, but a sword. Brother will war against brother, a man's household divided against him. They shall run to the hills for safety, but shall find none. They shall cry out for the stones to fall upon them and crush them in their misery, but the stones will not hear them. As surely as I stand before you, the son of man will be lifted up, bruised fruit on the tree of blood. The Temple of God's glory will be destroyed. He, who hears, let him also understand."

Objections came from a group of pious religious men, a sect of theologians and teachers of Hebrew law. One of them, a heavy man with a long beard cried out to him in accusing tones.

"Do you dare say that the Temple of God will be destroyed? It is blasphemy to speak such things! Surely your words are contrary to the heart of God."

Yeshua looked at the man. "Truly I say that the Temple of God's glory will be destroyed. Yet in three days I shall raise it up again."

The sect of men behind us erupted with cries of "Blasphemy!"

The man tore his own clothing. "Your words are from the dark one," he yelled. "The works that you do are performed by the power of Beelzebub, the lord of darkness!"

"A house divided against its self will not stand; the works that I do come from the Father of Lights. His kingdom is among you, here now, in your sight." Yeshua's gaze fell directly upon Ariel. "The violent shall take it by force."

"Blasphemy!"

Ariel turned to the religious man. "Hold your tongue," he said. The man gave him an angry look. Ariel stepped directly in front of him, his eyes boring into the man. "Hold your tongue, or I shall tear it from your open mouth!"

I placed my hand on Ariel's shoulder. "Let it go, brother," I said.

He turned around, his face full of fire. He pointed his finger at me, trembling.

"You did not tell me! Surely you knew."

"I do not understand your meaning," I said.

He pointed at Yeshua. "He is not Adam reborn. He is the very presence of the I Am. His body is the Temple of Heaven. Yeshua is the Kingdom of God!" His face contorted. His eyes looked both frightened and pained. "I am the violent one. It is I who will take him by force. It is I who will cause the Temple of God to be destroyed!"

"This cannot be," I said.

"It is, Saruel. I heard him deep inside my being. For this very purpose I was created."

"You were created a Watcher of Heaven."

Ariel shook his head.

"No. We all do his will. Even our rebellion, our terrible fall, all of it is part of his master plan."

He turned from me and walked away.

"Ariel," I called. He did not turn around.

The religious men saw Ariel's departure as a chance to continue their verbal assault on Yeshua and began again to accuse him of blasphemy.

Yeshua held up his hands. Several of his closest disciples waded into the water, climbing onto the boat with him. Marah was among them. Where she had come from, I do not know. I had not seen her earlier. Yeshua took her by the hand and lifted her from the water. She sat beside him. She was so beautiful, wearing a robe of light green against her white skin, her autumn hair. Her smile, not meant for me, but for Yeshua.

The disciples paddled the boat out into the water, away from the land, heading toward the other side of the Sea of Galilee. They lifted the sail and the wind took hold of it.

Marah looked with love upon Yeshua as the boat carried them away.

CHAPTER 36

Azazel fed upon the young man, grunting and swallowing, feverishly sucking at the wound in the man's throat, bringing to my mind the image of Eve devouring the Fruit of Carnal Knowledge, her lust unfettered, dark blood pouring from her greedy mouth.

"Enough!" I said. "You will not commit murder in my dwelling."

Sangruel waved a hand in Sarai's direction, and she pulled the young man away from Azazel, who looked at her with pleading eyes. Blood poured down his chin, staining the front of his fine white shirt. The color of his skin, ashen and pale before he fed, took on a healthy hue.

"More," he begged, "I must have more!"

"You shall have more, my brother," Sangruel said, "all that you desire, after you divulge the location of Erozel and his mistress."

Azazel turned toward Sangruel. "You force your curse upon me and then demand that I help you? I refuse."

"You will not refuse," I said. "Erozel is no longer your master."

Azazel glared at me, his eyes red with blood. "You will never see your precious girl again."

I knelt down, grabbing him by the collar of his shirt. "She has wronged no one. What does Erozel want with her?"

"Her very life is an affront to him. She lived and Asherah died. Did you believe he would never discover the truth?"

I stood up, releasing my hold on him. "Where is she?"

"I will not tell."

I placed my hand in my pocket, feeling the iron cross I had removed from Sangruel's neck.

"You are forever altered, a creature of the night. Erozel will despise you as he does Sangruel."

Azazel glared at me with pure hatred. "It is not out of loyalty to Erozel that I refuse to help you. I long to see you brought down to the abyss. I will delight in your suffering. I tire of your self-righteous judgment."

Moving quickly, I pulled the cross from my pocket, holding it up to Azazel. Sangruel hissed, turning away in terror. Her teeth bared, eyes averted, Sarai stepped between Sangruel and me, protecting him from the view of the cross.

Azazel stared fixedly at the cross, unable to look away. He looked both puzzled and terrified. His body shook, his face grimaced in pain. He struggled to turn away, but could not. I stepped directly in front of him, holding the cross inches from his face.

"Sangruel was cursed twice," I said, "firstly for partaking of the blood of the fruit and secondly for drinking the blood of the Son of God. I see that the curse carried to you through his blood."

I inched the cross slowly toward him. It felt suddenly hot in my hand. "Where is Marah? Tell me, or I swear by all that is holy that I will fasten this cross around your demon neck and fly with you into the light of the sun."

"Please," Azazel said, his voice shaking. Bloody tears formed in his eyes. "We are brothers."

I pushed the iron cross hard against his brow. It made a hissing sound, burning into his angelic flesh. Black tendrils of smoke rose from the cross. Azazel screamed. Tears of blood poured from the corners of his eyes. I pulled the cross away from his charred flesh, holding it in front of him.

"You will tell me," I said, surprised at the coldness in my voice. I moved the cross toward him again. He cried out.

"Corruption!" he cried, staring with terror at the cross in my hand. "You are to meet him in the place where his love met corruption."

I looked down at Azazel's pitiful image. How had I ever called this pathetic creature my captain? I returned the cross to my pocket. Azazel fell, face down on the floor. I turned to Sangruel.

"I will not forget this," I said.

"Go in peace, Watcher," Sangruel answered.

CHAPTER 37

I remained in the chambers Marah and I had shared. Gabrielle worried for me, bringing me food and water. I ate and drank nothing. Her troubled face etched with worry and distress at my state. She brought full plates and gathered full plates again. I waved away her worries and pleas for me to eat.

After a few weeks, she was troubled about more than my welfare. Her eyes fell on my perfectly healthy face and body, which showed no signs of weakness or weight loss. I had sat for weeks, motionless upon my bed. I had not bathed or shaved, yet I was perfectly groomed and fresh. I knew it was important to hide my true nature from her, but I no longer cared about such things.

I have listened to lectures and read the works of theologians and scholars over the years, interested always in those whose work and study focused on angels and demons. There are as many fallacies as there are truths in such theology.

Why would angels fall? Once Fallen, did angels retain their power and beauty? Did they dwell with humankind or were they cast into Hell? You now know the answers to many of these questions.

I retain my power and immortality, a curse as much as a blessing. Had the Creator stripped me of immortality and power, forcing me to live as a man lives, had my memories faded over time, my punishment, my fall would be much easier to endure. I remember everything in detail. My memory never fails. Time does not diminish it. I recall Heaven with unerring clarity, the sights, colors, smells, beauty beyond mortal imagination, making the most glorious sunset appear by comparison as the darkest night.

I remember my creation, the very moment I heard the tender voice of the Great I Am and looked upon His face. I know exactly what I am missing, every painful detail. Men lose their loved ones, to death, to the arms of others, but with time, most wounds heal. Broken hearts mend as memories fade. I dwell in eternal fall. My angelic heart, once broken, will never heal. The memory of my loss will never fade. I remembered the day I first saw Marah—the feelings, new and wonderful, that sprang to life in me when first I touched her, held her close to me; the sound of her singing, the sweetness of her lips, her face, her form, her grace, her loving kindness and warmth.

Through the window, I watched the early morning light give way to midday. Darkness fell, giving way again to morning, day after day, night after night, week after week. Marah did not return to me.

Jealousy gripped me at the thought of her with Yeshua, though I understood the absurdity of it, for my own heart longed to dwell with him. He was not a man, though in every way he was. I longed for both Marah and the I Am. To have both would answer my every prayer. Forced to choose, well, I already made that choice. In doing so, I lost them both.

One night, Gabrielle came in to remove my untouched food. I saw the worry and fear in her face. I remembered the things Marah had done to her on the very bed where I sat. Overcome with emotion, I wept. Gabrielle placed the plate down and, sitting beside me, put her arms around my neck, holding me close to her. I allowed my tears to flow, my heart to break in front of her. She wept with me.

"I love her, too," she said. "I love you both."

She kissed my face, ran her fingers through my hair. For the first time, I realized her hurt. How we had wronged her. She loved us as her own family, having no husband or children of her own. She had only been with Marah and, despite the abuse, loved her.

I returned her kiss. "I have wronged you," I said.

She looked at me, her shoulders quavering. "You have not wronged me," she said. "I was free to leave at any time. I remain here, a servant not of compulsion, but of love."

"Yet you have never known a man, never had a child."

"I would not trade what I had with my mistress or with you. I wish only that I had more, that my mistress remained with us. I desire her touch, whether cruel or tender."

I stood up from the bed for the first time in weeks. "You must know. I am not a man, not a son of Adam."

She nodded, wiping her eyes.

"My lord, in my heart I knew this, but only now, seeing you these many weeks in your grief, do I realize it. You neither eat nor drink, yet you wither not."

"I am an angel come from Heaven."

She stared at me for a long time, wondering at my words.

"I love you no matter what you are," she said.

I took her by the hand and pulled her gently to her feet. She stood before me, trembling. I removed her robe, letting it fall to the floor, exposing her naked body. I removed my own robe. We stood, looking at each other, two broken hearts seeking comfort. I leaned into her and she pressed herself against me. I guided her back to bed, my lips finding her neck, her breasts, my member pressing hard against her. She arched her hips, pushing her chalice toward me.

"Take me, my lord, enter me!"

She spread her legs wide and I entered her. She gasped, her eyes wide, her chalice pushing against my member, desiring more. I gave myself to her in my agony and grief, our hearts broken by the same woman. I pushed thoughts of sorrow away from me, losing myself in her body. Passion masked my pain and I devoured and ravished her, tenderly, dominating, lovingly, greedily. Gripped in ecstasy, she cried out, her body a spasm of pleasure, her juices flowing onto the bed I had shared with Marah. She pressed herself against me and I held her as she wept in my arms. In time, she fell asleep.

She awakened in my arms. Morning light shone through the window. She blinked sleep from her eyes and looked up at me. I kissed her.

"My lord," she said, "let me arise and serve you. Eat something today, I pray you. Move from this bed, this chamber."

"I will eat," I said.

We breakfasted together in the sun on the rooftop. She glowed with happiness and it warmed me to see it. She stood up and, coming behind where I sat, held me in a soft embrace.

"My lord, it is not too late for you. The world has never known a love like the love between my master and my mistress."

"She is gone from me," I said.

"She could not leave you anymore than her spirit could leave her soul, or her marrow could leave her bone. Go to her now, find her and you will see."

I looked at Gabrielle, my eyes filling with tears. "You are a good and faithful servant."

"I love my master and mistress," she said.

I rose into the air, hovering above her. She cried out in astonishment and wonder. I flew from her, looking back to see her on the rooftop, watching me as I went.

I found Yeshua in the city of peace. More and more people followed him, having heard the tales of his mighty miracles and teaching. He was easy to find. Wherever the crowds were, he was. In order to rest, he went into the hills, his disciples doing their best to keep people at bay. I flew high into the air and landed by where he sat alone, resting against a tree.

"Saruel," he said. "Why are you here? You have had your reward."

"Lord of Heaven," I said. I knelt on the ground, my head bowed. "Was my reward to lose the one I love?"

"I delivered her from the bonds of forbidden love."

"Then she no longer loves me? Please, I wish only to hear it from her lips with my own ears. Then will I seek her no more."

"Heaven belongs to her. Will you pry it from her hands? Should she choose to dwell with you, never knowing the joys of your former home? Is that love?"

"If she chooses Heaven, then I will not deter her, for my love is not selfish. I wish only to see her, to speak with her once more."

Yeshua looked at me.

"I have renewed her, cleansed her of all that was before. She remembers nothing of her time with you."

His words gave me hope. "Then that is why she did not return to me," I said.

"Perhaps," Yeshua said.

"Should she not be allowed to choose? You are the Tree of Life in her garden. With only one tree, she has but one choice. How can she decide between Heaven and our love, if she is not aware of my existence?"

"Do you want for her to choose? If you let her go, she will never know sorrow and will never die. She will be with me in Heaven."

I shook my head. "I want her to know Heaven as I once did. I long for her and to be without her is, to me, Hell itself. Yet, I love her more than I love the joy she brings to me."

Yeshua looked thoughtfully at me. "Is that your decision then, Fallen spirit?"

"It is," I said.

"Then depart in peace."

I bowed low to the ground before him, then, standing, I lifted into the air.

CHAPTER 38

Though I chose live without Marah, my heart still longed for her. My thoughts could not escape her. From time to time, wanting only to see her again, I watched over Yeshua, knowing she would be nearby.

One night, I hovered above the Garden of Gethsemane. At the base of the Mount of Olives, campfires burned as followers of Yeshua made ready for the night. Marah was not among them. I turned to leave, but movement caught my eye.

Two shadowy figures hovered in the air on opposite sides of the mountain, their hooded faces staring silently down at the Earth below them. They were Sangruel and Hemael. They had returned, each to the place of his particular curse: Sangruel above the place of the skull, where once stood the Tree of Carnal Knowledge; Hemael above where the Tree of Life had grown.

Yeshua, wearing a robe of white, knelt on the ground, a stone's throw away from three of his sleeping followers. He was weeping, his eyes turned toward Heaven.

"Let this cup pass from me. Am I not a man? Is she not a woman? Must I turn myself over to death? Must my blood be poured out for others?"

He looked up at Sangruel, who hovered in the shadows above the place of the skull. "Those who desire my blood can wait for another time."

He turned, looking toward Hemael. "Those who seek my life can wait. Father! My spirit is willing, though my flesh is weak."

I watched, my heart aching, for I once stood upon that very ground, facing the same choice. I had chosen Marah over the wonders of Heaven. Would Yeshua follow the will of God, or the desire of his heart?

"Father!" he called. Sweat poured from his brow. He buried his face in his hands and wept, groaning. Great drops of blood fell from his brow. He stared down at the blood, trembling. "Nevertheless," he said, "not my will, but yours be done."

He stood to his feet, wiping the remaining blood from his face and hands with the hem of his garment. After nudging his three followers awake, he walked with them to the camp below. From my spot above the garden, I saw a band of men carrying swords and torches, temple guards and officials, heading toward the Garden of Gethsemane.

Yeshua reached the camp moments before they did. He stood, looking in their direction, waiting. The band of men stopped under the shadow of a large tree. One of them, a close follower of Yeshua, walked to where he stood and greeted him with a kiss. Yeshua held him close. Tears filled his eyes.

"Do you betray the son of man with a kiss?"

The guards and temple officials moved from their hiding place and surrounded Yeshua. The captain of the guards stepped in front of him. "We seek the one called Yeshua of Nazareth. Are you that man?"

Yeshua held his hands out to them. "Did I not walk freely among you and teach in your synagogues? Do you now come to me in the night with drawn swords?"

"Are you Yeshua of Nazareth?" The captain of the guards demanded. Yeshua met his eyes. Fear and astonishment filled the man's face. He stepped back, lowering his head.

"I Am he," Yeshua said. At his words, the guards and temple officials fell backward, knocked off their feet by an unseen force. Yeshua looked down at them. "Arise," he said. The captain of the guards stood, looking troubled. He bowed his head and put his sword away.

"My Lord," he said. "I do only what I am commanded to do."

Yeshua placed his hand on the man's arm. "Do not fear. I will go with you."

CHAPTER 39

"Crucify him! Crucify him!"

The Fallen swarmed like shadowy vultures in the skies above Jerusalem, looking down at the shouting mob below. The Watchers walked as men in the streets, mingling among the crowd. Ariel stood near the seat of judgment, watching the Roman Governor, Pontius Pilate. I stood with the crowd, my head and face covered with a shawl.

Roman soldiers had draped a purple cloak across Yeshua's shoulders in mockery. They placed a crown of thorns roughly upon his head, crying, "Behold the king!"

Dark blood soaked through his white robe. Blood poured from where the crown of thorns cut deep into his scalp. His legs trembled under the weight of his body. His hands, which had known no violence, were shackled together in front of him. He kept his eyes toward Heaven.

The governor raised a hand to quiet the crowd. Soldiers brought him a basin of water and he made a great play of washing his hands before the people, holding them up while a servant dried them.

"My hands are free of blood! May the blood of this righteous man be upon you and upon your children."

"Let it be!" Several in the crowd shouted, "Upon us and upon our children!"

The governor turned to the Roman centurion. "What you must do, do quickly."

At the centurion's order, soldiers released the shackles from Yeshua's wrists. They forced him to carry a heavy wooden beam, the instrument of his own execution. He struggled with it, carrying as much of it as he could on his shoulders, dragging the rest through the dust behind him. The mob surrounded him, jeering at him, laughing and cursing, kept barely at bay by the armed soldiers. Music played in the streets and children danced.

I heard Marah's voice.

"Yeshua! My Lord!"

I turned to see her. She pushed against the jostling crowd, trying to see him through the chaos, her eyes red with weeping. She wore mourning robes of black. Miriam, the mother of Yeshua and two other women walked with her.

I wanted to help Yeshua, to relieve him of his burden and minister to his wounds. He fell several times under his heavy burden. Each time, the crowd shouted their approval and the soldiers kicked him, pulling him roughly to his feet by the hair of his head. His wounds bled freely, staining the white of his robe dark crimson. He reached the foot of Golgotha.

I stared with horror at what I saw. Ariel waited on top of the stony cliff, above the place of the skull. He wore the uniform of a high-ranking Roman officer and carried with him an iron spear. Yeshua stumbled, falling to the ground under the cruel gaze of the skull, trembling, exhausted. The soldiers kicked him, cursing.

"Enough!" Ariel commanded in a loud voice. The soldiers recognized his uniform and stopped their assault. "Find a man to help the condemned carry his burden."

One of the soldiers pulled a young man from the crowd and placed the beam of wood upon his shoulder.

"Carry your king's load," he ordered. The young man cursed in anger and spat on the ground at Yeshua's feet.

"I serve only Caesar. This man is no king!"

The soldier prodded the man forward with the tip of his sword. Yeshua stood, his legs shaking, his face turned to a silent Heaven. Earth groaned under my feet. Dark clouds formed to the east. Step after painful step, Yeshua climbed the stony path to the top of Golgotha.

Yeshua looked at the young man who carried his burden. The young man glared back with defiant hatred. Yeshua reached out and touched him. His face was tired, caked with dust and blood. His eyes filled with love. He spoke softly, words only the two of them heard. The hatred in the young man's face vanished, replaced by terrible sorrow. He fell to his knees before Yeshua and wept.

As Ariel watched, the soldiers stripped Yeshua of his garments. He stood, naked, his bruised and beaten flesh exposed for all to see. Bone and sinew showed in places where the whip had removed the flesh of his back. Miriam, his mother, cried out at the sight. The soldiers placed a second beam on the rocky ground, twice the height of the beam Yeshua had carried, notched near the top to accompany the shorter beam. Connecting the two beams, they formed a cross of about twelve feet in length. They turned to Ariel, waiting for instructions. Ariel looked out over the mob, his eyes falling upon me. Finally, he pointed his spear at Yeshua.

"Crucify him," he said.

"My Lord!" Marah called, pulling Miriam, Yeshua's mother, by the hand as she pushed through to the front of the mob.

My heart broke. How had it ever come to this? I fell to my knees in the dust and wept, not only for Yeshua, but also for Marah and Ariel.

The soldiers took hold of Yeshua, forcing him down, the cross against his naked back, pulling his arms out wide. Though agony showed on his face, he did not resist. I looked again in the direction of Heaven. Where was his deliverance? The only angels in the sky were Fallen. Their lord flew from the eastern skies to a spot high above the place of the skull.

I heard the steady pounding of iron against iron. Yeshua screamed, loud and anguished. The crowd shouted. I looked at Marah. Miriam wept in her arms. An iron spike fastened Yeshua's right arm to the cross at the wrist. His eyes rolled back into his head. The soldier with the hammer threw water on Yeshua's face and shook him back to consciousness.

"You do not want to miss this," he said with a cruel smirk.

He drove the second spike into Yeshua's left wrist fastening it to the rugged wood. Again, Yeshua screamed. Dark clouds filled the eastern skies, moving toward Golgotha. The Earth trembled under my feet, groaning. Lightning flashed in the distance, followed by thunder.

I stared at Yeshua, horrified. His body convulsed, his legs bucking against the soldiers, who struggled to hold them in place, crossing one leg over the other. A soldier held a long, thick iron spike to the spot where his leg joined his foot. The soldier with the hammer drove the spike through, fastening both legs to the wood. Yeshua's screaming was unbearable. His body jerked against the spikes, causing him even more torture. The soldiers worked together, lifting the cross, before placing it into a carved hole in the rocky ground.

The mob jeered at him.

"If you are the Son of God, save yourself! Come down from the cross!"

"You saved others. Save yourself!"

Yeshua looked toward Heaven again. He cried out with a loud voice in the Aramaic tongue. "My God, my God, why have you forsaken me?" He scanned the crowd below him, finding his mother near the foot of the cross. "Mother, behold your son."

"My son! My darling boy!" Miriam wailed, her hands reaching up to him. She fell to her knees, Marah embracing her. Yeshua looked at Marah.

"Miriam of the Towers," he said, using the Greek word for the Towers, Magdala. I remained on my knees, my face hot with tears. His eyes found mine. Turning again to her, he said:

"Remember."

Her eyes grew wide. Her hand went to her heart and it appeared she would faint. Her face turned pale. She looked up to the sky, searching for me.

Yeshua cried with a loud voice. "Two trees, one spirit, the other flesh." He looked down at his broken body. "Behold before you, the tree of blood and the tree of life, blood and spirit."

"He is mad!" someone shouted.

Yeshua looked at the mob below him. His face held compassion, love.

"My tongue cleaves to the roof of my mouth."

Ariel turned to the soldiers. "Give him drink."

One of the soldiers produced a goblet of iron, filling it with the drink customary for crucifixion, vinegar and gall. He soaked a small piece of cloth in the liquid, fastened it to a wooden pole and held it up for Yeshua to drink. Yeshua looked toward Heaven and cried out.

"My enemies compass about me. They wag their heads and gnash their teeth. They cast lots for my garments and give me vinegar for drink."

When Yeshua refused the drink, the soldier lowered the pole and spilled the vinegar onto the ground. Tears mixed with the blood on Yeshua's face. He stared down at the crowd.

"Father, forgive them. They do not know what they are doing!" He looked down at his mother and Marah. "Into your hands I release my spirit. It is finished."

He hung his head and died, suspended between Heaven and Earth. I remembered the Garden of Eden. Adam, newly created, speaking with the I Am.

"Is what he said true, Father? Will I, too, fall beyond redemption?" The I Am said nothing. He held his hands out wide and hung his head.

Miriam, Yeshua's mother, wept. Marah stood, unmoving, her eyes fastened upon the cross. I did not know what I expected. Perhaps that he would spring to life again and remove himself from the cross. Perhaps the angels of Heaven would come to Earth to claim his body and exact vengeance on his executioners. The soldier who had nailed him to the cross stood before the people, pointing up at Yeshua. He laughed with scorn.

"He died as a dog, not a king!"

I had to stop myself from killing him where he stood. Father, forgive them...

Ariel stepped toward Yeshua, the spear in his hand. With one fluid movement, he pierced Yeshua's side with the spear. Blood and water flowed freely from Yeshua's side in impossible amounts, streaming down the length of the cross. I turned to see the Son of the Morning lowering in the sky, triumph upon his face.

There was an earthquake.

Taken by surprise, I lifted several feet into the air before I could stop myself. The crowd of people fell to the ground, as the earth below them shook and rolled. Stones fell from the cliff above, hitting several people. The dark clouds rolled in from the east, eclipsing the sun. Day became night, as if nature herself wished to cover Yeshua's shame. Chaos ensued. The crowd panicked, running in every direction, trampling the ones who fell, reduced from a murderous mob to frightened sheep without a shepherd.

A figure darker than pitch landed before the cross, his shadowy robes flowing about him, hiding his face. His bony hand, white marble, stretched out to Yeshua. A mist of light the colors of God's rainbow flowed in torrents from Yeshua's body to Hemael. The Earth groaned again, shaking violently as Hemael lifted into the air with Yeshua's spirit, flying toward the abyss. I watched him until he vanished over the horizon. All at once, the Earth settled, the quaking stopped.

I heard people screaming as new terrors set upon them in the darkness. Shadows moved among the crowd with preternatural speed, wolves among the sheep. Half a dozen servants of Sangruel fell upon the frightened people, tearing throats open in a frenzied lust for blood. Two of them sprang upon the soldier who had driven the nails into Yeshua. He screamed in wide-eyed terror, as one tore his arm from his body while the other sank sharp teeth deep into his scalp. Sangruel stood at the heart of the slaughter.

Everywhere, men and women ran, stumbling in the darkness, trying to escape the horrors around them. I searched for Marah and found her sitting on the ground, yards away from the cross, holding Miriam in her arms. I flew to them just in time to stop a servant of Sangruel who was moving toward Marah. Taking hold of him, I pushed with all my might, propelling him far into the air. I knelt before Marah.

"Do not fear. I have come."

Marah squinted to see me in the darkness.

"Saruel," she said.

Sangruel stood in the midst of his servants, no more than twenty feet from us. He stared steadfast, eyes upon the cross and the blood flowing from the wound in Yeshua's side.

"Life is in the blood," he said.

It was the night of his curse all over again. The land had succumbed to the seasons and elements, no longer the lush paradise it had once been, but the image of the skull remained. The rugged cross, dripping with holy blood, stood where the Tree of Carnal Knowledge once had.

Sangruel stood before the cross. His servants joined him. Fresh blood covered their faces and garments. They were very old, judging by the way they dressed and their mannerisms, made by Sangruel perhaps hundreds of years earlier. One of them, a Phoenician by his looks, spoke.

"Master, you do not feed."

Sangruel did not answer. His attention remained on the cross.

His servant looked up at Yeshua. "Does my master desire the blood of this man? He has succumbed to death. Speak the word and I shall find you living blood."

"Living blood," Sangruel said more to himself than to his servant. "He is the life and life is in the blood."

"Your desire is my command," the Phoenician said. Looking around him, he found the goblet the soldier had abandoned. He picked it up and approached the cross, placing the goblet against it, catching Yeshua's blood.

He turned to Sangruel and bowed low before him, offering the goblet of blood. Sangruel took the goblet from him and raised it to his lips. He drank. He lowered the goblet, his lips wet with Yeshua's blood.

At first, nothing happened.

Sangruel dropped the goblet as if it had suddenly burned him. He stared down at it. The Phoenician before him trembled violently. His flesh boiled, his body writhed under his skin. Black smoke filled the air around him and blood poured from the corners of his eyes. He burst into flames, thrashing, screaming. Fire sprang from the cross, engulfing Sangruel and his servants. A tortured cry escaped Sangruel's lips as he lifted, a burning effigy, into the dark sky, fleeing the cross. His servants tried to follow, but fell, consumed by the flames, never to rise again. Sangruel's pale skin was charred black, falling away from his body. His face melted, twisting as he flew, a fiery skeleton with sharp, wicked teeth.

I took Marah's hand and pulled her to her feet.

"Take Yeshua's mother and return to the city." She gave me a look of deep sorrow. "Go," I said.

She nodded and turned from me, leading Miriam by the hand. She looked once more toward the cross. Her gaze fell on the goblet lying below it. Quickly, she picked it up, hiding it in her robes. I stayed behind, looking up at the lifeless image of our Creator. What men had done to him! I knelt down on my knees and prayed.

Ariel landed next to me. He placed his hand on my shoulder. I pulled away from him.

"You lifted your spear against the Great I Am!"

He did not answer. He looked up at Yeshua.

"How could you do such a thing? He was pure and holy. He showed only love, brought only good will."

His eyes remained on Yeshua. "Saruel, my brother," he said. I moved away from him in my anger. No brother of mine. He looked at me. "Piercing his side is the one holy thing I have done since my fall."

"Holy! You call it holy?"

"It is holy and good to perform the will of the Great I Am. As hard as it may be to understand, this is his will and doing. He made me for this purpose and he was born to this end. Is it by accident or chance that his cross stands above the place of the skull, where Eve gave her life to know Adam, and Adam his life to remain with Eve? You speak always of love. Is there any greater love than that a man would lay down his life for another?

I lifted from the Earth without another word, leaving Ariel, searching for Marah.

I followed her to the house where Miriam stayed. I waited. The door to the rooftop balcony opened, and Marah stepped outside, standing alone, her eyes searching the dark skies. I hovered a moment, absorbed by her beauty, before revealing myself. Her eyes were red and swollen with weeping. Dust covered her black robes. I heard the voices of men and women mourning inside the house.

I lowered slowly to the rooftop, and landed beside her. She looked at me, her face filled with the most terrible pain and sorrow. I wanted to hold her, comfort her with the peace of angels, but I did not. I stood wordlessly before her. She looked at me with a mixture of love and heartache.

"I did not remember you," she said. A single tear ran down her face. "You must have thought that I had abandoned you."

"It was, perhaps, for the best," I said.

She reached out, caressing my face with her hand, and then turned away.

"I never thought it possible that I could feel this way about another. I love you, Saruel, and always have."

"And now?"

She turned back to me, clasping her hands together.

"I still love you, but I love another as well."

"Yeshua," I said.

She nodded, meeting my gaze.

"He is the Great I Am," I said. "Loving him is the duty and pleasure of all creation. He is not just a man."

"Yet he is a man. He was born of woman, raised as a boy, like any other. He knows hurt, he knows sorrow and is acquainted with grief. He loves as a man loves."

I stared at Marah in disbelief.

"He is the God of All That Is. His mere Word called me into light from the shadows on the day that He made me. Have you stolen the heart of the one who sits upon Heaven's throne? Is it even possible?"

"He declared his love for me and I accepted it. I knew you not. Your love was as far from my memory as the east from the west."

I was dumbstruck, reeling with what she said.

"Did you couple with the holy one?"

She shook her head. "There was no sin in him. He loved me with all purity of heart and soul, as I loved him." She hid her face in her hands, taken again with weeping. "What good was any of it? Murderous hands have taken him from me. Will my eyes never see him again?"

I placed my arms around her and she did not resist. "I, also, must confess," I said. "In mutual grief your servant Gabrielle, and I, sought comfort in each other's arms. We both love you and were heartbroken."

Marah stepped back from me, lowering her eyes. "It sickens me to recall the things I did to her. How could she love me? I was a beast to her, filled with unnatural longing and sins of the flesh." She looked up at me. "It is a good thing that you showed her kindness and shared yourself with her."

"What do we do now?" I said. "Will you dwell with me again or walk in the new path Yeshua placed your feet upon? I covet Heaven's light for you, though I myself behold it not again. You will dwell in Heaven's grace and behold the face of the I Am. You shall see Him as He is."

She turned her face toward the place of the skull. "I do not know," she said.

I returned to the Towers, leaving Marah with Yeshua's mother and his followers. Gabrielle heard me come in.

"My lord," she said, bowing. I lifted her up by the hand. "You are distraught," she said, "what has happened?"

"I spoke with Marah," I said.

Gabrielle's face lit up. "My mistress! Is she well? Will she return to us?"

I shook my head. "I do not know, for she loves another. The flame of that love may burn brighter than her love for me."

Gabrielle looked crestfallen. "Surely not! For her heart belongs to only you."

"The one she loves holds my heart in his hands as well. She will make her choice and I will support her in whatever path she chooses."

Gabrielle stood on her toes to kiss me, holding my face in her hands. "She will choose you." She then stepped away from me, dropping her gaze, frowning nervously.

"What is it, Gabrielle?"

"My lord," she said, "do not be angry with me, for I know you are not a son of Adam and such knowledge causes me great fear."

"Fear not," I said.

She looked up at me. "I am with child," she said.

The news of Gabrielle's pregnancy astonished me. I had coupled with Marah year after passing year without producing offspring, never considering that Marah might have been barren. Gabrielle had the glow of a woman with child. I placed a hand on the growing roundness of her belly.

She studied my face. "Are you displeased?"

The child kicked within her; my child. I could scarcely believe it.

"I am pleased," I said. I held her close to me. "It is a wondrous gift."

I thought of Marah. What would her reaction be? It was one thing for me to couple with Gabrielle. Marah had done far more than that with her. Had Marah wanted children? I did not know. What of the child, would it be like me? Could such an offspring ever know Heaven? Most of the children born to the Watchers were as wicked as they were.

"I am not a man," I said, "and the child within you is unlike the children of men. It will grow very quickly. You must rest. I will hire a chambermaid to wait upon you."

"Yes, my lord," she said.

Bending down, I kissed her belly. The child moved beneath my kiss. "Call me Saruel," I said. "You are the mother of my child."

I found the daughter of a poor widow woman, a girl of about sixteen years, and hired her to serve Gabrielle.

CHAPTER 40

I returned to Jerusalem the next morning, to the home where Marah stayed. I hoped to see her, but she never came out. I flew to Golgotha, finding the skies around Jerusalem thick with the presence of the Fallen, a dark cloud hovering high above the Garden Tomb.

Feeling the eyes of the Fallen on me, I lowered to the ground, pulling my shawl over my head, walking as a man. Roman soldiers barred the entrance to the garden. Several more guarded the tomb itself. A large stone covered the mouth of the tomb. Followers of Yeshua tried to enter the garden from time to time, but the soldiers stopped them.

A group of women in black mourning garments stood a distance away. Miriam was among them. She stared in the direction of the tomb with sad eyes. I made my way to the women, offering the customary greeting of peace.

"Peace be with you," they replied. Miriam remained silent. I followed her gaze to Yeshua's tomb.

"He was your son," I said. She nodded. Her face twisted in sorrow. I placed my hand on her shoulder. "Be at peace, Mother." I felt her relax a little under my touch. She turned to me. I lowered my hand.

"Who are you?"

"I am Saruel, your servant."

"I have seen you before," she said. "Did you follow him? Are you a believer?"

"Yes," I said. "I believe, and tremble."

Her eyes brimmed with tears. She looked again at the tomb and the Roman soldiers guarding it. "They will not let me near him. I want only to see him before his body knows corruption." She buried her face in her hands and wept. "Forgive me, sir, but I am brokenhearted. It was not supposed to end this way. My son is dead."

"Let me assure you, Mother," I said. "It is not the end. You of all people should know who he is. I heard him say with my own ears that the Temple of God's glory would be destroyed and in three days he would raise it up again."

The women standing with Miriam turned toward Herod's Temple. I shook my head.

"No, dear women, not a temple built by hands, but one in which flesh and blood is the dividing veil. Did you not hear that the veil in Herod's Temple rent in two in the same hour that Yeshua died? The true Temple of God was destroyed, but shall be raised again on the third day."

Miriam looked at me, wiping tears from her eyes. "Can this be?" she said.

I took her by the hand. "If anyone knew him, you did."

Hope battled grief on her face, as she considered my words. She glanced at the tomb again. Releasing her hand, I flew from her as fast as I could. To the women with her, I appeared to vanish. I smiled at their astonished gasps. I slowed, hidden from sight above them. Below me, Miriam rejoiced.

Did I not tell you that I am no devil?

I heard a sound in the air to my left and turned to see the Son of the Morning. His face showed madness. Madness is the word. To think that any creature would venture to usurp the place of the Great I Am! He halted, hovering in front of me.

"I heard your foolish words, Watcher. Why do you comfort the woman with lies and false hope? The Son of God is dead. Why do you side against me? I am not the one who bound you to the Earth. You are Fallen, your sin equal to mine in Heaven's eyes. Be glad of my victory. Join me and together we shall take Heaven by force."

"You call my words foolish? You of all angels know the great power of God. He had no beginning and shall have no end. He spoke the universe into existence. By His thought and spoken word, you and I have life. Only by His mercy do we continue to live."

The Lord of the Fallen answered.

"You speak true. I know His power like no other angel. I have lived longer than any other creature. I beheld all creation and saw what is beyond the veil of the Holy of Holies. I have not lost my sanity, Watcher. I know what you do not. What I know could bring Heaven to its knees."

"Though you lived a thousand times longer, it would make no difference. He is your Creator. He sits upon the throne. He always has and always will."

A smile formed on his lips. "And yet, for a second time have I destroyed one He calls His son. If He is so powerful, so perfect, how could I do such a thing?"

"Your mouth spews blasphemy," I said, "and you are blind. Do you still believe that Yeshua is Adam reborn, a new creation of God?"

His mouth tightened into a grimace. "He was a man fashioned in the image of the I Am, the second Adam. And he is no more," he said.

"Then seeing, you do not see, and hearing, you do not hear. He was the Son of God. That is true. It is likewise true that he was the son of man. Yet he was so much more. God created me as He created you, calling me into being, bringing me to His bosom."

The Son of the Morning scowled. "What does that have to do with Yeshua?"

I met his eyes with mine. "It was Yeshua who created me. He is the one who called me by my name. He was there."

Several emotions passed across the face of the Lord of the Fallen: mockery, worry, and then fear. "You speak lies," he said. "You cannot know such a thing."

"I speak truth. He knew me. He remembered my creation. He is not just the Son of God. He is the Creator, the Great I Am. I do not understand how. His ways are above my ways, but it is true, nonetheless."

"This cannot be, for he was born a child, a mortal human."

"He watched you fall as lightning from Heaven. With His little finger He cast you into the abyss."

The Son of the Morning looked horrified. "Who told you this? How do you know such a thing?"

I smiled. "Yeshua told me," I said.

CHAPTER 41

Early on the morning of the third day, I flew to the garden. A band of Roman soldiers stood outside the tomb, looking bored with the duty of guarding a dead man. The sun was a faint glow, rising in the east. I saw a multitude of heavenly angels on the horizon, coming with the dawn. The light of their bodies added a shimmer of gold to the rising sun. In the skies opposite to them, the Fallen arrived, their shadows forming a dark cloud. One side of the sky was darkness, the other light. I hovered in the middle. Fallen and holy alike watched the tomb below me. The Lord of the Fallen looked troubled, his eyes roving between the tomb and the angels of Heaven. I saw the faces of holy Watchers among the heavenly angels. They showed little expression, eyes fastened on the scene below. Had I once been so passive?

A white-robed figure flew from where the heavenly angels hovered. A rainbow surrounded his head. He stopped, hovering over the garden, between sky and Earth. The Lord of the Fallen gnashed his teeth, his eyes blazed with anger and madness at the sight of Enoch.

Enoch descended and landed squarely in front of the soldiers. They fell to the ground as if dead. Enoch touched the large stone covering the mouth of the tomb. Looking upward to the heavenly angels, he called, "Who is worthy to remove the stone from the mouth of the tomb?" None answered him. "Is there not one worthy among you?"

He looked directly at me.

"Saruel!" The sound of my name startled me. "Come, for you have been chosen to roll away the stone."

I did not move. I hovered there, confounded by this sudden turn of events. The Lord of the Fallen fastened hateful eyes on me. I looked toward the heavenly multitude. Their expressions were not much different than his was. Finally, I found my voice.

"Enoch, son of the Most High God, I am Fallen, unworthy to roll the stone away from the Master's tomb."

Enoch motioned to the stone.

"Yet you alone ministered to our Lord after his temptation. You caught him when he fell. You are Fallen, a wicked, willful servant cast from Heaven. Still, the Lord has chosen you for this honor. Come, Saruel, Fallen spirit, roll the stone away."

I lowered to the ground in shocked obedience, ignoring hateful murmurings from the Fallen and surprised gasps from the holy. When the soldiers saw me descending, they stood and ran, crying out to a multitude of false gods, some of them my fellow Watchers.

Enoch looked at me with the same sadness he had when I failed to enter the Holy of Holies. I approached the stone with hesitation, sensing the sanctity of my duty. Placing both hands on the great stone, I rolled it away from the mouth of the tomb, revealing pitch darkness inside.

"Behold, Yeshua," Enoch called, "the Great I Am!"

The Fallen shouted curses and denials. I looked up at their lord, the Son of the Morning. He remained silent, focused on the open tomb. The holy angels were likewise surprised at Enoch's proclamation. I returned to my place in the sky, watching the entrance to the tomb.

For several minutes, nothing happened. Nervous laughter grew among the Fallen. The Son of the Morning silenced them. He kept his gaze on Yeshua's tomb. Still, nothing happened. There were questioning looks and murmurs even among the holy angels. Laughter started up again among the Fallen.

Sudden movement above us and a flash of rainbow colored light silenced holy and Fallen alike. Hemael appeared, wrestling with the light, which could be nothing else except Yeshua's spirit. He held it in a failing grip, struggling against it with every bit of his strength. He flew, rolling and falling as he went, dragged along by the spirit. Finally, the angel of death released his hold, falling to the Earth.

Light filled the tomb, every color of the spectrum, brighter than the noonday sun, more lovely than a thousand sunrises. The Lord of the Fallen trembled. The heavenly angels worshiped. In the entrance of the tomb, the light gave way to a form, the silhouette of a man.

Yeshua stepped out.

A rainbow surrounded his head. The light flowed around him, forming a heavenly robe. Darkness fled the skies as the Fallen scattered in every direction, crying in terror. Their lord remained, watching Yeshua with angry eyes. Enoch knelt before Yeshua, bowing his head and worshiping. Yeshua motioned for him to rise. Enoch stood and, turning to the holy angels in the sky above him, shouted with a voice of triumph.

"Behold the mystery of godliness! God became flesh and dwelt among men. He came unto his own and they did not know him, despised and rejected, a man of sorrow and grief. Yet he was wounded for the transgressions of all humankind, bruised for their iniquity. With his blood are they made whole!"

Below me, a solitary figure—a woman in mourning garments, her face veiled—made her way along the path leading to the Garden Tomb. Yeshua spoke to Enoch, who quickly joined the holy angels in the sky. The rainbow and glowing white robes around Yeshua vanished, replaced by a seamless robe of white cloth. He walked to the woman.

"Who do you seek?" he said.

The woman kept her eyes to the ground. "I seek Yeshua, the Nazarene. I have come to anoint his body and to mourn for him."

"Why do you look for the living among the dead?"

For the first time, she looked up at Yeshua. Gasping, she tore the veil from her face, letting it fall to the ground. I nearly fell from where I hovered in the sky. The woman was Marah. She tried to embrace him, but he pulled away from her.

"Do not touch me, for I have not yet returned to Heaven."

"Take me with you," she said.

Tears filled my eyes. She had made her decision. I considered the foolishness of envying the Creator. I shook myself from such thoughts. I would honor Marah's choice, though it condemned me to eternal sorrow.

"It is not yet time," he said. "Go and tell the others what you saw here today. Then return, for there is much I have to show you."

Marah bowed her head. Yeshua vanished in front of her. She lifted her eyes, finding herself alone. She looked into the sky. I made no effort to hide myself.

"Saruel," she said.

I placed both hands over my aching heart.

I had chosen Marah over the loftiest rank and position afforded to my kind. If need be, I would suffer eternal sorrow in exchange for her happiness. I loved Yeshua, as I loved Marah. Yet I could not escape the crushing feeling of loss, the terrible aching of my heart.

Marah returned to the Garden Tomb in the early evening. A fine robe of delicate purple replaced her black robes of mourning. A white flower adorned her hair. She cast furtive glances toward the part of the sky where she had last seen me. I remained a great distance above the Earth, beyond the limits of human sight. Yeshua appeared in front of her as suddenly as he had vanished earlier in the day. When she saw him, her face lit up with joy. She threw her arms around him.

"My love!"

How her words pierced my heart. Still, the joy and delight in Yeshua's face made me glad for him. To me, he was as beautiful as Marah. He returned Marah's embrace, kissing her cheek. She wept and held him close to her.

"The things evil men did to you!" she said.

He wiped her tears with the gentle touch of his hand. "I am alive," he said, "and will return to my place beyond the stars. Come with me, for you must choose."

"I have chosen, my love."

"I cannot accept your choice, for you have chosen without full knowledge. You must see Heaven with your own eyes."

I felt a spark of hope. Perhaps not all was lost. Yeshua held his hand out to Marah. She took his hand. They vanished in the blink of an eye. I tarried for several moments, looking down at the empty Garden Tomb. Would it end this way? Would I spend eternity separated from both Marah and the Creator? The thought paralyzed me. For the first time, I wondered whether I had made the right choice in choosing Marah over Heaven. If I had known the end of it, would I have remained with her, or would I have returned to Heaven to dwell in the Holy of Holies?

I returned to the Towers. Coming into the house, I made my way to Gabrielle's chambers. The young chambermaid bowed her head when I entered. Gabrielle lay upon the bed, great with child, her face aglow. She smiled sweetly at me.

"My lord, come! Look upon your handiwork. See how your child has grown in just these few days!"

"Our child," I said, sitting next to her on the bed. I marveled at the size of her belly. "Not mine, but ours together. I am no longer your lord and master, but Saruel, your lover."

The chambermaid stared at Gabrielle's roundness. "How can this be?" she said.

I turned to her. "I charge you to tell no one about this."

She looked bewildered. "But…"

"Swear to me," I said.

She looked at Gabrielle, and then nodded. "I swear it, my lord."

Gabrielle looked at me. "What news is there of my mistress?"

I frowned. "Marah has abandoned us."

"No, dear Saruel, I cannot believe such a thing. If there ever was eternal love, it is the love shared by you and my mistress. She will return."

"She is gone," I said. "Her affections belong to another. I have lost her."

Gabrielle's brown eyes glistened with tears. She touched my cheek. "She will return to us. You will see."

I bowed my head. "I pray for her sake that she does not."

CHAPTER 42

Yeshua returned to Earth without Marah. I watched him every day until his final ascension into Heaven forty days later. I had to stop myself from flying to him, begging him to return Marah to me, as he lifted from Earth in clouds of glory. How I longed for her. How destitute was my heart without her!

Although only a month and a half with child, Gabrielle looked ready to deliver. Her chambermaid stayed at her side night and day. Two elderly midwives remained in the house, prepared for the birth of our child. The constant grace and tenderness Gabrielle showed to me was all that kept me sane.

I returned every evening to the Garden Tomb where I had last seen Marah, gazing toward Heaven. On such a night, returning to the rooftop of my house, I heard bustling and clamoring in the rooms beneath me, and Gabrielle in the moans and pangs of childbirth. I rushed down to her chambers and opened the door. Gabrielle lay naked upon the bed. She looked up to see me, smiling warmly through obvious pain. The chambermaid stood next to her, wiping sweat from her face with a cloth. One of the midwives shooed me away.

"Not for husbands. No men here, mind you. You will bring bad luck upon both the child and the mother."

I returned Gabrielle's smile and left the room. Her moans started up again, along with the coaxes and coaching of the midwives and soothing words from her chambermaid. A torrent of emotions filled me. The idea that I would soon be a father thrilled me. My joy mixed with sorrow, for, though Gabrielle was warm, beautiful, worthy of my affections, I did not love her as I loved Marah.

Several minutes went by before Gabrielle gave a final moan, followed by the cries of a baby—a sound that, until that moment, I had never associated with joy and love. My heart pounded in my chest. I rapped on the chamber door. One of the midwives opened it. Without a word, she nodded to Gabrielle. Gabrielle lay upon the bed, her face weary but happy, dark hair falling like a shawl over her shoulders. She held a baby to her chest.

"You have a son, Saruel," she said.

I sat beside her on the bed, looking with awe upon the infant. His small pink body radiated health. He looked up at me with eyes the shade of Heaven's throne; my eyes. Gabrielle held him out to me. Despite mild protests from the midwives, I took him from her. He felt solid and strong in my hands. He was flesh and blood. Human, yet not human. The midwives had no need to worry over his safety. I held him to my chest. He looked up at me. His features were a perfect blend of Gabrielle's and my own. I loved him instantly, the love of a father for a son. He reached up with his little hand and touched my face. I wept tears of joy.

"I have a son," I said, "a child made in my own image. He shall be called Jonathon."

After a time, I returned to the rooftop and looked up into the night sky. I had witnessed the birth of the glittering stars above me. Such beauty have I seen, such wonders have my eyes beheld. The sight of my newborn son eclipsed the births of a million stars.

CHAPTER 43

Cool wind whistled past me as I flew away from San Francisco, surrounded by darkness, my heart pounding in my chest. I remembered Erozel in the Garden of God, pain etched into his lovely face, holding Asherah's decaying corpse to his bosom.

The garden was a place of beginning. There Adam and Eve were given life. There they found death in the place of the skull. The most pivotal moments of human history hinge upon that spot. It was the site of the first sacrificial lamb. It lies within view of the Field of Blood where Cain slew Abel. Nearby, Abraham offered up Isaac and Solomon built the Temple of God. There Yeshua died upon the cross. There, according to Azazel, I would find Marah.

I flew until I reached the cave where I had first given Marah the Fruit of Life. No trail or path led to the mouth of the cave, and the mountain's sheer surface would daunt even the most fearless rock climber. A formation of rock and leafy growth hid the entrance from sight. I squeezed through the overgrowth of bushes and vines, hunching my shoulders, my hair scraping the ceiling of rock as I made my way into the cave. A large round stone formed a false wall in front of me. I had placed it there myself in the remote chance of someone discovering my hiding place. Taking hold of the stone with both hands, I rolled it away. Soft golden light sprang forth from behind it, lighting the cave. A small alabaster box glowed on the cave floor, lit from within by what remained of the Fruit of Life. There was so little of it left! The knowledge that I could not keep Marah alive for all eternity troubled me. How long would the fruit last?

Morning gave way to midday, as I flew across time zones, holding the alabaster box in my hands. I reached Jerusalem at sunset. I looked down upon the place of the skull, following it across the Field of Blood to where the Tree of Life had been. My gaze fell finally on the Garden of Gethsemane, where Yeshua had prayed on the night of his betrayal.

I have heard many theories and ideas concerning the original location of the Garden of Eden. Most are wrong. Earth's face has changed dramatically since creation. What was once a single land mass is now divided into continents. Seasons and climates have changed. Deserts span where flowers once bloomed and rivers once rolled. The I Am is omniscient, knowing the end from the beginning. There is a method to apparent madness, a rhythm to what looks like chaos. Where man was lost, there he was found, where the blood of the lamb was spilled, so the blood of the Lamb of God. Where the tree of death and the tree of life grew, so Yeshua hanged upon a tree, both death and life.

I landed, looking around me. A man stepped out from a grove of trees. His face held a wary expression.

"Jonathon?" I said. "What are you doing here? How did you get here?"

Erozel stepped out from under the grove. As lovely as ever, he wore a white shirt. Frills of lace adorned the neck and sleeves, the buttons were pearl. His long blonde hair fell in a braid behind him.

"I brought him here," he said.

In anger, I took a step toward Erozel, my hands clenching into fists. He held up his hand.

"Remember that I have your girl. Will you risk my wrath by striking me?"

"Why did you take her?" I said.

Erozel frowned, narrowing his eyes. "You know why, Saruel. In this very spot, your act of omission stole Asherah from me. You could have saved her with a small part of the Fruit of Life. Instead, she died in my arms."

"Asherah lives," I said. "I know your secret, as you know mine."

Erozel's delicate hands closed into tight fists. Rage flared in his eyes. "Asherah is dead, a walking corpse. Her soul remains in the abyss to this day. Her body, her carnal desires an empty reminder of what you did to her."

"I did not kill her," I said.

"You let her die when you had the power to save her. What is that in your hand? Is that not the fruit of the Tree of Life? Did you have it long ago when she lay dying in my arms?"

I held the alabaster box tight with both hands and stepped between Jonathon and Erozel. "Why did you bring Jonathon? He has no part in this."

Erozel laughed. "He has everything to do with this, Saruel. I did not take your girl, though not for lack of trying. Jonathon, believing Andrew had betrayed you, rescued her, killing him in the process. I found him before he could return her to you, and told him my story." His beautiful face twisted in rage, "How you allowed Asherah to die. He gave your girl to me, freely, without a fight."

I looked at Jonathon. His face turned red. "Tell me you had nothing to do with this."

"I did it, Father," he said. "I delivered your beloved Marah into the hand of your enemy. I told your well-kept secret. Erozel retrieved your altar stone, and I tied it to Andrew's leg."

I stared into the face of my only son.

"How could you? You love Marah as I love her."

Jonathon looked angry. "Love her? The very sight of her sickens me! Every minute she lives reminds me of what I lost. My mother is dust in the ground. You let her die when you could have saved her."

I had thought that my heart could not break anymore, but I was wrong. If ever I had hated my immortality, I did at that moment. I wanted to die.

My son, my only son.

Erozel fingered the braid of his hair. "It seems that you have a pattern of such behavior," he said. "Your sins of omission have found you out. What other lives were destroyed for your romantic affair?"

To Jonathon I said, "Your mother loved Marah, and Marah loved her. She chose to die. I wanted to keep her alive, but she would have none of it."

"She chose death because she knew you loved her less than Marah. Was she a dog, to live off the scraps that Marah left for her? She loved you with her whole heart. You betrayed her by letting her die."

My son, who had brought such joy to my heart, looked upon me with pure hatred. His eyes, blue like mine, were cold as death.

"Jonathon," I said, "what have you done?"

"I did what needed to be done, Father. Marah is your weakness, your fall. You say that she loved my mother. That is good, for she shall soon join her in death."

I fell to my knees in front of him. "You are my son, I am your father."

He did not answer. I faced Erozel. "Brother," I said, "If there remains within you any love for me, I beg your mercy."

Erozel smiled cruelly. The atmosphere trembled. My brother Watchers, followers of Erozel, landed, one by one, surrounding me. The last one to arrive held a bundle wrapped in scarlet, the shape and size of a small child. Erozel turned to them, his cruel smile never leaving his lips. He motioned to the bundle.

"Behold, Saruel."

Standing, I moved toward the Watcher, reaching for the bundle in his arms. He pulled away from me, before dropping it. I cried out. The scarlet cloth pulled back, revealing white, ashen skin. Dead flesh. I fell to my knees, stunned. Would it end this way? Had I lost my only love?

"Marah," I said. My voice shook.

Erozel stepped between me and the small body, his cruel smile a terrible sight on his lovely face. "How does it feel to lose the one you love? Now do you understand? Upon this very ground I held Asherah in my arms. I begged for your help, but you denied me." He pointed to the small body on the ground. "I condemn you to Hell, as you once condemned me."

He stepped aside, clearing a path to the body. I stood to my feet, fastening my eyes on the scarlet bundle. Did I want to see her? The sight of her dead body might drive me to madness. Still, she deserved my grief. Love bound me to her. I approached, hesitantly. Bending down, I peeled back the scarlet cloth, revealing a cavernous hole in a smooth child's chest. The heart was gone. Laughter came from the Watchers behind me. I closed my eyes and pulled the cloth away. It took every bit of my resolve to force my eyes open again. I looked in horror at a young girl's face. Her dead eyes stared at me, accusing. Laughter from the Watchers echoed in my ears. My body went numb. She was Andrew's daughter, who I had left in Jonathon's care.

I stood and faced Erozel. "What is this?" I said. "Where is Marah?"

Erozel waved a dismissive hand toward the dead girl. "Marah yet lives. You will see her once more, Saruel. I am not quite finished with her." He lifted off the ground and hovered in the air above me. The Watchers joined him. "Come," he said.

I followed Erozel the short distance to Golgotha. A silvery moon replaced the last orange light of the sun, casting the former Garden of God in a dismal light.

"Look and see, Saruel," he said.

An altar of stones stood where Yeshua's cross once was. Marah's small body lay naked upon the altar. Asherah stood facing her. She wore a white, revealing robe. A small golden crown adorned her head. Her hand held a long, silver dagger. A group of men and women in white robes knelt in a circle before the altar of stones.

"Marah!" I cried.

Two of the Watchers took hold of me: Asriel on my right and Sodomel on my left. I struggled to free myself, but they held me fast.

"All in good time," Erozel said.

We landed several yards away from the circle of humans, the two Watchers still holding me. Erozel forced the alabaster box containing the Fruit of Life from my hand. He hovered above the altar of stones.

CHAPTER 44

Two years passed. Jonathon grew at an amazing rate. He appeared to be around ten years old. Gabrielle's chambermaid became his nurse. She held true to her oath of secrecy, considering Jonathon's strength and rapid growth to be a miracle of God. He possessed a brilliant, inquisitive mind. He was physically powerful—stronger, even at his young age, than ten full-grown men. I had cautioned him to keep his strength a secret. His advanced rate of growth forced us to keep him away from people.

How I enjoyed talking with him, being near him, his hand in mine. Gabrielle loved him. Such a mother she was! Her natural warmth and gentleness turned my house of sorrow into a home. I loved her, but not with the love that she deserved. I shared my bed with Gabrielle, but my heart, broken as it was, belonged to Marah. Every sunset found me hovering in the skies above the Garden Tomb, looking toward Heaven.

To avoid suspicion over my agelessness and Jonathon's accelerated growth, we moved from our house in the Towers. I regretted leaving the home I had shared with Marah, but I saw no other way. We departed for Greece. Days became months, months became years. Jonathon grew to adulthood before his tenth birthday.

"Where do you go every evening, Father?"

We sat together on the balcony of our new home, a large estate overlooking the ocean. It was nighttime, and I had returned from the Garden Tomb.

"I watch the setting of the sun," I said.

He studied me. "Your departure fills Mother with sadness. Seeing that it causes her sorrow, why do you continue to leave?"

"I love your mother," I said, "and wish only for her joy and happiness. Still, I covet my time alone. Would you deny me an hour of each day?"

"I would deny you nothing, Father. I love you with my whole heart. I love my mother, also. You love her. That is plain to see. Yet you keep her at a distance."

I took Jonathon's hand in mine. "There is much that you do not know."

"Tell me, Father, for I am no longer a child."

For the first time, I told him my story. The telling of it took several hours. He listened in quiet astonishment.

"You are not a man," he said when I finished. "What, then, am I?"

"You are my son," I said.

"Mother is mortal flesh. Will you extend her life as you extended the life of your first love?"

I hesitated. He frowned.

"I see, then, that you have given it little thought. Would you allow the mother of your only son to perish? Would you withhold life from one who loves you as she does? You gave up Heaven for this Marah, yet, faced with the same choice, she left you. Mother would not do that."

"Perhaps not," I said, "but my heart loves as it loves."

Jonathon turned his back to me. "Then to you, my mother is only a servant."

"Your mother is my only earthly friend. I do love her."

"Would you have traded Heaven for such a love?"

I did not answer. He left me alone on the rooftop.

For the most part, all returned to normal between us. I endeavored to show Gabrielle affection and tenderness, especially in Jonathon's presence. She delighted in this, and her delight contented Jonathon.

Jonathon loved Greece. He devoured Grecian literature, listened to minstrels in the marketplace as they played stringed instruments and recited stories of the thirteen gods of old. How the gods came to Earth and coupled with women, who bore children, great and powerful men. Of course, he immediately saw the similarity between the stories of the Greeks and my story.

"The stories are true, Father. Are they not? The thirteen gods were you and your brothers. Did they have children with women as you did? Are there others like me?"

We stood together on the balcony. Stars above us glittered in the night sky. Silvery moonlight lit up Jonathon's excited face.

"The stories are legends, contrived by men. Yet there is a thread of truth in them. Men worshiped my brothers as gods, but there is only one God. One Creator made both men and angels."

"Where are your brothers? Do they have sons and daughters?"

"They had children in the past," I said. "I avoid them, for they are full of violence and perversion. Like them, their children loved abominations."

Jonathon stood, and looked out at the dark ocean. "Where do they dwell?"

"Do not seek them out, my son. They are evil spirits, without natural affection."

"I must know, Father. Will you keep this knowledge from me? They are your brothers."

I placed my hand on his shoulder. "They dwell in Rome," I said. "Promise me that you will not seek them out."

"I am alone, Father. The idea that there may be others like me..."

"You are never alone. I am with you always."

He turned from me, his gaze returning to the ocean.

For forty years, we lived among the Greeks. I managed to find a sliver of happiness. In Gabrielle's love and Jonathon's company, I found refuge from constant despair.

I spent each sunset in the skies above the Garden Tomb, looking to Heaven without expectation, the act little more than a ritual.

Returning home one night, I found Gabrielle waiting for me on the rooftop. I landed next to her. She looked up at me, tears in her eyes.

"What is it, my lover?" I said.

She touched my cheek. "Your constant sorrow grieves me. I have tried these many years to bring you happiness. Yet your sorrow remains. Is there no help for you? Will you never recover from your broken heart?"

I took her hands in mine. "You are a balm for my heart's affliction," I said.

"A balm, but not a cure," she said. "Will your heart never heal? I am old and will soon go the way of all flesh. What will become of you then? Who will ease your suffering?"

I looked at her, for the first time truly seeing her age. I thought about the fruit of the Tree of Life in its hiding place.

"You can be young again," I said.

She shook her head. "No. That is for my mistress on the day of her return. I do not seek eternal life. I have lived a good life with the one I love. I want nothing more, save one thing."

"Anything," I said, "speak it and it is yours."

She touched my face. Tears moistened her eyes. "I want you to miss me when I am gone."

I pulled her close. "Remain with me," I said. "Marah would want you to partake of the fruit. Be young again."

"No, my love, I choose the natural course of life. I want only to be missed by you, for my memory to occupy a place in your heart."

I wrapped her in my arms. "I will miss you," I said. "I will hold you dear for eternity."

CHAPTER 45

Erozel hovered above the altar of stones, staring down at Marah's tiny form. He opened the alabaster box and removed what remained of the fruit of the Tree of Life. Its golden light cut through the gloominess of night. Asherah watched Erozel with unblinking eyes, holding the wicked dagger in her hand. The white-robed humans kneeling around the altar looked up at him with adoration.

"Tonight is the final Festival of Hearts," Erozel said. "For thousands of years, the Queen of Heaven survived because of the sacrifice of others. That has come to an end. I hold life in my hands: not the life of the body only, but of the spirit."

He ran a finger across the fruit, caressing it.

"Then release Marah," I shouted. "You have what you want!"

Erozel motioned to the Watchers holding me. Sodomel, standing behind me, clamped his hand tightly over my mouth.

"It is true that I have what I want. I have the Fruit of Life and your precious Marah. Her heart pumps blood mingled with the life that is within this fruit. Imagine what consuming such a heart may do for Asherah." He looked at the fruit in his hands. "Alas, so little remains. I will not let Marah's heart go to waste. I will certainly not let her waste it on loving you."

I struggled against my captors, trying to break free. Erozel held the fruit of the Tree of Life above his head. He looked down at the men and women in white. "Let the festival begin," he said.

The humans removed their white robes and stood naked before the altar. Erozel pointed a hand toward them. The atmosphere trembled. Desire and lust filled their faces. They fell upon each other with unbridled lust. Asherah dropped her robe as well, lust apparent on her face. She trailed a finger along Marah's nude body. Her other hand held the silver dagger. The other Watchers stared at the writhing tangle of humans. Gomhorel removed his clothing, followed by the others, except for Sodomel, who kept a firm hold on me. Asriel, who had helped to restrain me, undressed as well. Members erect, they joined in with the humans. Asherah held the tip of the blade above Marah's chest, waiting, gazing up at Erozel.

I flew.

With all my strength, I rose into the air, kicking my feet against

Sodomel, flying full speed toward Marah. Erozel lowered in front of me. I hit him hard and knocked him to the ground. Marah's salvation was narrowly, but surely, within my reach.

No human being could have seen me at the speed I flew. Yet, somehow, Asherah did. She lowered the dagger, slicing into Marah's chest at the same moment I grabbed her hand. I pushed Asherah away from the altar. To my great relief, the wound in Marah's chest was not deep. I had won. Marah and I would be halfway around the world before the Watchers could follow. A figure in black slammed me into the altar of stones with such force that the ground trembled around me. Shocked, I looked to see who it was.

"Ariel," I cried. "Release me. They will kill her!"

Ariel looked down at me without emotion. "Yes, Saruel, they will kill her."

"Release me, Brother. You are not my enemy."

Ariel tightened his grip on me. He had the strength of a Warrior. "They will release her from the bonds of flesh, and, in doing so, release you from your curse. I am not your enemy. I do this for your good. You have lost who you were over the love of this woman."

Erozel rose into the air, looking down at me with hatred. "You have interrupted the ceremony, Saruel." His eyes found Asherah. "It is of no consequence. After all, ceremony is not the true heart of the matter."

The Watchers laughed. Ariel remained quiet, holding me to the ground. The humans around the altar, lost to Erozel's fever, were oblivious to the commotion around them.

"It is time you learned that love does not conquer all."

"I beg you, Erozel," I said. "Do not do this thing."

He turned to Asherah. "Kill the girl and remove her heart."

Asherah plunged the silver blade into Marah's chest. I screamed, struggling against Ariel with all my strength. Blood poured from the gash in Marah's chest. She opened her eyes. Her young face showed pain and fear before the light in them went out, leaving the dull sheen of death.

I cannot describe the terrible agony, the feeling of loss at the sight of Marah's dead body. The fight in me vanished. I watched numbly as Asherah removed Marah's pulsating heart, holding it up with a bloody hand, the heart that had loved me for generations.

In that moment, I knew the true meaning of Hell.

CHAPTER 46

I hovered alone above the Garden Tomb, watching as the sun set over an orange horizon, my face turned toward Heaven, my thoughts on Gabrielle. She was ill and fading fast. I held the fruit of the Tree of Life in my hand.

"You have been gone for a long time," I said. "My love for you has not changed, but I do not want to be alone."

The final rays of sunlight gave way to night. I remained, watching in silence, waiting. Would Marah appear suddenly, declaring her undying love? Stars shone down from an empty sky. Marah was in Heaven, with Yeshua. She had made her choice. I placed the Fruit of Life in the pocket of my robe and flew to Gabrielle.

Jonathon was waiting for me on the rooftop when I arrived. I landed in front of him. His eyes were red with weeping.

"What is it?" I said.

"Mother is on her deathbed," he said, "and still you leave us to pine over your lost love."

Reaching into my robe, I removed the fruit of the Tree of Life. It shone with soft, golden light. Jonathon stared at it in wonder.

"This will heal her?"

"It will make her young again," I said.

"Then let us go to her at once."

I glanced toward Heaven once more before following him to Gabrielle. The chambermaid, then in her mid-fifties, knelt next to the bed, running a comb through Gabrielle's long white hair.

"How is she?" Jonathon asked.

"She rests."

"Leave us, please," I said.

She nodded and, offering Gabrielle's arm a tender pat, left us alone, shutting the door behind her. Gabrielle stirred and opened her eyes.

"Do I hear the voice of my beloved?" she said.

I sat beside her. "I am here," I said.

She reached out to me and I took her hand in mine. Her other hand reached for Jonathon. He held her hand and sat down on the other side of the bed.

"I go the way of all flesh," she said.

"No, Mother," Jonathon said. "Father will give you life again."

Gabrielle fixed her brown eyes on me. "I take it, then, that you have brought the fruit to me, despite my wishes?"

I squeezed her hand softly. "I do not want to lose you," I said.

"The fruit is for my mistress when she returns. I am old and content with the life I have lived. When my eyes close in final sleep, they will close upon a life of joy, filled with love and happiness."

Jonathon shook his head. "No, Mother, they would close upon a son in despair and a husband in sorrow. Please, take of the fruit, and live. The woman you speak of will not return. You have taken her place in Father's heart."

Gabrielle looked at me. "Is it true, my love? Do I now own your heart? Tell me, where were you this evening at the time of the setting sun? You were not here by my side. Marah is your Rachel, while I am your Leah."

"It matters not," I said, "for I am here now. Eat of the fruit, rise from your bed and live."

"Where your love is, so is your heart. If she were here, would you worry over losing me as you do now?"

"Father loves you," Jonathon said, "and I love you."

Gabrielle smiled weakly at him. "I do not doubt your love, or the love of your father. He does love me, I am sure of that. Yet it is one thing to feel love, but another to be in love."

I pulled the fruit from my pocket. Golden light showed every detail of Gabrielle's ashen face. She stared at it for a long moment before shaking her head.

"It belongs to my mistress," she said, "I will not eat of it."

Jonathon let go of her hand. Blotches of red appeared on his face. "You are no longer a chambermaid. You are free from your service to her. If she returns, it will be only to find you in her former place."

Gabrielle reached for his hand. "You do not understand, my son. She will always be my mistress, as your father will always be my master. I love them both, you see. You are certainly old enough and knowledgeable of the ways of the world to comprehend my meaning. She was more than a mistress to me and I was to her more than a chambermaid."

Jonathon stood, watching her, his eyes growing wide. "You loved her as a woman loves a man, according to the flesh? You had sexual relations with her?"

"I loved her, not only with my body, but with my heart and soul, as I do your father. Do not look upon me with such surprise. Perhaps your father loved me with only half a heart, but my mistress loved me with the equal half of hers. Together they loved me fully."

Jonathon stood, staring, as though seeing his mother for the first time. He turned to me. "Is my mother unworthy of the fullness of your love? Will I lose her because you refuse to let go of the one who abandoned you? She used my mother as a concubine and you did as well."

"No, my son," Gabrielle said, "I was never a concubine, nor was I forced against my will. I was free to come and go as I pleased. I was in love with two people, and I still am." She looked tenderly at me. "I count myself fortunate. I release my spirit with gladness, having lived a good and abundant life."

"Please," I said, holding the Fruit of Life out to her.

"No, my lover," she said. "All I want is for you to miss me when I am gone."

Try as I might, Gabrielle refused the Fruit of Life. She died early the next morning, before the rising of the sun.

I buried her in her own country near the village where she grew up. Jonathon and I stood by her grave under the shadow of a juniper tree, the moon our only light. I wept. Tears wet Jonathon's face. I placed my hand on his shoulder, but he shrugged it away.

"You could have saved her," he said.

"She made her choice, my son. This is what she wanted."

He looked up at me, his beautiful face full of anguish. "She would have stayed with us until the end of time, if not for your divided affections."

"It is the way of all flesh," I said.

Jonathon shook his head.

"Leave me, Father. I do not wish to see you again for some time."

"I am sorry, my son. I share your grief."

He did not answer me. I lifted away from him, rising slowly into the dark sky. There I hovered, out of sight, allowing Jonathon his privacy. I wished for a way to wipe the tears forever from his eyes, to remove the pain of loss from his heart.

A dark figure moved in the air at the edge of my vision, robes of shadow like tendrils of black smoke. I turned to see Hemael staring down at Gabrielle's grave. Looking down at Jonathon once more, I turned and flew toward Jerusalem, to the Garden Tomb.

CHAPTER 47

Asherah held Marah's pulsating heart in her bloody hand. I started toward Marah, but Ariel stopped me with a firm grip.

"It is finished," he said.

I watched, horrified, unable to turn away, as Asherah, standing where Eve had partaken of the Fruit of Carnal Knowledge and Sangruel had fallen from grace, lifted Marah's heart to her lips.

In that instant, Sangruel dropped suddenly from the night sky, hitting Asherah with devastating force. His sharp teeth found her throat. His monstrous face showed rapture. He flew quickly away, carrying her off as he drank from her. Erozel screamed, his lovely face twisting with rage. He took to the skies after Sangruel.

I ran to Marah. Ariel made no move to stop me. Taking her tiny body in my arms, I flew. None followed me. I held her body close to me, cradling her, flying without thought or direction, drifting between Heaven and Earth. The night surrounded me. Marah's blood soaked through my shirt. I wept, a lost spirit condemned to Hell, my anguished voice swallowed by darkness.

I turned my face toward Heaven. "Are we destroyed for love?" I cried.

Heaven did not answer.

A figure, blacker than night, appeared in front of me. Hemael's cadaverous face stared out from his shadowy hood. I turned toward him, clutching Marah to my chest.

"Why have you come, reaper grim?" I called.

Hemael pointed a skeletal finger at Marah.

"No! You will not have her."

Turning from him, I flew toward Heaven, glancing behind to see if he followed me. He hovered, unmoving, watching me with hollow eyes. I increased my speed, flying toward Heaven, holding Marah close, protecting her body from the heat of Earth's atmosphere. Still, Hemael did not follow. Several miles outside of Earth's atmosphere, I reached the invisible barrier, set there by the word of God to keep Fallen angels from Heaven. Bracing myself, I drew near to it. A rainbow-colored light moved toward me from the direction of Heaven, until I could make out the figure of a man in robes of heavenly light, a rainbow around his head. It was Enoch. I stopped, the Earth a bluish orb far below, surrounded by dark space. Enoch flew the rest of the way to me.

"Fallen spirit," he said, "I am sent to you by the Great I Am."

I held Marah's lifeless body out to him. "Take her, I implore you. Deliver her from death's hand. Let her dwell in Heaven with the Creator."

"No, Saruel. She made her choice. The Great I Am will not interfere with her freewill."

"He loves her as I love her. Take her, I pray you. He will not turn her away."

"I am here to stop you from returning to Heaven. You are a Watcher, she a daughter of Eve. Her end has come, and, with it, the day of her judgment."

"Why did you come to me, then? Is there not a barrier between Heaven and Earth?"

Enoch motioned toward Heaven. "Had I not come, you would have flown all the way to Heaven's gates. No barrier can withstand selfless love."

"Then is not that evidence of the purity of our love, though I am of Heaven and she is of Earth?"

Enoch shook his head. "You disobeyed the law of Heaven. The wages of sin is death, and after that, judgment. Marah's judgment, postponed for thousands of years, is now upon her. Death will have her, Saruel, and the abyss. No sin shall enter Heaven's gates."

Without another word, I flew toward Heaven, leaving Enoch behind. The barrier could not have been far ahead, but I felt no resistance as Earth's gravitational pull released me to the vacuum of space. I had passed through the barrier!

The voice of Enoch sounded behind me. "I cast you to Earth, Fallen spirit."

An unseen force took hold of me, pulling me backwards.

I lost control of my body, paralyzed. Marah remained against my chest, but I could no longer hold her. I fell to Earth, propelled downward by the word of Enoch, through the atmosphere. Thankfully my body still protected her from the heat of our entry. Earth's gravity took hold of me. Marah slid from my limp embrace. From the corner of my eye, I saw Hemael flying in the direction that the wind had taken Marah. I struggled for control of my body, praying a wordless prayer of supplication, a plea for mercy. The wind grew louder, humming in my ears, as Earth raced up to meet me. I hit the ground with meteoric force; a falling star. The ground shook with a sound like thunder. The force of my body formed a deep crater, burying me, surrounding me in darkness.

CHAPTER 48

Three years after Gabrielle's death, I hovered over the Garden Tomb at sunset, my eyes turned toward Heaven. Despair consumed me. Loneliness drove me to the edge of madness. My thoughts were of Jonathon, who still blamed me for Gabrielle's death. How I missed him. I took little notice of the happenings on the Earth beneath me.

The sound of a woman's voice pulled me from my thoughts. I nearly fell from the sky. I knew that voice. God in Heaven, I did. How many times over nearly fifty years had I jumped at the sight of any woman similar in appearance to Marah? How many times had I thought that I heard her voice, only to be mistaken? I dropped from the sky, slowing just above the Garden Tomb. Marah stood where I had seen her last. She wore the same robe of delicate purple. The same white flower adorned her autumn hair.

She cried out when she saw me. "Saruel, my love!"

I landed in front of her, my heart pounding in my chest, my arms aching to hold her. My eyes brimmed with tears. "You are here," I said.

She threw herself at me, weeping suddenly. I put my arms around her. "What of Heaven? What of the Great I Am?"

Marah looked up at me. Tears trailed her lovely face. I wiped them away with my hand. "I love Yeshua, and Heaven is beyond description. All that you told me of its glory and beauty is true." I felt her tremble in my embrace. "Despite its glory, I could not remain there. Sorrow filled me instead of rapture. The light of Heaven paled when compared to my memories of you. Without you, I felt no peace, no joy. For you are my Heaven."

I held her close to me, feeling the soft curves of her body against mine, breathing in her fragrance. "I thought I would never see you again," I said.

"I left you for but a moment's time. Did you give up on me so quickly?"

"My darling," I said, "fifty years have passed since the day you left me."

Marah's eyes widened.

Realization dawned on me. My time with Gabrielle, the birth of my son, Gabrielle's death, had seemed like minutes to her.

"Heaven is eternal, my love," I said. "A day there is as a thousand years, a thousand years as a day."

Her brow furrowed. "Fifty years? What of our beloved Gabrielle, is she well?"

"She chose to leave this world," I said. "She went the way of all flesh."

She stepped back, studying my face. "The Fruit of Life, Saruel, did you offer it to her?"

"I did. She refused it."

Marah lowered her eyes. "How I wronged her, forcing her into my bed even before she understood fleshly desire. Because of me, she never knew a man. I twisted her emotions with my abuse, until she lusted after the female form."

"She loved you," I said.

Marah looked up at me. "You remained with her, then? You showed love to her?"

"I took her as my wife," I said.

She stared at me. Sadness and regret showed on her face.

"It is good that you gave your love to her. I cannot fault you for it, for I love her as you do. If she were yet alive, I would gladly share you with her."

"There is one more thing," I said. "Gabrielle bore me a son."

"You have a son?"

"Much has happened in fifty years," I said.

"I want to meet him. I will hold him dear to me for Gabrielle's sake as well as for yours."

Picking her up, holding her against me, I lifted into the air. I flew toward Greece, noticing for the first time in a long time the beauty of the setting sun.

CHAPTER 49

Darkness enveloped me. I lay entombed in earth, unable to move. I thought only of Marah. Had Hemael cast her spirit into Hell? I felt the subtle warming and cooling of the soil above me as night turned to day and day turned to night again, repeating the process. Three days passed while I lay trapped beneath the ground. If I never saw light again, never a sunset or sunrise, it made no difference, for what was my life without Marah?

Slowly, I recovered control of my body. Still, I did not move, choosing to remain there. What waited for me in the land of the living? My own son had betrayed me. Marah was dead. I imagined her small body, lying broken on the ground, susceptible to the elements and decay. The thought spurred me from that earthly grave. I had to find her body. She deserved that from me. Soil exploded in every direction as I shot from the ground into a reddish sky.

I scanned the Earth below where I had last seen Marah's body. I searched from that point, circling outward until I covered more than a hundred square miles. I broadened my search, moving eastward in the direction of the abyss. Still, I could not find her. I flew on, searching, until I reached the ocean. If her body had fallen into the ocean, my chance of finding it was small.

The ocean turned to an inky black. The waters churned and boiled below me as I drew nearer the abyss, to the mouth of Hell. I hovered, looking down into the darkness below. I imagined Marah's spirit, falling, screaming in terror, Hell's mouth opening to receive her.

Hell. It is the utter absence of joy, a cavernous abyss, where imprisoned spirits cry out into eternal darkness. There is no returning, no escape. I remembered my time before man's creation, watching over the abyss with Ariel, both of us holy angels of Heaven. How much had changed! I felt a tremble in the air behind me and turned to see Hemael, watching me silently. He lowered his hollow gaze to the mouth of Hell.

"Did she remember me?" I said. He looked up at me from the shadow of his hood. I moved closer to him. "Tell me, Hemael, does she suffer there alone? May I join her?"

"Would you choose to suffer the torments of Hell for her?" he said.

"I would," I said, "if it meant seeing her again."

"You do not understand what you ask. Hell's torments are unknown to you. Though she stood directly in front of you, your only thought would be to free yourself from that place."

"I am already in Hell. My heart could never know more sorrow, more suffering. You have never loved another, therefore you cannot understand. If I am with Marah, though Hell surrounds me, yet I am in Heaven."

He looked down at the abyss. "I know what love is," he said. "I am a lover of life. I eschew death. It is for that reason the Great I Am condemned me to this curse. I delight in life and weep at its destruction."

"Then, if only for love, open Hell's mouth."

Hemael stared at me for several moments before returning his attention to the abyss. He pointed one skeletal hand at the abyss. The whirlpool churned and boiled under his gaze, reversing the flow of the current. A black hole appeared in its center. I stared down into Hell's open mouth. I heard cries of suffering, shrieks of terror and pain coming from the darkness below.

"None return from that place," Hemael said.

With a slight nod, showing him that I understood, I descended into the mouth of Hell.

Misery, suffering, despair, darkness as Heaven is light. Hellfire surrounded me, fire that burns not flesh, but spirit, devouring life and happiness. It felt as though I had never known joy. Memories of laughter were far from me, my life before Hell a fleeting dream. I cried out, my voice joining the cacophony of tormented voices around me as I fell, tumbling headlong into the bowels of Hell. My only thought was to escape, to free myself from that place. I knew nothing else.

For how long I continued to fall, I cannot tell. A suffocating blanket of depression surrounded me as I fell, afraid that I would hit bottom, afraid that no bottom existed. In the deepest recesses of my mind, I remembered a glorious city, a place of pure light. I remembered a bluish throne. Where had that been? Surely, all I had ever known was suffering and torment, miserable darkness.

I remembered a pool of clear water. Had there ever been such a thing? I remembered standing near the pool of water staring with such wondrous emotion, not at the water, but at a bathing woman, her white skin reflecting the morning sun. The sun, I remembered the sun. The woman had been singing, and her song eclipsed the choirs of Heaven. I remembered again the place of light, the bluish throne.

The darkness wrapped cold tendrils around me, seeking to extinguish my memory of light, my thoughts of the warm sun. There had been no Heaven, no pool of water, no woman and no song. I knew only Hell.

No.

There had been a Heaven. There had been a sun. The woman had been real, in a time before this eternal darkness. Cruel laughter came to me from every direction, mocking my memories of light and beauty. There had never been beauty. I had always been in Hell.

I cried out, struggling to hold to the fading memory of Heaven, of the woman. What had she looked like? What were the words of her song? I felt her memory slipping from me.

"Marah!"

Darkness loosened its grip. My memory of the woman returned. Who was she? Darkness encircled me again, tendrils of fog groping at my mind. There had never been a woman.

"Marah!"

Why had I screamed that name? In my mind, I saw the woman, not in the pool of water, but in my arms, looking up at me with eyes filled with love. What was love? There was no love, only sorrow. Who was the woman? She had never been. Darkness, misery and suffering were all I had ever known. How did I get here? For what terrible sin had I been judged?

Being here was my choice.

More cruel laughter from the surrounding darkness told me the foolishness of my thoughts. Who would choose to come to this place, and why?

Yet I had chosen.

I saw the woman in my arms again, the pleasant fullness of her breasts against my chest, the sweet aroma of her body, the way she looked at me. In that instant, misery, depression, fear fled from me. I knew only love.

I stopped falling.

The darkness surrounding me shifted and pulled away from me, repelled somehow, becoming a thin mist instead of dark pitch. I could see other tormented spirits around me, some falling, others floating in thick darkness. I looked up. How far had I fallen? I flew upward, wanting nothing more than to leave that place.

Marah.

I stopped. I knew. Love and longing filled me. I had to find Marah. I called her name. The cries of the anguished damned were my only answer. I flew, looking for her, searching the faces of the lost. I had never seen such misery, such hopelessness. It is far better to have never existed than to end up in that place. As I drew near to them, they reached for me in desperation, begging for deliverance. What sin warranted such punishment? I kept on, calling her name.

"Marah!"

A woman called to me from my right. I turned excitedly. Finding my way through a sea of damned souls, I flew to the voice.

"Marah!"

The woman called to me, speaking in Aramaic, the everyday language of

Israel two-thousand years ago.

"Here, Saruel, come to me, my love!"

Spirits of the damned surrounded me. Marah was not among them.

"Marah!"

"Saruel!"

The voice came from behind me. I knew it. It was not Marah's voice. I turned around. Gabrielle floated before me. Her haunted eyes stared at me in disbelief. Darkness wrapped itself around her.

"Can it be?" she said. "Do I look upon my beloved, or is this more of Hell's cruelty? Does Hell show me what I lost only to increase my despair?"

I had never considered that Gabrielle would be cast into Hell. I had never known a better person, good and kind. Surely, she did not deserve to be there.

"I am here, Gabrielle." I drew close to her. "How did this happen? Why are you here? Was there ever a more faithful and truer heart than yours?"

She met my eyes. "I am guilty of the sin of love," she said. "My love for you and for my mistress is abomination in the eyes of Heaven."

"Until this moment," I said, "I did not know that you were here. You belong in Paradise."

"Then why are you here? Why do you call the name of my mistress?"

"Marah is here, in this place of torment. I am searching for her."

The darkness thickened around her. Sorrow filled the features of her face. She turned her eyes away from me. "You seek your true love."

"I did not know you were in this place, Gabrielle."

She looked up at me. "You would not have come for me," she said.

I reached for her, but she pulled away.

"No, Saruel, for seeing you, only to lose you once more, is far worse than the torment I already endure. Your touch would only add to my misery. Leave me. Rescue the one you love."

"I am not here to rescue her," I said, "for I am imprisoned here, as you are. I came to share in her judgment, to be with her in eternal damnation. Your words pierce my heart, for you are very dear to me."

For a moment, the darkness shrank from around her. A small light of hope glimmered in her eyes. "Did you miss me?" Did you remember me with fondness?"

I reached for her again and she allowed my touch. Her spirit felt surprisingly solid under my hand. I pulled her close to me. "Always," I said. "I remembered you always. Besides Marah, you are the only woman who ever touched my heart."

She smiled up at me. "You bring joy to me even in the midst of Hell. Go, find my mistress and be with her. Tell her that my love for her remains."

I looked at the darkness all around us, at the tormented souls numbering as far as the eye could see through the misty darkness. How could I possibly find her among so many?

"Come with me," I said, "we will find her together."

I took her hand in mine and flew with her, calling Marah's name into the surrounding darkness.

CHAPTER 50

Gabrielle and I searched the faces of the lost for what seemed like an eternity. Thousands, tens of thousands, spirits without number, cried out to us, cursing us as we passed them by. The darkness around us grew, thickening, as we descended into the lower parts of Hell. How long could I fight the despair of that place?

Evil men and women inhabited the lower parts of Hell, their faces contorted and hideous, the true images of their wicked souls. They gnashed their teeth at us, reaching for us with twisted hands. Surely, Marah could not be among these. Still, I descended further.

Gabrielle trembled, clinging to me, hiding her face from the ghoulish apparitions. The darkness wrapped itself around us, a constricting serpent, seeking to swallow us whole. Gabrielle cried out, overwhelmed by despair.

I stopped. The spirits here had never known love; they had never admired beauty. Marah could not be among them. She could not be in such a hellhole. I looked up, toward the mouth of Hell, miles above us. That is where she had to be.

I began to ascend, longing to leave the darkness.

"Wait," Gabrielle said, "listen."

"What is it?" I said.

Through the cries and curses all around us, I heard a woman weeping, far below, in the pitch darkness. The small voice was nearly lost amidst the screams and cries, the sound of her weeping a chord out of tune with Hell's somber orchestra. I stared down into the oppressive darkness. What creature was worthy of such a place? What transgression merited such a judgment?

Gabrielle followed my gaze. "It is my mistress," she said. "She is in torment. We must go to her."

Tendrils of despair coiled around Gabrielle and me, suffocating us, seeking to quench our last spark of hope, as we descended toward the anguished voice in the darkness below. Gabrielle held me tight, her own moans echoing the sounds of weeping.

"Marah?" I called.

The weeping stopped suddenly.

"My mistress?" Gabrielle called.

"Here," Marah answered. "I am here."

My heart pounding in my chest, I lowered further into the darkness. What I saw caused me to cry out.

Marah, as she had looked as a young woman, hung in space, naked, her hands held above her head by tendrils of darkness. Red lashes appeared on her white skin, as an unseen whip flogged her repeatedly, and though she was a spirit, blood appeared to flow from the cuts. I heard the cracking of a whip as another lash appeared across her chest. She moaned in pain. There came again the sound of a whip. A cut appeared on her beautiful face. Blood poured down her cheek.

"Marah," I cried.

She lifted her eyes to me. I looked at the tendril of darkness. I reached out and touched it. It felt solid to my touch, a rope tied tightly around Marah's wrists. I heard the unseen whip crack again. Marah groaned.

"Leave me to my punishment, Saruel," she said, lowering her eyes from me. "I deserve every stripe."

"No, my love," I said. "Your crimes against God do not warrant this. Your only sin is your love for me." Another lash appeared, this time across her right breast. I saw that the other cuts on her body were healing.

"My sins are many," she said. "For thousands of years, I have piled up transgressions, defiling myself with temple prostitutes." She looked at Gabrielle. "I corrupted and abused my chambermaid. What other woman in the history of the world has committed as many sins as I have?"

Suddenly, her hands pulled forward, held tight in front of her, bending her body at the waist. The whip cracked. A welt appeared on her buttocks. A silhouette stepped behind her from the darkness. It was not a spirit, but the featureless shape of a man, with a very large, erect member, formed from the same darkness as her bonds. The shadowy form grabbed the cheeks of her buttocks and spread them, before pressing violently against her and entering her forbidden part. She cried out again, her eyes filled with tears, her body moving back and forth with the shadow's thrusts. She moaned in pain, turning her eyes to Gabrielle.

"How many times have I defiled you in this fashion? Surely I have earned my torment."

"No," Gabrielle said, moving closer to Marah. "I love you. You did not force yourself upon me. I longed for you, desired you. You were to me the sweetest pleasure."

Marah's eyes filled with tears. "It saddens me to see you," she said. "You were but a girl, a servant in the house of my father. I robbed you of your innocence, forcing my depraved desires upon you, defiling your body. I am ashamed."

The shadowy form behind her grew more violent, its dark hands tearing into the flesh of her back with sharp claws, thrusting hard against her.

Marah cried out, her face twisting in pain.

"My mistress," Gabrielle said, "if I could return to the time that I was a girl in your father's house, I would not change the course of my life, but would gladly endure the sting of your desire. My heart yearned for you, my loins burned for you. I loved you."

At Gabrielle's words, the shadowy form behind Marah trembled, its constant thrusting slowed.

An idea occurred to me then. What was the opposite of Hell? Love, love was the answer. It was love that had shaken me from my despair and confusion when I had entered the mouth of Hell. Love overcomes all things.

"I love you, Marah," I said. She looked up at me. I heard the sound of the whip. A lash appeared across her back. She cried out in agony. The shadow form behind her started to thrust with renewed energy, more violent than before. Marah wept.

"Because of me, you lost everything," she said. "Never again will you see Heaven. You will never dwell in the Holy of Holies. Is there any sin greater than this? I caused a holy angel to fall."

I reached out and touched her beautiful face. "No," I said. "I lost nothing, but, instead, gained everything. I love you with all that is within me. I do not regret our love, or its consequences." I lifted her head and met her eyes. "I love you."

The shadowy form behind her shook violently and broke apart, before scattering into a thousand pieces, to be absorbed by the surrounding darkness. The tendrils binding Marah's wrists snapped in two, releasing her. She stood in the thick darkness before me, tears running down her face.

"I love you, too" she said.

Gabrielle rushed forward and embraced Marah. They held each other, weeping. My heart swelled with joy, seeing them together again, no matter that we were in the deepest parts of Hell. The heavy darkness sprang sharply away from us, churning and roiling, tendrils seeking to regain lost ground.

I put my arms around Marah and Gabrielle, completing love's embrace. The darkness retreated further away from us. Holding Marah and Gabrielle, I flew upward toward the mouth of Hell. Darkness fled from all around us. Hell groaned. I heard a rumbling coming from every direction. The higher we rose, the lesser the darkness.

The mouth of Hell appeared above us, a vortex of darkness and hellfire, spiraling downward, an inescapable gateway from the land of the living; an entrance, but never an exit.

"What will we do?" Marah asked, staring down into the darkness.

I kissed her, holding her tight against me. "We will remain here," I said. "If we cannot escape this place, then we will make it a place of love instead of torment, joy instead of sorrow, Heaven instead of Hell. We have love, and love is all we need."

Hell shook violently, as what must have been every lost soul in Hell cried out at once. The thick darkness below boiled and churned. Above us, the vortex roiled away from us. I considered all of this. I remembered Enoch's words before he had cast me to Earth.

No barrier can withstand selfless love.

CHAPTER 51

Holding Marah and Gabrielle in my arms, I lifted upward toward the mouth of Hell. Flames of hellfire reached for us from above. I filled my mind with memories of Marah, concentrating, remembering all the glorious feelings of love. The vortex trembled above us, the hellfire faltering before reaching us.

"Fill your heart with thoughts of love," I said, "for the gates of Hell cannot prevail against it."

I looked at Marah. How wonderful it felt to hold her in my arms again. Gabrielle stared upward at the vortex of darkness and hellfire. Her face showed fear.

"Gabrielle, look upon me and upon Marah. Remember our love."

With great effort, she pulled her gaze away from the mouth of Hell. Another bout of violent shaking rocked the foundations of Hell as the spirits of the damned wailed in unison. I lifted toward the swirling mass above us, staring into Marah's beautiful face.

"Love," I shouted over the thunder of voices. "Think only of love!"

The fiery vortex shrank away from us. Black tendrils of darkness reached for us, striking out like venomous snakes. I continued to rise, ignoring the turmoil. I remembered Marah's song on the first day that I ever saw her, our first embrace, our first kiss. I remembered the years we spent together in the Garden of Eden.

Gabrielle screamed, slipping away from my embrace. I reached down for her, grabbing hold of her hand. Hellfire leapt at her feet from below, darkness reached up for her. She stared down into the depths of Hell.

"Hold on!" I shouted. "Do not look down!"

She looked up at me, her eyes wide with terror. A tendril of darkness wrapped itself around her ankle. Hell rocked again, the voices of the damned thundering up to us.

"Love," I said, "only love can free us. Remember our time together!"

Gabrielle's face filled with despair and hopelessness. A second tendril of darkness shot up to her, wrapping itself around her waist. "Did you ever love me? Was I ever more to you than balm for your broken heart?"

Marah reached for Gabrielle, taking her by the arm. "We love you,

Gabrielle! You are dear to our hearts."

I slammed into a barrier above us. Darkness from below rose toward Gabrielle. She screamed, looking down. "Gabrielle!" I called. "Think only of love!"

She gazed up at me one last time. Hellfire surrounded her. Losing her grip on my hand, she fell, screaming, into Hell's waiting grasp, vanishing into the darkness below.

Marah cried out. I stared after Gabrielle, wanting to follow her, knowing that I must not do so. Instead, I focused on Gabrielle's love for me, recalling the lifetime we spent together, she accepting my divided love without complaint.

Hell shook again. Darkness swirled beneath us, shooting suddenly up toward us with volcanic force. The mouth of Hell opened and the darkness exploded, purging itself, catapulting me high into the night sky. Cool air surrounded me. I panicked, for my arms were empty. Marah was gone.

I cried out, searching in desperation for her. A soft, effervescent light floated to me, slowly taking the shape of Marah, a spirit without a body. I descended to a place in front of her. She stared down at the abyss.

"She suffers for all eternity, and I am to blame for it," she said.

I tried to embrace Marah, but my hands found no substance. Although seemingly solid in Hell, my hand now went right through her. I felt a trembling in the atmosphere and looked up to see Hemael descending toward us. I moved in front of him. He hovered in the air before us, his hollow eyes on Marah.

"She will not return to that place," I said.

"She is spirit, without flesh and blood," Hemael said. He looked down at the mouth of Hell. "Only one has ever escaped the clutches of the abyss. I fought to return his spirit, but he defeated me. Hell could not hold him. Death could not stop him." He looked up at me.

"If you return my love to that place," I said, "I will only find her again. Love overcame the grave and released Yeshua from the bowels of Hell. Love released Marah and me. You are powerless against it, reaper grim. It is the greatest power in the universe. By love and in love, the Great I Am called the universe into existence. For God is love."

Hemael spread his hands in a gesture of peace. "Fear not, Watcher, for I have not come to deliver her again into Hell. I tire of my curse."

"Then you will let us leave this place?"

His eyes turned down to the abyss. What could have been sadness showed on his face. He nodded. "Go."

Turning to Marah, I said, "Can you follow me?"

"I do not know."

Marah floated beside me of her own accord, free from the law of gravity, altering between formless ephemeral light and her own image. We flew together, returning to San Francisco just before the rising of the sun. I landed on the balcony of my dwelling. She glided down beside me, her feet sinking through the marble balcony floor.

Once inside, she examined my collection of sculptures and paintings, most in her image, the different stages of her many lives. She had lived with me in my dwelling a little more than six years earlier before partaking of the Fruit of Life.

"I see that you added a few to your collection," she said.

It was so good to be with her, though bittersweet, not being able to hold her in my arms. She looked out through the window. We stood together, watching the rising sun paint the sky in purple and magenta. I moved to hold her hand, finding no substance. She turned to me.

"Let us commission a sculpture of Gabrielle. Her memory deserves a place among your collection." Her lovely face crumpled. "To think of her in that place torments me."

We spent the rest of the day loving one another, a joy mixed with sorrow over Gabrielle. We watched the sunset together. Darkness fell.

Early in the morning, before sunrise, I felt a tremor in the air and looked to see Hemael landing on my balcony. He stood, watching us through the open doors. I stepped outside.

"What brings you here, reaper grim?" I said, frowning.

"Do not fear, Watcher. Your woman is safe from me. I have not come to bring death, but life."

"Life?" I said. "God alone has power over life and death."

He turned away from me, ascending slowly into the dark skies above. "Bring the spirit of your woman. Follow me."

Hemael flew ahead of us, the ocean below. We flew for several hours, because Marah could not match my speed. The whole time, Hemael remained silent. Morning turned to night. Finally, land appeared below us, then the lights of a city, Jerusalem at night. Hemael stopped, hovering above the Garden Tomb. A figure in shadowy robes, Sangruel, stood upon the ground, looking up at us. Hemael landed by him. I hesitated.

"Come, Watcher," Hemael called.

Marah beside me, I landed in the Garden Tomb, formerly the Garden of Eden.

"What is this?" I said.

Sangruel answered me, "Patience, my brother, your questions will soon be answered." He looked at Hemael. Hemael reached a bony hand into his shadowy garment and pulled out a fruit of the Tree of Life, illuminating the garden around us with its golden light. A small part of the fruit was missing: a single bite.

"How can this be?" I said.

"I paid dearly for this fruit," Hemael said. "I returned for it the morning after my judgment, finding it where I had dropped it." He stared at the glowing fruit with visible longing and regret. "Life flows within, beautiful and pure. Year after year, I have taken life from humankind. I thought one day to give life, waiting for one worthy of such a gift." He looked at Marah. "I have found the one."

"I thank you for your offer," I said, "but it is too late. Marah is spirit without flesh and blood, unable to partake of the fruit."

"Come," he said. Hemael rose into the air and Sangruel joined him.

They flew to Golgotha. I followed, landing in the dust, Marah's spirit beside me. A naked girl's body lay before us on the ground—Marah's body, a gash in the chest where Asherah had removed her heart. Hemael held the Fruit of Life in his bony hand.

"I stole the Fruit of Life," he said. "Sangruel stole the Fruit of Death."

Sangruel held his hand out, revealing a fruit of the Tree of Carnal Knowledge, dried, bloodless and shriveled.

"I returned for the fruit of my fall as well," he said looking at me. "Perhaps it was for a time such as this."

"The Fruit of Life," Hemael continued, "gave spiritual life to humankind, while the fruit of blood gave life to the flesh. For the life of all flesh is in the blood. Humankind died spiritually, ruled by the dictates of their Fallen bodies."

Sangruel looked at the fruit in his gnarled hand. "Two trees, each the opposite of the other," he said. "Eve partook of the fruit of blood, Adam with her. I drank from the same fruit. Hemael ate of the Fruit of Life. We were angels, not human, and cursed for our actions. I have often wondered what would happen if I were to now eat of the Fruit of Life and Hemael of the fruit of blood."

I stepped forward. "Are you mad? Do you not remember your terrible judgment? Have you not learned?"

Hemael shook his head. "Peace, Watcher," he said, staring at the Fruit of Carnal Knowledge in Sangruel's hand. "It is our memory of the judgment and our curses that prevented us from trying." He looked at Marah's small body on the ground in front of us. "Marah is human, however. There is a reason why the Warriors took the two trees from the Garden of God. If humankind had partaken of the Fruit of Life and the fruit of blood, they would have lived, Fallen, but eternal, as we are."

I heard the whistling of wind above us. The atmosphere trembled. I looked up into the dark skies and saw Erozel and his followers, hovering together, looking down upon us.

Hemael turned to Marah. "Decide quickly, woman. Will you risk judgment for a chance to live again?"

Marah looked at me. She nodded. "I have nothing left to lose. What must I do?"

The Earth shook as Erozel and his followers landed hard on the ground, forming a circle around us. Hemael moved quickly toward Marah's small body. I watched in wonder and terror as he placed the Fruit of Life into the gaping hole in Marah's chest.

Erozel rushed forward, reaching for Marah's lifeless body. Sangruel turned on him, fangs bared, eyes red with rage. Hemael knelt beside the small body, covering it in the shadow of his robes. Marah's spirit hovered beside me, her eyes watching Hemael.

"Move no further, Erozel," Sangruel hissed. "Remember, I have the life of your beloved Asherah in my power." Erozel stopped, his eyes wide, questioning. "Yes, Erozel, she remains alive. Did you think me so cruel as to destroy the one you love?" His eyes glowed, blood red in the night. He bared his teeth. "I am not the monster that you are. Her blood is sweet, flavored with the essence of the fruit in the Garden of God, but I left enough to sustain her."

I moved toward Erozel. "How did you know we were here?" I said.

A look of disdain crossed his feminine face. His voice held mockery. "Your son, Saruel, your precious son told us of your journey into the depths of Hell. I must say, I am impressed." He looked at Marah's spirit hovering behind me. "Upon hearing it, I sent a Watcher to follow Hemael, assuming that he would collect her spirit." His eyes found Hemael still protecting Marah's body with his own. "I did not expect a scene such as this. What are you doing here with a decaying corpse?" He looked hard at me. "I held a corpse in my arms near this very spot."

"You lie," I said, "for Jonathon knew nothing of my journey into Hell."

"I speak the truth," Erozel said. "Your only son betrayed you." He turned to the Watchers behind him. "Take the body and destroy it with fire."

The Watchers moved toward Marah's body. Sangruel flew to a spot between them and Hemael. Three Watchers surrounded him, while the remaining flew to Hemael. I started toward them, but Erozel grabbed me from behind. Turning back to him, I struck him hard in the face, knocking him backward.

The Watchers fell on Hemael, pulling hard to separate him from Marah's body. I flung myself at them. Two of them leaped at me, and wrestled me to the ground, holding me fast despite my struggling. Erozel joined them.

"It is fitting," he said. "My love is flesh without spirit, while your love is spirit without flesh."

"Asherah's spirit is tormented in the bowels of Hell," I said. "You speak of love, but know it not. You loved only her body, delighting in her sexual depravity. I love Marah's very soul."

He raised his hand to strike me.

Suddenly, as if out of nowhere, Ariel landed behind him, and grabbed him by the wrist.

"Leave him be," he said.

Erozel turned to him, his face contorting with anger. "Do you now defend your old friend, after joining with us?"

Ariel's eyes flashed with violence. His voice was a low growl from between gritted teeth. "I joined with no one. Leave him be."

He moved suddenly, fluid lightning, striking Erozel hard in the face and knocking him several yards backward. He turned to the Watchers holding me, pulling them off me with the strength of a Warrior. I marveled at this. He was a Watcher. Had he always had such strength? Did God place the desire for war within him, and with it a Warrior's strength?

I flew to help Sangruel, throwing myself at the Watchers. Ariel joined alongside me, moving with impossible speed and agility.

Free from his attackers, Sangruel flew toward Marah's body, holding the Fruit of Carnal Knowledge in his outstretched hand. In my peripheral vision, I saw Erozel flying toward Sangruel from the side. I cried out: "Sangruel!"

Erozel hit him hard, sending him into a spin, knocking the Fruit of Carnal Knowledge from his hand. It tumbled and turned through the air. I lifted from the ground, flying toward the fruit with all the speed in me. Erozel reached it first, plucking it from the air with a shout of triumph, before lifting into the night sky, holding the Fruit of Carnal Knowledge in his hand.

He looked down at me with a hateful smile. "It is finished!"

Hemael moved faster than any creature I have ever seen, nearly invisible, even to my eyes. One moment he was on the ground, the next, he hovered before Erozel, holding Marah's small body in front of him. Erozel's eyes remained on me, unaware of Hemael's presence, as he flew directly into Marah's body. His hand holding the Fruit of Carnal Knowledge lodged deep into the open wound in Marah's chest.

Erozel turned, looking at Hemael in astonishment. He tried to pull his hand from Marah's chest, but some force held it there. His eyes grew wide. He screamed and fell to Earth, dragging Marah's body with him to the ground. I moved to catch her body, but Sangruel held me back.

"Do not touch her," he said.

Lightning flashed in the night sky. The clouds grew dark, releasing their water in a sudden torrent of rain. The Earth shook.

Blood poured and golden light shone from the gash in Marah's chest as the Fruit of Life and the Fruit of Carnal Knowledge joined for the only time in history. The mixture of blood and light flowed down Marah's corpse, growing in brightness and abundance as more and more blood and light streamed from the gash in her chest. Water fell in sheets from the dark clouds above, soaking her body, mingling with the blood. Sangruel watched intently.

"The water, spirit and the blood," he said.

I looked up into the dark, raining clouds. I saw the image of a man, a rainbow about his head. Could it be? Yeshua looked down at us, then, turning, ascended into the dark clouds above, out of my sight. The blood and light moved from Marah's chest, reaching out for Erozel, covering first his hand and arm, then his torso. He looked at it in fear, finally able to pull his hand from Marah's body.

A mist of golden light drifted from where I had last seen Marah's spirit, to her light-covered body, disappearing into the brightness. Erozel screamed a final time as the blood and light enveloped him completely.

I waited.

Moments seemed an eternity. Rain drenched my clothes and ran down my face. The light covering Marah and Erozel grew increasingly brighter until it shone like the noonday sun, causing me to fear for Marah. Would it consume her? Over thousands of years, I had witnessed the power of the Fruit of Life, each time fearing the results. Would she be a small child, or a young woman, an infant? I could never tell. What would happen to her now?

The light burned brightly for several minutes before showing any sign of dwindling. White light changed to golden, diminishing in size. Everything stopped. Nothing mattered to me but Marah. The light went out. Two bodies, both fully grown, lay on the ground, covered in thick, gelatinous blood.

I knelt beside Marah's body, looking for any sign of life. She was not breathing. Erozel lay beside her, as lifeless as she was. I reached for her, but Ariel stopped my hand with his.

"Do not touch, brother, for it is blood of the forbidden fruit."

Hard rain fell in sheets, slowly washing away the blood, revealing white skin underneath. Ariel placed his hand on my shoulder.

"She is not breathing," I said. "What have we done?" I looked at Hemael. He hovered silently nearby, watching Marah's body, his face hidden by shadow. "Her spirit, Hemael, do you sense its presence?"

Wordlessly, he shook his head.

My heart broke. Grief and pain flooded through me, more than I had ever known. Despair gripped me, smothering me, darker than the deepest parts of Hell. I turned toward the Watchers standing nearby.

"You are responsible for this!" My pain and grief fanned the fires of my rage. "She was pure and good, everything lovely and beautiful. You helped to destroy her, who even the Creator made flesh fell in love with. Your sins are many, but this is the greatest sin of all." I stood, glaring at my former brothers, meeting every face. One by one, they lowered their eyes in shame.

"I asked nothing of you. I wanted nothing, other than to love Marah. Her spirit is bound to mine. Her death is my death, a death I must suffer for all eternity. In destroying her, you have destroyed me. Were you not my brothers? Have we not loved one another since our creation?"

"Love! I tire of your endless ramblings about love!"

I turned, shaken from my anger at the sound of Erozel's voice. He sat on the ground, water pouring down his face, washing the blood from his naked body. I looked hopefully toward Marah, but she remained as she was. Erozel stood up, his feminine beauty marred by congealing blood.

"Love is but an emotion," he said. "Lust is emotion as well. Is there any difference? You love with your heart." He ran a hand along his chest, fondling his full, womanly breasts. His other hand groped between his legs. "I love with my body. Both the heart and the member are made by the Creator."

I stepped toward Erozel, my rage a consuming fire. He looked at the other Watchers.

"Bind him, hold him," he said. "Let us end this. The abyss waits for him."

The Watchers did not move. Their eyes fell away from him. I took another step toward him. He looked at the Watchers. Rage twisted his lovely face.

"Fools, all of you! Do you believe his words? Did I not teach you the wonders of human flesh? Will you now listen to this foolish talk of love?" He looked back at me. "Very well, then, I will deliver him myself into the mouth of Hell."

He struck out at me. His hand glanced harmlessly away. He looked at his hand, bewildered. He struck again, grazing my face, the blow weak and ineffective. This time he cried out as if in pain, clutching his hand to his body, eyes wide with fear and confusion.

Sangruel stepped forward, eyes on Erozel. "Flesh," he said, "Erozel is flesh. Human blood flows within him."

Erozel looked down, examining his body, his face frantic with fear and disbelief.

"This cannot be," he said, "I am a god!"

Sangruel reached out, running a sharp yellow nail across Erozel's womanly chest, leaving a line of red blood. "Do gods bleed human blood?"

Erozel gasped, trembling, staring down at his bleeding chest. I watched him in wonder. How had this happened? How had an angel become human? As I watched, the wound on his chest healed, the flesh knitting seamlessly together, leaving no trace, only pure white skin.

"Yes," Sangruel said. "You are flesh, but eternal, as Adam was in the Garden of God."

"This cannot be!" Erozel said. "I am a god!"

Sangruel hissed, baring fangs, staring hungrily at Erozel. "You are now what I desired to be. You have what I never will. I am cursed for wanting to be a man." He stepped toward Erozel, his lips curled, sharp teeth showing. "Perhaps I should show you what being a human in my presence can mean."

Erozel coiled back, away from Sangruel.

"No, Sangruel," I said. Erozel looked at me, fearful eyes pleading. "Let him be. He is our brother."

Something moved behind Erozel.

"Behold!" Ariel said.

I turned to see Marah, sitting up, looking around her.

"Marah!" I cried. She looked at me.

Erozel leapt toward her, screaming in rage, murder in his eyes. It happened so quickly. Before I could think to stop him, he was on her, knocking her to the ground, his hands wrapped around her throat, furiously choking and shaking her. I heard the breaking of bone and the grating of crushed cartilage.

I flew, hitting him with full force, regretting it instantly, when his body slammed into hers, shattering her chest under his weight. I screamed. Grabbing Erozel by the back of his neck, I squeezed hard, crushing his spinal column. He stopped moving. I threw his body aside and looked down at Marah.

Her neck was twisted at an odd angle, the print of Erozel's fingers purplish on her throat. Blood poured from her mouth, her eyes open, staring, unseeing, at the night sky. She was not breathing. I fell to my knees in front of her, feeling numb. I picked her up and held her to me. Tears ran down my face.

"Marah," I said, pressing my cheek to hers, "my love."

Sangruel picked up Erozel's body with one clawed hand, looking at him with disgust and hatred.

"You should have given him over to me," he said.

Erozel moved suddenly in Sangruel's hand, looking up at him with horror. Sangruel snarled at him.

"You live again. That is well. Hell is too good for you. Come, let me show you what true suffering is."

With that, carrying a screaming Erozel, Sangruel flew, vanishing into the night.

Hemael stepped up behind me. "Saruel," he said, looking down at Marah. "I sense life within her."

She moved in my arms. I felt her body shift, the broken bones in her chest mending, cartilage popping into place. Her neck straightened, the purplish welts on her throat vanished. She took a deep breath. Her eyes focused on me.

"Eternal," Hemael said, "she is eternal, as we are."